BAD GUYS

BAD GUYS

by

ANTHONY BRUNO

G. P. PUTNAM'S SONS
New York

G. P. Putnam's Sons
Publishers Since 1838
200 Madison Avenue
New York, NY 10016

Published simultaneously in Canada.

The author gratefully acknowledges permission to quote the following material:
"Physical" by Terry Shaddick and Stephen A. Kipner. Reprinted with permission of Terry Shaddick Music and SBK Songs/Stephen A. Kipner Music, copyright © 1981.
"Be My Baby" by Jeff Barry, Ellie Greenwich, and Phil Spector. Reprinted with permission of Trio Music Co., Inc., and Mother Bertha Music, Inc., copyright © 1963. All rights administered by WB Music Corp. All rights reserved.

Library of Congress Cataloging-in-Publication Data

Bruno, Anthony.
Bad guys.

I. Title.
PS3552.R82B34 1988 813'.54 87–7313

ISBN 0-399-13340-2

Printed in the United States of America
2 3 4 5 6 7 8 9 10

FOR MY SWEETIE

BAD GUYS

PROLOGUE

September 23, 1984

Lando parked the Caddy in the small lot behind Gilberto's, turned off the ignition, and stared at the odometer. There were only 12,000 miles on this car when he'd started this job. Now there were 43,621. Many miles and a lot of time, a little more than two years. Still it wasn't an accurate gauge, not the way he felt. It felt like he'd been on this assignment forever.

He got out of the car, locked it, and walked across the asphalt lot with his hands in his pockets. Even here in Brooklyn it was finally beginning to feel a little like fall. On his way in from Huntington that morning, he'd noticed a few trees just beginning to turn. He thought about his kids and wondered how they were really doing in school this year. The visits were regular enough, but now they were always like formal occasions, a big meal, the kids wearing their best clothes, his wife straining to make everything smooth and perfect. It was worse than being divorced and having to make do with court-ordered visitation rights. It was more like coming back from the dead. They always had that momentary look of amazement whenever he walked in the door.

Other guys at the Bureau had warned him to expect this. It just comes with the territory when an agent goes undercover for an extended period of time, his buddy Tozzi had told him. You have to live away from your family for their own protection, and inevitably you become a stranger to them.

Well, at least he wasn't a stranger to himself. That was supposed to be pretty typical too, getting so comfortable with your cover you forget who you really are. Fortunately that hadn't happened to him. In hindsight, he felt it was good that he hadn't taken an Italian cover. To the mob, he was Arnie Silver, the Jew accountant. It was good that they thought of him as the Jew, a trusted employee but not quite one of them. Some of Mistretta's associates had their doubts about him at first, but the boss himself liked the idea of having a Jew doing the books for his loan-sharking operations out on the Island. Jews are good with numbers, Mistretta's *consigliere* Richie Varga had reminded the boss, look at what Lansky did. After a while they began to refer to him as "Mr. Spock."

He had gotten his degree in mathematics from Carnegie-Mellon, and when you came right down to it, the FBI picked him for this job for the same reason the Mafia took him in. The Jew was good with numbers.

Goddamn Tozzi, he thought, smiling and shaking his head. He was originally supposed to take this undercover. But when they found out the Mistretta family was in need of a bookkeeper, the plan was changed. The Bureau had other agents working undercover in the mob as wiseguys, which was what they had in mind for Tozzi. But the opportunity to have someone on the inside with access to the books was too good to pass up. What a resource you'll be, Special Agent in Charge Ivers had said. Just imagine the information—the names, the places, the felonious events—you'll be able to feed back to us. It was all true, but every now and then Lando wondered what would've happened if Tozzi had gone undercover in the Mistretta family instead of himself. He would've been right in his element with these guys. He would have loved it. But not enough to turn. Not Tozzi, never. He, if anybody, knows who the good guys are. The lucky bastard.

Lando mounted the back steps of the restaurant. Come through the kitchen, Varga had told him on the phone yesterday when he invited him to this shindig, a surprise anniversary party for Mr. and Mrs. Mistretta. Well, at least the food would be good. Lando buttoned his top button and pulled up his tie, thinking about veal cutlets.

He tried the door but it was locked. When he knocked, Richie Varga poked his head out.

"Arnie, come on in," Varga said, taking his hand.

"Hey, Richie, how you doing?" Lando shook his hand, pumping Varga's weak grip. Varga was a strange dude, nothing like the other mafiosi he'd met. He always seemed so slow and lethargic to Lando, and there was something vaguely effeminate about him. And he always seemed to get a little heavier every time Lando saw him. Still he must've had something on the ball. How else do you become *consigliere* to the three most powerful Mafia bosses in New York?

"Mr. Mistretta's not here yet. I forgot Mrs. Mistretta always goes to twelve-o'clock Mass on Sunday. But come on in and have a drink at the bar."

Varga put a hand on his shoulder and led him down the tiled corridor. Lando didn't like this sudden chumminess. He wondered if Varga was coming on to him.

As they rounded the corner and entered the kitchen, something immediately caught Lando's eye. The first image that flashed through his mind were chickens, trussed-up chickens hanging in the window of the kosher butcher's shop in his old neighborhood in Buffalo. But these weren't chickens, they were men in rumpled suits hanging from meat hooks, hanging by the handcuffs locked around their wrists. Two men without heads, hanging by their arms like chickens.

His stomach lurched. He tried to think. How would Arnie Silver react to this? How would anybody react to this? He felt sick, and he bent forward. Varga was helping him bend forward, holding his wrist behind his back.

"Hey," Lando gasped as someone grabbed his other wrist. He struggled, but a sudden kidney punch stiffened him with pain. His arms were pulled back, and he felt cold metal on his wrists. Then he heard the click of handcuffs locking.

"You recognize them?" The voice wasn't Varga's.

Lando tried to get a look at the face of the other man behind him, but the bastard was jerking the chain on the cuffs up, keeping him bent over. "Who the fuck—?"

"Never mind who the fuck I am," the man said. "Walk."

Lando was shoved forward and he stumbled into the kitchen. When he looked up, he saw Varga standing over a chopping block. On the block there were two heads on a metal tray. One head was propped up by the other. The eyes were gone.

"Do you recognize them now, Lando?" Varga was smiling.

He couldn't breathe. He blinked to keep his eyes open.

"These are your paisans from the FBI, Lando. Mr. Novick and Mr. Blaney. They were sneaky little bastards who saw too much. Just like you, Lando. And when an outsider, especially a fed, sees what he shouldn't see, this is what has to happen."

"No . . . no . . ." He couldn't breathe.

"Okay, Steve," Varga said. "Come on."

Lando felt his cheek hit the moist wood of the block. He felt the man's knee in the middle of his back holding him down. Varga grabbed him by the hair with both hands and put all his weight on his head, crushing his ear. He saw the man's arm, caught a glimpse of the blade.

"No . . . please, no . . ."

The butcher's long knife was the last thing Lando saw.

ONE

July 1986

''You wanted to see me, Mr. Varga?''

''Wait in the living room, Vinnie. I'll be with you in a minute.''

Vinnie ''Clams'' Clementi nodded. He looked at Varga standing over a ledger open on the dining-room table. Richie Varga was a weird guy, Vinnie Clams thought. He had a shape like a woman and a mind like a snake. He'd invite you in, let you get warm and cozy, then strike. Vinnie was glad he was working *for* Varga and not against him. ''I'll be right out here when you want me, Mr. Varga.''

Varga stared blankly at the obese drug dealer until he disappeared, then he shut the ledger and eased his wide hips into one of the dining-room captain's chairs. Stroking his cheek softly, he stared at the two sleeping dogs, one a few feet away at the edge of the rug, the other across the room blocking the doorway to the kitchen. They were big dogs, Rottweilers, black with brown markings on their bellies, paws, and faces. One was named Blitz, the other Krieg.

''Blitz,'' Varga said evenly to the dog at the edge of the rug, the pitch of his voice just slightly higher than you'd expect from such a large man.

The dog didn't move.

He plucked a grape from the fruit bowl on the table and called the Rottweiler again, but the dog didn't respond.

Suddenly he whipped the grape across the room and it smacked the dog's shiny black flank. The dog raised her head and growled.

In the same even voice, he said, ''Quiet.''

The dog stopped growling, tilted her big square head, and looked at her master in puzzlement. A moment later she settled back down to her nap.

Varga picked a few more grapes from the bunch and set them down on the edge of the table, then reached for the red Trimline phone on the sideboard and started punching numbers.

It rang four times. ''Hello?'' a child's voice answered.

''Is your father home?'' Varga asked.

''Just a minute.''

He heard the kid calling to his father, then the sounds of plates and silverware and people moving around a crowded space. No one told him to have six kids.

''Hello?''

''It's me.''

''I know. What's up?''

''Is everything set for Paramus?''

''All set, don't worry.''

Varga didn't like it when people told him not to worry. ''Who do you have doing the job?''

''The jockey. He's good.''

Varga didn't say anything. He stared at the dog for a moment, then flung another grape at her. This one hit her on the ear. She whipped her head up and growled at him again, baring teeth this time.

''Quiet, Blitz,'' he said calmly. The dog hesitated, then dropped her head and closed her eyes.

The man on the other end didn't have to ask. He could picture those nasty dogs—overweight Dobermans, as he preferred to think of them—sitting in the looming shadow of their master. Poor animals.

''You use him a lot,'' Varga finally said. ''Do you have anyone else on tap besides the jockey?''

''There's one guy who used to work for Mr. L's people. He's experienced, but unfortunately the will isn't there anymore. I've got a kid I'm bringing along. In time I think he'll work out very well.''

Varga picked up another grape and beaned the dog in the face. The pissed-off bitch got up on her front paws, bared her full set of choppers, and alternately barked and growled at him.

''Quiet, Blitz.''

The dog snarled once, then was quiet.

''I was wondering,'' Varga suddenly asked, his voice higher. ''Would you be interested in doing another catering job for me? You know, something like what you did in Brooklyn.''

''No thanks.''

''You put out a very nice spread, Steve. I'd like to have that fancy platter again. Maybe not *that* fancy, but something . . . impressive.''

Steve pictured the three eyeless heads arranged on blood-soaked paper doilies. ''I don't think so.''

Varga could hear one of the kids wailing in the background. He picked up another grape. ''I can make it worth your while.''

''How much?''

''Thirty g's.''

''Let me think about it.''

''You think about it and let me know. Soon, though.''

''Right.''

''Take it easy now.''

''You too.''

Varga hung up the phone and rolled the last grape between his thumb and forefinger. He glanced at Krieg sleeping in the doorway, then looked at wary Blitz, who was already growling low, anticipating his intention.

Suddenly the grape flew from his hand and hit her in the eye. She was up on her feet, charging and snarling, a blur of teeth, spit, and tongue. Blind rage carried her to his knees, but when the flat of his palm slapped down on her forehead, she froze. ''Quiet, Blitz.''

It was like a faith healer's touch. The dog slumped down between his ankles, panting hard, brows furrowed.

Varga almost smiled.

''Vinnie,'' he called. ''Come on in.''

Mike Tozzi splashed cold water on his face, then stared at himself in the bathroom mirror. He stared at himself for a long time, wondering what the hell he was doing there. He was sick and tired of lying, afraid that he was lying to himself now. He used to think of himself as a man with a purpose in life, but now he wasn't so sure. Maybe his life had no purpose at all.

''Hey, what're you doing in there?'' she called from the other side of the bathroom door.

Alice. Tozzi had to remind himself that her name was Alice because she didn't look like an Alice. A nice girl from south Jersey up here for the housewares convention, she said. A real sweet kid with real nice legs, looking for a little fling at the convention. Everybody does it at the convention, she said. Probably has a boyfriend back home. But if she was such a nice kid, what was she doing in bed with him? Tozzi wondered.

"Did you fall in or what, Mike?"

"No," he called back, then pressed a towel to his face and forced a smile before he opened the door.

She was lying on the bed with nothing on but a deep blue slip with lace trim along the hem. Her hair was short and dark and stylishly punky. He guessed she was about twenty-three, twenty-four. She was perky, like those models you see in panty-hose commercials, the kind of girl you dream about having a one-nighter with. Tozzi sighed and looked out the window. Across the highway at the Meadowlands sports complex, the racetrack was all lit up. He could just make out a pack of trotters coming around the backstretch.

He sat on the bed next to her, looked into her perky dark eyes, and kissed her, running his hand over her silky hip. She giggled and seemed even younger than she was. Tozzi wished he didn't feel like he was doing something wrong. He wished he could stop thinking and just enjoy this.

She rubbed his bare back, working her hands down to his belt buckle. "Tell me the truth. You're not really in housewares, are you?" she asked as she undid his belt.

"What do you mean?"

"Well, you don't look like a salesman. I mean, come on, what kind of salesman wears Levi's to a big convention?"

"I told you I was a salesman. Why don't you believe me?"

She grinned slyly. "Who's Vinnie Clams?"

Tozzi glared at her in the dim light, but she didn't pick up on it.

"Come on," she said teasingly. "You're not a salesman. You're a cop or a bounty hunter or something like that. Am I right?"

Tozzi didn't answer. He could hear his own pulse throbbing.

Finally she realized that he was very upset about something. "Hey, come on, Mike, don't get mad. I was just looking around for a Kleenex and I found that piece of paper. I only looked at his picture and read his name. I thought it was funny."

Tozzi sat up and whipped open the nightstand drawer. He pulled out the folded piece of paper. He opened it and stared at the fuzzy picture of the fat man in the upper left-hand corner. It was a copy of the top sheet of Vinnie Clementi's FBI file.

"Why are you so interested in this?" The muscles in his neck were tight.

"I told you, Mike. I just happened to find it. I wasn't snooping or anything." She started to sit up. She looked scared. Or guilty, he thought.

"Why do you think I'm a cop?" he demanded, pushing her back down. He reached under the bed. "Did you happen to find this too?"

Her eyes shot open when she saw the gun in his hand.

"Huh? Answer me," he said through clenched teeth. He pressed the muzzle of the revolver into the hollow of her cheek. He was digging his fingers into her tit. "Say something!"

Her face crumpled and her lips trembled. She started to sob in soft squeaks. "No, don't . . ." she cried.

"Get out," he yelled, bouncing off the bed. "Get out," he repeated, but she was frozen in fear. He yanked her up by the arm, then gathered up her clothes from the armchair and thrust them at her. "Just get the fuck out!"

She stood motionless, clutching her dress to her chest. Her contorted expression was caught in the moment just before the crying begins.

He picked up her shoes, grabbed her arm, and pulled her to the door. "Just get out of here," he said as he pushed her into the hall and slammed the door shut.

Turning away from the door, he threw the .38 into the pillows at the head of the bed as hard as he could. He fell into the armchair and kneaded his temples with one hand.

What the fuck is wrong with me? She was a nice kid. What's wrong with me?

Suddenly he bolted up from the chair and went into the bathroom for his shirt. He had to get out of there before she called the cops.

This'll be over soon, he kept telling himself as he got dressed. This one and two more, then it's done.

TWO

Vinnie Clams squinted as he emerged from the shadows of the Lincoln Tunnel, tailgating a bus loaded with commuters heading home to Jersey from their office jobs in Manhattan. He flipped down the visor and gunned the accelerator to pull up alongside the crawling bus so he could get a look at the face on the blonde he'd been watching all the way through the tunnel. Her sexy hair had given him a hard-on, which was putting undue stress on his already overstretched size-48 burgundy double-knits.

He leaned over the expansive pearl-gray leather seats of the Lincoln Town Car and tapped on the horn to get the blonde's attention. "Yo! Honey babes!" he yelled through the closed window. "How'ja like some salami?"

The blaring horn turned heads on the bus, including the blonde's. She reminded Vinnie of a young Joan Rivers, a pinched fox face with heavy makeup. Not bad, he'd had worse.

Like everyone else on the bus, she squinted to see through the dark-tinted windows of the black Lincoln swerving alongside the bus.

Vinnie Clams laughed and snorted, delighted that he'd gotten a rise out of the blonde. He waved goodbye to her, then hauled himself back up behind the wheel. He had business to attend to.

The hood of the Lincoln sparkled in the late-afternoon haze as it sped up the ramp that connected with Route 3. Vinnie was in a very good mood because he felt insulated from the world. It was hot and sticky outside, but the whispering whoosh of the air conditioner kept him nice and cool. Untouched, clean. Get a job where you keep your hands clean, they always said back in the old neighborhood. Truer words were never spoken.

The Lincoln zipped under the big sign that announced the New Jersey Turnpike turnoff, veering around a jacked-up Chevy Nova flying the Puerto Rican flag from its antenna.

''Fuckin' spics,'' Vinnie Clams muttered appreciatively. If it weren't for spics and niggers and jooches, his hands wouldn't be so clean. But they could be cleaner, and in a few months, if things worked out, they would be.

A cassette was sticking out of the customized Blaupunkt stereo system the Clam had installed. He pushed the tape in and instantly Olivia Newton-John was singing to him from six speakers. *''Let's get physical, phy-si-cal . . .''* It was the only tape he kept in the car, and that was the only song on the tape he really liked.

Spotting a pothole in the road up ahead, Vinnie Clams aimed for it on purpose. The front left tire hit hard, and Vinnie frowned at the soft thud he heard. He glanced down at the odometer. Seventeen thousand miles and the suspension's already shot. A few scratches on the doors, too. It was time for a new car, maybe a Seville this time or a Mercedes. If they're not too cramped up front. But what the fuck? After this pickup, he could spring for a stretch limo—easy. The Clam smiled.

Vinnie Clams believed that the secret of his success was caution, and even though it went against his better judgment to jinx himself by getting cocky, he couldn't help himself today. This was his biggest score to date, three hundred grand, cash. The smile stretched wider across his meaty lips. He'd come a long way from the days of selling nickel bags to high-school kids in Washington Square Park.

As Vinnie saw it, the turning point in his life came three years earlier when he was busted on a relatively minor possessions charge. Normally his lawyer would have plea-bargained the charge down to a fine plus probation, but that goddamn eager-beaver assistant DA wouldn't play ball. In his closing argument the asshole made Vinnie sound like some kind of child molester, and that old bastard of a judge sentenced him to six months upstate. When you're five foot seven and you weigh two sixty-five, sharing an eight-by-ten cell is no fucking fun. By the time Vinnie was let out, he'd lost thirty-seven pounds and swore to God that he'd never ever see the inside of a goddamn jail cell again.

Just thinking about that prison cell made him panicky. A day didn't go by that he didn't remember sitting in that cell, heaving and wheezing for air, promising himself over and over that he was through with penny-ante shit. He would tell himself every single day that when he got out, he'd work big drug deals for big payoffs. It would be less work and he'd be off the streets. He swore that he'd never get caught with shit on the street again. He'd learned his lesson. It was stupid even to be in the vicinity of a dope deal . . . not when you can get someone else to do it.

The Clam's plan wasn't original; it was more or less traditional in his line of work, the established way a street pusher works his way up. A junkie will kiss his connection's ass, lick it clean, then lap up the turd off his shoes, just as long as he gets his fix. All of Vinnie Clams's regular customers were like that. So like many others before him, Vinnie Clams figured that he could take advantage of this available labor pool and form a small company of very loyal bagmen, whom he would pay with quality dope. There was only one problem with this: Vinnie Clams worked for the Mistretta family, and Mr. Mistretta, like a few of the other New York bosses, had these stupid old-world ideas about honor and decency. Vinnie thought the old man's rules were crazy. It was okay to sell dope to dealers; Mistretta just didn't want his people directly involved with the street action. The families considered selling dope directly to the junkies "nigger business," even though they handled better than sixty percent of all the dope sold in Harlem.

Sitting in jail, the Clam had worried that this would be a problem, but by the time he got out things were different. It was a whole new ballgame. After Richie Varga everything was different. It was incredible. The families had made Varga a prince, but the guy ended up screwing them all. What balls! Turned state's witness and fried their asses. When the Clam got out, the families were in chaos, their people scattered, their power just about gone. And with all the *capi di capi* either in jail or about to go, New York belonged to the small-timers, guys like Vinnie Clams. When Varga's testimony ruined the families, things really started to percolate in New York. Before long, disorganized crime swept through the city like a plague. And it was still going strong.

But for guys like Vinnie Clams, the disruption of the families was both good and bad. Sure, it freed him to operate the way he wanted to without all that outdated Code of Honor bullshit, but without the backing of the Mistrettas, he had nothing to start up with, no connections, no cash, no credit, nothing. So with no family affiliation, Vinnie Clams found himself out on the street again, an ex-con scrounging around his old neighborhood in Brooklyn, Gravesend, fencing hot VCRs and TVs. But that's when he got a call from a certain interested party, someone who wanted to invest in Vinnie Clams's drug expertise, someone who was getting in touch with a lot of the poor schlumps who were left high and dry without the families.

This interested party told Vinnie that he was taking in the best men left from the three families so that he could start up his own family. He told Vinnie that he could put him in touch with reliable suppliers and that he could provide him with seed money, just as long as he pledged his allegiance and, of course, agreed to cut the new family in for a piece of his action. He told the Clam that if things worked out, down the line there might even be something better for him in the organization, something safe without so much risk, like gasoline hustling or insurance scams. That certain interested someone was Uncle Sam's little rat, Richie Varga, who said he was going to run the whole thing by remote control from the Justice Department's Witness Security Program. It was fucking beautiful. The Clam heard opportunity knocking, and he accepted Varga's offer gratefully.

With the seed money he got from Varga, Vinnie bought himself some inventory—cocaine, heroin, dust, crack—both to sell and to pay the help with. The Clam set himself up in a newly renovated apartment building on Lafayette Street in lower Manhattan, a building full of upwardly mobile types, people with small noses and good posture, the kind of people Vinnie hated. It was a very good place to be, though, because it was convenient to his men working the streets in the East Village and on the Bowery. All Vinnie did was sit on the couch, set up the deals on the phone, give his junkies their assignments, then collect the profits. His only afternoon chore was making out the "payroll," measuring out what he felt his employees deserved for their labors—he even doled the shit out in brown payroll envelopes—rewarding some guys with purer doses, punishing the ones who got out of line by stepping on their dope a few more times than he normally would. Now and then a bagman would OD on him, but so what? The way Vinnie figured, the average dope fiend normally doesn't have a very long life expectancy, and who gives a fuck about a junkie anyway?

Besides, there was always an unlimited supply of applicants drooling all over themselves for an entry-level position in his company.

And yet, with all the money he had coming in, Vinnie Clams was still nervous. He had it easy, sure, and he was making it up the wazoo, but he still had nightmares about being locked up in that cell. He knew that no matter how cautious he was, there was always a good chance that he could go back there—and for a whole lot longer than six months. He knew that the only way to eliminate that risk was to stop handling shit altogether. That's when he decided to promote a few of his junkies and make them handle *all* the dope.

Ramon Gonsalves, for example, was a coke freak and his best bagman. He ran a small bodega on Avenue C and sold shit out of the store, which kept him going, since not even his own spic neighbors would buy the rotten plantains those people eat, not from that pigsty. But despite his crummy store, Ramon was okay and Vinnie Clams trusted him. But he didn't trust him enough to handle a sizable portion of his inventory. Not yet. The Clam needed some insurance first.

Ramon had a family: Teresa, his wife, and two kids, Ramon Jr. and Wanda, ages eleven and nine. Vinnie Clams started getting chummy with the Gonsalves family. He'd drop by with a couple of six-packs and throw little parties behind the bodega, meet the kids after school and give them rides home in his big Lincoln. The Clam soon found out that like their old man, the kids liked to get high too. He'd slip them joints regularly, and after a while he started adding angel dust to the weed. Within a month, Ramon Jr. and Wanda had developed quite a taste for the stuff, a real craving. As for Teresa, she was an easy mark. An ex–heroin addict struggling to stay clean? Come on. The Clam just showed up with the horse one afternoon when Ramon was out, and Teresa was all ready to ride again.

Now with his whole family hooked on dope, Ramon had no choice but to play it straight with Vinnie Clams. The Clam made it clear that if Ramon fucked around with the inventory, he'd cut them right off, leave the four of them high and dry. Ramon wasn't dumb; he figured out that altogether his family had something like a twelve-hundred-dollar-a-day habit. They needed Vinnie Clams bad. So when the Clam called him up and told him to go to a meet, Ramon did it. And when Vinnie Clams told him to stash the cash at a certain drop, Ramon did that too.

That's why Vinnie Clams was on his way to the Meadowlands right now. To make a pickup from one of Ramon's regular drops, a very nice pickup, which was a just little overdue, as Mr. Varga had reminded him the other day.

The Lincoln crested a rise in the highway, and like magic, the three massive structures that make up the Meadowlands sports complex appeared on the horizon: Byrne Arena, where the Nets and the Devils play, the racetrack, and Giants Stadium. Vinnie Clams fixed his gaze on the stadium and unconsciously gave the Lincoln a little more gas.

Turning off the highway, the Clam scanned the endless parking lots that surround the Meadowlands. They were empty except for the cars parked in the employee sections. He guided the Lincoln around the ribbons of service roads that led to the stadium and headed for the far end of Lot W. Swinging the long car around, he abruptly threw it into reverse and backed up to the concrete barrier where the lot ended and the tall reeds of the wetlands began. Vinnie Clams never liked to walk too far.

Examining the shifting cattails in the rearview mirror, the Clam decided that they'd grown at least another two feet since he'd last been here a couple of months ago. He pushed the door open and wedged his big belly out from under the tilt steering wheel, rolling out of the cool car into the oppressive heat. He coughed up some phlegm, slammed the door shut, and spat. "Fuck."

He pulled a crumpled handkerchief out of his pocket and mopped his face as he peered across the lot to get his bearings. Two, three, four, five, six, seven—he mentally counted the lampposts from the right-hand corner of the lot—eight, nine, ten, eleven, twelve, thirteen, fourteen. Lucky seven times two. He squinted and showed his teeth, then stuck the handkerchief over the sweaty flab under his chins as he walked toward the fourteenth lamppost.

He stepped carefully over the low concrete barrier and minced down the embankment with his arms outstretched like a tightrope walker. His heart was pounding when he got to the bottom. "You need a fuckin' machete down here."

There were reed stalks everywhere, crowding him like prison bars. And mosquitoes and flies, the big black ones that bite. The fat man got excited and started swatting at the reeds, fighting to make room. Shit . . . where the fuck is it? He looked all around, but nothing looked familiar. Maybe I counted wrong . . . shit. His breathing became short; he wanted out of there fast. But then he spotted a path of recently broken reeds, and his panic subsided. The oil drum, Ramon's path to the oil drum.

Vinnie Clams headed down the path, fearless now. He could see it in his mind. That rusty old oil drum half-buried in the wet dirt, the rim jutting out like an iceberg on the water. His greed got there before he did. Just reach around through the rusted-out side and he'd feel it. A Hefty bag, a heavy-duty Hefty bag full of cash—*Madonn'!* Vinnie Clams was running now, light-footed for a fat man, his feet barely leaving an impression on the soft, moist earth.

I'm coming to get you, baby, I am here for the—

Up ahead a lean muscular figure glanced over his shoulder and looked at the fat man. The back of his black T-shirt was tiger-striped by the reeds.

The Clam stopped dead in his tracks. "Hey! What the fuck're you doing here?"

Tozzi stared at Vinnie Clams, his eyes dark shadows under the ridge of his brow. "I'm taking a piss," he said indignantly. "What're *you* doing here?"

The Clam looked down. The fucker was pissing on the oil drum! Pissing on the cash!

Tozzi didn't move, but he kept his eyes on Vinnie Clams, waiting for an answer.

The Clam felt stupid and obvious. He had to say something so he wouldn't look so suspicious. "I'm taking a piss too," he said.

"So take a piss."

Vinnie Clams didn't like the way he said that. He didn't like this guy at all. And besides the fact that he was standing right over the oil drum *and* pissing on it, there was something vaguely familiar about this asshole. Vinnie Clams had a feeling he knew this guy from somewhere.

Reluctantly the Clam turned his back on him, unzipped his fly, and pulled out his dick, trying to remember where he knew this guy from. He started to relieve himself and then it suddenly dawned on him—those pictures Varga had sent him a long time ago!—and he peed on his shoe. This guy's a fucking fed! One of those two FBI guys who were on his ass all last winter trying like crazy to get something on him. Damn, he'd thought they'd given up on him. Goddamn.

The Clam didn't move. Slowly he reached into the side pocket of his jacket for his gun. Sweat was running into his eyes. Son-of-a-bitch.

Vinnie Clams clicked the safety as he turned, leveling the small automatic at—

Where the fuck—? The guy was gone.

The Clam quickly dropped down on one knee and stuck his hand into the oil drum. Empty. The humid smell of the fed's piss was in his face and on his hand. Vinnie Clams stood up and angrily wiped his hand on his pants.

''Where are you, you cocksucker!''

The reeds stared back at him, whispering in the stagnant breeze, closing in on him again. He thought he heard something to his right and squeezed off two quick shots. Then he listened. The reeds were still talking about him.

Heart pounding, he barreled through the overgrowth, hoping to find the bastard doubled over holding his bleeding gut. But there was nothing. The Clam wheezed and coughed, gazing bug-eyed all around him. Nothing but those fucking reeds.

''Yo! Fat man! Over here!''

Vinnie Clams fired wild and ran even though he wasn't sure where the voice was coming from. ''Where are you, you rat bastard? *Where's my money?''*

The Clam ran hard, thinking about all that cash in a big pile on the living-room carpet in his very air-conditioned apartment, trying very hard to ignore the pain that seared through his chest. He fired again without thinking. Then suddenly he saw something flying over his head. The green Hefty bag sailed through the sky in a high arc and then disappeared in the reeds.

Vinnie Clams went after the money, thinking about Richie Varga's warning about being late, thinking about those two dogs of his. ''Get away from that garbage bag, you fucker! Just clear out, you hear me!'' He thought he was shouting, but his voice was little more than a hoarse whisper.

He plunged through the reeds, then slipped and fell, dropping his gun. The Clam was wheezing and wincing as he hauled himself up, grabbed the gun, and kept on running and running. All he found, though, were more reeds.

Jesus Christ Almighty! I *need* that cash. People got to be paid. Varga wants his cut. Shit, fuck, piss— ''I want that dough, man,'' he said. A terrifying image flashed through his mind—the empty eye sockets of three heads on a silver platter—and panic filled his gut.

The Clam swatted furiously at the reeds, his throat constricting, the pain like a crowbar being bent around his chest. Suddenly a sharp pain spiked his lower back. It wasn't until he was down on the ground that he realized he'd been kicked from behind.

"It's all over, fat man."

Fucking wiseass, Vinnie Clams thought as he rolled over, ready to blow the fucker's head off, but suddenly a lightning bolt went through the Clam's chest and his hands went numb. His eyes shot open, and a purple-blue tongue was trying to jump out of his mouth. His vision blurred. He didn't recognize the black hole of the muzzle right in front of his face.

"Oh, no, Clams. You can't have a heart attack on me now," Tozzi said. He hauled Vinnie Clams to his feet by the lapels as if he were a featherweight. "No, that's much too kind for a slime like you."

The Clam made a noise like a balloon with a slow leak.

"No, Clams, no. It's got to really hurt when you die. It's got to hurt you the way you hurt those kids, man, those kids you turned into junkies. You know what I'm talking about, Clams, I know you do. I've been wise to you for a long, long time. You thought you were beyond the law, but no one is immune forever. Your time has come, pal."

Vinnie Clams's face was like a Jersey tomato—red, ripe, and about to burst. Then his vision cleared enough to recognize the pig-snout muzzle of a .44 Bulldog. He felt the barrel sinking into his waterbed belly.

Tozzi breathed in his face. "I hope this hurts."

The Clam gasped for breath. There was some feeling coming back into his hand, and he realized he was still holding his gun. "Hold on a minute, Mikey," he slurred. "Just hold on—" He jerked his hand up as far as he could, squeezed the trigger, and blew a hole in the mud next to Tozzi's foot.

Tozzi acted instinctively, firing the .44 point-blank. The explosion ripped through fat and flesh.

"That's for the Gonsalves kids," he whispered. "This is for the Patterson boy."

A second blast shattered bone.

"And this is for the Torres kids."

The final slug penetrated bloody mush, nicked the spinal column, and passed out the other side.

The bloated corpse dropped to its knees, then toppled sideways.

Tozzi, his eyes wide and wild, pulled a folded piece of paper out of his back pocket, crumpled it up into a ball, and forced it into the Clam's open mouth, ramming it in tight with the barrel of his gun.

Breathing hard, he stared down at the obese drug dealer's gray-blue face, replaying the last thirty seconds in his mind.

''How the fuck did you know my name, you bastard?'' he asked out loud. Then he turned and disappeared into the reeds.

THREE

Gibbons waited as Brant Ivers, Special Agent in Charge of the Manhattan FBI field office, finished paring his fingernails. Most people just clipped or cut their nails; Ivers *pared* his.

Gibbons didn't say a word—didn't ask why he'd been called in, didn't initiate any kind of conversation. Ivers would get around to it eventually, and anyway Gibbons had plenty of time. He was retired.

Inappropriate furnishings for an FBI field office, Gibbons thought, looking around the room. He'd always thought so. Eleven-by-thirteen Bokhara rug. Oversized mahogany desk. Swiss mantel clock next to the IBM pc. Color picture of the president on the wall over Ivers's head. Strange yellow-beige color on the walls, the color of eggnog. Gibbons looked around for a picture of J. Edgar, but he couldn't find one. J. Edgar wouldn't have approved of eggnog-colored walls. He wouldn't have approved of yellow walls. Just white, plain white.

Ivers's clothes wouldn't have sat well with the Old Man either. Three-piece, navy pinstripe. Sapphire stickpin in a powder-blue silk tie. Matching silk handkerchief carefully arranged in his pocket. Pastel blue shirt with a white collar. Blow-dried hair. Very ostentatious, even for the SAC of the Manhattan field office.

Ivers swept his nail parings into his hand and deposited them in the wastepaper basket. It was the only varnished wood wastepaper basket Gibbons had ever seen in his life.

''Well, Bert,'' Ivers finally said, ''how's retirement treating you?''

No one called him Bert, and no one ever referred to him by his real first name, Cuthbert. It was Gibbons, just Gibbons. He could have corrected Ivers—again—but this time he didn't bother. It was good to hear these false familiarities every once in a while; it reminded him who his real friends were.

"Retirement is . . . quiet," Gibbons said. "I get a lot of reading done."

Ivers nodded, a dopey grin on his face. He probably thought that expression was enigmatic and inscrutable, but it wasn't.

"You didn't *have* to retire, you know? You met all the physical requirements, Bert. I'll bet you could've gone on to sixty. I could've fixed it with Washington . . . if you'd only have asked me."

Gibbons exhaled, long and slow. This could almost be funny. No one wanted him out more than Ivers. He knew damn well what Ivers thought of him: an asshole from the old Bureau, one of "Hoover's goons." He knew what Ivers was thinking right now: Look at this dinosaur, still wearing J. Edgar's regulation summer outfit, the seersucker suit, white shirt, regimental striped tie, black lace-up shoes (shined), summerweight straw snap-brim hat. But what the hell did he expect? After thirty years of being one way, a man isn't interested in changing his style.

"Well, Ivers"—Gibbons paused to relish the SAC stiffening as he heard his name used casually and without title—"fifty-five is old enough for an agent, don't you think? Old warhorses just hold up the campaign." Gibbons smiled like a crocodile.

Ivers fingered his chin and smiled back. "I always liked your quaint allusions to the Roman Empire, Bert. Reading your reports always reminded me of my prep-school Latin exams. Do you still think of the FBI as the Roman legions enforcing the laws of the empire? Keeping the *pax*?"

"Absolutely."

Ivers nodded slowly; he tried too hard to be clever.

Gibbons uncrossed his legs and pulled on his earlobe. "Are the pleasantries over now, Ivers?" Gibbons was never very good at niceties. "You want to tell me why I'm here, or shall we talk about the kids next?"

Ivers leaned back in his chair. "There's one kid I want to talk about."

"Who's that?"

"Mike Tozzi. Have you heard from him lately?"

Gibbons shrugged. ''Not since the Bureau—in its infinite wisdom—decided to transfer him out to the graveyard.''

''Do you know why he was being sent out to Butte? Because he was a cowboy, a hothead who had to learn how to take orders.''

Gibbons grinned nostalgically. What a character Tozzi was. The only partner Gibbons ever got along with. ''Well, he did come over to us from the DEA,'' he pointed out to Ivers. The guys at the Drug Enforcement Administration were all cowboys, or at least that's how it seemed a while back. When it came to nabbing drug smugglers, they believed the means always justified the ends. Gibbons pictured Tozzi riding shotgun through the Everglades on one of those propellered swamp buggies, whatever the hell they're called. ''As I remember, at one time you liked having a cowboy on board. He was good for the dirty work, you said. The attack dog in our stable, you once called him, I believe.''

Ivers didn't seem very interested in Tozzi's history. ''You say you haven't heard from Tozzi since you left the Bureau?''

''He was my partner, not my wife.'' Thank God.

Ivers glared at Gibbons, who was beginning to enjoy himself.

''Tozzi has become a problem, a potential embarrassment.'' Ivers's tone was solemn now. ''A potential scandal.''

''What's he done?''

''He's disappeared,'' Ivers said. ''I think he may have gone renegade.''

A renegade agent? Tozzi? Never. He's crazy, but he's not stupid.

''The Bureau hasn't had a renegade agent in some time,'' Gibbons said speculatively.

Ivers picked up a file folder and handed it to Gibbons. ''You recognize these.''

Inside the folder there were three pieces of paper, each one crumpled and carefully smoothed out again, then encased in its own lock-top plastic evidence bag. Gibbons scanned them; they were photocopies of top sheets from confidential FBI files. Each one had been routinely signed by the agents assigned to those cases, ''C. Gibbons'' and ''Michael Tozzi.'' The last sheet was from the file on Vincent ''Clams'' Clementi.

''These are cases Tozzi and I worked together,'' Gibbons said matter-of-factly. ''No convictions on any of them. Lack of sufficient evidence, supposedly.''

''Be more specific,'' Ivers said.

Gibbons flipped through the plastic bags on his lap. ''Harrison Lefkowitz, radical lawyer, celebrity, royal pain in the ass. Tozzi and I had him on harboring escaped cons, quote-unquote political prisoners. We had video and we had wiretap tapes to prove it, but for some unfathomable reason you nixed the bust, Ivers. As I recall, you said that while the evidence was fine for a routine felon, for a lawyer of Lefkowitz's cunning, the case would have to be superlative. Five weeks after we were taken off the case, one of these so-called political prisoners we observed at Lefkowitz's country house killed three people in a bank robbery in Putnam County, then went on a spree—''

''Never mind that,'' Ivers interrupted. ''What about the other two?''

''Congressman Danvers . . .'' Gibbons smirked and shook his head. ''Tozzi located his funhouse in the woods. Bucks County, Pennsylvania. Queers—or should I say the congressman's associates—making it with eight-, nine-, ten-year-old boys, all of them orphans or runaways. The congressman himself was into bondage. A regular leather boy. Washington ordered us to close that investigation. I guess it pays to be in the right party.''

Ivers was staring out the window. ''And Clementi?''

Gibbons scowled. ''Another guinea scumbag drug dealer. Mafia-connected, of course. Used to work for Sabatini Mistretta, then went out on his own after Mistretta's organization fell apart. The Clam set himself up with a network of junkies doing all his dirty work, junkies whose wives and kids were hooked on dope too, thanks to him. Clementi's a clever bastard, I'll give him that. Tozzi and I had him under surveillance for over a month, but we couldn't get anything on him that would stick in court.''

Ivers formed a steeple with his fingers. ''Interesting.''

''Why am I here, Ivers?''

''Clementi, Lefkowitz, Congressman Danvers . . . all dead, murdered.''

Ivers let his statement hang in the air as if it meant something.

''Good,'' Gibbons finally said.

''A United States congressman is murdered and you say 'good'?'' Ivers seemed hurt and disappointed by Gibbons's reply.

''I can't say he didn't deserve it.''

''That's not the point.''

''Then what is?''

Ivers exhaled slowly to compose himself. "Each of the victims was found with the Xeroxed top sheet from his own file crammed into either his mouth or . . . some other orifice."

Gibbons couldn't hold back his grin.

"Furthermore those copies were made in this office, on the copier in the File Room."

"And that's why you think Tozzi killed them? To borrow a phrase, insufficient evidence, Ivers."

"The bullets that killed Lefkowitz came from a thirty-eight. Clementi was killed with a forty-four, the congressman with a nine-millimeter automatic of some sort."

"Tozzi does like to change guns a lot. Always in search of the perfect weapon." Gibbons was getting nostalgic.

"Is that all you have to say?"

"The MO could fit Tozzi. Good work, Ivers. That's how you build a good case."

"Cut the shit, Gibbons," Ivers snapped, finally blowing his legendary cool. "The first murder happened six days after Tozzi went AWOL. He's left his goddamn signature on each corpse. Of course he's the killer. He wants the world to know it's him. Why? Because he's got some kind of fucked-up romantic notion that he's a hero, a Robin Hood—no, a Superman—that he can make justice happen all by himself with a couple of slugs. Well, he's not a hero. He's just another killer, just another crazy with a gun and a cause. I want him neutralized, Gibbons. That's why you're here."

Gibbons let it all sink in for a minute. "You're telling me that you want an old man to come out of retirement to put out a young stud with a mission?" He laughed out loud. "You're shittin' me, Ivers. Can't your men find him? Christ, he's only one guy."

"I'm not asking, Gibbons," Ivers said grimly.

A mean grin spread across Gibbons's lined face. "You guys can't find him, can you? And I'll bet you haven't even put him on the Most Wanted List because he'll make the Bureau look bad. Tozzi must be a better agent than I thought. I imagine this whole situation is pretty embarrassing for you, Ivers."

"Look, Gibbons, the Bureau has the right to recall any agent in an emergency. You know Tozzi better than anyone who's currently active. Besides, you're intimate with his family. As of right now you're reactivated. Your orders are to find Tozzi and neutralize him." Ivers avoided

Gibbons's eyes and stared at the pulsating green cursor on the screen of his computer.

Gibbons glared at Ivers. He was not intimate with Tozzi's goddamn family. Just Lorraine. And that was none of his business anyway. "And how the hell am I supposed to find him if the whole goddamn Bureau can't?" Gibbons asked angrily.

"The whole goddamn Bureau doesn't know anything about Tozzi. This is still an internal matter confined to this field office. Tozzi was your partner. You knew him better than anyone. I'm giving you carte blanche on this. Do whatever you have to. Just find Tozzi and"—Ivers paused and looked down at his blotter—"eliminate him before he hits anyone else."

Gibbons mulled it over for a second, revealing nothing in his face. He wasn't convinced that Tozzi was responsible for these killings, but if it was true—well, he had broken the law and the law had to be enforced. "What about expenses?"

"Don't worry about that. I'll get you whatever you need."

"I'll need access to the files on everything he worked on, including the cases he had before we worked together."

Ivers nodded. "You'll have complete access to the files, plus unrestricted use of the computer. All Bureau field offices will be notified that you're on special assignment. You'll get total cooperation with no questions asked." For just a moment, Ivers looked sad and disturbed.

Gibbons pulled on his lower lip, still mulling it over. "Sounds good," he finally said as he stood up to leave. "I accept your kind offer, Ivers. Retirement is a fucking bore anyway."

"One more thing," Ivers said as Gibbons reached for the door. "Do you need a weapon?"

"Nope." Gibbons closed the door softly behind him.

FOUR

Bill Kinney filled his glass from the bottle of Beck's on the table in front of him. The waitress came by then and refilled Varga's coffee cup as she set down his hamburger. Kinney glanced at the crowded plate, French fries and coleslaw piled high on either side of the burger. He hated watching Varga eat.

Varga reached for the ketchup and poured out a neat mound at the edge of the fries. "So," he said, "am I supposed to worry about this guy Tozzi?"

Kinney sipped his beer and shook his head.

Varga drew a ketchup circle on his burger. "You sure?"

Varga was getting to be an old lady. He knew damn well he had nothing to worry about. There was no reason for this meeting. "Tozzi doesn't know anything about you. He's got his own agenda."

"And what's that?" Varga picked up the burger and took a bite. The fat under his chin shook as he chewed. Kinney looked away.

"He's getting back at all the guys he couldn't put away fair and square. The Clam just happened to be one of them. I'm sure Tozzi doesn't know he was connected to you. I'm the one who did the postmortem report on his apartment. Tozzi had been there, but I'm convinced he didn't find a thing. He tore the whole place apart, which just indicates how frustrated he was. Believe me, I know these things. Anyway the Clam was too smart to keep anything that incriminating around the house."

Varga didn't look convinced. He dug into the coleslaw but didn't seem to be enjoying his meal. Eating was just a routine to him. A strand of milky cabbage hung out of the side of his mouth as he chewed. He was disgusting.

"Tell me," Varga said, wiping his mouth, "how is it that you got to do the report on the Clam's apartment?"

"After you called me and told me he was dead, I hung around the office and made myself available. I was the only special agent around when Ivers got the call on the Clam's body."

Varga nodded and speared a few French fries. Kinney looked past him into the mirrored wall behind the booth and focused on Feeney sitting at the bar, slumped over a draft. For the life of him, he couldn't understand why Varga kept that skinny incompetent punk as his bodyguard. All brass and no balls. Stupid little mick.

Silence fell between them as Varga concentrated on his hamburger. Kinney knew from experience that Varga would be preoccupied until all the food was devoured. He could keep talking, but he knew Varga wouldn't be listening, so instead he just waited, sipping his beer and staring into the mirror at the neon-blue haze around the bar. Stanzione's Bar and Grill was a typical lower-echelon mob meeting place down by the docks in Elizabeth. The walls in the back were paneled entirely with mirrors. Mafia joints usually have a lot of mirrors so you can always see who's behind you. Bosses, of course, never sit facing a wall, mirrors or no mirrors. He noticed that Feeney was looking down the row of booths and waving to him in the mirror, flashing that cocky grin of his. He ignored him.

Varga finished up the last of his French fries and washed it down with coffee. He looked up at Kinney then, his sleepy eyes hard and penetrating beneath the heavy lids. "What's Ivers doing about Tozzi? I'm still concerned."

"He's called Tozzi's old partner out of retirement to find him. A guy named Gibbons."

Varga looked skeptical. "What has Washington got to say about all this?"

Kinney grinned and shook his head. "Ivers is stonewalling it. He's worried about his career. He figures if he can find Tozzi before Washington gets wind of it, he can save himself the embarrassment of having to explain a renegade agent coming out of his office. Only a few others at the field office know about it now. He's working very hard to keep a lid on it."

Varga drained his cup of coffee. "I want you to get involved. Just so we know what Tozzi's doing."

Kinney resented Varga giving him orders when it concerned his work with the Bureau. That was his province. "I've already thought that through. When the time is right, I'll suggest to Ivers that I team up with Gibbons on the hunt for Tozzi. When Ivers thinks about it, he'll realize that I'm the only logical choice. Besides Gibbons, right now I'm the only other field agent who knows about Tozzi because I did the investigation on the Clam's apartment. I've never worked with Tozzi so he doesn't know my face. If Gibbons doesn't find him in a week or so, I'll go in and have a talk with Ivers. I'm sure by that time he'll be so crazy worrying about the renegade he'll go for it."

Varga just stared at him. He was thinking. "Okay," he said softly, nodding his head slightly, then he reached over and took Kinney's beer bottle and drank what was left in it. "Will this affect your other work?"

Kinney shook his head. "Don't worry. I've been getting down to Atlantic City at least once a week. I've already got one store lined up, and I'm working on four more in the area. We've got the warehouse in Margate, and I've got a line on a torch who lives down near there. He's a little crazy, a Vietnam vet who can't find work anywhere, but he's got a clean record. I've checked."

Varga didn't react one way or the other, the fat bastard. A little approval would be nice.

"Let me know if you get tied up with this Tozzi thing. I want to get the Atlantic City operation rolling soon."

"Don't worry about it. I'll have everything ready in six weeks. Eight weeks max." What a fucking old lady.

Varga started nodding again. "Have you thought about the 'catering job' I asked you about?" he said, abruptly changing the subject.

"Yeah. How many this time?"

"Just one."

"Who?"

"Orlando Guzman. He's an independent dealer from East Orange who thinks he doesn't need me. He's got a very big mouth, and I don't like that. The other independents have to see that they can't work alone anymore. Do you know what I'm saying?"

"You want to make an example out of him. I understand."

"So are you interested?"

Kinney swirled the beer in his glass as he thought about it. Killing was no big deal, and when you came down to it, taking a man's head off was no worse than putting a few bullets into his chest. The result was the same—dead is dead. Lopping heads off was just something he could do that no one else could seem to stomach. It wasn't that he enjoyed it or anything. Not really.

"You said thirty thousand, right?"

Varga nodded. "I'll make all the arrangements. You just show up."

Kinney picked up an unused butter knife from the table and held it like a scalpel with his index finger over the back of the blade. "Do I have to bring my own?"

Varga shook his head. "I'll have knives there waiting for you."

Kinney scratched the back of his head. He was considering his chances of bargaining for a higher fee.

"Tell me," Varga suddenly said. "How're the kids, Steve?" He was grinning like a sultan.

"Fine." Kinney put down the knife. "All right. I'll do it." You fat bastard.

"I'll give you the details next week sometime." Varga pulled a twenty out of the side pocket of his jacket and threw it down on the table, then he raised two fingers and waved to Feeney.

In the mirror, Kinney saw the punk get off his stool and face Varga, standing there with feet spread apart and his head cocked to one side like a Jimmy Cagney tough guy. What a joke.

"I'll be talking to you," Varga said, hauling himself out of the booth.

"Yeah, take it easy."

Varga stood over him and looked him in the eye. "Yeah . . . you too."

Kinney started thinking about his house in the suburbs, the layout of the first floor, where the ground-floor windows were and which ones were partially covered by high shrubs. He wondered how much it would cost to put in a good alarm system. He glanced into the mirror and saw Varga's enormous hips going out the door. Fat bastard.

FIVE

Tozzi wanted to unbutton his collar in the worst way, but he knew he couldn't. It would be out of character for a bank executive. Instead he consciously sat up straight, one leg neatly crossed over the other so as not to wrinkle his pants, and flipped through a back issue of *Datamation* magazine. He stopped at an article on CAD/CAM systems for small manufacturers because it looked like something a bank vp would probably read. He read the first couple of paragraphs, wondering what the fuck a CAD/CAM system was. He glanced up at the receptionist, who was busy scribbling down a telephone message on one of those pink while-you-were-away pads.

Would a banker get off on a shelf like hers? he wondered. Sure, why not? He kept on admiring her anatomy until her intercom buzzed and she suddenly looked up at him.

"Mr. Thompson?" she said, holding the phone to her ear as she flashed him the sweetest smile he'd gotten from a woman in a long time. "Ms. Varga will see you now."

Tozzi smiled gratefully at the fetching brunette who smiled back so cordially. The company logo hung on the wall over her head, squat chrome letters that spelled out DATAREACH, INC. "Go down this hallway all the way," the brunette said, "then turn right. Ms. Varga's is the corner office."

"Thank you," he said. He picked up his briefcase, which was empty except for a 9mm Beretta folded inside a copy of yesterday's unread *Wall Street Journal*. Tozzi didn't like having his weapon there, out of reach, but his good suit, the blue European-cut double-breasted, was too tight for a shoulder holster or even a belt clip, and for this one the image was more important than accessibility to firepower.

He turned right down the carpeted corridor, mindful of his strides. Cops have a certain walk, a woman once told him. If you know the walk, you can spot a cop a block away. Unfortunately she never told him what it was about a cop's walk that gives him away. Anyway, technically he wasn't a cop anymore, he was a fed. Tozzi glanced into the open doorways of the offices he passed. Each one contained an intense-looking executive with a phone on his shoulder and a faithful computer terminal beaming green by his side. None of these guys looked over thirty.

At the end of the hall just outside Ms. Varga's office there was a big picture window. In the foreground two squat futuristic black-glass-and-steel office buildings squared off like robot pit bulls across a blacktop parking lot. In the background the Garden State Parkway raced by.

Tozzi poked his head through the doorway. "Ms. Varga?" he said, forcing that cordial smile. "Robert Thompson."

This brunette stared hard at him from behind an oversized desk. The high cheekbones gave her a cunning hard-ass look, like a female Jack Palance. She was wearing a gray worsted suit over a peach silk ascot-collared blouse with a gold stickpin; she wore her clothes like armor. Her eyes were oval, dark, and slightly upturned. They were classic suspicious Sicilian eyes, just like her old man's.

"Have a seat . . . Mr. Thompson." There was a sardonic edge to the way she said that. Tozzi immediately wished he had Gibbons working with him on this one. Gibbons was always better at playing a businessman. WASPs always seemed more normal in an office, more believable.

He noticed the brass nameplate on her desk as he sat down, JOANNE C. VARGA. Why the hell did she still use his name? But then it occurred to him that her maiden name might be just as awkward for her in the business world. Tozzi somehow felt better thinking of her as Joanne Collesano, though.

Tozzi reached into his breast pocket and pulled out the phony business card he had ready: Robert W. Thompson, Vice President, Customer Relations, Citibank. She ignored the card and abruptly stood up and went to close the door.

Tozzi got that sinking feeling that he was blowing it before he even got started.

"Ms. Varga, we have a rather unusual problem and I'm hoping you can help us. You see, your ex-husband—"

"We were never divorced," she said, cutting him off curtly as she went back to her desk.

"Oh . . . Well, to get to the point, Mr. Varga had purchased several certificates of deposit from Citibank, all with long-term maturity dates, and now they've matured. These CDs are currently worth in excess of eighty thousand dollars. Our problem is that obviously we can't locate him to find out whether he wants to reinvest this money in new CDs or cash them in."

Tozzi thought he'd made a mistake the moment he heard himself say "cash them in." There had to be a more professional banking phrase for that. But he couldn't stall now. The best thing to do was to keep talking and hope she didn't suspect anything.

"We've tried to get in touch with him through the Justice Department and I personally discussed the matter with the people there in charge of the Witness Security Program, but that was eight months ago and I still haven't gotten a satisfactory reply. Legally, Citibank is in an rather sticky situation here. We can't hold on to his money without his expressed intention of how he wants it invested, and yet we can't treat this the way we would treat, say, the estate of a deceased customer. So, Ms. Varga, we were hoping you could help us get in touch with him . . . if that's possible."

She stared right through him, those hard Sicilian eyes just waiting for him to hang himself.

"Who the hell do you think you're kidding?" she said.

"Pardon?"

She lit a cigarette and just held it poised between her fingers, her elbow resting on the desktop. Her nails were Chinese red.

"Mr. Thompson, when I was in second grade, I came home from school one day to find three strange men sitting in the living room with my father. They wore dark suits and overcoats, and they kept their hats on in the house. One of them tried to be nice to me, asked me how my day at school was, but my father told him to shut up and leave me alone. Then he told me to go into the kitchen with my mother for cookies and milk. By the time I came back, everybody was gone, my father too. They were federal agents, there to arrest my father."

I bet one of them was Gibbons, Tozzi thought.

"I've seen a lot of cops in my life, Mr. Thompson. Local cops, state cops. All kinds of federal cops, FBI agents, Treasury agents, marshals. As you might imagine, the daughter of a big bad mobster eventually becomes sort of an expert on cops. There's something about cops, all cops, whether they're in uniform or undercover, no matter what their rank is. It's something I can smell. And you know what, Mr. Thompson? You reek."

He couldn't hold back the grin. He was beginning to like her.

"Ms. Varga, are you suggesting that I'm a policeman?" He wasn't very good at righteous indignation either, but so what? The jig was up.

"I'm *sure* you're a cop of one kind or another. I called Citibank this morning. They have no Robert Thompson in Customer Relations. You shouldn't have made an appointment in advance. Most undercover cops just show up, apologize, and say they just happened to be in the neighborhood, something lame like that."

"You're not the type to see visitors on the spur of the moment, Ms. Varga, not even from Citibank. Corporate vice presidents tend to insist that you make an appointment."

She smiled and leaned back in her high-back leather swivel chair. "Life is tough." And it could get tougher, she thought.

Tozzi unbuttoned his collar and loosened his tie. "I don't know what to say."

"Oh, come on. You're not giving up that easy, are you?"

Tozzi covered his lips with his fist and nodded thoughtfully. "Okay . . . suppose I am a cop. What do you think I want with you?"

"Well, since you came in with that cock-and-bull story about Richie's CDs, I assume it has something to do with him."

"So what is it I want to know about him?"

She picked up a carved jade letter opener and held it lengthwise between her index fingers. She knew what he wanted. "Now that's an interesting question, seeing that you guys have him socked away in the Witness Security Program. Don't tell me that after all this time you're beginning to doubt the gospel according to Richie Varga?"

"You're referring to Varga's federal grand jury testimony against your father and the other"—he paused deliberately as if searching for the right word—"reputed mob bosses?"

"Hallelujah," she muttered. Where'd they find this one?

"I take it you think your husband did your father dirty?"

"That's putting it mildly. Do you know how many lives he ruined with his testimony? Do you know how many people were killed because of him? Do you? Richie put terrible doubts into people's minds. They couldn't trust each other after Richie started telling his tales. And in any business, Mr. Thompson, if you can't trust someone, you don't need him.'' Sometimes she startled herself with this forthright sincerity. It wasn't easy keeping a straight face.

''These people you're referring to are the other bosses Richie fingered?''

''Not just them. Everybody on down the line under them.'' She shook her head. ''You guys never got it, did you? Richie Varga *destroyed* the New York families. He violated their trust and screwed them royally, blew the entire system to pieces. And goddamn Richie did it all by himself.'' Those hard eyes were glinting with fury now.

''So what's left? *Capo*s, lieutenants, soldiers—all of them either dead or in hiding,'' Tozzi said. ''No one answers to no one anymore. It's all freelancers and rookies out there now. And a lot of people are getting hurt as a result.''

''That's right, Mr. Thompson. But if you know all this, what do you want from me?'' I want Richie, Ms. Varga.

''I want to know about Richie.''

''Why don't you go talk to him yourself? He likes to tell stories.''

When Tozzi didn't answer, she leaned forward and laid the letter opener on the blotter. She studied his face for a moment. ''You're *not* a cop, are you? You want to know where Richie is. Somebody finally put a hit on him.'' She relaxed her face for the first time and hoped she was convincing.

Tozzi said nothing.

She looked at the ceiling and shook out her thick dark hair. ''Boy-o-boy, do I ever wish I could help you.''

''You don't know where he is?''

She glared at him. ''If I did, he wouldn't be breathing now. My father would see to that.''

''If your father still has connections, why can't they track Richie down?''

Joanne picked up the letter opener again and held it by the tip as if she were going to throw it. ''Who're you working for?''

Tozzi just stared at her.

''You're not working for my father, I know that. So it's got to be either Giovinazzo, Mistretta, or Luccarelli. Or maybe all three of them.''

She wondered how he'd react to her mentioning names. Would he think she knew more than an innocent woman should?

"Why would I be working for them?"

She laughed out loud. The answer was obvious. "Betraying a family is one thing, but betraying the three biggest families in New York and getting away with it is unimaginable. There's a lot of besmirched honor at stake here. In their eyes, Richie *has* to die."

"How about you? Do you want him dead?"

"Let's just say I wouldn't be a grieving widow."

"But you wouldn't take up a collection to buy the bullets?"

"Look, Mr. *Thompson,* I'm not a Mafia princess, if that's what you're insinuating. I've worked for this company for six years and I'm proud of my position here. What my father and his buddies do has nothing to do with me."

"But you were married to Richie Varga, not exactly Mr. Clean."

"My old man arranged that when I was nineteen. Richie was pretty good-looking back then, before he turned into a blimp. He was a big spender, and my father loved him like the son he never had. I liked what money could buy and I wanted to please my father, so I married him. Pure and simple."

"Did you love him?"

Joanne rocked in her chair and gave him a sarcastic what-do-*you*-think look.

Tozzi looked embarrassed.

She swiveled toward the window and stared out at the cars rushing by on the parkway. She sighed and wondered how tenacious this guy was going to be. "Richie is somewhere out there with a new name, a new address, maybe a new wife, who knows? I've heard that the government even arranges for plastic surgery for some witnesses. If it was available I'm sure Richie got himself a new face too. Richie takes whatever he can get. It's funny, though. He did so much damage, yet he wound up a hero because he cooperated with the federal prosecutors. A real all-American boy. He fucked us all . . . and he got away with it."

Tozzi pressed his lips together and nodded. After a moment, he grabbed his briefcase and got up to leave. She turned and looked up at him. He seemed frustrated. Maybe he didn't like the idea of sympathizing with Jules Collesano's daughter, of all people.

"Just one more thing," he said, standing over her desk. "Does

Richie have any distinguishing features, characteristics, mannerisms, something that can't be fixed with plastic surgery, anything that might give him away?"

She looked away, a wicked little grin playing over her lips. "Well, there is one thing . . ." She let it hang coyly.

"What's that?"

She glanced at her wristwatch. "Take me to lunch, Mr. Thompson, and we'll discuss it."

SIX

This was getting boring. Gibbons finally took off his jacket and hung it over the back of the pink vinyl kitchen chair he was sitting in. He rolled up the sleeves of his white shirt but left his collar buttoned and his tie up. Back in the old days, it was against the rules for an agent to loosen his collar while on duty. It had become a habit with Gibbons.

The small apartment was hot and stuffy, but he hadn't opened any windows. Open windows just broadcast your presence. But it wasn't the heat that was bothering Gibbons, it was the place itself, the furnishings, the invisible presence of the old lady.

The kitchen was permeated with the smell of garlic, tomatoes, and anisette. There was a crucifix in every room, a crimson-robed statue of the Infant of Prague enshrined on the dresser in the bedroom, and a portrait of the Virgin Mary over the TV. Even the light-switch plates had saints on them. Gibbons wondered where the hell you could buy these crappy things. Maybe Catholics traded them like baseball cards.

He stayed in the kitchen because the living room was excruciating. Clear plastic over imitation baroque furniture, plastic roses in little white vases, stupid porcelain party favors from too many weddings, and pictures of the old lady's guinea relatives everywhere. Gibbons hated Italians. If they weren't all in the Mafia, they were penny-ante crooks begging to get in.

Of all those photos scattered around the living room, Gibbons had given a second look to only two. One was a faded color snapshot in a small gilt frame on the end table by the sofa. A dark-haired little kid, maybe six or seven years old, sitting on a Shetland pony and scowling at the camera. A monkey on a pony. He was pretty sure the monkey was Tozzi.

The other was a five-by-seven of a tall, giddy-looking girl in a cap and gown. It was Lorraine at her college graduation: Barnard, class of '60.

Gibbons glanced at his watch. He'd been waiting for four hours and eleven minutes, and it was just beginning to get boring. He could remember being on plenty of plants that went on a lot longer than this. Plants were never fun, but he'd learned how to do it. You just took it all in stride. That was what being an agent was all about, really. If Tozzi didn't show up this morning, he'd just keep digging until he found another lead, another place, another connection.

Gibbons fingered the butt of Excalibur, his .38 Colt Cobra, the revolver he'd carried during his entire career as an FBI agent. He sniffed his fingers, getting a familiar whiff of gun oil and leather to counteract the smell of the old Italian lady. The other thing that bothered Gibbons about this apartment was the stagnant feeling of loneliness the place had, the imprint of one person winding down her life all by herself in three tiny rooms. It reminded him too much of his own apartment.

He glanced at his watch again. It was a little after seven A.M. If Tozzi was camping out here, he'd probably be back by now. Even if he'd been out all night with some woman, Tozzi had never been the type to stick around for scrambled eggs and small talk.

"Shit," Gibbons muttered. He thought he had him this time. It had been two and a half weeks since Ivers had reactivated him, and in that time Gibbons had studied the Bureau files on the three hits, interviewed other agents about Tozzi, tailed all the old girlfriends he could recall, checked Tozzi's old hangouts. But he came up with nothing.

He then took a trip to the neighborhood where Tozzi grew up, Newark's Vailsburg section, and tracked down Tozzi's sister and a couple of cousins. In Gibbons's experience, people who do desperate acts sometimes return to their hometowns, figuring there's more safety in familiar surroundings. Sort of like running home to mommy. He didn't think Tozzi was one of those, but it was worth a shot. No one had heard from him since he'd been reassigned to Montana, or so they claimed.

One of the cousins, Sal Tozzi, sold car insurance out of a storefront on South Orange Avenue. Sal looked a lot like Tozzi but was much shorter. When Gibbons dropped in on him, he was wearing a black knit shirt under a cream-colored sports jacket, and he didn't stop smiling the whole time Gibbons was there.

"Hey, tell me the truth," Sal suddenly said to Gibbons in the middle of their conversation. "Mike's up for a big job down in Washington, am I right? That's why you're here. Character check and all that stuff."

Gibbons almost laughed out loud. "Could be," he said.

"I knew it!" Sal slapped his desktop. "I always knew Mike'd be the one to make us proud. I mean he *has* made us proud. You know, locking up drug pushers, chasing down Mafia guys, all that stuff. He's got balls, that cousin of mine. And he's smart too. My old man was always throwing it up to me how my cousin always got A's. You should never compare kids, you know that? It gives them an inferiority complex, and that stays with you all your life. I admit I was kinda lazy, but that Mike, man, he was always a real hard worker. And a real hardhead, too, sometimes. A one-track mind, his mother used to say. But I can see why the government would want a guy like him for a special job. Tell me, what's he up for?"

A life sentence, the way he's going, Gibbons thought, suppressing a grin. "I'm really not at liberty to say, Mr. Tozzi."

"It must be real top-secret. Just tell me one thing—is it something domestic or will he be working overseas? The Middle East maybe. That's what it is, I'll bet. I had a feeling that whole Montana business was just cover for something big."

Gibbons shook his head. "Please, I really can't talk about it. I'm sorry. I have to go now."

Gibbons pictured Sal running a concession on the boardwalk selling Mike Tozzi T-shirts and key chains.

"Hey, you know, I just thought of something." Sal tapped his forehead. "You ought to talk to my cousin Lorraine. She was real close with Mike. She'd be a real good character reference."

"Oh, yeah?"

"Yeah, she's a lot older than me and Mike, but they always got along. They were the two smart ones. Lorraine used to baby-sit for Mike when he was a little kid. You ought to talk to her."

Gibbons just nodded.

"She teaches down at Princeton. Her name is Lorraine Bernstein. Bernstein is her married name. I don't know why she kept it, though. The marriage didn't even last a whole year. After the wedding, she found out he was queer, the bastard. Personally I don't think she ever got over that. Hell of a thing to happen to a person."

Gibbons didn't say anything. Sal didn't seem to notice.

"Poor Lorraine. I haven't seen her in years. She's been going out with some old guy from the FBI, I don't know his name. From what I heard she supposedly met him before Mike hooked up with the FBI. Over ten years she's been seeing this guy. I don't know why the hell he doesn't marry her, the jerk." Sal laughed nervously then. "Hey, I better shut up. For all I know, *you* could be her boyfriend."

Gibbons shook his head. He thanked Sal for his time and left, wondering if that might be the way Lorraine felt about him sometimes. He felt a little depressed recalling that he and Lorraine had been together long before he ever knew Tozzi. He never thought of his relationship with Lorraine in terms of years. Walking to his car, he figured out that Tozzi must've been a rookie with the Boston PD when he and Lorraine first met. Hard to believe.

Tozzi had been married once upon a time, but never happily according to him. Of course, Gibbons realized that partners like to gripe to each other, even when things weren't really that bad. It's just the nature of the job: Digging for bad guys brings out the badness in you sometimes. It occurred to him that maybe Tozzi's wife wasn't the bitch he always made her out to be. There must have been something good about her for him to have married her in the first place. Maybe now that he was out in the cold, his better memories of her might've turned golden and drawn him back for some comfort. Gibbons decided to drive up to Rhode Island to have a talk with the former Mrs. Tozzi.

He found her in the showroom of her father's lamp and chandelier factory outside of Providence. She wasn't the kind of sexy dish he usually associated with Tozzi. She was excruciatingly neat, perfect bangs, not a pale blond hair out of place. Gibbons took note of the pleats in her skirt, which were equally perfect. He didn't think women wore pleated skirts like that anymore. Her voice was high and sweet, and she spoke with measured precision in a thick New England accent. As soon as he asked her if she'd heard from Tozzi lately, the dim confusion in her finely mascaraed eyes told him that this had been a wasted trip. There was definitely no solace or simpatico to be found in this china doll. But since he was there—and since he'd always been a little curious about Tozzi's past—he decided to ask her a few questions for the hell of it.

She offered him a cup of coffee in a shallow, fragile-looking cup, exhibiting the same kind of mechanical cordiality that she must have used on buyers. He took the saucer and cup and frowned at it. The delicate cup had one of those stupid little handles that didn't fit a man's finger.

"Do you mind if I ask you a few more questions, Ms. . . . ?"

"Of course not. And I go by my maiden name, Howard."

"When *did* you see Tozzi last?"

"Oh . . . it must be about four years ago. In court." She said *court* like *caught.*

"Any children?"

She shook her head and Gibbons wondered if she was capable of reproducing.

"Why did you get divorced, if you don't mind my asking?"

"Will this help you find him?" She must've been annoyed by the question because the lines around her mouth appeared briefly. It was the most character she'd shown so far.

"It might help. The more I know about him, the easier it'll be for me to figure out how he thinks."

"Legally, could you make me tell you? Like with a subpoena or something like that?"

"If I thought it was that important, yes," Gibbons lied.

"Well . . . it's been four years, so I guess it doesn't matter now."

"Probably not." Gibbons smiled and nodded encouragingly, the way he thought an understanding father might.

She looked him straight in the face, her violet eyes as wide as could be. "My father told me to."

Gibbons knew better than to be judgmental. "Why did your father want you to divorce him?"

"Because Michael wouldn't go into the business." She made a sweeping gesture toward the lamps and chandeliers glittering all around her, like one of those girls who point out the prizes on TV game shows. "My father wanted to take him in, make him a vice president. Anything to get him to quit the FBI."

Gibbons set down his dainty cup. "Does your father have anything against the FBI?"

"Not really, no. I mean he has had his books audited, but everyone in the lighting business gets it from the government sooner or later. No, my father just thought being an agent was too dangerous."

"Are you an only child, Ms. Howard?"

Her eyes got wider. "No. I have an older sister, Lori. She lives in California."

Gibbons nodded sagely. "Thank you, Ms. Howard. I think I have all I need. You've been very helpful."

He got up, put on his hat, and left the wide-eyed china doll standing in the dazzling glare of the showroom.

The next day Gibbons had the Research Department at the Manhattan field office do a universal search on the name "Tozzi" in every newspaper in the country east of the Mississippi for the past two years. He wasn't looking for anything specific, just hoping something might pop up. Something did.

Research came up with twenty-one Tozzi mentions. One was an obit in the *Newark Star-Ledger* for a Carmella Tozzi of Bloomfield, New Jersey. It had appeared in a Saturday edition fourteen months ago. The deceased, as it turned out, was Tozzi's aunt. On a hunch, Gibbons started to check into Carmella Tozzi and discovered something very curious at the apartment building where she'd lived. Her name tag hadn't been removed from the neatly arranged buzzer grid in the front hallway. It was a nice neat building in a nice neighborhood full of senior citizens. It was the kind of building where apartments don't stay vacant very long and buzzer tags are kept up-to-date.

A plaque next to the buzzers said that the building was managed by Blue Spruce Management, Inc., in Montclair, so Gibbons paid them a visit. He purposely waited until lunch hour and predictably scared the shit out of a skinny teenager working in the office for the summer. His broad-nosed, narrow-eyed, hard-ass Aztec deity face scared the shit out of a lot of people. The skinny blonde, who was alone in the office, actually squeaked when he produced his ID. She didn't dare object when he asked to see the file on Carmella Tozzi, 1005 Broad Street, Bloomfield, Apartment 4K. She nervously apologized and said that all the files were on the computer, then immediately led him to the computer in the boss's office and called up the file on Mrs. Tozzi.

According to the management company's records, Carmella Tozzi's rent was paid up to date. The apartment hadn't changed hands in twelve years. As far as Blue Spruce Management was concerned, Carmella Tozzi was still breathing.

When he politely asked what bank the company used, the skinny girl told him without hesitation. He thanked her for all her help, then walked into the blistering July heat, crossed the street to a Greek coffee shop, and ordered a cup of coffee and a piece of French apple pie. When he finished his second cup, he called Ivers's office from the pay phone in the rear between the bathrooms and told the SAC's assistant that he needed some bank records, the Blue Spruce Management account at First People's Bank of New Jersey. The next morning at the Manhattan field office, there was a white eight-by-ten envelope waiting for Gibbons, photocopies of all the checks written to Blue Spruce Management from Carmella Tozzi for the past thirty-six months.

He found a secluded cubicle in the File Room and compared the old lady's handwriting on the checks. The FBI had handwriting experts in Washington, of course, but over the years Gibbons had picked up enough about handwriting analysis to tell him what he wanted to know. Anyway he hated sending evidence to the labs; when all you wanted was a simple yes or no, they always gave you a goddamn term paper.

Carmella Tozzi's handwriting was delicate and florid, slanted very slightly to the right. She crossed her sevens the way most Europeans do. At some time in her life, she must have practiced her penmanship assiduously, perfecting the little serifs she embellished her letters with. Gibbons noticed that the serifs on the checks written last spring and summer weren't so perfect or so delicate, but by the winter, they were back to their old form. The first check to show sloppy serifs was dated last June 1. The obit in the paper said that Carmella Tozzi died on May 12.

Not bad for an amateur, Michael. But not good enough.

It looked like Tozzi was paying the rent out of his aunt's checking account, forging her signature so that he could use the apartment. Pretty clever.

But what Gibbons wanted to know was where Tozzi was right now. There was no question that he'd been here, but whether he was living here now was hard to tell. In the bedroom, Gibbons had found two pairs of men's pants, a few shirts, a dark blue suit, some underwear, athletic socks, and a scuffed pair of Pony high-top leather basketball sneakers. Not much stuff if he really was living here. The refrigerator was depressingly bare too. Gibbons was a little disappointed that there was nothing getting moldy in the fridge; he'd always thought of Tozzi as the type who'd just let things go bad.

But as dawn became early morning and sunlight streamed through the kitchen window, Gibbons realized that Tozzi could be anywhere right now, possibly somewhere stalking another target.

Shit . . .

Gibbons got up, put on his jacket, pushed the chair under the table the way he'd found it, and headed for the door, vaguely wondering where the hell he'd start looking for Tozzi next, convinced that he'd be hearing about another murder soon. But for the moment what he really cared about was getting something to eat and then getting some sleep. As he unlocked the dead bolt and turned the doorknob without a sound, he decided he'd worry about Tozzi's whereabouts this afternoon.

Suddenly the door whipped open, smashing Gibbons in the shoulder and knocking him into the cluttered hall table. Knickknacks hit the floor and broke. Instinctively Gibbons went for Excalibur before he even saw his assailant. He clicked the safety with his thumb as he pushed against the wall behind him with his left hand to get back on his feet. Gibbons caught a glimpse of the back of the man's head from behind the door. Then the door slammed shut and a lightning roundhouse kick struck Gibbons's gun hand. He took the punishing blow but didn't let go of his weapon.

Forgetting his exhaustion, Gibbons crouched, lunged, and tackled his assailant before the man regained his balance and attempted another fancy martial-arts maneuver. Together they slammed against the opposite wall in the narrow hallway, and it was only after Gibbons heard the man's cursing grunt that it registered that his assailant was Tozzi.

Instantly Gibbons got to his knees and pointed Excalibur in Tozzi's face. His eyes were locked onto his old partner's, but he could feel the muzzle of Tozzi's automatic digging into the flesh just below his sternum.

"How long have you been out there?" Gibbons demanded angrily. He was pissed off at himself. He should have sensed that someone was waiting for him behind that door. "How long, Tozzi?"

"I don't know—over an hour at least." Tozzi tendered the back of his head with his free hand, then glanced at his blood-smeared fingertips. "Fuck."

"How'd you know I was in here?"

Tozzi smirked and shook his head. "You never did know how to pick a lock, Gib. Fresh scratch marks all over the cylinder. You left your card."

Gibbons had never liked Tozzi's arrogance. "I ought to blow your fucking—"

"You do and I'll blow *your* fucking whatever off, too," Tozzi said.

Gibbons looked down at Tozzi's 9mm Beretta. Suddenly it seemed very peculiar for his partner to be holding a gun on him. It didn't make any sense.

Tozzi was laughing, shaking his head and laughing.

"Is it that funny, Tozzi?"

"No, not really. But then again maybe it is, I don't know. It's just that I had this weird daydream a while back that they'd sent you out to get me. Like a knight in shining armor out to slay the dragon. And now, lo and behold, here you are."

"You killed them, didn't you?"

Tozzi looked insulted. "Of course I fucking killed them. Jesus H. Christ, if the Bureau can't figure that out, they're more fucked up than I—"

"Why?" Gibbons cut him off.

Tozzi just stared at him. "I don't believe you, man. If *you* don't know why, then I may as well stick this gun in my mouth and forget about it."

Gibbons waited for one of Tozzi's typically flamboyant gestures, like turning the gun on himself for dramatic effect. But this time he didn't do it.

"How should I know why you killed those guys?" Gibbons asked.

Tozzi was yelling. "I feel like shooting you, you bastard, I really do. I didn't kill just any three guys, I killed *those* three guys. And you want to know why? Because when we were working their cases, no matter what we did, we couldn't put them away. The rules, the fucking rules and the fucking legal system, man. Guilty as shit, all three of them. We knew it, they knew it, everybody knew it. But we had to go by the fucking book, the fucking system. And the goddamn system let those guys fly, man. A drug kingpin, a child molester who happened to be a U.S. congressman, and a lawyer who sheltered killers."

"That's not much of an answer."

"What are you, fucking senile, Gibbons? A year into retirement and you forgot everything. Let me give you a refresher course in reality, man. It was *you* who clued me into the way things work at the Bureau, *you* who told me how justice really works in this country. All those hours we spent on all those plants, you bitching to me about how Ivers flushed all our good work down the toilet, bending my ear about how rich people buy themselves out of trouble, how judges jump on the small-time criminals but invite the big-timers to dinner. Is any of this coming back to you, Gib?"

It was, but Gibbons didn't say anything.

"I'm just doing what we always talked about doing," Tozzi continued, still spitting venom. "I'm taking justice into my own hands—there, I said it, plain as could be. Eliminating a handful of career criminals is a hell of a lot better than working within a system that makes me totally ineffectual. That's how I see it."

Gibbons exhaled slowly. There was nothing he could say in response. He agreed with everything Tozzi had said, and he did remember all the growling tirades in the dark when he'd said those exact same things to Tozzi. But with him it was always just talk, blowing steam. Tozzi was actually doing something about it.

"And after you've wiped out everybody on your hit list, what then?"

"I've made plans. I've got relatives . . . out of the country."

Gibbons stared at him for a long moment, then sighed and holstered his gun.

"What're you doing?" Tozzi demanded. "You're supposed to shoot me—no, what's the word they use?—'neutralize' me. They sent you to neutralize me, man. So come on, get with it. You're the fucking company man—do it!"

The gun was shaking in Tozzi's hand. Gibbons had never seen him so upset and it made him uncomfortable. He slowly laid his hand on the doorknob.

Tozzi abruptly pointed his gun in Gibbons's face. "I don't want to kill you, Gib, I really and truly don't, but I'm not through yet. I'm onto something big, really big, and I don't want any interference."

There was a hollow, gnawing sensation in Gibbons's gut. He stared at Tozzi's gun, avoiding his eyes. "I've gone through our old files. My guess is that you're next target is either Felix Kramer or Reverend Miner."

"Neither one. There's just one more name on my hit list . . . but I don't know who he is yet." Tozzi waited for Gibbons to look him in the eye. They stared at each other, but Tozzi seemed to be sizing up his old partner, wondering whether Gibbons could still be trusted. Suddenly Tozzi lowered his gun. "Sit down, Gib. There's something I've got to show you."

SEVEN

Reluctantly Gibbons sat down on the edge of the plastic-covered sofa while Tozzi went into the bedroom. It crossed his mind that Tozzi could come back out with guns blazing, but he resisted the urge to pull his weapon. Tozzi wasn't like that. Even if his old partner had gone renegade, Gibbons felt he could trust Tozzi that way.

A moment later Tozzi emerged from the bedroom, an ugly look on his face. He was carrying a stuffed manila envelope, which he dropped on the coffee table in front of Gibbons. "Take a look at these."

Gibbons opened the envelope and pulled out a curled sheaf of eight-by-ten black-and-white photographs. They looked like surveillance shots. He flipped through them quickly—guys in parking lots, on the street, sitting in cars, getting out of cars—then he slowed down when he started to recognize faces. They were all FBI agents from the Manhattan field office.

"Did you take these?" he asked Tozzi.

Tozzi took the pile away from him and shuffled through the photos quickly. He pulled one out and showed it to Gibbons. It was a picture of the two of them seated at a lunch counter.

"Where did you get these?"

Tozzi sat down next to Gibbons. "Remember Vinnie Clementi? The pusher?"

"Yeah?"

"I found them in his apartment after I did him. There are twenty-six pictures here, thirty-eight agents in all." Tozzi was breathing fast. "And get this, he knew my name."

"Who knew your name?"

"Clementi. The scumbag was standing in my face, begging for mercy, and he called me by my name. He called me 'Mikey.' "

Gibbons stared down at the photos scattered over the coffee table. Some of these faces he'd known for over twenty years. "Clementi knew your name was Michael," he murmured absently, searching for the angle. He looked at his own face in the picture. It was tired and creased, an old man's face. "Somebody's been tailing agents," he said sadly.

"Damn straight. And that means somebody's been *fingering* agents," Tozzi said. "Somebody who knows us. Somebody on the inside."

Gibbons's stomach started to ache. His temper suddenly flared. "What the fuck is this, Tozzi? You go AWOL and turn into a vigilante, and now you're trying to tell me you're onto a bad agent? What're you trying to pull?"

Tozzi looked him in the eye, then looked away. "I didn't *want* to find these pictures."

"Why did you toss Clementi's apartment, tell me that. You did a real job on the place. The guy who did the report on the apartment said the perp was clearly looking for something, looking for something pretty badly."

"Who did the report?" Tozzi asked.

"Why do you want to know?"

"Anybody I know?"

"Some new guy—I don't know his name—just transferred to New York from the Philly office. What were you looking for at Clementi's?"

"Address books, ledgers, anything that might lead to his connection."

"So you could go execute him too?"

"Since when do you start taking up for drug dealers, Gib?"

"When some asshole starts taking the law into his own hands."

"Fuck you, Gibbons. You and I both know this is the only way to get these guys. They're too big, too smart, they buy the best lawyers. I've thought this through. It's the only effective way to put these guys out of action."

Gibbons wasn't about to argue with that. He let out a slow breath until the testiness ran out of him. "You said you stumbled onto something big. Give it to me. The Bureau will handle it in-house."

"The hell they will. Whoever's responsible *is* in-house. I'm sure of that."

"So what do you think?" Gibbons asked. Tozzi had to have a theory: in all the years they'd worked together, Tozzi always managed to cook up some kind of Sherlock Holmes solution.

"Hang on, let me show you something."

Gibbons watched Tozzi go through the photos. He picked out two and laid them down next to the picture of the two of them at the lunch counter. He watched Tozzi's hands, long and quick, gambler's hands, just as he remembered them. The sweaty forehead was something new, though.

"Here." Tozzi pointed to a picture of an agent in a heavy overcoat emerging from a car on a busy Main Street somewhere. You could see his breath in the cold. "Dave Simmons, right? Look in the background." Tozzi pointed to a blurry movie marquee in the background. "See what it says? *Terms of Endearment*. That movie was released in the fall of eighty-three, I checked. It was the big movie that year, stayed in the theaters all that winter. This means they've been watching our guys for—what?—almost three years?"

Gibbons thought it was interesting that Tozzi referred to the agents in the pictures as "our guys." In all his years with the Bureau, he himself never thought of it as a brotherhood.

"Now look at this." Tozzi snatched up their picture. "Look on the counter, next to my coffee."

There was a small white bottle in front of Tozzi, a crumpled-up napkin next to it.

"Cold pills. I remember, three winters ago, I had a stupid cold that I couldn't shake and I was taking those pills that're supposed to keep you going. They didn't work for shit, and my nose was running all over the place. Now the way I figure, this had to have been taken somewhere on Staten Island. We were checking out that construction company, remember?"

Gibbons nodded. "I remember. It was February, March of eighty-four."

Tozzi dropped their picture and grabbed the third one. It showed a crowd of standing men, most of them smoking, some looking around, others studying racing forms. There was a row of betting windows in the background. A circle had been drawn around two of the men standing together in the crowd, both in their mid-thirties. One was wearing a leather jacket over a crewneck sweater, the other a light-colored suit with no tie. "Kozlowski and Driscoll. I'm positive this was taken at

Aqueduct.'' Tozzi tapped the picture with his index finger. ''They were undercover at the time, had a warehouse setup somewhere out on Long Island. They were posing as small-time fences looking for some big-time action. I remember this distinctly because Kozlowski came to me to show me this shitty little goatee he'd grown. He wanted to know if I thought he looked Italian enough.''

''What'd you tell him?''

''I told him he looked okay, but it was his rotten kielbasy breath that would give him away.'' Tozzi laughed, but Gibbons could tell his heart wasn't in it.

Gibbons stared at the faces of the two agents. ''These guys were undercover, and somebody knew who they were.'' He shook his head. ''This is bad . . .''

''And it gets worse.'' Tozzi grabbed the envelope and pulled out a handwritten list. Gibbons immediately recognized Tozzi's hasty block printing. ''These are the names of the guys I picked out of the pictures. Thirty-eight agents in all. But who's missing?''

Gibbons scanned the list quickly, then went back over it one by one. What was Tozzi driving at? He shrugged and shook his head.

''If these pictures were taken in the winter and early spring of eighty-four, there are three very obvious omissions here.''

Three. Gibbons stopped breathing. Of course. Lando, Blaney, and Novick. Jesus Christ . . .

He rubbed the back of his neck and looked hard at Tozzi, his gut churning. Lando, Blaney, and Novick—three guys who hardly knew each other but whose names were permanently linked, always mentioned in the same hushed breath, three names that still made federal agents swallow hard and think anxious thoughts about their kids and wives. Everybody knew the story, but for those agents who were active at the time, it would never go away and would always be a startling reminder of what could happen on the job.

It started out as a gruesome puzzle, didn't even concern the Bureau at first. Three bodies found in the middle of a field of high grass behind a grammar school in Stamford, Connecticut. Three male bodies without heads. It was late September 1984.

Then, a few days later, on the last Saturday of the month, a postal worker drove up to a mailbox on a fairly busy road near Van Cortlandt Park in the Bronx to make his first pickup of the day. He found a large package on the ground next to the box, the corners crushed and torn as if someone had tried to jam it in but couldn't make it fit. He picked it up, immediately thinking that the damn thing would have to be returned. It was heavy, thirty, forty pounds from the feel of it, and he was sure there wasn't enough postage on it. He turned the box over on the hood of his Jeep and saw almost thirty twenty-cent stamps plastered down the right-hand side of the package in uneven overlapping lines, lines of American flags ripped from a roll and haphazardly pasted down. No return address. Then he noticed the carefully printed address done with a black felt-tip pen:

DIRECTOR
FEDERAL BUREAU OF INVESTIGATION
WASHINGTON, DC 20535

The postal worker set the package down gently, crossed to the other side of the street, and flagged down the next police car that came by.

Two hours later the NYPD bomb squad trailer arrived on the scene and took possession of the package. The bomb squad truck looks like a giant chain-mail jelly roll and is specially designed to contain an explosion while in transit. They took the package to the police firing range at Pelham Bay Park on the other side of the Bronx for examination and detonation if necessary. As part of their routine procedure, one of the men on the bomb squad X-rayed the package to see just what he was dealing with. What he saw made his mouth go dry.

That afternoon the package was transferred to the city medical examiner, who opened it with an FBI lab tech in attendance so as not to lose any possible evidence, like fingerprints, lint, hair, or saliva. Inside they found what the bomb squad told them to expect, three human heads. But the bomb squad X rays didn't prepare them for the rest of it, not the smell or the first sight of the mottled yellowed faces, and certainly not the gouged-out eyes. Three heads lined up on a stainless steel tray, six horrible raw holes looking at nothing. Lando, Blaney, and Novick. Gibbons remembered the ME's report saying that in each of the victims there were signs of clotting in the torn optic nerves, indicating that the eyes had been ripped out before death.

Lando, Blaney, and Novick. Before they were killed, they had each been working alone, undercover, infiltrating organized crime in the New York families. They posed as eager-beaver hoods, anxious to find a regular gig with the mob. They were swimming with sharks. Lando had an office over a plumbing-supply company in Uniondale where he took care of the books for Sabatini Mistretta's loan-sharking operations on Long Island. Blaney was running numbers for a lieutenant in Phillip Giovinazzo's family, working out of a car wash on Twenty-third Street in Manhattan. Novick was working for a trucking business owned by one of Joe Luccarelli's associates, driving oranges, grapefruit, and cocaine twice a week from Florida to the farmers' market in Newark. They swam with sharks, and they got their heads bitten off.

Tozzi stared out the window and mumbled into his fist. "I keep thinking about Nina Lando. And the two girls. The older one must be in high school now. He was my first partner in the Bureau. He used to look out for me, have me over for dinner, that kind of stuff. Even tried to fix me up with his sister-in-law once. He was the kind of guy you could talk to about real things . . . Good man . . . I was supposed to have that undercover . . ."

Gibbons stared down at the pictures. "Lando, Blaney, and Novick fingered by another agent . . . that's a pretty serious charge."

"I've considered every other possible alternative." Tozzi shook his head gravely. "It's got to be a bad agent. How else would a flea like Clementi have pictures like this? It has to be."

Gibbons's head was throbbing. "If the mob knows who we are and they have known for almost three years, why haven't they tried to get rid of all of us?"

"Why? Because it would be stupid, that's why. If they started gunning down agents, the Bureau would just replace them with new men the mob wouldn't know. But as long as they know who the feds are, they can watch out for us, keep us at arm's length, run us around in circles. It's the perfect situation for them."

Tozzi did it again. He kept saying "us" when he referred to the Bureau. Gibbons rested his elbows on his knees and stared at his shoes. "The perfect situation," he murmured. "But what good did it do them? The Varga trials crippled the Mafia in New York. Luccarelli and Mistretta have been convicted and sentenced, and Giovinazzo is locked up in a hospital room playing possum and getting bedsores while his lawyers keep prolonging the agony. All their key men are serving time, and the few who got away are in hiding. So what the fuck good did it do them? Some perfect situation."

"That's what I keep asking myself, Gib, and you know what?"

"What?"

"It doesn't matter."

"Huh?"

"What does matter is that there's a bad agent somewhere in the Bureau, and we've got to nail him."

"What do you mean 'we'?"

"We can't turn this over to the Bureau. You don't know who we can trust there."

Gibbons shook his head. "You are one paranoid son-of-a-bitch, you know that?"

Tozzi's face contorted in contained fury; his fists were trembling. "Will you fucking listen to me, man? The shit these punks on the street are pulling is getting worse everyday. There are shootouts out in public practically every week. A lot of innocent people are getting hurt. It's like Dodge City out there. So how do we know the bad guy in the Bureau isn't selling his info to the freelancers, huh? To guys like Clementi. These fleas out there now aren't as weird and ritualistic as the families were, but they sure ain't showing the kind of restraint the families did either."

Gibbons stared at the photos again, the faces he knew, men he'd worked with, men who kept framed color pictures of their families on their desks back at the field office. "Specifically what are you suggesting, Tozzi?"

"I have a few hunches, but I need room to move."

"In other words you don't want the Bureau on your tail. You want me to run interference, stay between you and them."

Tozzi nodded. "I'll also need access to Bureau files."

Gibbons sighed. "Great. Criminal use of confidential federal files should add what?—at least another ten years to our sentences when they catch us."

"Not if we catch them first." Tozzi was flashing that big nervous smile again.

Gibbons glanced at the pictures one more time. "If I were to help you—*if*—I don't want to be kept in the dark about what you're doing, understand?"

"We're partners, Gib. We always were."

Gibbons looked past him to the picture on the end table, the little kid on the Shetland, the monkey in a Daniel Boone outfit sitting on a pony. He knew this was wrong, that helping Tozzi would make him a renegade agent too. There was a heavy feeling in his chest. But Tozzi was right, there was no other way.

Finally Gibbons nodded slowly, and Tozzi laid a grateful hand on his shoulder. Gibbons glared at it. He didn't like being touched.

''So tell me, Sherlock. What's your hunch?''

''Okay. Lando, Blaney, and Novick worked for different families, but were obviously killed in the same hit. Very uncharacteristic for the mob. That kind of cooperation is almost unheard of. The families may have been tipped off about the undercovers at the same time, but why would they get together for the punishment?''

''I give up. Why?''

''I don't know,'' Tozzi said, ''but I do think there's someone who may know, someone who was intimately connected with Luccarelli, Mistretta, and Giovinazzo.''

''Richie Varga?''

''You got it. He was their golden boy before he ratted on them. They loved him. I've got a feeling Varga may know something.''

Gibbons laughed out loud. ''Boy, are you whistling Dixie! You ever try to question someone under witness protection? To do it legit, you've got to put your business in writing, then submit it to the Justice Department. Then, when and if they get around to it—''

''Fuck the Justice Department,'' Tozzi said, grinning. ''I've got my own channels.''

Gibbons shook his head and smiled slyly. ''I don't doubt it,'' he said.

EIGHT

Joanne Collesano Varga stuck her tongue in Tozzi's ear. "Wake up, Mr. Thompson," she purred. "I've got to get to work."

Tozzi stretched under the sheets, then rubbed his nose. The clock-radio on her side of the bed was tuned to a classical station. The volume was low—a string quartet playing something modern and atonal—just loud enough to be annoying.

"Turn that shit off," he groaned.

"Don't tell me you're the type who listens to rock first thing in the morning." She seemed mildly disappointed.

"No." He was lying. He could really go for some Springsteen or maybe Dire Straits right now. That and another go-round with Joanne.

He turned toward her, pulled her close, and kissed her, and again he was surprised by the tobacco taste in her mouth. He didn't smoke himself, but he could live with the taste. Considering what came with it, who wouldn't?

He palmed the back of her head, felt the glory of her thick dark tousled hair, and grinned under that kiss. She was the first really Italian-looking woman he'd ever slept with.

She pulled away from him slowly. "I've got to go to work," she whispered.

"You're a vice president. They won't can you if you're late. Call in sick and we'll spend the day in bed."

She shook her head and grinned. A stray lock of raven hair curled up salaciously under her eye and gave him another hard-on.

"It's a tempting offer, Mr. Thompson, but . . ."

"But what? You never had it so good. Admit it."

Under the sheets she ran her fingernail up the length of his dick. "Not with Richie, that's for sure."

"Poor bastard," Tozzi said. "Married to you and out of commission. Tragic."

"Unfortunately, he didn't exactly see it that way."

"No?"

"Hope always sprang eternal, even if he didn't. We'd try it, he'd fall down on the job as usual, then he'd slap me around to work off his frustrations. It didn't happen often . . . but often enough."

"Did he hurt you?"

"Only once."

Tozzi shook his head. Those violins were driving him nuts. "I can't believe your father would let him get away with that. I'd have thought ole Jules'd make him live to regret the day he laid a hand on his little girl."

"Richie was the golden boy, the heir apparent. Jules Collesano just told his little girl to go back home and try harder, that it would all work out, don't worry. My father took for the bastard." She turned on her back and looked at the ceiling. "Richie was like a little dog, always eager, always loyal, ready whenever my father wanted him. That's why he loved Richie, because he never disappointed him. Until the shit double-crossed him, that is. But before that my father considered Richie the ultimate 'nice boy.' Christ, he'd known Richie since he was a little kid."

"Yeah?"

She pushed the curl out of her eye. Tozzi wished she'd left it.

"Richie's half-Cuban," she said. "Did you know that? His father worked in a casino my father owned down in Havana before Castro took over. When Batista was in power."

"No, I didn't know that." Tozzi stared at her as she stared at the ceiling and talked.

"When the revolution came Richie's family left Cuba and came to America. They were pretty desperate, apparently, when Manny—that's Richie's father—went to see my father. Manny had always been a good guy as far as my father was concerned, so he gave him a job running one of his bars in Camden. Nothing very glamorous, but my father-in-law was honored to work for Jules Collesano. You know, all that beholden Latino 'I-am-forever-indebted-to-you' crap. By the way, Richie changed his name, did you know that? It's really Vargas. After his father died, he dropped the *s* so it would sound more Italian."

"No shit." Tozzi wished the fuck those violins on the radio would drop dead.

"Anyway, Manny pushed Richie into the business, always making a big show out of his kid paying respect to my father and his mob buddies. My father ate it up with a spoon. After Manny died, my old man took Richie under his wing, the son he never had. After a while it was just sort of understood that we'd get married."

Just like Ricky and Lucy. "How long were you married?" Tozzi asked.

"I told you, technically we're still married. I suppose I could divorce him now, but with him in hiding it hardly seems worth the effort. And can you imagine what an incredible hassle it would be trying to take him to court, with him in the Witness Security Program?"

"While you were married—together I mean—did you ever get an inkling that he wasn't on the up-and-up, that he really wanted to fuck your father over?"

She glared at Tozzi and squeezed his dick hard. "Why are we talking about him? I'm not about to take the morning off just to talk about that asshole."

Tozzi grinned and got up on one elbow. As he kissed her again, running his tongue over her teeth, he reached over and spun the dial on the radio. He found a stronger station and David Bowie blared across the room. Quickly Tozzi turned down the volume and started to mumble-sing along with the radio. *"Let's dance, ba-da, ba-da, bum, bum, bum, ba-da-dum, dum, dum. Let's dance . . ."*

He cupped her ass in his hands, buried his face in all that beautiful hair, and bit her earlobe. Bowie would do just fine.

He felt her reach down and take his balls in both hands. She started to guide his rigid dick into her, arching her back to meet him. He was surprised to find that she was already wet and satiny. Suddenly he was in up to the hilt and she was pulling him closer, grinding into him, gyrating her hips around him.

"Get up on your knees," she whispered.

When he did, she wrapped her arms around his back and pulled herself up into him, thrusting again and again with sweet, slow deliberation. She kept up the rhythm, twisting just a little with each thrust to change the angle of projection and drive him crazy.

Then he felt it rising in him, and he tried to stop it, straining to keep from coming before she did.

"Don't hold back," she said, licking his lips. "Let it go."

Her hips slammed against his and he couldn't hold it any longer. It was like coming over the crest of the scariest part of a roller-coaster ride, a rush in the pit of your stomach as you go over the top, then falling fast out of control, rushing for the thrill. As it was happening, in the blur of ecstasy, he vaguely realized that he'd never experienced anything like this with a woman before. Not even remotely close.

The phone rang while Tozzi was in the shower. Joanne answered it in the kitchen.

"Hello?"

"What's going on in there?"

She paused and took a sip of coffee from a deep blue mug. "He's in the shower now. I'll get him out of here in a half hour."

She could hear his breathing on the other end. She knew he was mad.

"I think he's in love with me," she said, grinning into the phone. "We did it twice last night and once more this morning."

"I hope he's got AIDS."

She laughed. She knew he'd be pissed, and she loved it. Richie was so proprietary.

"Everything's all set," he said. "Don't take all day."

"Don't worry. We'll be out soon."

She hung up the phone, picked up her mug, and headed back to the dressing room to finish putting on her makeup.

It was a little after ten, and they were standing in the parking lot behind her building making out like teenagers, him sitting on the fender of his cousin's 300ZX, her in a navy-blue business suit leaning over him with her arms draped around his shoulders. They both wore shit-eating grins.

This is outrageous, he thought.

"I, ah, think I better get going," she said with a throaty laugh, then ran her tongue over his lips.

"You been saying that since seven o'clock this morning."

"Yeah, I know."

Tozzi glanced up at the elderly gentleman glaring down at them from his balcony. He had that pissy look of someone who'd paid two hundred grand for his small two-bedroom condo and for that price didn't need two hot bods down in the parking lot showing him what he wouldn't be getting anymore, if he'd ever gotten any in the first place. Tozzi was a little concerned, though, that the old guy might call the cops, and that kind of attention he didn't need.

"Well," he said, "I guess you're right. We better break this up before your neighbor up there has a coronary."

She didn't bother to look up at the neighbor, just pressed her weight against Tozzi and ground her lips into his, her tongue going like mad. The springs of his cousin's car squeaked under the weight of that incredible kiss. Tozzi suddenly remembered the term "soul-kissing" from high school.

When they finally let go, she ran her hand affectionately over his cheek, kissed him once more lightly, and said, "I have to go." She turned and walked away.

"Hey," he called after her, "Joanne, can we—will I be seeing you again?"

She turned and smiled coyly as she kept walking, her heels keeping time. "That's up to you, Phantom. You know where to find me . . . Mr. Thompson." She dug her keys out of her shoulder bag and unlocked the door of a maroon Saab 900 Turbo. It looked new. The engine had a nice quiet purr as she pulled out of her space, waved to him in the rearview mirror, and took off for work.

He waved back and got off the fender of his cousin's silver Nissan. If Bobby only knew that he had his precious car, he'd go nuts, Tozzi thought. But he'd never find out, not unless he checked the odometer. Tozzi imagined fat Bobby coming home from his regular business trip to California, unlocking his garage, starting up the car, letting the engine get warm, then staring down at the mileage and having a shit fit, wondering how the hell they got into his garage, took his car, clocked over a thousand miles, and got it back in as if it'd never been touched.

Tozzi reached into his pocket for the universal ignition key he'd "borrowed" from the Bureau and opened the car door. The day was already getting hot, so he took off his jacket and leaned inside to toss it in back. That's when he sensed that something wasn't right. It smelled different, like a cigar smoker's clothes. Bobby chain-smoked cigarettes, not cigars, not those shitty little crooked ones from Italy, the ones that smelled like this. Tozzi glanced through the windshield. That old man was still glaring at him from his balcony.

He backed out of the car carefully and crouched down to look under the dash. Then he contorted his body and tried to get a look under the seat. He noticed a bend of yellow wire that shouldn't have been there.

Tozzi stood up and backed away from the car, considering his alternatives. Call the cops to check it out, and he loses his wheels. Worse, they trace the registration to his cousin and the Bureau will automatically assume he took it. They check out who lives in the building and make the connection with Joanne Varga. No good.

But he couldn't just abandon the car. In a couple of days, the building superintendent would call a tow truck, and some dumb kid would get behind the wheel and get his ass blown to kingdom come. No, he couldn't just leave it here.

Shit. There was only one solution, which really wasn't much of a solution at all.

Tozzi backed away a few more steps to the hedges at the edge of the lot where he found a broken half of a cinder block in the dirt. He picked it up, weighed it in his hand, then remembered the old guy who was still up there watching him.

''What're you looking at, you old bastard? Get the fuck inside,'' Tozzi yelled up at him.

Tozzi could see him bristling. ''I said, get inside and mind your own fucking business!''

The old man sputtered something Tozzi didn't understand.

''Stubborn asshole,'' Tozzi muttered, and then gave the guy the finger, which sent him scuttling back inside, shouting indignantly that he was calling the police.

''Good, you do that,'' Tozzi murmured as he took aim with the piece of cinder block, swinging it nice and easy. He pitched it into the car like a horseshoe.

The cinder block skinned the edge of the door, hit the steering wheel, and landed on the driver's seat, which was just enough pressure to depress the concealed spring plate under the seat and make contact with what's generally known as a loose-floorboard bomb. Tozzi was already facedown on the asphalt with his arms over his head. The explosion made his ears pop. When he looked up, the inside of Bobby's 300ZX was a furnace, flames curving out the windows and licking what was left of the roof.

Shit. Bobby was gonna be pissed.

Tozzi stood up, brushed himself off, and started to walk away fast. Walk, don't run, just get away from the scene, pronto.

He looked over his shoulder and stared at the burning wreck for a moment. Well, that's why God made insurance, Bobby.

Gibbons had just bitten down on an Oreo when the phone rang. He closed the book he'd been reading on his finger and chewed thoughtfully. The book was a scholarly work on the influence of the Teutonic barbarians on their Roman conquerors, how their alien culture seeped into the empire and persevered despite all Roman efforts to eradicate it. Gibbons saw many parallels with the present.

The phone kept ringing. Gibbons sat up on the sofa and reached for the receiver, dropping his book in the process and losing his place.

"Hello," he said, still chewing.

"It's me."

Gibbons recognized Tozzi's voice, even though it sounded like he was underwater with traffic in the background. "What's up?"

"Someone tried to kill me this morning."

Gibbons picked up another Oreo. "No kidding."

"Bomb under the driver's seat."

"You get hurt?"

"No, but there could be problems."

Gibbons paused to swallow. "What kind of problems?"

"The car can be connected to me. It's my cousin's car. He's in San Diego on business and won't be back for another couple of weeks. But if they connect me with the wreck and where it is, it could fuck things up. Hey, your phone's not bugged, is it?"

"Hope not."

"Okay, listen. My cousin's name is Benedetto not Tozzi, so the connection won't be obvious right away. Plus, it happened in Jersey, out in Morristown, so if the Bureau gets called in, it'll be the Newark office, not ours."

Ours: Gibbons took note of that. "You sound paranoid again," he said. "Even if the New York office did get wind of it, how could a burnt-out wreck lead them to you now?"

"That's not what I'm worried about. The car was parked outside Joanne Varga's apartment. If they canvass the building, they'll find out Richie Varga's ex lives there. It's not a connection I want them to make."

"I don't get it."

"Neither do I. Not yet."

"You think she set you up?"

"I don't know. I don't think so. We were together sitting on the fender for at least twenty minutes, a half hour."

"Doing what?"

"Use your imagination."

Gibbons picked another Oreo out of the package and held it near his mouth. "You'll never learn, will you? Don't trust her."

"If she was setting me up, she wouldn't have hung around the way she did."

"Don't trust her," Gibbons repeated. "Just remember who the hell she is and where she comes from."

"I know, I know. She seems legit, but who knows? I just need to string her along for a while. I have a feeling she might be able to lead me to Varga."

Gibbons listened to Tozzi trying to sound like a hard guy. He knew damn well that Tozzi was sleeping with the broad and enjoying it too. He was getting sweet on her, the stupid asshole.

"Listen," Tozzi said, "I've been trying to make sense of all this. It's the sequence of events that bothers me. First, Varga double-crosses his father-in-law and feeds inside information to Mistretta, Giovinazzo, and Luccarelli, in effect giving them Atlantic City. Then Lando, Blaney, and Novick. Then Varga turns on his three godfathers and rats on them to the grand jury. Organized crime in New York is *supposedly* dealt a fatal blow, but in no time the heavy business gets worse than ever. Now what I want to know is who's fronting the money for these freelancers? Small-time dealers are buying in volume now—where are they getting the cash? They haven't been in business long enough to have that kind of capital. Guys like Vinnie Clams. How did he get so big so fast?"

"I give up, how?"

"I think there's a new boss, somebody we don't know, somebody working very cleverly behind the scenes. Maybe all the heavy action on the streets isn't random, maybe these guys aren't freelancers at all. Maybe this is a whole new family, a very powerful family who's got a monopoly on New York now that Mistretta, Giovinazzo, and Luccarelli are out of the picture."

"It's an interesting theory," Gibbons said. "You think you can sell it?"

"Too early to tell. The important thing now is that we find the rotten apple in the Bureau. I have a feeling that once we find him, everything else will start to fall into place. Including who killed Lando, Blaney, and Novick."

"What do you want me to do?" Gibbons picked up a blunt pencil and looked around for a pad. He rummaged through the piles of books on the coffee table, the books he'd been meaning to read for years. The pad was lost. Fuck it, he'd remember. What else did he have on his mind these days?

"Check the files on Varga," Tozzi said. "See who he worked with when he turned state's witness—you know, feds, prosecutors, marshals, everybody. Poke around for anything peculiar. Also, try to get a list of all the agents who worked undercover in the families in the past five, six years. It's possible that our rotten apple went over to the other side while he was working inside the mob."

"You got it," Gibbons said.

"I'll be in touch—"

"Hold on. I want to know one thing."

"What's that?"

Gibbons grinned into the phone. "Was she good?"

"What do you think?" Tozzi said just before he hung up.

The dial tone droned in Gibbons's ear, but he ignored it. He studied the Oreo he'd been holding and then ate it whole.

NINE

The next day Gibbons lucked out. It was Friday and Ivers wasn't going to be in that day. The New York SAC was taking a long weekend to pick up his son at summer camp in Maine. Gibbons had discovered that Ivers had an annoying habit of popping in unexpectedly when he was working with the computer and reading through files. He may have given Gibbons free access to the files, but he never said he'd keep his nose out of the investigation. Ivers wanted Tozzi's ass on a hook, and Gibbons was sick of giving him evasive answers, quoting him procedural chapter and verse on just what he was doing, how he was doing it, and what his goals were. Today, thank God, he'd be able to work in peace, and he planned to take advantage of the situation and get a lot done.

By one o'clock his eyes were burning. His cubicle in the File Room was stacked with the transcripts of Richie Varga's testimony at the federal grand jury hearings. The CRT screen tilted up from the desktop and glowed green at him. His head was throbbing, but he couldn't stop now. He was beginning to get a feel for what Tozzi suspected. Varga was intimately linked to three mob families in New York, a unique position for anyone. The three bosses of these families obviously had to have agreed on killing Lando, Blaney, and Novick, so if anyone was privy to such a pact, Varga certainly could have been. And if Varga had known about the plans for the hit, it was possible that he also knew who fingered the three agents.

Gibbons had put together a list of agents from the New York office who had worked undercover in the three families during the last ten years. Besides Lando, Blaney, and Novick, there were sixteen others—four in Mistretta's family, five in Giovinazzo's family, and seven in Luccarelli's. Gibbons studied the names. He knew some of them pretty well, the younger guys he didn't know at all. But that meant nothing. The rat could be your best friend, the most inconspicuous guy in the world, the one no one would ever suspect. It could be any one of these guys. Gibbons stared blankly at the yellow legal pad where he'd written the names down in a column with the Italian cover name each man had used in parentheses.

Before tackling the volumes of courtroom testimony, Gibbons had decided to read through the FBI standard file on Varga. Richie was born in Havana, Cuba, on September 3, 1949. Gibbons counted the years; Varga would turn thirty-seven in two weeks. His father had been some kind of gofer for the American mobsters who controlled the Havana casinos. Emanuel "Manny" Vargas, Richie's father, adored gangsters because they were macho and they were American. When Batista fled Cuba in 1959 and Castro's revolution drove the mob off the island, Vargas moved his wife and son to Philadelphia, where he found work with the mob, specifically running an after-hours gambling club in the basement of a bar called the Peppermint Lounge across the river in Camden, New Jersey. Like most of the Cubans who fled their homeland, Manny Vargas became a superpatriot in his adopted country, openly and frequently praising the United States, the great enemy of world Communism. He was very proud of the fact that his only son had the same first name as the great anti-Communist champion, then Vice President Nixon.

In the Philly organization, Richie's father answered to Jules Collesano, a loyal lieutenant who was generally known as a "good Joe" and a soft touch. Manny apparently encouraged his son to suck up to Collesano, who took to the boy, presumably because he had three daughters despite his wife's best efforts to produce a son. (Mrs. Collesano had suffered two miscarriages trying, in 1955 and again in 1956.) Richie grew up in an atmosphere of casinos, bars, and numbers parlors but was a quiet, studious kid. He graduated from St. Joseph's Prep in Philly, went on to Holy Cross in Worcester, Massachusetts, then eventually got his MBA from Temple. Collesano liked the fact that Richie was well-educated. He gave Richie a new car when he graduated from Holy Cross. For years, Jules and Manny had joked about making the match between Richie and Collesano's youngest daughter, Joanne. In the summer of 1972, after her freshman year of college, Joanne Collesano did marry Richie, who by this time had legally changed his name from Vargas to Varga.

There was a newspaper clipping of their wedding announcement in Varga's file. Gibbons studied the picture carefully. The bride looked frail, a small face lost in a lot of long straight hair, bangs covering her eyebrows, a real flower child. The groom had a kind of sleepy-eyed suaveness, dark wavy hair, long sideburns, and a droopy Zapata mustache over a toothy Latino smile. Not bad-looking, if you liked the type. Gibbons took note of the hippie influence in their hairstyles and was spitefully pleased to see that even the Mafia wasn't completely unaffected by the sixties.

Gibbons turned back to the terminal and started scrolling up, searching for more on the Atlantic City double cross. In the early seventies, Atlantic City was a quiet town, not a whole lot of action at what was then a decaying resort. Jules Collesano was getting older and wasn't much of a go-getter anymore, so the Philly mob sent him to Atlantic City to oversee what little they had going there. Jules was happy to be down the shore, and he took Richie and Joanne with him, putting his son-in-law the businessman in charge of the books. Eventually Richie was given responsibility for the day-to-day operations of everything in Collesano's jurisdiction—narcotics, prostitution, gambling, loan-sharking, protection, food suppliers, laundry services, garbage collection—everything. Jules knew that Richie was a good boy, capable enough and, if nothing else, trustworthy. Jules was very happy with this arrangement. He could hold on to his position of authority and still take it easy and enjoy his semiretirement.

But that was all before gambling became legal in Atlantic City. That's when things started to heat up.

Traditionally Atlantic City had always been the province of the Philadelphia boss, and when legalized gambling came into their territory, the Philly mob saw gold, Vegas East. But the other *capi* around the country had other ideas, particularly the three powerful New York bosses, Sabatini Mistretta, Joe Luccarelli, and Phillip Giovinazzo. They felt it was only fair that Atlantic City be an open city, the same as Las Vegas, so that everyone could get a piece of the action. Philly didn't see it that way and basically told them all to go fuck themselves. Jules Collesano assured his boss that he was prepared to go to the mattresses to defend his turf. Bolstered by a fresh crop of heavy hitters from the City of Brotherly Love, Collesano then let it be known that he'd come down hard on anybody who arrived from New York or anywhere else trying to get cute in his town.

Gibbons rubbed his tired eyes with the heels of his hands and imagined Collesano as a bullet-head centurion crammed into his breastplate, a good foot soldier once upon a time but promoted beyond his capability. He was ready to defend his walls to the death, but the thought of a fifth column never occurred to him. What a blow it must have been when he found out that his beloved Richie had been playing footsie with the New York bosses all along, feeding them inside information about his operations so that they could eventually take over Atlantic City as systematically as an epidemic.

Richie Varga may have looked like a jerk, but he must have had nerves of steel to do what he did. For over three years, he worked with Collesano while he was really spying for Mistretta, Luccarelli, and Giovinazzo. Finally when New York's hold on Atlantic City was strong enough, Richie made his true allegiance known, in effect spitting in his father-in-law's face.

The file didn't have anything about Varga's wife except to say that their marriage had never been a paradise. Gibbons simply assumed that when Richie betrayed his father-in-law, that was it for the marriage.

Gibbons kept scrolling. Jesus, this was a long file. He stopped for a moment and glanced out the tinted window at the blazing orange sunset beaming off the hard surfaces of the World Trade Center. It looked hot and hazy out there, in sharp contrast to the cool, dimly lit File Room.

He looked over at Hayes the librarian, who was poring over a stack of printouts. Gibbons stared at him, glassy-eyed. How the hell does a guy who looks like a pro linebacker and can't put three words together in the same sentence end up a librarian for the FBI? Gibbons stretched his back and cracked his knuckles, then finally went back to the screen.

He skimmed through Richie's involvement with the New York bosses, how he was instrumental in getting them to work together so they could all get what they wanted in Atlantic City. Mistretta, Luccarelli, and Giovinazzo were in love with the little asshole. Whatever Richie wanted, they got for him. They actually tried to outdo each other with expensive gifts. Nothing was too good for Richie. How fucking stupid. If he did it to Collesano, why didn't they think he'd do it to them?

It was odd, though, how his turnaround seemed to just come out of the blue. One day Richie's their prince, and the next day he's spilling his guts out to the federal prosecutors. Very strange. By all indications, his conversion was totally unmotivated. He was sitting pretty under the protection of three of the biggest Mafia bosses in the country. Why give all that up? What happened? Did he suddenly get scared? Of what? Maybe he found religion, who knows?

Gibbons rubbed his mouth and looked at the two thick volumes sitting in front of him on the desk, Varga's grand jury testimony. Not today. He decided to take it home and look at it over the weekend.

He rolled his head on his shoulders and listened to his neckbones creak, then he hit the scroll key again, stopping it at random to skim the rest of the file. He passed over the parts about Richie's testimony and the resulting convictions—he knew all about that. Dozens of mobsters were sent to jail, including Luccarelli and Mistretta. Giovinazzo's trial was still pending as he was recovering from an alleged stroke reportedly triggered by the news of Richie's betrayal. The file ended with an abrupt paragraph after the litany of Richie's victims.

> Richie Varga is presently living under the auspices of the Justice Department's Witness Security Program. His identity has been changed for his own protection. Inquiries of Varga, which pertain to ongoing investigations, must be submitted in writing and sponsored by a Special Agent in Charge. Appropriate written inquiries should be forwarded to the Assistant Attorney General in charge of the Witness Security Program.

Tight as a clam's ass, Gibbons thought.

But just when he thought he was finished, Gibbons was annoyed to see that there was a short addendum to the file, miscellaneous information about Varga that had been collected after he entered the program, mostly inconsequential personal stuff. One item did catch Gibbons's attention: "Varga diagnosed for testicular cancer, 1979. Surgical removal of affected testis; St. Jude's Hospital, Upper Darby, Pennsylvania; March 1980. Eighteen-month course of radiation and chemotherapy followed thereafter."

Gibbons shut off the terminal and leaned back in his chair, staring at the black screen. Cancer of the nuts. "Surgical removal." He shuddered and rubbed his crotch.

He quickly removed his hand when he heard the door to the File

Room opening. Fluorescent light spilled through the doorway as someone came in, someone Gibbons didn't know. One of the younger guys, he assumed.

"Hi . . . Bert?" the guy said as he walked toward Gibbons, his hand outstretched. "Bill Kinney."

Gibbons sized him up in a glance: young SAC material. Tall, trim, broad smile, crinkly eyes, athletic-looking. In a way he sort of reminded Gibbons of that asshole singer from the Rockies, what's his name, John Denver, but not so anemic. He wore a trim blue suit that was a shade lighter than navy and a pale yellow linen tie, Cub Scout colors. Gibbons shook his hand—firm grip, heavy college ring with a big garnet stone on his fourth finger. He slipped his other hand into his pants pocket, very casual, and Gibbons noticed a gold chain hooked onto his belt that looped into his pocket. Probably not keys, given his Ivy League looks; probably grandpa's old pocketwatch. Definitely SAC material, Gibbons thought.

"I heard you've been looking for me," Kinney said. "I was out of town for a few days."

"Yeah, Ivers told me. I wanted to ask you about Vinnie Clementi's apartment," Gibbons said.

"Did you read my report?"

Gibbons nodded. "I just wanted to know what your impression of the place was. If you got any . . . impressions, you know what I mean?"

"Well . . ." Kinney pulled up a chair and sat down on it backward, resting his forearms on the seatback. He even looked neat doing that. "I think it's all pretty much in the report. I wouldn't say there was anything that unusual about Clementi's apartment. Modern, predictably garish, but not cheap stuff. The whole place had that look as if he'd bought all his furniture in the same day. Not a whole lot of care, no little touches, none of the little items that seem to clutter up a place after you've lived in it for a while."

Gibbons thought of the stacks of books in his own living room, the books he'd meant to read years ago. He knew exactly what Kinney was talking about.

"Six ounces of coke in a box of Frosted Flakes in the cupboard, some crack too. Not much for the kind of dealer he was reputed to be. There was also a plastic bag full of cash behind the refrigerator, a little over two thousand dollars. Again, not much for a big dealer.

Nothing in the fridge. Jug of white wine, a few beers, ketchup, no real food. Clementi probably wasn't much of a cook.''

Kinney grinned and shrugged. Gibbons wondered what he found amusing.

''And other than that,'' Kinney went on, ''there wasn't much else. Lot of good stereo and video equipment, projection-screen TV, all top-of-the-line merchandise. But oddly enough, I only found three albums, a few cassettes, and just one blank videotape.''

Gibbons nodded slowly, imagining what the apartment looked like, wishing he could've examined the place himself before they rented it out again. Too late now.

''You and Tozzi were on his case a while back, weren't you?''

''Yup. We followed him around for a month. He was a cunning bastard, did everything over the phone and always made it sound like he was calling out for pizza. The guy never went anywhere near street-weight quantities.''

''So what happened?''

''Ivers ordered us to drop the investigation. Unless we could rope in a big haul of dope with the bust, he said it was a waste of time, that Clementi would fly in no time. He likes getting on the six-o'clock news, standing over a table full of dope, cash, guns . . . you know.''

Kinney nodded thoughtfully. ''I've heard that about him.''

They fell silent. Gibbons was thinking about Clementi's apartment, Tony the Tiger on the Frosted Flakes box, the big TV screen, the fancy stereo equipment. He was hoping something might click, but nothing did.

''Well . . .'' Kinney went for that chain in his pocket. He pulled out a gold watch, hexagonal-shaped with large Roman numerals on the face. It was a very unusual piece, the kind of heirloom a crusty old Boston banker might pass on to his favorite son. Gibbons had never seen one like it before. ''I've got to be on my way,'' Kinney said. He stood up and held out his hand again. ''Nice meeting you, Bert.''

Gibbons took his hand. ''Yeah, you too, Bill.''

''By the way, how's it going?''

''What?''

Kinney nodded at the transcripts on the desk. ''Your case. Any progress in finding Tozzi?''

Gibbons frowned and shook his head. ''Nothing solid yet.''

"Well, if I can do anything for you, let me know." Kinney got up and went for the door. "So long, Bert."

"Yeah, take it easy."

Gibbons couldn't believe it. In his entire career as an FBI agent, this had to be the first time another agent actually *offered* to help him on a case. Even if Kinney didn't mean it, it was still incredible. Maybe the guy wasn't half-bad, even though he did look like a SAC.

TEN

"I love the names," she said, flipping through the pages of one of the volumes. "Pat 'Irish' Facciano . . . Louie 'the Flea' Musso."

She laughed, but it was strained. Gibbons knew she was worried about Tozzi. He studied her face and focused on her throat. Her skin was tight under her chin, like one of those aging movie stars who'd had several face-lifts to look twenty-five again, but whose neck told the tale. Gibbons's gaze slipped to the mostly exposed breast hanging out of her open kimono. Lorraine still had nice tits for a forty-seven-year-old.

Gibbons leaned back in her creaky desk chair and watched her skimming through Richie Varga's testimony, her face alternating between gravity and that false mirth. She was a real sketch. Lorraine Bernstein, tenured professor of medieval history at Princeton, leaning over an open tome on an antique podium in her tome-lined study, the sound of birds singing in the pines outside her window, all her weight on one foot conqueringly positioned on the camel saddle she'd brought back from a trip to Morocco, her wonderful tits hanging out of the open front of a full-length painted silk kimono, her wonderful snatch hidden in the rosy shadows of the fuchsia-colored silk lining, her thick dark silver-threaded hair hooked around one ear. The sight of her standing there suddenly made him sad, wondering why the hell they'd never gotten married.

He knew the answer to that, of course. At least, the excuse they gave each other. The victims of two bad marriages do not a good marriage make. She'd put the Chaucerian touch on the phrase and it had become their motto over the years.

What they had together, in Gibbons's words, was "a good intellectual friendship with sex." They got a real kick out of being a Mutt-and-Jeff couple and delighted in their differences: the stoic Roman versus the capricious medievalist, the hard-ass fed versus the knee-jerk liberal, the troll under the bridge versus the hookah-smoking caterpillar, his dingy three-room apartment in Weehawken versus her comfortably shabby Cape Cod in the farm country of the Hopewell Valley. But Gibbons didn't like to think about the particulars anymore; it made him uncomfortable. He had liked their differences, probably because it kept them together yet slightly distanced in a safe, nonconfrontational orbit.

He took a sip from the mug of coffee she'd brought him. It didn't have the metal-polish taste of the diner coffee that was his standard, and even that made him sad. Gibbons sighed quietly. Why the hell couldn't they have made a life together?

She laughed through her nose. "Charlie 'Tailpipes' Riccodelli? Where do they get these names?"

Gibbons shrugged. "You know why they use the nicknames?"

She shook her head and took a sip of her own coffee.

"Wiretaps. Mobsters talk in code, almost. They started using these nicknames to cover themselves in court. If you tried to connect them with something they said on a phone tap, they'd deny everything, say they were talking about tailpipes, not killers."

"Interesting," she said.

"A lot of these guys get their names when they're 'made.' "

"What's that mean?"

"Made is when you're officially brought into the Mafia. It's like getting knighted." He flashed a wry grin at her.

"Yeah, I'll bet." She flipped over another page and glanced down at it. "Here's one I like. Nicky 'Two Quarts' Salerno." She forced another laugh.

Gibbons could've cried.

"Do you really think any of this is going to help you find Mike?"

"I found him," he said.

She stared at him for a moment. Anger flashed in her eyes, then disappointment. "Why didn't you tell me?"

"I thought you'd be better off not knowing anything. Legally, I mean."

"Where is he? What's he doing?"

"He's onto something very big," Gibbons said, getting up from the chair. "I've decided to help him."

"With the Bureau's sanction?"

He sat on the edge of the desk and looked her in the eye. She knew the answer to that one.

She tried to conjure up a picture of her cousin—as an adult, not as a kid. Nervous energy was what always came to mind. Dark and good-looking, but always those dangerous flashing eyes. Whenever she thought of him, she always thought of a picture he'd once shown her in a copy of *National Geographic*. It was a vivid stop-action color photo of a pouncing leopard about to overtake a fleeing antelope. He had been about ten years old at the time. She remembered thinking how his eyes flashed just like the leopard's if you watched them closely.

"So how is he?"

"He's okay." Gibbons reached for his coffee and pulled the transcript he'd been reading across the desk.

"Good." Lorraine nodded, feeling locked out again. She knew better than to ask too many questions. Gibbons would just clam up. She pulled her kimono closed and walked over to the windows to see the morning. The only times she saw it this early were when Gibbons stayed over. Fear for her cousin gripped her as she pondered just how much trouble he was in.

Gibbons picked up where he'd left off in the transcript. Varga was giving testimony to an assistant federal prosecutor named Denise Monkhouse about the murder of Pinkus Litvak, an Israeli who'd tried to stiff the Mistretta family for their share in a diamond heist.

> MONKHOUSE: Mr. Varga, how was Mr. Litvak's proposal received when he originally approached the Mistretta family with his idea?
>
> VARGA: Mistretta's people had some reservations. Litvak claimed to be intimately connected with the gem trade on Forty-seventh Street, but he wasn't a Hasid and that made them suspicious. They figured the only people really intimate with anything on Forty-seventh Street were the Hasids. But by then Litvak had made friends with a couple of Mistretta associates, Ray Bilardi and John DiMarco.

MONKHOUSE: How did Mr. Litvak's friendship with Mr. Bilardi and Mr. DiMarco affect Mr. Litvak's relationship with the Mistretta family?

VARGA: Bilardi and DiMarco told Mistretta's people they'd spent some time with Litvak and could pretty much vouch for him. On their say-so, Mistretta's people decided to hear the guy out.

MONKHOUSE: How and where did they hear Mr. Litvak out?

VARGA: There was a meeting at the Roman Treat, an espresso bar on Mulberry Street. As *consigliere,* I was present at that meeting. Anthony Trombosi was also at that meeting. Anthony Trombosi is Sabatini Mistretta's underboss, his second-in-command.

MONKHOUSE: And what took place at this meeting?

VARGA: Litvak told us about a group of upstart jewelers in town who were buying diamonds from a new supplier who was getting his stones from Russia. Litvak said that a large shipment of Russian diamonds was scheduled to come into Kennedy Airport via Sweden on March 10, 1983. Litvak had apparently done his homework. He knew what flight the diamonds were coming in on, what warehouse they'd be kept in overnight, what kind of safe the stones would be kept in, and what kind of security the warehouse had. We were all impressed with him. He told Mr. Trombosi that he could pull off the heist if he could use Bilardi and DiMarco as well as three other hoods who they had suggested. Trombosi told him that his proposal would be considered and that they'd let him know.

MONKHOUSE: Why, Mr. Varga, do you think he went to the mob with his plan? Couldn't he have attempted this robbery on his own? Hired manpower from other sources?

VARGA: Yes, he could have, but what Litvak was after was more than just manpower. He wanted assurances. He knew that if he went ahead with the job on his own and word got out that he was the one who did it, he'd have every punk in New York trying to hit on him for the diamonds. However, by cutting in the Mistretta family, he'd have protection. No jerk with half a brain, Ms. Monkhouse, would dare touch someone involved in a mob-sponsored operation, and God forbid if some idiot did, because he wouldn't be around very long. That's how the Mafia works. They provide advice, protection, and assurance for those kinds of criminal entrepreneurs who naturally cannot get these services through regular business channels. You can think of the Mafia as a combination consulting firm, savings and loan, insurance company, and police force. It's a multiservice conglomerate for extralegal activities.

MONKHOUSE: There is a growing organization in this country commonly known as the Israeli Mafia. Do you have any idea why Mr. Litvak didn't go to his own, as it were, for these "services," as you call them?

VARGA: He was asked that at the Roman Treat meeting. He simply said he wanted to work with professionals, not thugs. Those were his exact words. When Mr. Trombosi reported this back to Mr. Mistretta, Mr. Mistretta was very pleased with his high regard for the organization.

MONKHOUSE: Now when Mr. Trombosi got back to Mr. Litvak after consulting with Mr. Mistretta, what did he tell Mr. Litvak?

VARGA: Trombosi told him that the Mistretta family wanted thirty percent off the top of whatever the diamonds brought in. As part of the deal, the Mistretta family would provide the vehicles and the guns, and afterwards they would take care of fencing the diamonds. After the family took its cut, the five men involved in actually pulling off the job would each get ten percent of the balance. The rest would be his. Litvak did some figuring on the calculator in his wristwatch before he answered. He figured out that his cut would be the same as thirty-five percent off the top. It was a fair deal. He agreed to it, and the heist was pulled off as planned.

MONKHOUSE: Based on your knowledge, as an intimate of the Mistretta family, what happened after the diamonds were stolen?

VARGA: Sometime before dawn on March 11, Litvak and Ray Bilardi were driving south on Ocean Parkway in a van with roughly 1.7 million dollars' worth of Russian diamonds in two briefcases on the seat between them. They were heading for a dry cleaners in the Bensonhurst section of Brooklyn, where they'd been instructed to deliver the diamonds. Litvak was sitting in the passenger seat with a cannon in his pocket, a Smith & Wesson 645. When they came to a red light at the intersection of Avenue Q, Litvak pulled out the gun, pistol-whipped Bilardi, reached over him to open the driver's door, and pushed him out.

I imagine Litvak was anxious to knock out Bilardi in one shot, but he didn't realize how hard he hit him. Litvak wasn't experienced in this kind of thing. Sometime later, I'm not sure how long, a cabbie spotted Bilardi lying in the road. The cabbie chased down a patrol car and informed the officers about it. Bilardi was taken to King's County Hospital, where he was treated for a severe concussion that resulted in a partial paralysis down the right side of his body.

MONKHOUSE: Were you with Sabatini Mistretta on March 11?

VARGA: Yes, I was. I was attending a breakfast meeting at his home.

MONKHOUSE: And how did he react when he received news of Mr. Bilardi's condition and the aborted plan?

VARGA: He just looked at Trombosi and said, "I want the Jew by noon."

MONKHOUSE: And did Mr. Mistretta get his wish?

VARGA: His men found Litvak at Newark International Airport before nine o'clock. He was getting ready to board a plane for Montreal. According to the tickets they found on him, he'd planned to make connecting flights to Athens and then Tel Aviv. All along he'd planned to stiff everybody and take off with the diamonds to Israel where he'd probably have them recut and eventually resold. It didn't work out that way, though.

MONKHOUSE: What happened to Mr. Litvak?

VARGA: At about eleven o'clock, Mr. Mistretta, Mr. Trombosi, and I were having coffee and *biscotti* in Mr. Mistretta's study when a Polaroid picture was brought in. It was a picture of Litvak's body. The front of his coat was covered with blood. It was reported to Mr. Mistretta at that time that Litvak's body was disposed of in the backseat of an old Ford, which was then compacted to the size of a steamer trunk.

MONKHOUSE: What was Mr. Mistretta's reaction to this news?

VARGA: He just nodded, then he leaned over toward Mr. Trombosi and said, "Make sure Ray knows." We continued with our meeting after that.

What struck Gibbons about this story, like all the other incriminating stories that Varga had told, were the details, the particulars. It was almost as if he had taken notes when these things had happened, planning to use the information later. His recall about times, dates, places, attitudes, chain of command, who knew what, and who ordered what was just too precise. He must've been planning to rat on the bosses someday from the moment they took him in and made him their *consigliere*.

Gibbons took another sip of coffee, which by now was lukewarm. He didn't notice, though, because he was thinking about loyalty and the glaring absence of it in Richie Varga. Over the years, Gibbons had done his best to refute the image of the Mafia as an association of honorable men standing firm in a dishonorable world. That *Godfather* crap was a load of bullshit, but as much as he wanted to, he couldn't deny the fact that for them, loyalty was a way of life. Each little schnook knew his place in the hierarchy, and they all knew to respect their system. The boss was their father. And like a father, the boss took care of his sons. "Make sure Ray knows." It was truly remarkable.

He began to wonder if this ironclad loyalty really was what made them so strong. It was a quality that certainly wasn't very evident in the rest of the world. He'd always believed that Brant Ivers's first loyalty was to his own career, not the FBI. Even Tozzi had jumped ship, even though his intentions were theoretically good.

And what about me? Gibbons thought. Where were his loyalties supposed to be? To his partner the renegade? Or to the organization he'd been with for over thirty years? Loyalty means not questioning authority. But what happens when authority has its head up its ass?

Gibbons threw a pencil into his place in the transcript and looked over at the woman in the painted kimono staring out the window.

And what about Lorraine? What kind of loyalty did they have for each other? Just what the hell was "a good intellectual friendship with sex"?

Gibbons sighed.

He walked over to her and pressed himself against her back, running his hands over her hips. She turned around, almost looked surprised, and he kissed her. His thick fingers touched the angle of her jaw. He felt guilty. He wanted to make it all up to her.

She unbuttoned his shirt blindly as his lips found her aging throat. There was nothing wrong with her aging throat, nothing at all.

By the time her fingers had gotten to his belt they were on the floor, the cool silk kimono spread out under them, like young lovers on a picnic. She pulled him close and kissed him desperately. He knew she was worried about Tozzi.

"Don't worry. He'll be all right," he said.

She nodded and smiled. "He can take care of himself. He always has." She ran her fingers over his bare chest and kissed his skin.

They made love by the morning light with the birds singing in the pines outside their window.

Afterward, lying on his back in the sun, holding Lorraine's hand and feeling her delicate fingers, Gibbons could've cried.

But he didn't.

ELEVEN

It was two-fifteen Friday afternoon, and Bobo's Video on Springfield Avenue, just over the Newark border in Irvington, was packed—kids, young blacks and Hispanics tired of looking for work, a couple of old guys just hanging out, even an on-duty cop who had his cruiser double-parked out front while he looked for a movie. The linoleum floor was filthy and the place smelled like an all-night poker game. Whenever an empty videotape box fell off a shelf, the clientele just stepped over it and eventually on it, unless of course it was a Clint Eastwood film or one of the *Friday the 13th* movies, which were the hands-down favorites at Bobo's and were treated with due respect. But despite its shabby-verging-on-sinister appearance, the place was a goldmine. Tozzi watched Bobo Bocchino and the black kid who worked for him checking out tapes behind the counter. It cost two dollars for one night's rental, and Bobo must've raked in fifty bucks in the time Tozzi had been there looking over the considerable porno collection, which couldn't have been more than ten, fifteen minutes.

"Hey, Bobo," a little kid wearing a white T-shirt with a picture of a cross sticking out of a fire-engine-red flaming heart yelled over the crush. "Where's *I Eat Your Skin*?"

"Out." Bobo rubbed his nose furiously.

"Still?"

Bobo shrugged. "I'm getting another one."

"When?"

"I don't know, when it comes in."

The kid scowled. ''You been saying that for three weeks.''

''What do you want me to tell you? I got it on order, and the company hasn't sent it to me yet, okay?''

''Fuckin' liar.'' The kid in the Sacred Heart CYO T-shirt left in a huff.

Bobo looked like Yasir Arafat, or Ringo Starr, depending on how you felt about him. He shaved maybe once a week, and he usually wore designer jeans that were loose in the ass and a dress shirt with stains down the front. The slob hadn't changed much since high school. Tozzi remembered him always spilling shit all over himself. But it was strange seeing someone from so long ago, someone you thought of as a jerky, acne-ravaged teenager now with thinning hair and a big beer belly. Then something caught Tozzi's eye that would have definitely been out of character for the old Bobo, a very classy-looking gold watch hanging loose on his hairy wrist.

Tozzi waited for the cop to leave before he went up to say hi to his old classmate from St. Virgil's.

''Bobo,'' he called out, pushing his way up to the counter. ''How's it going?''

''Hi, how ya doin'?'' Bobo said automatically. He didn't recognize Tozzi at first; it had been a long time. Then Bobo squinted at him; there was something familiar about the face. ''Toz?''

''I knew you couldn't forget me.'' Tozzi appeared to be smiling warmly. Of course Bobo couldn't forget him. Tozzi knew that Bobo knew he was a fed, and Bobo knew that Tozzi knew he'd served time.

''How the hell could I ever forget you, Tozzi? Be serious.'' Bobo stuck the burning cigarette in his mouth and held out his arms in a grand gesture of bullshit magnanimity. Tozzi wondered if he was offering to be frisked.

''Bobo, I gotta talk to you,'' Tozzi said, coming around the counter and jerking his head toward the back room.

''Can't we talk here? I got customers.'' Bobo looked nervous.

Tozzi put his arm around Bobo's shoulders. ''C'mon, I just want to ask you something. Your man here can take care of things.''

The black kid didn't look at them. He knew better than to pay attention when strangers showed up to see Bobo.

''C'mon. I just want to ask you a couple of things.'' Tozzi smiled warmly again and led Bobo into the back room where there were hundreds of videotapes in brown plastic boxes lining the walls, floor to ceiling.

"I heard you were moving out west, Toz," Bobo said, grinning like a weasel. "What happened? You come back?"

"That was canceled." Tozzi glanced at a stack of VCRs on the floor behind the door. "So tell me, how've things been with you?"

Bobo looked confused. "Ah, not bad. Can't complain."

"I mean since you got into this." Tozzi pointed toward the shelves full of tapes. "After your boss went to jail."

Bobo coughed up a weak laugh and nervously flicked cigarette ashes on the floor. "Who's that, Toz?"

Tozzi grinned and shook his head. This was to be expected. Guys like Bobo never admitted that they worked for people like Joe Luccarelli, except when they were bragging to each other. He looked at the stack of VCRs again. "Those for sale?" he asked Bobo. "I'm looking for a good machine."

"Those? No, sorry, Toz, they're not for sale."

"No? Then what are they doing there?"

"They're broke. People bring 'em in to be fixed."

Tozzi looked around the room. "I don't see any tools, Bobo."

"Well, I don't do it myself. See, I got this guy comes in, picks 'em up, fixes 'em at home. I'm just the middleman, you know what I mean?"

"I don't see any tags on those machines, Bobo. How do you know which one belongs to who?"

Bobo pulled on his bottom lip. "Hey, Toz, is this a social visit or what?"

"I'm just asking."

"It's all kosher. Believe me."

Tozzi's warm smile reappeared. "I'm glad, I really am. Because it would be a real shame if someone came in here asking for paperwork on those machines. You know they could give you a hard time about possession of stolen property, and that would be a real shame."

"You come here to bust balls or what? What the fuck do you want with me, Tozzi?"

"Don't get mad, Bobo. Please. I just want your opinion on a certain matter, that's all."

"What? What is it?"

"Well, I'll tell you. I look around in the neighborhoods—New York, Newark, Jersey City, Brooklyn, the Island, everywhere—and I see that there's a lot of shit going down. You know, gambling, hookers, protection, narcotics. The kind of things you used to know all about. Right?''

Bobo shrugged. He wasn't admitting to anything.

''Now here's what I can't figure out. The families aren't what they used to be, everybody's doing time it seems like. So where's all this heavy action coming from?''

Bobo kept flicking his cigarette. ''Hey, Toz, you weren't born yesterday. If there's a buck to be made out on the street, there's always gonna be somebody—''

''But hold on!'' Tozzi laid his hand on Bobo's arm and Bobo flinched. ''I'm not talking about small-time shit. I'm talking big deals, professional stuff. Somebody's got to be financing it. The way I figure there's got to be an angel somewhere backing up this kind of volume. Who could that be, Bobo? Who's putting up the money?''

''Tozzi, you're out of my league. I don't know nothin' about that kind of stuff anymore.''

The warmth in Tozzi's smile turned cold. ''You got a nice business here, Bo. What's really nice about it is that it's all cash. How many tapes you rent in a day? Hundred and fifty, two hundred, two-fifty. That's four, five bills a day times seven days a week—all cash. Even if you report just half of what you make, you're still way ahead of the game.''

''What're you saying here, Tozzi? You saying I don't run a legitimate business here?'' Bobo's jitters were making him belligerent now.

Tozzi stared hard at him. ''What I'm saying is that I can get the IRS on your ass in ten minutes if that's what you want. And believe me, they really like guys like you, Bo. They'll look into everything. Those guys'll get so cozy around here, you'll begin to think they're in bed with you at night.''

''Give me a break, will ya?''

''And even if they don't prosecute—which is a long shot given your record, pal—the fucking back taxes and penalties will kill you. Do you doubt me, Bobo?'' Tozzi looked down at the VCRs again and tapped the bottom one with his shoe. After a long pause, he asked, ''So what do you think, Bo?''

Bobo's face was sweaty. He kept rubbing his mouth and pulling on his lip. ''You don't know what you're asking me for, Toz,'' he muttered. ''This is very heavy, man. Heavy-duty.''

''Yeah? Tell me about it.''

Bobo abruptly walked to the back door. He was all hunched over as if he had bad stomach cramps. He looked like he was beginning to shrink. Tozzi followed him. "I shouldn't be telling you this," Bobo hissed.

"I won't tell anyone where it came from," Tozzi said.

Bobo's mouth was dry. He was having a hard time breathing. "There's a new boss. There's a whole new fucking family." Bobo glanced out to the front of the store. "Richie Varga."

Tozzi wasn't surprised. But how the hell could Varga run a family while he was under witness protection? "Keep talking, Bo."

"Don't ask me how he's doing it or where he is 'cause I don't know, I swear. All I know is that his people are creepy as hell. A lot of them are leftovers from the old families, but some of them nobody's ever heard of before, especially the enforcers. It's like these guys popped up from nowhere. And that's why they're so creepy. They're invisible."

Bobo's eyes suddenly widened. He looked at Tozzi and the thought crossed his mind. Tozzi? Nah, not Tozzi.

"I don't believe it." Tozzi shook his head. "Varga was a little nothing. Even when the big boys took him in for helping them dump Collesano, he was still a little schlump. How could he get that kind of power?"

"Varga may look like a jerk, but believe me, he's not. When he got to New York, he started making connections, doing little deals here and there, building up his bank account."

"Come on, will ya? What kind of connections could Varga make in New York? Sure, the bosses were happy to have his help against Collesano and the Philly mob, but they weren't that in love with the guy. They kept him on a short leash, they had to. You can't tell me Luccarelli, Mistretta, and Giovinazzo just let him pull whatever deals he wanted. With those guys, you play by their rules."

"Not with Varga, Toz. With him it was different. They were like broads with him, they loved him. They let him get away with murder."

"Why?"

Bobo looked very panicky and very pale. "Because he proved himself," he whispered.

"What do you mean 'he proved himself'?"

Bobo seemed to be having a hard time breathing. "This is only what I heard, you understand? I wasn't there. This is just what I heard, okay?"

"Yeah, I understand."

"Okay . . . okay . . . See, Varga wanted to prove to them that he was on the up-and-up. He screwed his own father-in-law right up the ass, so he didn't want the big boys to have any doubts about his loyalty to them. Now I don't know how he knew this, but he told them that he found out there were feds working undercover inside the families, at least three that he knew of."

A gunshot went off in Tozzi's brain. Lando, Blaney, and Novick.

"The bosses wanted to hear names, but Varga said he'd take care of it for them. About a week later he called for a meeting—the back room of this restaurant in Brooklyn, Gilberto's in Sheepshead Bay. Luccarelli, Mistretta, and Giovinazzo all sitting together, suspicious as hell of each other, waiting to see what Varga had for them. Finally Varga comes in pushing one of those dessert carts." Bobo couldn't seem to catch his breath. He swallowed hard and went on. "On the cart there's this long tray with one of those clear plastic lids you can see the cannolis and stuff through. But right away, everybody can tell it's not pastry under there. Varga whips the lid off to show the bosses. Three heads. I heard the eyes were scooped out, too. Because they saw what they shouldn't have, you know. The bosses recognized them. One from each family. Varga goes in his pocket then and pulls out their badges to prove that they really were feds. Gave 'em to the bosses as souvenirs. But you didn't hear it from me. You understand, Toz? You did not hear it from me."

Tozzi wasn't listening. His vision blurred. He was thinking about Joel Lando. He wanted to break something. "You're full of shit, you fucking liar. Could never have happened, *never*. Varga had no muscle of his own back then, and that limp prick sure as hell didn't do it himself."

"I heard it was his bodyguard who actually did the job. Varga just ordered it."

"Who's the bodyguard? What's his name?"

"I don't know, Toz, I swear. All I know is that they call him 'the Hun' because he looks like a fucking Nazi even though he's Italian. That's all I know, Toz, I swear." Bobo raised one hand and laid the other on a video box lying on a shelf. "I swear to God, Toz."

The Hun, the Hun . . . it didn't ring any bells with Tozzi. He tried to think of German-looking guys, light blonds with clear blue eyes and square heads, tall well-built guys, but he couldn't come up with any grown-up Hitler Youth in the mob. But his head was racing, and he couldn't think straight—he was too angry to think straight.

He grabbed Bobo's coffee-stained shirtfront. "I want to know the Hun's name."

"I'm telling you, Toz, I don't know any more than I told you. I—"

Tozzi's hand slammed into Bobo's throat, forcing his head back into a shelf. "You think I'm fucking around here? I want that guy's name, do you understand me? I want to know who Varga's bodyguard was and I want to know right now."

Bobo's face was red, his arms hanging helplessly at his sides like stiff salamis. He was too scared to defend himself. "Toz, I don't—"

"Two hours, asshole. That's how long it'll take me to get a couple of IRS agents down here." Tozzi was putting all his weight on Bobo's throat.

"Listen . . . listen," Bobo croaked. "I swear to you, I don't know who this Hun guy is, but I know someone who probably does. Okay? Someone who's been doing a lot of work for Varga lately. You know Paulie Tortorella?"

Tozzi shook his head and let up a little on Bobo's neck.

"He's crazy, the kind of guy who'll do anything for a buck as long as there's a thrill in it. Used to be a nobody, a hanger-on. Did little stupid jobs for Giovinazzo's people every once in a while. These days he calls himself a specialist, a torch. He's a real arrogant little son-of-a-bitch."

"Where do I find him?"

"I don't know where he lives, but he hangs out at this place on Ferry Street in the Ironbound. A Portugee bar, Leo's I think it's called."

"How do I find him?"

"You can't miss the little fuck. He looks like a jockey, five-feet-nothin'. And a real loudmouth."

Tozzi let go of Bobo's throat and pulled the man's face up to his own. "If I don't find this Tortorella where you say, I'll be back. Okay?"

Tozzi didn't wait around for a response. Bobo just stood there, paralyzed, watching as Tozzi shoved his way through the front of the store.

"Hey, Bobo." The black kid poked his head through the doorway. "We got somethin' called *My Bloody Valentine*?"

Bobo shook his head and closed his eyes.

TWELVE

Tozzi unwrapped what was left of his veal-and-pepper sandwich and tossed it out the window to a mutt pawing through the garbage inside a ripped plastic bag. The dog was all black, and in the dark of the alley, it was just a pair of tawny eyes. Tozzi stared at those fearful, suspicious eyes as the dog sniffed the sandwich. He felt like giving somebody a break because no one was giving him one.

He punched the buttons of the Buick's silent radio in frustration as he looked at the front door of Leo's Tavern, nervously trying to make something happen. The car, a '77 copper-brown LeSabre, belonged to a man in his aunt's building who was laid up in the hospital. Tozzi was "borrowing" it. For the past two hours, he'd been staring at that door and the flickering neon Rheingold sign in the window. His back was sore, his underwear was all crammed up his ass, and he had a throbbing headache. Sitting tight on a plant could be fucking torture.

Since seven o'clock that evening, he'd mentally taken note of everyone who'd gone into the tavern, then one by one accounted for them as they left. At eight-twenty he went in, sat at the bar, ordered a beer, and looked around for anyone small enough to have been a jockey. There were a couple of short stocky guys, but they were all Portuguese immigrant stonemasons, still wearing their work clothes, their shoes and pant legs white with mortar dust.

Tozzi nursed his beer, then ordered another. He struck up a conversation with the bartender about the World Cup games and this wonder that Argentina had on their team, Diego something or other. Tozzi didn't know shit about soccer, but the bartender was a fanatic, so it was easy for Tozzi to make the guy carry the conversation by just acting enthusiastic. It was one of those bullshitter techniques Tozzi had become good at.

After he finished his second beer, he waved so long to the bartender, who was busy uncorking a bottle of wine for the stonemasons, and went back to the car where he'd been sitting ever since. Now it was twenty to midnight. The bar would be open till two, but Tozzi had a feeling Tortorella wasn't going to show tonight. He didn't have a good reason, he just had a feeling. He reached for the key in the ignition and thought about Gibbons. Gibbons would wait for the place to close. Gibbons always went by the book. Tozzi preferred his instincts. They always used to argue about that.

Anyway, to hell with Tortorella. He had a better idea.

He fired up the engine and pulled the long metallic-brown sedan away from the curb. Tozzi was nervous and he had to move. He knew where he was going, but he wasn't sure why he was going there. He just told himself something would happen when he got there.

"What?" Her voice on the intercom didn't sound pleased.

"Hi," he said, leaning into the intercom box. The fluorescent lights in the vestibule were too bright. He felt exposed.

"Who the hell is this?"

"It's me, Thompson. Your lover boy." He felt like an asshole as soon as he added that.

She didn't respond. After a few seconds, the buzzer buzzed and he pushed through the glass door.

On the elevator up to her floor, he suddenly wondered what the hell he was doing there. But by the time the elevator doors opened on her floor, he wasn't worrying about that. Tozzi told himself he didn't need reasons; only bad guys needed reasons.

Turning a corner in the hallway, he suddenly spotted her leaning against her open doorway, wearing a long blue caftan. Her hair was tousled and loose, her eyes smoky and subversive. Young Lauren Bacall with a little Sophia Loren thrown in. She didn't say a word; she didn't have to.

"How ya doin'?" he said. He hoped a boyish grin would do the trick. If he had a boyish grin.

She didn't say anything. So much for his boyish grin.

"Okay. So now that we both know I'm an asshole and that I shouldn't be pulling this kind of shit at my age, why don't you accept my apology and invite me in for a drink? Two fingers of rum with a splash of soda. And a piece of lime if you've got any."

"I don't like rum. Will Chivas do?"

"Sure, fine."

She turned and headed for the kitchen. He followed, watching the bottoms of her bare feet play peekaboo under the hem of the caftan. She seemed to have pretty big feet for a woman. Roberta had little square feet. Fred Flintstone feet. Joanne's were big but narrow and graceful.

"You had a bad day, right?" she said sarcastically as she pulled down two rock glasses from the cupboard. "And you just had to see me."

"You sound like you've heard this before."

"Yup."

"From Richie?"

She gave him the finger.

"Okay, okay. I won't even mention him. I promise. Anyway, I didn't exactly have a bad day, just an unproductive one."

"For me, that's a bad day," she said, handing him his drink.

"Salute," he said, and clinked her glass. He thought about mentioning the bomb in his cousin's car, but then decided not to. There was nothing to be gained from bringing it up. Joanne didn't like to reveal much of herself in the way of emotions; she didn't even bother to fake it. Whether she was playing straight with him or not was going to remain her business and hers alone.

"I just came because I wanted to see you," he said.

"Uh-huh." She sipped her scotch and looked at him over the rim of her glass. Vintage Bacall. He'd always thought Bacall was hot.

"Yeah, well on second thought, maybe it has been a bad day," he said. "But I don't really want to talk about it."

"I know you don't want to talk about it." There was a wry laugh in her reply. "Tell me, are you still going to be 'Mr. Thompson' with me?"

He thought about it for a minute. He'd slept with her, for chrissake. If she was involved with the mob, she probably already knew his name, just like Vinnie Clams did, so it wouldn't matter if he told her. He had a feeling she wasn't involved, though. Oh, what the fuck. "My name's Tozzi, Mike Tozzi."

"That's better." She raised her glass to him and smiled.

He grinned and put his drink down on the kitchen counter. He looked her in the eye and they started to laugh at nothing. Then he pulled her close and kissed her, a silly, sloppy, delicious kiss. She didn't taste so much of tobacco this time.

"That's better," he said. He smoothed the material over her ass and the back of her thigh. She wasn't wearing anything under the caftan.

"The kitchen floor isn't my style, Tozzi." She disengaged from his embrace, picked up her drink, and walked out of the kitchen.

Tozzi grabbed his drink and followed her into the bedroom. It isn't her style, she'd said. It was too uncool just to say no. From the living room, he could see her standing by the bed, pulling the caftan over her head. She stood there looking back at him, resting one fist on her naked hip. She took another sip of her drink, and the rim of the glass underlined those beautiful dark eyes. Entering the bedroom, Tozzi wondered if Bacall ever said something wasn't her style in any of the Bogart movies.

He embraced her and kissed her again, running his hand down her hip. She grabbed his belt buckle and pulled him down onto the bed. He unbuttoned his shirt and turned off the bedside lamp as she undid his belt.

When he was naked, he loomed over her and covered her breast with his mouth, slowly circling the nipple with his tongue as he gently stroked her labia, feeling the warm wetness materializing to his touch. She let out a little moan and threw her head back into the pillows as she tugged on his cock.

He was hard but he was in no hurry. He wanted to give it to her slow, make it last, drive them both crazy. He entered her all the way, undulated his hips awhile, then suddenly pulled out until only the tip was pressing on her clit. She moaned sharply in surprise. He moved ever so slightly, rubbing in and out. She clawed at his chest hairs, rolling her head in the pillows.

Then without warning, he went in again, halfway, then pulled out completely. She screamed and he immediately stuck his cock back in slow and easy, stopping halfway again and rocking gently. Gradually he started to pull out again until his cock was just touching the edge of her clit.

"No . . ." she moaned. "Don't stop . . ."

He worked her clit, moving as little as possible without coming out. She breathed harder, moaning louder. He kept going, his head starting to spin, the merry-go-round going faster and faster. It felt so good, but he wasn't ready to let go, not yet.

She dug her fingernails into his back and stiffened, her squeals of delight rising in pitch. He kept going, spinning faster and faster. She was coming now, thrashing her head in a tangled nest of her lush hair.

He grinned and stopped then.

''Don't stop,'' she rasped frantically, and he started again, working with his tip, which felt like it was about to explode. Suddenly he couldn't hold back any longer. He started coming, slow at first, like a wave building momentum far out in the ocean, gaining height and power as it approached the shore, forming a towering curl that seemed to hang suspended in the air for longer than it naturally should, then finally crashing into the sands with a deafening roar.

After that he fell over onto the sheets, and the foamy remnants of the wave retreated from the sands and slipped back into the ocean.

It was almost three A.M. Joanne couldn't sleep. Tozzi shifted position in his sleep and pulled the sheets off her. She pulled them back and frowned. He was a light sleeper, damn it. She turned her head and looked at the phone, frustrated.

If she could just get to the phone in the kitchen, she could call Richie and tell him Tozzi was there. He'd have a couple of his men there in an hour. But she was afraid Tozzi would wake up again if she got out of bed. He might be in deep sleep now, but she didn't dare risk it. When she'd gone to the bathroom a half hour ago, he was wide awake when she returned.

''What's the matter?'' he'd asked in an alarmed whisper.

She soothed him and told him to go back to sleep. He pulled her close and eventually drifted off again.

She sighed now. This was maddening. It was the perfect opportunity to get rid of him, but she couldn't do a thing. She briefly considered killing him herself, but rejected the idea immediately. Her father always said, ''Keep your hands clean, no matter what.''

Well, there is one consolation to having him around a little longer, she thought, resigning herself to the situation. He is a great fuck.

She grinned and settled back into her pillow, smugly wondering whether he'd admitted to himself that he was in love with her.

* * *

Tozzi was staring out the window at the passing clouds. Joanne was playing with his chest hairs. He glanced at the clock-radio and saw that it was 8:34. He was surprised; he thought it was later. They must've gotten up very early.

"What are you thinking about?" she asked.

An ex-jockey turned torch. Some guy named the Hun. Your husband. You. "Not much," he said.

"You look like you've got a lot on your mind. What's the matter?"

He turned and looked at her. "Last night you said that a bad day for you is an unproductive day. I don't know what that means. In your business, I mean. Don't computers pretty much run themselves?"

She looked at him funny but answered anyway. "Sure, they run fine by themselves, but they've got to have something to run for us to make a profit. The hardware is useless unless we've got data to process."

"So what's an unproductive day for you?" He was lying on his side now, watching how the end of her nose moved when she talked.

She laughed at what was obvious to her. "An unproductive day is a day when we don't sign up new clients."

"What kind of clients?"

"DataReach handles data for big corporations, insurance companies, hospitals, universities, municipalities. Our main-frame computers hold their personnel data, their files and records, the kind of information that used to fill up warehouses with paper."

"I thought big companies all had their own computers these days. Why do they have to use yours?"

"For some midsized companies it's more cost-effective to rent time and equipment from us than to buy their own hardware and hire staff to run it. Then there are the big companies that haven't decided on how they want to computerize so they use us as a temporary measure. A lot of the insurance companies we serve are like that. Of course, insurance people are very slow to do anything. They're notorious for their inefficiency and indecision. I'll be retired before most of them get their acts together and set up their own systems."

"How'd you get into data processing? You know, from being married to what's-his-name."

"I went back to school. For business, not computer science. I got my MBA and took a sales job with another data-processing firm up in Clifton. I was good at it, very good. Word got around, and DataReach lured me away. They weren't very big when I started with them back in . . . eighty-one I guess it was. But I've grown with the company, and we've been good for each other. Besides, computer services is the growth industry right now, and I want to be where things are happening."

Tozzi nodded. He was only half-listening, remembering where he was when she was getting her MBA. Hotshot narcotics detective with the Boston PD.

"What about you?" she asked. "Did you always want to be a cop when you were a kid?"

Tozzi shook his head. "I always wanted to bust balls and go against the grain. When everyone else was dropping out of college to drive cross-country or bum around Europe, I dropped out and became a cop. This was up in Boston. I was so good at it I surprised myself. That's because I thought I was playing cops and robbers. But I didn't get along with the rank and file; I didn't fit the department profile. In other words I wasn't a mick with roots in Southie. After four years and five medals of valor, the brass had no choice but to kick me up to detective. They figured, Hey, this guy's a cowboy, he'll get his head blown off sooner or later. No loss."

"What did you work? Homicide?"

"Narcotics."

"You're not a city cop now, though. How did you get to be a federal agent? You are a fed, aren't you?"

Tozzi looked her in the eye before he answered. Used to be a fed, he thought, then he nodded to her question. "The Drug Enforcement Administration heard about the boy wonder up in Boston and they invited me to become a fed. At first I resisted their offer—city cops generally don't think much of the federal law-enforcement agencies—but then they showed me what a wild-West show they were running down in Florida. Seaplanes, choppers, swamp buggies, submachine guns, kilos, smugglers—it was romance. It was my big chance to make up for missing out on Vietnam. You can see where my head was at the time."

He looked out at the clouds again. That had been a weird time for him. He liked to believe that business about Florida being his Vietnam, but in truth, he took the job to spite Roberta.

"I was married then," he said, breaking the silence. "She wouldn't move to Florida, said she couldn't stand living in the South because of all the prejudice. I pointed out to her that there weren't too many black faces at her father's factory in Providence, but that didn't penetrate. She had a gift for repelling anything she didn't want to know. It was like an invisible force field. What a mistake marrying her was."

Tozzi fell silent again and stared blankly out the window. His marriage to Roberta was the one time in his life that going against the grain didn't work for him. He tried to make it work—at least he thought he did at the time—but in looking back he had to admit he didn't try very hard. Roberta had made it clear from the start that she didn't want to be married to a career agent, and she was prepared to sit tight in Boston and hold her breath until she got her way. He had never had any use for tight-asses in his life, but he treated it like a game at first. Eventually it became a battle of wills. He deliberately ignored his marriage and forced her to make the first move. It took over a year for her to do it. When he was served with papers, he cussed her out and trashed his living room in Lantana. But even then he knew he was just going through the motions.

For the first time in a long time Tozzi started counting the years. Fourteen years in law enforcement, four since the divorce, seven since they really lived together. Suddenly the loneliness of his life became overwhelming and the hard facts gathered in a lump in his throat. His failed marriage never bothered him much before. But that was when he still had the Bureau to call home.

Why the fuck am I thinking about her? he thought angrily.

"Hey, what's wrong?" Joanne said. "All of a sudden you look mad at the world." She started to knead his shoulders.

He sighed and muttered. "Just thinking about the past."

"How about some breakfast?"

"I'd like to meet your father sometime," Tozzi said out of the blue. "That all right with you?" This was a real long shot, but he figured he'd ask anyway for the hell of it.

"Why do you want to meet my father? So you can bust him?"

"Bust him for what? I just want to meet him. I'm curious."

"My father's not a curiosity."

"Don't get hot. It was just a suggestion. I didn't mean anything by it."

She threw the covers off and reached for her caftan on the floor. "All right . . . since you're so 'curious.' I haven't been down to see him in a while. Let's go today."

Jesus Christ. He couldn't believe it.

"Sure, fine."

"You'll probably be very disappointed," she said sarcastically. "He doesn't look like the Godfather or anything."

"I didn't say he would."

She gave him that wry grin again. "How do you like your eggs, Tozzi?"

He shrugged. "Over easy."

"So do I. You make them. I don't cook."

She walked into the bathroom and left Tozzi naked on the bed.

He wondered whether Bogie had ever made eggs for Bacall. He let his head fall back into the pillows as he listened to her shower running and imagined her naked and wet. He'd never felt so good about a woman before, not Roberta, not anybody. Maybe this was love, he thought, and immediately grimaced at the word, recalling Gibbons's warning.

"But what the hell does he know?" Tozzi muttered, getting out of bed.

THIRTEEN

"Dad?" Joanne leaned over and touched his shoulder.

Jules Collesano was oblivious to his daughter's presence. His eyes darted around the table as the croupier, a petite black girl in a red vest, white shirt, and black tie, dealt out cards from the "boot." She had a Cleopatra hairdo that didn't move at all. Jules looked confused and upset as she nimbly flipped out cards to the three other men huddled over the table, then quickly scooped them back up. It was as if it were the first time he'd ever played blackjack and he just couldn't understand how his money was disappearing so fast.

"Daddy?" Joanne repeated. She said it so pathetically Tozzi wondered whether this was the same woman he'd spent the night with.

"Not now, honey," he said, a little too loudly. "I'm all set, see?" He raised a tall glass of orange juice from the table to show her. A screwdriver, Tozzi guessed. The old man's fingers were thick and stubby, and Tozzi noticed that he shook a bit. Suddenly Jules scowled meanly when Joanne didn't go away. He thought she was the cocktail waitress.

"No, Daddy, it's me."

He snapped his head up, still scowling. It took at least twenty seconds for him to realize that this was his daughter. Joanne smiled down at him with steadfast benevolence, like a plaster saint. This was apparently her way of dealing with his senility.

Gradually his face started to relax, then suddenly it blossomed with love and recognition.

"Joanne," he said sweetly, touching her cheek with the flat of his rough-looking hand. *"Quanto sei bell'!"*

That phrase instantly triggered a memory: his Aunt Carmella's parlor and the smell of her anisette cookies. Tozzi remembered her always saying the same thing to him whenever his mother brought him over for a visit.

Joanne hugged her father, but the old man's mind was still on the game as he squirmed around to see what the croupier was doing. The other men at the table kept their eyes on the game and nothing else. Gamblers only pay attention to where their money is going.

"I knew you'd be here," she said with a disapproving frown.

"And where the hell else should I be? With the senior citizens playing shuffleboard? Shit on that."

He picked up his screwdriver and took a long drink. His hand actually shook a lot more than Tozzi originally thought.

"Hey!" he suddenly said, pointing a stubby finger in the croupier's face. "This is my little girl here. You hold my place, you hear? I'll be back later."

The black girl smiled diplomatically but didn't respond. The pit boss, a short blonde in a gray suit, perked up when she heard Jules's command. Like all the other pit bosses here, she looked like a bank manager, only happier. Jules was so out of it he'd forgotten that croupiers have to change tables frequently and so there was no guarantee that the black girl would be at that table when he returned. Smartly the black girl said nothing to him, knowing that even the hint of collusion with a customer could mean her job.

"You don't have to yell, Dad."

He leaned into Joanne's face and said in a stage whisper, "You gotta talk to *moolinyahms* like that. Otherwise they don't understand."

Tozzi could never understand how some old guys got away with saying racist crap like that without violent consequences. The croupier waited for Jules to pick up his chips before she started the next game. The pit boss's smile returned when he got off his stool.

"Daddy, I want you to meet a friend of mine," she said, leading him away from the table. "Daddy, this is Mike Tozzi."

It sounded strange when he heard her say his name out loud. He was used to hearing her call him "Mr. Thompson" with that ironic skepticism of hers.

Tozzi extended his hand to Joanne's father. "*Come stai,* Mr. Collesano?"

Jules smiled broadly and grabbed Tozzi's hand, pumping it vigorously with a surprisingly strong grip. Tozzi had a feeling his *come stai?* would go over well with him. Jules was that type. To guys like Jules there were three classifications of people: niggers on the bottom of the pile, whites in the middle; and Italians, meaning only ''*Sicilian*' '' and ''*Napoletan*','' on top. He hoped Jules didn't try to continue the conversation in Italian because other than food and curses, Tozzi only knew a few phrases.

''You want a drink?'' he suddenly said. Then without waiting for an answer, he called to a bleached blond cocktail waitress at the next table. ''Miss . . . *miss!* Two more of these things.'' He held up his glass to show her he wanted screwdrivers. Jules seemed to think in short bursts that translated into immediate explosive reactions. Between the explosions, his mind wandered and his face smoothed out to a sort of helpless innocence.

''No thanks, Mr. Collesano,'' Tozzi protested. ''It's a little early.'' It was just after eleven.

''Hey, you listen to me,'' he warned. ''This is fresh-squeezed, the best. I don't drink it otherwise. Anyway they're free for high rollers like me,'' he said, laughing hoarsely. ''So take it.''

Joanne just smiled and said nothing. Apparently she figured it was easier to just go along with him and not object. When the bleached blonde came back with the drinks, Joanne took one even though she wasn't even asked if she wanted anything.

The waitress was no kid but she put up a good front. She did have great legs, which was probably what kept her here. The cocktail-waitress uniform in this casino, the Imperial, was spangled black leotards, black tights, and black spiked heels. Tozzi noticed that her bare shoulders were covered with freckles. Roberta had freckles all over her body. Tozzi remembered how much his ex-wife hated them. He picked up the other screwdriver from the bleached blonde's tray, and when Jules called ''*Salute!*,'' he took a sip to be polite. It was excellent orange juice, and they weren't stingy with the vodka either.

The old man waited for his reaction to the drink, nodding with a big I-told-you-so grin. ''What'd I tell you? Only the best for Jules Collesano. This is *my* town.''

Tozzi looked at Joanne, who looked back with pain and pity in her eyes. She'd warned Tozzi that her father wasn't always totally coherent. He had a tendency to slip back in time to the days when he was boss in Atlantic City, she'd said. The Imperial was his regular casino, so the people here played along with him. It was when he went into other casinos and tried to throw his weight around that problems started.

Jules then started laughing softly for no reason, a sad, knowing laugh. "It's still my town," he repeated, but not so loudly.

Joanne turned her face away.

"Too noisy in here," Jules said, and wandered off toward the nearest exit.

"Hey, you all right?" Tozzi put his hand on Joanne's arm.

"Yeah, fine." Her face was still turned away. "I'll be right back," she said, and abruptly headed for the ladies' room.

Tozzi followed Jules through the purple-black tinted glass doors that kept the casino in a state of perpetual midnight. The slanted sunlight streaming into the vestibule was so strong it looked like the old man was at the bottom of the stairway to Heaven about to go up and meet his Maker. Tozzi went over to the window where Jules stood looking out at the boardwalk and the ocean beyond. The sun was hot on Tozzi's face, and it made him squint. Jules stared at the waves, his skin almost white in the sunlight. He was like a sad little ghost.

"Do me a favor," he said to Tozzi. "Be nice to her."

Tozzi didn't know how to respond to that. "Sure . . . I mean, why wouldn't I be nice to her?"

Jules laughed scornfully. "Richie was a real son-of-a-bitch to her. I don't want that to ever happen to her again."

"Well . . . I'm not Richie."

Jules didn't answer that. He was frowning at the ocean.

Tozzi wasn't sure how much about Varga he should let on that he knew. He wished Joanne would get back.

"She used to tell me that he hit her," Jules said, squinting up at Tozzi. "I don't think he ever did, though. Not really."

"Why do you say that, Mr. Collesano?"

Jules gulped his drink. "Wasn't his style." He wiped his mouth with the back of his hand. "The guy was a sneak. He'd never hit anyone. He was afraid they'd fight back. Even with a woman, he was afraid, I bet."

"Yeah?"

"Oh, yeah, he was something. Yeah, I remember at a confirmation party one of my men threw for his kid. Matty O'Brien's oldest boy, it was. Some punk from Matty's crew thought Richie was making eyes at his wife, and he called Richie on it, right in front of everybody.

Richie just stood there stuttering and mumbling and getting red in the face like a real dummy. The guy roughed him up, right in front of everybody, and Richie just let it happen. I wanted to kill the jerk myself, I was so mad. How do you think it made me look? My goddamn son-in-law, my right-hand man, acting like a fucking mameluke in front of all those people."

"Maybe he acted that way on purpose," Tozzi said. "To make you think he was a mameluke."

"He *was* a mameluke! He was a little yellow, back-stabbing sneak. You think that fat-ass pencil pusher would've ever been able to run a crew like a real man? Never. There was no way in the world he'd ever get made on his own, not the way he was going."

Tozzi nodded and sipped his drink. Keep talking, Jules.

"But he *wanted* to get made. He told me all the time. I told him to be a good boy and stay with me. I gave him a good job, you know. Better than he deserved. But I guess a lot of guys do that when their daughters get married—am I wrong? Even big businessmen. I took care of the bastard . . . and then he took care of me."

Jules shaded his eyes with his big hand and peered out at the ocean. There were half a dozen ships far out on the horizon. "Who's that? The Russians come to bomb us?" Jules asked. "They don't like fun, the Communists. People have too much fun here at Atlantic City. They like to bomb places where people have fun." He laughed, but it wasn't convincing.

"I would think they'd hit New York before Atlantic City," Tozzi speculated.

"I wouldn't shed any tears if they did." Jules gulped down the rest of his drink. "No tears at all."

"They put Richie up to it, didn't they?"

"Of course they did," Jules said bitterly. "What do you think? They promised to make him in New York if he helped them get rid of me. Richie knew it was the only way he could ever get made, so naturally he went along with it. He was ambitious, my son-in-law. He associated with big men—Mr. Luccarelli, Mr. Mistretta, and Mr. Giovinazzo." Jules swiped the fingernails of one hand under his chin, the old Italian gesture that meant "May they spit blood."

Joanne poked her head through one of the tinted doors then. "There you are," she said, and she walked over to put her arm around her father and kiss him on the cheek. "How've you been, Daddy?"

Tozzi was touched by the sight of this sophisticated lady in a silk top, linen slacks, and high-heel sandals doting over her old man, but then again he'd never known people to use their office persona or, God forbid, their bedroom persona with their parents.

"I love you, Daddy." She hugged him tight.

Jules squeezed her close in a way that would have made her seem like a little girl if she didn't have four inches on him.

"Okay, enough of this," he declared brusquely, and suddenly let go of her. "Don't want people to think I'm fooling around with young girls again, do you?" His booming laugh filled the vestibule.

"Lunch," Jules said. "You gotta eat"—he sized up his daughter's slender figure—"and don't say no." He turned to Tozzi. "You're hungry, no?"

Tozzi smiled. "Sure."

"We'll have the clams oreganata. They know how to make them here. Nice, not all bread crumbs. You won't believe."

He grabbed his daughter's hand and started to lead her away, then made an about-face and pointed at Tozzi. "You like calamari?"

Tozzi shrugged and nodded.

"I'll bet you never had it the way they make it here. Tender like you won't believe. Come on, Richie. Let's eat." Jules pushed the door open and pulled Joanne with him.

Tozzi caught a glimpse of the pained expression on her face as she went through the doorway.

Joanne leaned back in the passenger's seat and stared through the windshield as Tozzi drove. She was wearing a pair of oversized Jackie O sunglasses. Tozzi noticed her fidgeting with the straps of her purse as if they were a set of rosary beads. The Saab had a nice ride, but it took some getting used to. He kept glancing at the dash, making sure things were where they were supposed to be because the ignition on the floor under the stick shift had thrown him for a loop.

Joanne had been crying, but she'd stopped now. Jules had gotten a little boisterous at lunch, and she couldn't get him to settle down. It was hard for her to see him acting as if he were still the big man in Atlantic City. It must've been even harder hearing him promise her the moon, assuring her that the next time she got married it would be "beautiful." And Jules didn't say things just once. She'd kept up a good front all through lunch. It was only after they'd said goodbye and Jules went back to the blackjack tables that the tears came.

"I know I shouldn't, but I avoid coming down here to see him," she said. "He seems to get a little worse every time I see him."

Tozzi went to shift, then remembered to clutch first. It had been a while since he'd driven a standard transmission. "Your father seemed okay when I was talking to him."

"What did you talk about?"

He glanced at her, then returned his gaze to the road. "Richie."

He looked at her again.

"Your father brought him up," he said. "I didn't."

"Did he tell you how he and his pals are going to find Richie and make him pay?"

"No."

"I'm surprised. That's one of his big topics. In fact, I'm surprised he didn't ask you to help."

Tozzi kept his eyes on the road. "If he'd asked, I might have said yes."

She didn't respond.

They fell silent. After a while Joanne put a tape in the cassette deck. Tozzi hoped it wasn't classical music. It was, but as he listened he was relieved to hear that this music was very soothing and meditative, more traditional than that cat-screech string quartet in her bedroom. He liked it.

"What's this?" he asked.

"Telemann fugues," she said. "Turn left here. I'll show you how to get back on the Parkway. The expressway's always jammed on Saturdays."

Tozzi followed her directions and drove down a wide residential street lined with large homes, old Victorians alternating with more modern houses. The newer homes were either one-story ranches with expensive stone facades or center-hall colonials with big pillars on the front porches. The lawns were all neat and manicured. A solid upper-middle/lower-upper-class neighborhood. Tozzi imagined banker-types living in these houses.

Joanne sat up and stared at one of the colonials, a white house with big pillars and red geraniums in clay pots flanking the front steps. She seemed very interested in that house.

"Somebody you know?" he asked.

"What?"

"That house. You know who lives there?"

"Somebody I used to know," she said. "When I was a kid."

She was quiet for a moment. ''A girl I went to grammar school with used to live there. Linda Tuckerman was my best friend in third grade. We used to play there all the time until one day after school the maid rushed out as we got to the porch and told me I had to go home, that I couldn't come in. A big black woman from Jamaica. She shooed me away like a chicken. I didn't understand at the time. Turned out that Linda's father was running for councilman and he didn't want to be discredited by his daughter's association with Jules Collesano's kid. It was so cruel.'' She leaned her head against the headrest.

''Did your father find out about it?''

''Oh, yeah. I told him all about it, bawling my eyes out.'' She sighed and shook her head. ''You know what he did? He sent one of his men to Mr. Tuckerton's office bearing gifts. Linda's father got an anonymous ten-thousand-dollar campaign contribution . . . and a broken hand. A few days later when I came home from school, there was a new Barbie doll and a Ken doll in my room with the complete Barbie and Ken wardrobes and every Barbie accessory available, the little sports car, the boudoir, everything. I already had a Barbie and some clothes, but getting the whole thing in one lump was a little girl's dream come true. That night at dinner I asked my father where it came from. He told me not to worry about it, just enjoy it. From then on Linda and I played at my house after school.''

Tozzi raised his eyebrows. ''Fathers and daughters,'' he murmured.

''Take a right at the stop sign,'' she said, and turned up the volume so that the music filled the car.

Fathers and daughters, she thought wistfully as she looked into the side mirror and saw the terraced lawn in front of the big white house with the geranium pots on the steps, her father's house.

FOURTEEN

Gibbons sat down opposite Brant Ivers, who ignored him as he studied the papers on his desk. The SAC was wearing a pastel pink shirt and a contrasting paisley tie under a gray double-breasted suit. The desk's writing slide was pulled out where Ivers's lunch awaited him: a spinach salad in a clear-plastic container and a cup of strawberry yogurt. Gibbons stared at the fare. J. Edgar would've croaked if he'd ever seen this.

"Well?" Gibbons finally said.

Ivers peered over his half-glasses. He didn't say anything. Gibbons assumed this was supposed to be meaningful.

"You called me in here, Ivers. What do you want?"

Ivers took off his glasses and dropped them on top of the papers he'd been reading. Gibbons wasn't sure what the SAC meant to convey with this gesture. It could have been the prelude to either a pep talk or an ass-reaming.

"I just read your last report, Bert." He reached for the cup of yogurt, pried off the lid, and started to stir it with a plastic spoon. "It's a little . . . spare."

Gibbons watched him stirring up red glop from the bottom of his cup. "Sorry to disappoint you, but that's what I've got so far." Gibbons resented being called in to explain himself. What he and Tozzi were onto was a hell of a lot more important than playing games with Ivers. He wished he could tell the SAC to fuck off.

Ivers dug into his yogurt a little more, then set it aside. "Have you forgotten that you're required to include everything you've done during the previous week in your reports? Even leads that bear no fruit?"

Gibbons smiled with his teeth. "Yes, Brant, I do remember how to write a weekly."

"Then why did you omit your work with the Varga files?" Now Ivers was showing his teeth.

When the immediate flash of hate passed, Gibbons cooled down and realized that Ivers had been working on that line all morning. Dropping a bomb was one of Ivers's favorite ploys.

"The Varga stuff was a dead end," Gibbons said. "Just a bad hunch."

Ivers nodded and went for his yogurt again. He shoveled a drippy spoonful into his mouth. The sight nearly turned Gibbons's stomach. "I'll bet you're wondering how I know you went into the Varga files."

"Hayes the librarian told you." That big dumb-ass.

Ivers shook his head, smiling like the cat who caught the canary. "We've got a new system with the files. It was installed after you retired. Every Monday I get a printout of all the files that were called up and who requested them during the previous week. It includes hard copies too since Hayes records all traffic in the File Room on the computer. From what I see here, you spent a lot of time with the Varga material. It took you that long to figure out you were running up a blind alley?"

"I'm very thorough." All of a sudden Gibbons had heartburn. He had Rolaids in his pocket, but he'd be damned if he was going to let Ivers see him popping them.

"I'm curious. What did you think Varga had to do with Tozzi?"

Gibbons was in a corner. He didn't want Ivers to know anything about his research into Richie Varga. Fucking Tozzi. Why didn't he say something about this goddamn new monitoring system in the office? The asshole never did think about the details. Well, fuck me, Gibbons thought, I've got to say something. Sometimes you've got no choice but to throw down a good card.

"I thought Tozzi's next target might be Richie Varga. It seemed crazy enough for Tozzi."

"I don't follow you, Bert."

"Tozzi thinks he's on a roll. He's three for three with this vendetta business. I thought he may be ready to take on something more challenging."

"Like gunning down a guy hidden under the auspices of the Witness Security Program." Ivers squinted skeptically. He was digging through his yogurt again, staring into the cup as if he were reading tea leaves. "Why would he go after Varga? Varga cooperated with the prosecutors.

A lot of hoods were put away thanks to him. Varga turned out to be a good guy.''

Yeah, so are you, Brant.

Bile was burning the back of Gibbons's throat. ''Tozzi didn't think so. I remember some comments he'd made about Varga at the time of his grand jury testimony. He thought Varga was just as dirty as the guys he was ratting on.''

''And that's why you thought he might be after Varga? Sounds pretty weak to me.''

''It was just a hunch,'' Gibbons said. ''And not a very good one, as it turned out.''

Ivers set down the yogurt and picked up Gibbons's weekly report. He had a feeling the SAC was going to pick through the whole thing, point for point. What an asshole. Gibbons shifted in his seat. On top of everything else, his goddamn hemorrhoids were acting up.

But just as Ivers was about to say something, his intercom buzzed. He picked up the phone and listened. ''Send him right in,'' he said.

A second later the door opened and in walked Bill Kinney. Gibbons noticed *his* paisley tie and the matching handkerchief artfully stuffed in the breast pocket of his navy blazer. The young heir apparent to the SAC's paisley throne, Gibbons thought, then realized that he was just in a bad mood. Kinney wasn't such a bad guy.

''Sit down, Bill.'' Ivers pointed to the chair next to Gibbons.

Kinney pressed his lips together into a smile and nodded to Gibbons as he took his seat.

''Bert, your investigation is going too slow. Tozzi has to be found before he strikes again. I've decided to assign Bill to this case. You'll work together on this.'' Ivers's tone suddenly turned pompous, as if he were orating to a roomful of recruits. Gibbons knew this was all for Kinney's benefit.

''Bill, I want you to go over Bert's reports and read the file on Tozzi. Then consult with Bert and see if you can take a new approach to this investigation. This is top priority, Bill, so do whatever you feel is necessary to find Tozzi. You two are partners now on this.''

Kinney threw a sympathetic glance at Gibbons. That was a real low blow. It was understood that this was Gibbons's case, even if Kinney was being brought in to help. By stating that they were partners on the investigation, Ivers was letting them both know that from now on Gibbons's seniority meant shit.

''Now I have a lot of respect for the old gumshoe method of investigation,'' Ivers continued. ''It's how the Bureau made its name back in Hoover's day. But you've got to take advantage of the available technology. The labs in Washington are there for a reason. Use them. Also, the files. Don't think of it as a vast library full of isolated reports. Now that everything is computerized, you can make the files work for you. Employ a little creativity in calling for universal searches. You may come up with something unexpected. Talk to Hayes. He can help you there.''

Gibbons's asshole was on fire. This was just a lot of bullshit, meant to show him what an antique he'd become. In thirty years with the Bureau, no one had ever complained about the ''gumshoe method,'' as Ivers called it. The fucking ''gumshoe method'' got results. Always did and always would. The fucking ''gumshoe method'' already found Tozzi, you goddamn nitwit.

Kinney's arms were crossed. Gibbons could see that it was even uncomfortable for him to have to listen to this crap. Ivers was using him, making him the sounding board because the SAC didn't have the guts to tell Gibbons this to his face, the spineless jellyfish.

Ivers sat up straight and folded his hands on the desk. He looked like a politician making a campaign address on TV. ''Now, Bill, I expect you to give Bert a little refresher in what's developed here at the Bureau since he retired. Bert, I think Bill will save you from making any more time-consuming detours, like the Varga business. You two will make a good team, I think. Expertise combined with experience.'' Ivers looked at Kinney and nodded as if he were very satisfied with this marriage.

''Any questions?'' Ivers asked.

Gibbons waited for young Kinney to ask something bright to show the boss he was on top of things. But he didn't say a word. Gibbons was impressed.

''Are we through?'' Gibbons asked testily.

''Bert, we won't be through until we've caught Tozzi.'' Ivers was such a clever bastard.

''Well then, I've got business to attend to,'' Gibbons said, getting up. ''I'll talk to you later, Bill.'' He abruptly headed for the door.

''Results, Bert,'' the SAC called after him. ''Keep that in mind.''

Gibbons shut the door behind him, thinking only about finding some Preparation H.

* * *

After he took care of his immediate problem, Gibbons went back to his desk, which was in the big room with all the other special agents' desks. The desks here used to be arranged in lines and were usually empty because special agents spend most of their time out of the office. Since Gibbons's retirement, though, the room had been remodeled with modular partitions that gave each desk its own private little cubbyhole. Gibbons didn't like the arrangement. What did a guy need this kind of privacy for? To pick his nose? Call his mistress? If you needed this much privacy, you had no business doing it at the office. Anyway, with the old arrangement, you could always see at a glance who was in and who wasn't. Now all you could hear was muffled, disembodied voices because you couldn't see anyone over the tops of these things. It turned the room into a stupid rat maze and all for what? It was just another good reason for being pissed off at Ivers.

"Bert?"

Gibbons turned around. Bill Kinney was standing at the entrance to his cubbyhole.

"What's up?" Gibbons had a knack for making innocuous little phrases like this sound like he was saying "fuck off." He knew it, but he never made much of an effort to change his tone.

Kinney sat down in the beige molded plastic chair, the only other seat in Gibbons's office. "I feel bad about his little performance before." Kinney's voice was low, and he deliberately avoided referring to Brant Ivers by name. "It was embarrassing and entirely uncalled for. I think it sucks."

Gibbons picked up a paper clip and started to unbend it. When the paper clip was as straight as he could get it, he twirled it between his thumb and forefinger. "Yeah, I'd say it sucks too."

"I also feel bad about him saddling you with me." Kinney leaned forward with his elbows on his knees. "Tozzi was your partner, and this is your investigation. I don't want to horn in on what you've been doing. I've got a full plate with my own cases, so I don't need any more."

"Did you tell him that?"

Kinney nodded. "He didn't want to hear about it. I think he was only interested in busting your balls."

"Short-term gains are his specialty." Gibbons bent the paper clip into an L so that it spun faster when he twirled it.

"How about if I do the computer work on Tozzi that he wants to see while you go about your business on this case? Keep me posted on anything I need to know in case he corners me. Otherwise it's all yours."

"Fine with me," Gibbons said.

"Great." Kinney smiled. "I appreciate this, Bert."

"No problem."

Gibbons wondered if he should tell Kinney that he hated being called Bert.

Kinney pulled out that gold stop-sign-shaped pocketwatch and checked the time. "Shit. I've gotta run." He clicked the watch closed and got up to leave. "Lunch date."

After he was gone, Gibbons pondered the term "lunch date." It sounded like the kind of phrase they use in fashion magazines. He imagined a woman in a tight skirt and a hat with a brim wider than a pizza, picking at a spinach salad but not really eating it. Kinney was okay, though, Gibbons thought. But for the time being he could still call him Bert.

FIFTEEN

When Gibbons got home that evening, he cracked open a beer and started making a big breakfast for dinner—three fried eggs, a few slices of pork roll, and rye toast. He would've liked home fries with that, but they were too much trouble to cook and anyway they never tasted as good as diner home fries when he made them at home. The radio in the kitchen was tuned to a classical station; the strains of a Liszt piano sonata competed with the sizzle of the frying pan. The music reminded Gibbons of fancy Viennese pastry topped with swirls of sweet cream and ribbons of icing.

He slid the eggs onto a plate, buttered his toast, and cleared the mail off the table. Gibbons drained the last of his first beer and got himself another to go with his meal. But as soon as he cut into his first egg, the phone rang. He watched the yolk ooze out of the wound and considered letting it ring.

"What?" he said, picking up the phone in the living room.

"It's me." Tozzi had a much better connection this time. It sounded like he was calling from across the street.

"What's up?"

"You ever hear of a wiseguy called 'the Hun'?"

Gibbons sat down on the couch. "Hmm . . . Doesn't ring any bells."

"He was Varga's bodyguard and, from what I hear, the guy who did the actual dirty work on you-know-who."

Gibbons looked through the kitchen doorway and watched the steam rising from his plate as Tozzi proceeded to tell him how he squeezed Bobo Bocchino for what he knew about Varga and the murders of Lando, Blaney, and Novick.

"Tomorrow why don't you see what the files have on this Hun guy?" Tozzi said.

"That could be a problem. The man in the corner office has been monitoring what I take out of the files. I'm beginning to feel his breath on the back of my neck." Gibbons told Tozzi about his meeting with Ivers that morning and his new partner.

"What about your friend Kinney?" Tozzi asked. "Is he going to be a problem?"

"No. He's your typical overworked agent, happy to do as little as he can get away with on this case." It seemed funny talking about the "case" to Tozzi. He *was* the case.

"So how do we find out about the Hun? He could be our missing link to Varga."

Gibbons suddenly remembered Brant Ivers's nasty comment about "gumshoe" techniques. He grinned into the phone. "We do it the old-fashioned way . . . we earn it."

"What's that supposed to mean?"

"I'll tell you some other time. What're you up to?"

"I'm looking for a little torch."

Gibbons could hear the contempt in Tozzi's voice. "Why?" he asked.

"I heard his current employer is Richie Varga."

Arson? It was an odd choice. Burning down buildings for insurance money seemed relatively small-time for someone who'd seen the bright lights of Broadway. The money in drugs was much bigger and much quicker. If Varga was back in operation, Gibbons guessed he'd be concentrating on narcotics.

"Have you located this guy yet?" Gibbons asked.

"Not yet. Maybe tonight. I'll let you know."

"Right. And I'll see what I can find out about the bodyguard. Take it easy."

"You too."

Gibbons hung up the phone and returned to the kitchen where the running yolk had already congealed on the side of his plate. He picked up the beer bottle and took a long swig, then sat down to eat. The eggs were still warm, but that didn't matter. Gibbons ate quickly and with gusto. He was going to pay a visit on someone tonight, do a little good ole gumshoe work.

He casually looked through his mail as he ate, throwing out everything but the gas-and-electric bill and a flyer for a lecture Lorraine was giving at Cornell on the differing concepts of war in the Christian and Islamic worlds in the twelfth century. She always sent him these announcements even though he'd never been able to attend any of her lectures. She used to write little messages on the flyers, but she didn't do that anymore.

Gibbons put the mail aside and concentrated on his dinner. He had to get moving if he was going to make visiting hours. On the radio, a sorrowful mezzo was singing a doom-and-gloom aria from some Italian opera. Gibbons didn't care much for opera. It was too dramatic.

When Gibbons stepped off the elevator onto the fifth floor, he glanced at the clock over the nurses' station. It was quarter of ten. He was expecting some nurse to give him flak about hospital visiting hours being nearly over, but the fat nurse with the long stringy hair sitting behind the desk didn't give him a second look.

He walked briskly, as if he knew exactly where he was going. He could find the room easily enough even if he didn't have the room number. It was the one with the cop posted outside the door. This uniform was a beefy, Irish-looking kid with a permanent scowl. Gibbons knew from personal experience that tough-looking guys always get stuck with this kind of guard duty. Superiors always figure that hard-ass types prevent trouble. They never realize that a certain kind of trouble—like a hit—cannot be sidetracked that easily and that tough guys just attract additional trouble from assholes who have something to prove. If he was a supervisor, he'd give this kind of duty to women because people tend to underestimate them.

Gibbons pulled out his ID folder as he approached the cop, who stared back at him through squinted eyes, clearly expecting trouble. The cop, who had been sitting by the door, stood up and broadened his stance, which amused Gibbons. Did the kid really think he was going to storm the door?

Gibbons held up his ID. "I have to talk to him."

The Irish kid took the folder out of Gibbons's hand and scrutinized it carefully. Gibbons wondered if he'd ever seen a real FBI identification because he took a good long time examining it.

"Nobody told me anyone was coming tonight."

Gibbons flashed a knowing grin. "When do the feds ever tell you guys anything?" He'd meant it as a chummy sort of remark, but he could see that the kid took it the wrong way. It was easy to understand, though. Feds had a bad—and not undeserved—reputation for pulling rank on local police.

"Can't let you in without prior notification. Court orders." He added the court business as if it was supposed to work on G-men like Kryptonite on Superman.

Gibbons took his ID back and put it in his pocket. "Okay," he said with a big sigh of annoyance. "I'll have to call the Special Agent in Charge of the Manhattan FBI field office, who's at home now. He'll have to call the night clerk at the Justice Department in Washington so that they can get someone to call the Staten Island DA, who's also probably at home. The DA will call your captain, who will call you to chew your ass out for obstructing an FBI special agent conducting a priority investigation. It's almost ten now. By the time your captain gets his call from the district attorney, it's going to be very late." Gibbons leaned up against the wall opposite the cop and crossed his arms. "It's your call. Shall we do it the easy way or the hard way?"

The expression on the Irish kid's face was priceless. He looked like he was trying to add up a lot of big figures in his head. It wasn't really that hard to figure out, though. Cops never like to get flak from the feds. It's an unwritten police rule that you steer clear of the feds when you can and just make way when you can't. When all this finally added up in the kid's brain, he nodded with a smirk of resignation. "Okay, go on in. It's your birthday."

Just as the cop stepped aside, a woman's voice came over the p.a. system announcing the end of visiting hours. Gibbons ignored it and pushed through the door. The first thing he saw was a stacked blonde with her hands over her head and her dress bunched up at her armpits as she shimmied into it. A pair of white pumps with spike heels were on the floor next to her.

That crooked little son-of-a-bitch, Gibbons thought. Court orders, my ass. He wondered how much the Irish kid was being paid to protect the privacy of these illicit rendezvous.

"Conjugal rights?" Gibbons said with extra acid in his voice as he held up his ID for the man lying in bed.

Phillip Giovinazzo squinted through his heavy horn-rimmed glasses, showing two rows of perfectly even pearly white teeth. It was that toothy salesman's smile that a staff cartoonist at the *Post* had made infamous after Giovinazzo took over the family from his uncle Rocco nine years ago. The mob boss sat up and nestled comfortably in his mountain of pillows, smoothing out the shirttails of his raspberry silk pajamas.

"What's he got there, honey?" Giovinazzo asked the blonde.

The blonde stepped into her shoes and squinted at Gibbons's ID. "I think he's from the FBI."

"I want to ask you a few questions," Gibbons said.

"See my lawyer," Giovinazzo said, running a hand over his thick mane of brushed-back dyed-black hair. "Now if you don't mind . . ."

Gibbons walked in front of the blonde, pulled up the orange vinyl armchair, and sat down, tossing his hat on top of the telephone on the nightstand.

Giovinazzo jerked his thumb at the door. "Hey, *guaio,* I said take a walk."

Gibbons just stared at him.

"Ah, Phil," the blonde interrupted. "I think I'm gonna be going." She leaned over and kissed him on the lips. Gibbons took in the great view he had of her ass and the backs of her legs. He wondered how much cash it took to get a bimbo like this to kiss an ugly guy old enough to be her grandfather.

Gibbons said, "Now I can see why playing possum isn't such a hardship for you, Giovinazzo."

The mob boss pushed the girl aside so he could see Gibbons. "This is harassment, pal."

The blonde backed toward the door. "I'll see you, Phil. Bye." No one was listening to her.

Gibbons crossed his legs and balanced his chin on the pad of his thumb. "Harassment? I'm just sitting here."

The blonde opened the door a crack. "So long, Phil," she said.

Giovinazzo turned toward her abruptly, flashing his teeth at her. "Yeah, take it easy, honey. I'll see you soon, okay?"

The girl broke out into a delirious smile, as if she'd just won the lottery. Phil must've paid her very well.

After she'd left, Giovinazzo returned his glare to Gibbons. "I've got nothing to say to you." He reached over to the nightstand for the remote control and switched on the TV. A baseball game appeared on the set mounted high on the wall opposite his bed. It was the Mets game. They were playing Philadelphia. Dwight Gooden was pitching. Mike Schmidt was at the plate with a man on second. The announcer was saying something about "power against power."

Giovinazzo suddenly changed the channel from nine to eleven, where

Phil Rizzuto was calling the Yankee game. The Yankees were losing to Toronto in the eighth. Gibbons and Giovinazzo watched in silence as Dave Winfield swung on a slider and struck out.

"Put the Mets back on," Gibbons said. "These guys suck."

Giovinazzo ignored him and kept the Yankee game on.

"How long do you think you can hold out here?" Gibbons asked matter-of-factly. "The U.S. district attorney is getting antsy, you know. You're keeping him from pitching his perfect game."

"I'm a very sick man," Giovinazzo said to the television. "My doctors have testified to that."

"Yeah, I know all about that. But you're messing up a perfect record. Every last schnook Varga testified against has been put away except you. Why prolong the inevitable?"

The boss responded by turning up the volume. Rizzuto was talking about his golf game. Even he was bored with the Yankees.

"I'd hate being cooped up in a place like this," Gibbons said to no one in particular. "Blondes or no blondes." He knew Giovinazzo liked the nightlife.

Giovinazzo suddenly bounced up on his bed. "I ain't talking!" he yelled. "You understand? I got nothing to say to you!" Then he slapped his hand over his mouth. Gibbons thought he was throwing up until he realized that Giovinazzo was removing the upper and lower plates of a pair of dentures. The mob boss defiantly threw the choppers into the top drawer of the nightstand. His lips had collapsed into his face. Suddenly he looked like a ninety-year-old Elvis impersonator.

"Well, fuck me," Gibbons murmured in disbelief.

Giovinazzo settled back into his pillows and glared at the TV.

Gibbons got up and looked down at him, scowling like the Aztec deity. "I'm gonna give it to you straight, Giovinazzo. I'm here to warn you to leave Varga alone. You understand me?"

The mob boss bolted up in bed. "What the fuck you talking about?" His lips flapped and spit flew he was so excited.

"Don't give me that shit. You sent your goons after Varga. They found his first hiding place, but they won't do it again. We don't intend to lose him to your guinea vendetta ethics."

"Bullshit! Bullshit! Bullshit!" Giovinazzo kept repeating himself, his face getting redder and redder.

"We know it was your guys who attacked the house in Ohio. Fortunately Varga didn't get hurt. He's been relocated, buried even deeper this time. But I'm putting you on notice. Call off the dogs or you'll be facing a few more serious charges.''

''You're full of shit!'' Giovinazzo screamed.

''Come off it. Your two boys came close, but they blew it. They got into the house, but they didn't make it to Varga.''

''They weren't mine, that's for sure,'' Giovinazzo said, gumming the words. ''I'd never send just two men after that fat fuck Varga. Not with that crazy Nazi of his.''

''What Nazi?'' Gibbons screwed up his face.

''His bodyguard, you fucking idiot. Varga never goes anywhere without him. At least he never used to.''

''You mean the Hun?''

''Who else? He's crazy. Nothing he won't do if Varga tells him to.''

''You think the government is paying to keep his bodyguard under witness protection. Wake up, will ya?''

''You wake up!'' Giovinazzo yelled. ''Varga goes nowhere without Pagano. And you guys better watch yourselves. He'll cut the eyes right out of your head.''

Lando, Blaney, and Novick. Pagano. Bingo. Varga did have a bodyguard nicknamed the Hun, whose real name is Pagano, and it appears that Mr. Pagano did do dirty deeds on Varga's orders. Like Lando, Blaney, and Novick. Gibbons had gotten what he came for.

''Look, my friend,'' Gibbons said, pointing his finger in Giovinazzo's face, ''you've been warned. Another attack on Varga and you'll be charged with it. It's as simple as that.''

''Stick it up your ass!'' the mob boss yelled as Gibbons stormed out the door.

Outside the cop greeted him with raised eyebrows. Apparently Giovinazzo's other visitors didn't get him quite so riled.

''You coming back?'' the cop asked.

''Is she?'' Gibbons asked pointedly.

He made sure the Irish kid saw him looking at his badge number before he turned and left. Heading for the elevator, Gibbons smiled maliciously to himself, knowing that the kid would sweat it out waiting for the reprimand that would never come.

Of course, maybe the dummy would do his fucking job now and, if he was smart, get the blonde's number for himself.

SIXTEEN

It was just past ten when Tozzi arrived at Leo's Tavern, and he knew the minute he walked through the door that he'd found the torch. The little man had a voice like a two-stroke engine on a cheap motorcycle, and his nonstop yammering made the room feel more crowded than it already was. Tozzi ordered a beer and sat down at the bar. He watched Paulie Tortorella in the reflection of the mirror behind the rows of liquor bottles.

Tortorella was sitting at a round table with a girl who couldn't have been more than sixteen and a guy in his late fifties. The man looked like he was made out of slabs of granite, all right angles, squat and rock hard. The girl was beautiful the way poor Mediterranean peasant girls are in the movies. Dark hair pulled back off her face, tight olive skin, big innocent liquid eyes, round but modest breasts under a white camp shirt. The only flaw Tozzi detected was under the table. Her ankles. She didn't have any. Her calves were solid piping right to her feet. Strong peasant legs came with the package.

Granite man and the girl sat elbow to elbow at one end of the small table, keeping enough personal space between them and the little loudmouth. They were sharing a bottle of wine while the dwarf was drinking something clear on the rocks.

Tortorella was a real sketch, a hood fashion plate in miniature. Burgundy silk shirt, heavy gold chain over the exposed chest, black doubleknits, pointy gray loafers with Cuban heels, and those sheer, faggy-looking nylon socks that wiseguys seem to like for some reason. Tozzi noticed that the toes of Tortorella's shoes just barely touched the floor. He had that kind of arrogant wiseass face that begs to be punched out. High cheekbones, slit eyes, permanent sneer, pug nose with piggy nostrils. Despite Tortorella's slick veneer, Tozzi couldn't help thinking of Knucklehead Smith.

"I'm telling you, Leo, this is a sure shot." He'd said that several times since Tozzi had walked in. "Can't miss."

Tozzi watched Leo the granite man—*the* Leo, he guessed—shake his big square gray head. "How can you be so sure?" he said, his accent as thick as his voice was deep. "Stocks are very risky business. No sure shots."

Tortorella shook his little apple head, a condescending smile scoring his face. "You ever hear of insider trading, Leo? What I've got is very similar, but better. My source is onto some very confidential information. I'm telling you as a friend. You invest in Futura Systems, and you won't have to worry about sending Carmen here to college." He eyed the girl as if he stood a chance with her. The little guy had more balls than brains, though. Portuguese fathers were known to maim for less, and Leo looked like a real bone crusher.

Leo refilled his glass with red wine and tipped a little more into his daughter's glass. There was a big plate of mussels in front of her, which she was eating slowly but steadily. Her liquid eyes rolled from Tortorella to her father to the plate of mussels in a slow, regular pattern. She ate slowly, placing the mussels on her tongue as if she were receiving Holy Communion. Tozzi noticed that she had a slight space between her teeth. She was sexy as hell. In another year or two she'd be worth tangling with Leo over, thick ankles or not.

"How do you know this stock will split?" Leo gave him the you-lie-you-die eyeball.

"Futura Systems is a subsidiary of Maks Enterprises. Forum International is a major stockholder in Maks and my source tells me that Forum is getting ready to mount a hostile takeover of Maks. Maks is going to fight it—"

"Buy up their own stock, you mean." Leo was no dummy and he wanted Tortorella to know that.

"Exactly," Tortorella said. "Futura is a very attractive company, one of the main reasons Forum wants Maks. That's why Futura stock is gonna jump as soon as it gets out that Forum is out to get Maks."

"Have you bought any?" Leo asked.

''Damn straight I have,'' the little man announced. ''Twelve grand worth.'' He wanted everyone in the tavern to hear the figure.

Leo threw his head back and held his gut. A second later he opened his mouth and let the bellowing laughter escape. ''You? Twelve grand? You're so full of shit, Paulie, you make me laugh.''

Knucklehead Smith's face turned very ugly then. ''Hey, I'm no five-and-dime jerkoff, pal. Those days are over. I got cash to burn now, my friend. As a matter of fact, I could buy this goddamn hole of yours with pocket change. I'm making real money now.''

Leo couldn't stop laughing. ''Yeah, yeah. Your big-deal boss Varga. You tell me all the time.''

''Go ahead, yuk it up. Mr. Varga likes to hear about people who think he's a joke.'' Tortorella's heavy irony was meant as a threat. Leo just waved him away with his enormous paw, but his daughter stopped eating when she heard the little man's statement.

The girl tilted her head toward her father and said something softly to him in Portuguese.

''No, no,'' he answered gruffly, then finished his reply in Portuguese.

''Tell me this.'' Leo turned back to Tortorella, frowning at him. ''If your Varga friend is such a big mafioso, why haven't I ever heard of him, huh? I think maybe you make him up.''

''So how the hell do you think I got the new Eldorado parked outside? I paid for that in cash. Varga money,'' he said in a stage whisper.

''Oh, yeah? Anybody can get a car loan, Paulie. You bullshitting me again, I think.'' A hard grin passed over the older man's thick lips.

Tortorella leaned into Leo's face to emphasize his point. ''Mr. Varga is everywhere and he's getting into everything, Leo. But guys like Mr. Varga don't take out ads in the paper for your benefit, Leo. Just take my word for it, the man is into a lot of things.''

Leo remained skeptical, but his daughter seemed to be spooked by Tortorella's ghost story. Her eyes were wide and she wasn't blinking. She clutched her glass of wine with both hands. Maybe she'd seen a movie where the nice old man who owns the corner candy store gets roughed up by the mob punks because he won't pay protection. Maybe she was afraid for her father. Maybe she was just grossed out by the little creep. It was hard to tell.

The argument continued with Leo putting questions to Tortorella about Varga that sounded vaguely philosophical. It was almost as if he were asking the little man to prove the existence of God. Tortorella's answers were vague and ambiguous. He didn't want to admit that he didn't know all that much about his boss.

Tozzi paid for his beer and headed for the door. This shit was going to go on for a while, and he'd heard enough. He'd wait for Tortorella outside. As he opened the door, he glanced back once more at Leo's daughter. She caught him looking at her and she pouted at him. Incredible, he thought. But the rush of appreciation he felt for the girl was immediately flattened by the wall of dead, humid air he walked into as he stepped out into the night.

It was five after midnight when Tortorella finally left Leo's. He unlocked the new black Caddy parked at the curb and hopped in, literally. His method of getting into a car was something like a high jumper making a backward vault. Tortorella's ego wouldn't allow him to step up on the rocker panels to get in. That would be the pussy way to do it.

Slunk down behind the wheel of the old Buick, Tozzi watched as the Caddy's red taillights came on, then the white backup lights. His hand on the ignition, he waited for Tortorella to pull out into the street before he started up the Buick. The tired old V-8 coughed before it roared. The idle was set too high, and the front end needed a lot of work. The car drove like it had high blood pressure. Fast but unsteady. Every time he got into that car, Tozzi wondered if it would be the last time she'd turn over for him. He tapped the accelerator to calm down the engine, then put it in gear and followed Tortorella.

Tozzi tailed the Eldorado down Ferry Street, thinking about Tortorella's boast about paying for the car in cash. That had to be at least a twenty-five-thousand-dollar car. Banks usually don't make loans to arsonists, even successful ones, which meant Tortorella probably did pay cash. Twenty-five grand plus twelve more to buy stocks. Tortorella was doing all right, much better than your average torch.

When the Caddy headed under the dark steel support beams of the Pulaski Skyway, Tozzi assumed Tortorella was going to follow the truck route past the Harrison dump toward New York, but when he turned onto the Turnpike entrance, Tozzi suddenly felt something was up. He just had a feeling that this wasn't Tortorella's regular route. Tozzi didn't know where the little man lived or where else he hung out, but south on the Turnpike didn't seem right. Once you passed Elizabeth and the docks, normal people lived down that way. Victims, not hoods.

Driving past the airport, Tozzi discovered what an erratic driver

Tortorella was. He stayed in the fast lane, but he'd work his way up to seventy-five, then suddenly drop back down to fifty-five. Maybe his feet keep slipping off the pedals, Tozzi thought meanly. But this kind of driving made Tortorella hard to tail, and Tozzi had to let him get far ahead whenever he sped up so as not to be too obvious. He hoped the little bastard was so busy watching for state troopers that he didn't notice the old brown LeSabre behind him. Fortunately for Tozzi, though, he wouldn't get out of the left-hand lane, so that whenever Tozzi did pull up close, he could ride in Tortorella's blind spot.

Staring at the Eldorado's taillights, Tozzi kept thinking about the Portuguese girl and how her composure was rattled when she discovered there was a real-live Mafia guy sitting at her table. She was so beautiful, so complete in that innocent tranquillity of hers until Tortorella mentioned the mob. Joanne was beautiful too, but it was a different kind of beauty. Her calm was cool; it came from knowledge, not innocence. She'd seen it all—certainly in terms of bad guys, she had—and the completeness of her experience made her tranquil and beautiful. It was almost fucking zen, Tozzi thought.

At Exit 11, the Caddy suddenly turned off the highway without signaling and got onto the Garden State Parkway going south.

"Where the hell is he going?" Tozzi wondered out loud.

A few minutes later Tortorella got off the Parkway at the first exit he came to, Woodbridge–Perth Amboy, then wound his way around local streets until he hit Route 27, a congested four-lane strip littered with small factories, cheap motels, chain restaurants, and discount outlets. On this road he had to concentrate on keeping two cars between himself and the Caddy, auto surveillance by the book, but he was still thinking about Joanne and the Portuguese girl. Eventually they blended in his mind and became two of the same person, both perfect and perfectly desirable. It had never been easy for Tozzi to think straight about attractive women. He'd often wondered if there was something wrong with his head.

At a traffic light, Tozzi noticed a WELCOME TO EDISON sign courtesy of the local Jaycees. Tortorella had beaten the light, and Tozzi anxiously watched the Caddy pull away, then turn into a parking lot about a hundred yards beyond the intersection. Tozzi could just make out the big yellow sign on a pole over the lot: $U$$MAN'S AUDIO-VIDEO CENTER.

After the light turned green, Tozzi cruised past Sussman's and turned into the next store's lot, a carpet outlet. He cut his headlights and circled around to the back of the building and parked in the shadows.

Tozzi sat in the dark and stared at the Caddy parked by the back door of Sussman's with the trunk open. Tortorella was unloading something, leaving it by the door. He shut the trunk, got back into the idling car, and backed it up to the embankment at the far end of the lot, where a collection of junk trees brushed the Caddy's roof with their drooping branches.

In the meantime Tozzi got out of his car and tiptoed to the edge of the shadows behind the carpet outlet. The little man got out of his car and walked across the lot to the back door, about thirty yards from where Tozzi was standing. Tortorella seemed to be looking for something. He bent down and picked up a discarded Styrofoam coffee cup that was on the ground next to the dumpster, then turned it over into his hand. Walking back toward the door, he threw the cup away.

When the door opened, Tozzi was certain that the key to the back door had been left in that coffee cup for a night visitor. By the dim light spilling out of the doorway, Tozzi could see that what Tortorella had unloaded from the car were plastic gallon jugs. Filled with something flammable, no doubt. He waited for the little man to bring his jugs in and shut the door behind him before he made a move.

SEVENTEEN

Paulie Tortorella went behind a counter and took out a headset radio from the display case. He turned up the volume, found his favorite FM rock station, put it on his head, and adjusted the volume back down. He liked working to music.

Billy Joel was singing "Uptown Girl." Paulie sang along softly with him as he fetched a gallon of gasoline and mounted the stairs to the second-floor showroom. On the way up he noticed that the carpeting was that fire-retardant industrial stuff. It didn't matter. The flames from the first floor would take care of the second floor. He just had to make sure the roof caved in.

He took a ten-penny common nail out of his pocket and punctured a few holes near the top of the plastic jug; then he went to work, squeezing the jug to douse the drapes, the satin promotional banners on the walls, and the ceiling. He was careful not to spray gas on the walls any lower than three feet from the floor. Investigators always look for excessive burn marks on the lower part of a wall, a sure sign that a flammable liquid was splashed around the room. Paulie prided himself on leaving no clues.

When he ran out of gas, he tossed the crushed jug downstairs and followed after it. He was thinking about Billy Joel in greasy coveralls making time with Christie Brinkley in the "Uptown Girl" video.

Paulie grabbed two more jugs and went down to the cellar, which had been left unlocked for him. He switched on a light and traced the water pipes until he found a rag tied around a section of pipe near the shutoff valve. He'd left instructions that a wad of candle wax be jammed into the pipe so that the sprinkler system would be choked off. By the time there was enough heat built up in the basement to melt the wax in the pipe, it would be too late for the sprinklers to do any good. Eventually the melted wax would flow out with the water, leaving no evidence of tampering. The rag marked the spot where the wax block was. Paulie noticed that somebody was even good enough to leave some broken wooden crates under the pipe just as he'd asked. He was very pleased with these arrangements.

Paulie punctured another one of the jugs and sprayed gas on the crates and stacks of cardboard boxes all around the room, gleefully taking aim at what he thought was the most expensive merchandise.

The deejay on the radio was giving the weather and complaining about the humidity. "Well, here's one for the heat," the deejay said. " 'Dancing in the Street,' the original by Martha and the Vandellas." Paulie was surprised and delighted that they weren't playing the Mick Jagger–David Bowie version. He loved old Motown. Puncturing the next jug, Paulie sang out loud with Martha. He was having a good time now.

When the jug was empty, he drop-kicked it behind a stack of Technics turntables. It clattered loudly when it hit the concrete floor. The nice thing about these thin plastic milk jugs was that they were consumed in the fire. No evidence. The not-so-nice thing about them was that you couldn't leave gas in them for too long. The gas eventually eats through the plastic and the jug leaks, which is not what you want in the trunk of your car. Paulie knew what he was doing, though. He knew how long you could trust these milk jugs once you filled them with gas. He also knew that you had to fill them right to the top with no air space. Air space makes fumes, and it's the fumes that are deadly. The fumes, not the gas itself, is what ignites and explodes. A good torch is always careful about the fumes.

Back on the first floor, Paulie picked up the last two jugs and assessed the room. They'd left a lot of boxes and cartons around the showroom the way he wanted. That was good. Electronics merchandise isn't so flammable that it doesn't need a little help. Especially when the carpeting is flame-retardant.

On a shelf near the cash register, there was an old-fashioned radio in a cathedral-shaped wooden cabinet. Paulie had asked that an old radio be here for this job. Standing on a chair, he turned it on with his knuckles, turned down the volume, then peeked around the back to make sure the tubes were starting to glow. Transistors don't get hot, but tubes do. Someone left this old mama on all night, a tube exploded, the wooden cabinet started to smolder, and that's how the fire started. At least, that's how it will appear to have started.

A fucking genius is what I am, Paulie thought to himself. He admired the old radio. *This* is real genius. That Stevie, man. You ask him for something, and it's always right there where you want it, no fail. Good man.

Paulie didn't give a shit what they said about him. Stevie Pagano was all right as far as he was concerned. Stevie always had jobs for him, good jobs like this one. When Paulie asked for certain things to be on the job waiting for him—rooms to be set up a certain way, wax in the pipes, whatever—Stevie made sure it got done. And Pagano always paid promptly. By the end of the week the cash just appeared in the safety-deposit box at Paulie's bank, like magic. Yeah, working for Richie Varga's family was all right.

There was a lot of good stuff on display in the showroom, and Paulie got a real kick out of dousing it all. It was the same feeling he got as a kid when he squirted lighter fluid on ant hills and set them on fire. One time, when he was home alone, he torched his sister's dollhouse. Just stood there and watched all the tiny furniture burn, room by room. The elegant dining room, the little rec room, the frilly bedrooms, the whole little place. It didn't look like the house they lived in; it was a house for rich people. These were nice little things, lots of things, and they all burned real nice. When the whole house was engulfed in flames, little Paulie's heart was pounding. In a panic he threw the dollhouse out the window, then ran outside and put out the fire with the garden hose. He put what was left of it in two paper bags and ditched them in somebody else's garbage around the corner. When his sister got home later that afternoon, she got frantic. Where was her dollhouse? Paulie said he didn't know. Maybe burglars took it, he said. That night in bed he thought hard about the little house on fire while he played with himself. It was the first time he ever beat off.

After draining the last of the final jug onto a big total-sound speaker that was nearly as tall as he was, Paulie tossed the jug behind a counter, then reached into his pocket for the matches. He pulled out a little box of wooden Blue Tips, which he preferred to paper ones. Wooden matches had a little weight; you could fling them farther.

Climbing the stairs to the second floor, Paulie couldn't help rubbing his crotch. This part always got him excited.

He scanned the big room, knowing exactly where he'd start and how he'd proceed, but before he struck his first match, he reached up and fiddled with the selector dial on the headset. His station was running a string of commercials, and he had to have music now. All the rock stations were playing heavy-metal shit at this time of night, either that or that little fag Phil Collins. But just as he was about to settle for a change of pace and go back to the classical station that was playing a Strauss waltz, he found the Ronettes doing "Be My Baby." He pictured the three girls in those tight sequined cocktail dresses and their outrageous beehive hairdos. Yeah.

Striking the first match, he gazed into the little flame and sang along with the backup. *"Oh, won't you be my baby?/My one and only baby . . ."*

He flicked the match at the satin wall hanging that advertised Bose speakers. It caught with a *phooop* so loud it drowned out Ronnie for a second. Before long the whole wall was on fire, flames beating against the ceiling panels.

He flicked another match at the opposite wall, and a flame ran down the length of the room and ignited the drapes at the front windows.

"Be my baby now-a-ow-a-wo-oh-oh-oh . . ."

He was dancing now.

Paulie ran down to the cellar where he stood on the stairway and tossed match after match until the room looked like hell.

". . . Be my baby,/My one and only baby . . ."

Paulie rubbed his crotch. He was dribbling.

Back up on the first floor, he sidestepped around the perimeter of the showroom, tossing matches, singing. Fire danced in his eyes.

Finally, at the back of the room, he stood before his creation like a conductor before his orchestra. It was beautiful.

". . . Be my baby now-a-ow-a-wo-oh-oh—"

"What the—"

The music suddenly stopped as the headphones were ripped off his head. He could hear the full force of the hiss and roar of the raging fire as the room spun and his back slammed against the wall. His feet were off the ground, and his twisted shirt was digging into his armpits.

Tozzi stuck his face right into Paulie's. He ground his fists into the little man's chest, holding him up against the wall. He'd always wanted to pin someone up against a wall this way with his feet off the ground. Tortorella was light enough to do it.

"Who's the Hun?" Tozzi shouted at him. "What's his name?"

Tortorella struggled and kicked to get free.

"I'll ask you once more," Tozzi yelled in his face. "You don't answer me, I throw you in the fire and lock the door."

The whites of Tortorella's eyes were showing as he glanced at the heavy steel door.

Tozzi didn't want to give Tortorella a chance to think about it, so he dragged him closer to the flames to show him that it wouldn't take too much effort to heave him in.

"You want to burn, you little fuck?" he yelled. "Then tell me. Who's the Hun?"

"Steve, Stevie," Tortorella shouted back, still struggling.

"Stevie what?"

"I don't know. I swear." In the glare of the fire, Tortorella looked more like Jerry Mahoney than Knucklehead Smith.

Tozzi swung him around like a sack of grain so that his legs dragged through burning cardboard. Smoke was overtaking the room, filling his lungs. He hoped he could hold out just a little longer than Tortorella could.

"Stevie what?" he yelled, swinging Tortorella over the flames again.

"Pagano," the little man muttered, then repeated it louder twice more to placate the madman.

"Where is he?" Tozzi yelled. "Where do I find him?"

Suddenly an explosion rocked the floor and threw Tozzi off-balance. The wiry little man landed on his feet and quickly kicked Tozzi in the groin.

Tozzi doubled over. Pagano, Tozzi repeated over and over to himself, holding himself together as the pain thrummed through his body. He scrambled to his feet, coughing. Steve Pagano. He couldn't forget it.

He saw Tortorella run out the back door and he stumbled out after him, breathing into the sleeve of his jacket. He couldn't stop coughing.

Outside the cool air hit him like a cold shower. He coughed and heaved uncontrollably. All his body wanted to do was get the smoke out of his lungs. He heard an engine starting and he saw the shiny black fenders of the Caddy moving in the dark.

Then suddenly he heard tires screech and the whine of a transmission in reverse. Taillights were rushing toward him fast. Tortorella was going to run him down.

Tozzi turned and made a running leap into the dumpster. He landed in a cushion of trash just as the tail of the Caddy bashed into steel.

The impact jolted him. He heard it and felt it vibrating all around him.

Tires screeched again. Tozzi stood up and saw the Caddy swing around the lot, heading for the driveway. He unholstered the 9mm automatic, leveled it against the edge of the dumpster, and squeezed off seven shots with quick deliberation.

The big car whooshed by him, making for the street. He jumped out of the dumpster and ran down the drive in time to hear the sound of a flat tire slapping madly against pavement. Tortorella wouldn't get far on that. At least it would slow him down for the cops. And the broken taillight pieces by the dented dumpster would place Tortorella at the scene of the crime. Good.

Tozzi smiled like a werewolf, still catching his breath. Shooting out the tires, he thought with satisfaction. He'd always wanted to do that too.

Then Tozzi heard the screams of approaching sirens and broke into a run for the Buick. He didn't want to be around when the firemen and the cops showed up.

EIGHTEEN

Hayes the librarian sat behind his desk in the File Room looking through a card-catalogue drawer, checking something against what was on his computer terminal. Gibbons was sitting at a cubicle watching him. There was a sugar doughnut on a paper napkin and a cup of coffee on Hayes's desk, and from time to time Hayes would break off a small piece of doughnut and eat it, leaning forward over his desk to keep powdered sugar off him and out of the keyboard. He was making that doughnut last the way little kids make things last, and it was aggravating the hell out of Gibbons. Why the hell didn't he just eat the goddamn doughnut and be done with it?

If the Manhattan field office was a village, Gibbons often thought, Hayes would be the village idiot. He looked like a pro linebacker stuffed into a Robert Hall suit, but he had a soft whispery voice and a vague, confused way about him. He'd started with the FBI as a special agent, believe it or not. His size was an asset, but he was never able to bring himself to use it as a means of intimidation. And, of course, once he opened his mouth, he didn't seem very intimidating at all. His main problem as an agent had been that he was too thorough. He did things the right way, which meant his methodology was impeccable but his results amounted to shit.

Gibbons sat at the cubicle with a yellow legal pad in front of him, trying to figure out how to overwhelm Hayes and throw up a smoke screen for Ivers. He had no choice but to use the files now, and Ivers would get his weekly printout of who called up what on the computer.

But if Gibbons called up a lot of stuff, all kinds of stuff, it might keep Ivers busy second-guessing him for a while.

Gibbons put together a list of names and events he wanted files on. There were twenty-six items on the list and eighteen of them had clear links to Tozzi, either cases he'd worked on, people he'd investigated, or crimes he'd tried to break. Seven of the items had more tenuous connections with Tozzi. Ivers would have to do some research to figure out why Gibbons might be looking into these things. This, he hoped, would obscure the information he really wanted, information on Steve "the Hun" Pagano.

Tozzi, that bastard, had wakened him from a deep sleep late last night and told him about his encounter with Paulie Tortorella and how he squeezed him for Pagano's name. Tozzi was so excited and incoherent, Gibbons didn't even bother to tell him that Phillip Giovinazzo gave him the same information. Tozzi said they needed to know more about Pagano and insisted that the FBI files were the only way. Gibbons didn't think it was such a hot idea, but at three A.M. he wasn't going to argue about it.

Gibbons stared at Pagano's name where he'd written it down on the list. Tozzi was probably right, going to the files was the only way—the only practical way. Gibbons had considered going back to Giovinazzo and leaning on him some more, but it was unlikely that he'd say anything crucial about a fellow gangster. *Omertà* and all that bullshit. Tozzi could go hit up on Bocchino the fence again, maybe pay visits on other small-timers to see what else he could find out about Pagano, but Gibbons didn't like the idea. Tozzi was a hothead, and his antics could draw unwanted attention. He was lucky he didn't get caught at that fire. Gibbons figured the less time Tozzi spent out on the streets the better. The files were the only practical way.

Gibbons tore off the top sheet from the pad and turned over the book he'd brought from home. It was the book he'd been reading about the influence of the Teutonic tribes on the Roman Empire. This was going to be another long, boring day, more so than usual because he was going to have to pretend that he was reading through all these files. That's why he'd brought his book. He planned to read about barbarians while he scrolled through the files to make it look like he was reading from the terminal at his cubicle.

As he walked over to Hayes's desk, he scanned the list. Pagano's name was the eleventh item on his list. He figured he'd have to wait till at least eleven-thirty before he could safely get to Mr. Pagano.

"I want whatever you've got on all these," he said to Hayes, dropping the list on his desk.

Hayes peered up, squinted with his usual confused look, then stared down at the list. This took a while.

Gibbons looked at his half-eaten doughnut on the paper napkin. It looked like a rat had been nibbling on it. "You gonna eat that?" he said.

"What?"

"The doughnut. You gonna finish it?"

"Why do you want to know?"

Hayes's mere existence irritated Gibbons, and he hated having to spend more than a passing moment in the man's presence. "Just asking," he said.

It took twenty seconds for Hayes to digest all that before he returned to the list. "Do you want them in this order?" he finally asked.

"Yes."

"All right," he said slowly as he swiveled in his tiny secretary's chair to face his keyboard.

Gibbons was reminded of that business about chaining a hundred chimps to a hundred typewriters for a hundred years and eventually one of them would type out *Hamlet*.

"I'll feed the files directly to your terminal," Hayes said. "When you want the next file, you hit the 'escape' key, then type 'n' space 'f'—for 'new file'—and hit the 'return' key. Okay?"

"Fine," Gibbons said, turning back to his cubicle.

"But give me a few minutes to get you on line," Hayes called after him.

"Sure. Take your time." You usually do, you big baboon.

Gibbons went back to his seat and picked up his book. He started reading, but his mind wasn't on it. He was thinking about this whole stupid ruse, annoyed with himself for having to waste the day making it look like he was reading through all those files. The fact that he had to be so devious made him angry. Especially because he had to do it for Hayes's benefit.

He got up and went back to Hayes's desk. "I forgot to ask you," he said. "If I want to cross-reference these files, can I jump around or do I have to take the files in order?"

Hayes nodded. At what, Gibbons hadn't a clue. He left his command post trailing Gibbons's list behind him and went to the Xerox machine. He was still nodding. When a copy of the list came out of the machine, he gave the original back to Gibbons. "Refer to your list," he finally explained. "I'll enter the files in this order. When you want the first one, enter 'n space f space 1.' For the second file, 'n f 2,' and so on. That way you can skip around." The ape lumbered back to his desk, dragging his knuckles. "It'll take me a little more time to get it set up for you this way. Just a little bit longer."

"No problem." Gibbons looked down at the crumbly half-eaten doughnut. It was really bothering him.

Well, this should save some time, he thought, scanning his list as he returned to his seat. His eye fell on Reverend Miner's name. Reverend Miner and the Empire of God. First Church of the Unholy Survivalist, Tozzi used to call it. That and St. Rambo's. The reverend had more guns and munitions stockpiled than the New York State National Guard. Tozzi was the one who found the warehouse up in Rhinebeck. Crazy son-of-a-bitch. He had no patience for long-range surveillance, and he seldom waited for backups. That time Tozzi walked right across a cow field in broad daylight with a Nikon around his neck, climbed the roof of the warehouse, broke in through a ceiling vent, and took the whole roll of Miner's arsenal. Then when some farm-boy believer caught him coming out of there with his camera, Tozzi told him he was just taking pictures of the cows. The farm boy was holding a hatchet, making it very clear that he wanted the camera. Tozzi, the crazy bastard, dangles the Nikon in front of the guy's face like a hypnotist's pocketwatch, then hauls off and coldcocks him. What a fucking cowboy.

The next item on the list was the Cartagena Connection, cocaine smugglers. Gibbons shook his head at the memory. These slimy Colombians were making a delivery at the East Hampton Airport on Long Island. Their cover was a helicopter shuttle service from Manhattan. Seven agents and a dozen local cops were undercover waiting for them to touch down and unload when some stupid rookie jumps the gun and starts yelling and waving his service revolver at the chopper. One of the Colombians was already out of the hull, but his buddy inside started yelling for him to get back in. The chopper was two feet off the ground, the engine revving, ready to take off again. The bullets were just about to start flying when out of the blue, Tozzi runs out onto the tarmac pushing a lawnmower. Nobody knows what the hell to make of this, not even the Colombians. All of a sudden Tozzi's swinging this lawnmower like he's gonna throw the hammer. Then he lets it fly, right into the chopper's tail rotor. The noise was enough to scare the shit out of anyone, and it was only afterward that they found out the chopper could've flipped over and exploded. Tozzi was unimpressed with that information, as Gibbons remembered.

Gibbons's grin of nostalgia gradually faded. Tozzi had a long history of being reckless. It was unlikely that being out on his own made him any more cautious, and that worried Gibbons. Did Tozzi really believe he could knock off all the guys on his hit list, then safely make it out of the country to one of his relatives'? Tozzi wasn't that stupid. At least he never used to be. Gibbons decided he better find out more about what Tozzi was doing with his time. Particularly what he was doing with Varga's wife. They had to be very careful now.

Gibbons frowned. He knew he was thinking like an old lady. After all, who was going to catch them? He and Kinney were the only guys assigned to the case, and Kinney didn't give a shit about finding Tozzi. Still, he was uneasy, and he knew why. Consulting Bureau files for the benefit of a felon is a felony itself. Before this he'd maintained a degree of skepticism about Tozzi's crusade and in his mind he felt uncommitted, but by going into the files now he was actively working with Tozzi, and this time it really felt like he was doing something illegal.

Hayes's head suddenly popped up over the edge of his cubicle. "Okay, Gibbons, you're on line. You can proceed."

Gibbons nodded absently. He called up the first file, thinking about Ivers's monitoring system, wondering if the SAC could get lucky and figure out that the renegade had a confederate within the Bureau. He scrolled randomly, then called up another file, lingering over it for several minutes before he switched to a new one, deliberately avoiding the Pagano file. He looked around the side of the cubicle. Hayes was still nibbling on that goddamn doughnut. What the hell, he thought. We're already in this far.

He keyed in "n f 11" and waited for the printing to appear on the terminal. There was a pause, then a short message appeared. "No file under that title. Searching for cross-reference. Please wait."

Gibbons's stomach sank. He pictured Ivers's face suddenly appearing on the screen, telling him that the jig was up. Gibbons told himself that he was being paranoid. The computer was just doing its thing, for chrissake.

It took nearly a full minute for the computer to find what it was looking for, and when it did, Gibbons was certain that it had goofed. The file that appeared was titled "Mafia Undercover Activities: Philadelphia Field Office, 1981–1983."

He started skimming. The file was more or less a routine intelligence summary of what the Philly field office had discovered about their local mob family during that three-year period. Gibbons had seen countless reports like this over the years. What they said was usually pretty predictable.

He scrolled down and kept skimming. Then, several pages into the report, he saw Pagano's name flashing in boldface. This was how the computer let you know that it had found what you were looking for.

Pagano's name was on a double-columned list with his nickname in parentheses. Gibbons scrolled up to the paragraph before the list, which stated that the following was a list of cover names used by special agents while working undercover.

Gibbons scrolled back down to the list and Pagano's pulsating name. Then he read the corresponding name in the column beside it.

His skin went cold. "Goddamn," he said in a whisper.

Late that afternoon, Bill Kinney went into the File Room. He was looking for Gibbons and he hoped Hayes might've seen him. Hayes wasn't at his desk, though. Kinney decided to wait for him, and as he stood there, he scanned the librarian's desk.

Something caught Kinney's eye right away, the copy of the handwritten list Gibbons had given Hayes that morning. He recognized Gibbons's cramped scrawl. He turned the list around on the desk and examined it closer. The entry for "Steve 'the Hun' Pagano" was circled. Next to it, Hayes had made a notation: *"No file—referred to Mafia Undercover Activities: Philly FO, 81–83."*

Kinney breathed slowly. His eyes glazed over. He knew what was in that file.

And now Gibbons knew too.

NINETEEN

Gibbons had a lot on his mind as he drove south on the Garden State Parkway. He was heading for Tozzi's aunt's apartment in Bloomfield. He'd tried calling Tozzi from a pay phone on Broadway that afternoon, but there was no answer, so now he was going out to find him. He had to tell Tozzi what he'd found out, and then they had to decide how they'd handle it.

Kinney's face lingered in his mind like a powder burn. Kinney the Yuppie. Kinney and his fine old gold pocketwatch. Kinney the Hun. Kinney the butcher. The devil had a face now, and Gibbons could see him everywhere he looked.

Gibbons had spent most of the afternoon in the File Room, killing time with the files he'd asked Hayes for, gazing blankly at the screen, wondering how he should approach this. He'd considered telling Ivers about Kinney, but he had no hard evidence. It was possible that they could go to Joe Luccarelli and Sabatini Mistretta in prison and ask them to testify against Kinney, but their cooperation could never be counted on, and anyway testimony from convicted gangsters could easily be discredited by a good lawyer. And on top of that, even though Luccarelli and Mistretta saw the heads, as far as he knew they didn't actually see Kinney butcher Lando, Blaney, and Novick.

He knew how Tozzi was going to want to handle this, but that was wrong. Executing Kinney would make him a public hero, for one thing, and besides, it would eliminate their only solid connection to Richie Varga.

Blackmail was another possibility, but Gibbons couldn't see someone as cold-blooded and nerveless as Kinney buckling under to a blackmail threat. And if it came down to a question of his word against Kinney's, Gibbons had a feeling Brant Ivers would tend to believe the fair-haired boy over the difficult old goat.

No, they couldn't move on Kinney, not yet. As guilty and detestable as he was, Kinney was still only small potatoes compared to Varga. Kinney was really just a tool, the line they needed to reel Varga in.

Gibbons had all his arguments ready for Tozzi by the time he left the field office late that afternoon and headed for Jersey. Rush-hour traffic through the Lincoln Tunnel had been normally insane, but Gibbons was unusually calm. Now that he'd had time to think about it, finding the bad agent was a relief, an opportunity. Having that information was like finally having all the supplies assembled for a big job. The anticipation was sweet, full of possibilities.

Turning off the Garden State Parkway at the Bloomfield exit, Gibbons switched off the air-conditioning and rolled down the windows on the big LTD. It was an unusually cool day for August, one of those days that hints at the coming fall. He breathed deeply, catching a whiff of fresh-mown grass. Bloomfield was a nice town. Old Victorians and big shade trees. Gibbons thought about waiting in the park across the street from the apartment building if Tozzi wasn't home yet.

He cruised down Broad Street and parked around the corner from Tozzi's building. As he walked toward the apartment, he ran over his arguments against Tozzi's certain bid for blowing Kinney's brains out. It was hard to reason with Tozzi when he got something into his head. Gibbons knew from experience that you had to treat him like a little kid when he got that way. Just be forceful and lay down the law.

As if Tozzi gave a shit about the law.

A black Firebird Trans Am was parked in front of Tozzi's building, one of those top-of-the-line jobs with the Firebird logo painted on the hood in gold and white. Gibbons noticed it right away. It definitely wasn't the kind of car the senior citizens in this neighborhood favored.

In the front passenger seat, a fat guy sat eating an ice-cream cone. He licked slow and lazy, concentrating on the cone, lethargic yet very methodical. Coming closer, Gibbons thought the guy looked like an oversized baby. It was then that he saw the two big dogs sitting upright in the backseat. Ugly black things with brown markings. They watched Gibbons pass but didn't bark, which surprised him. He thought all dogs in cars barked at people passing by.

In the vestibule Gibbons rang the buzzer next to Carmella Tozzi's name. He looked through the glass door and waited. No answer. He turned to go back outside, but just as he was about to push through the front door, a woman opened the inside door. She was in her sixties and very attractive. She walked like a model, back straight and head high. Sort of an Ava Gardner type, Gibbons thought as she descended the steps. She had a little white dog on a red leather leash, and she smiled at him as she passed. A Scotch terrier, he guessed.

Gibbons nodded to the woman, then frowned as he heard something that didn't sound right. When the inside door swung back, there was no click. It didn't lock automatically the way it was supposed to. He climbed the steps and tried the door, which opened easily. As he suspected, the latch bolt had been taped flat.

Gibbons ripped the tape off and rolled it between his thumb and forefinger as he stepped inside. Unconsciously he stashed the wad of tape in the pocket of his jacket, then reached for Excalibur. He released the safety and pointed the gun up as he mounted the stairs very cautiously. It had been a while since he'd done this kind of thing.

Why would someone leave the door open like that? There could be a hundred reasons, some criminal, some not, but one scenario immediately took shape in his mind. Tozzi buzzed in someone he knew who then taped the door so that the big baby with the dogs could let himself in later. He imagined Tozzi in bed with some woman who rolled away just as the fat guy burst in with a silenced automatic. Gibbons rounded the landing and moved a little faster.

Tozzi's place was on the next floor. Gibbons leaned over the railing and looked up the stairwell before he proceeded. It was empty. He walked quietly to the stairs and laid his hand on the banister. In the dim light of the hallway he didn't notice that the apartment door opposite the stairway wasn't closed all the way.

Before Gibbons took the first step, someone appeared behind him, threw a wire garrote around his neck, and yanked him backward. Either by luck or misguided reflexes, Excalibur got caught between Gibbon's neck and the piano wire, and the gun was pinned against his throat, the barrel pointed under his chin.

The killer yanked harder, grunting with the effort, frustrated and confused with the unsatisfactory results of trying to strangle a piece of metal.

Gibbons couldn't breathe. The gun was pressed against his windpipe, and the wire was burning into the flesh on the left side of his neck.

He was leaning back against the killer, but still on his feet. Instinctively he got a leg up and was able to push hard enough off the banister to drive the man with the garrote back into the doorjamb of the apartment he emerged from.

The attacker grunted again. The impact was enough to cause pain, but not enough to make him let go of the piano wire.

"Die, you motherfuckin' bastard," he hissed, bearing down on Gibbons, who was on his knees now.

With his free arm, Gibbons played his only option: he hammered with his elbow until he found the man's groin and kept hammering until he triggered his own funnybone on the guy's pelvis. Gibbons felt woozy and sick to his stomach. He was afraid he'd pass out at any moment. Then the wire loosened slightly, and Gibbons found the strength to start hammering again. He was determined to keep it up until the guy doubled over or he passed out, whichever came first.

Finally the killer dropped the garrote and, stooped over, stumbled down the hall toward the stairwell.

Gibbons raised his gun, but his vision was blurred and he was shaking so badly he didn't dare fire. What if he plugged Ava Gardner coming up the stairs with her Scottie?

The killer was gone by then, just leather footsteps on the tile floor and the glass door slamming shut.

Gibbons was losing consciousness and he felt like he was going to heave up his lunch. He sat on the floor, helpless, then minutes later he realized he was still holding Excalibur. He promptly holstered his gun. What the hell would people think if they came home and saw him sitting there, wheezing and dizzy, holding a piece?

The pounding in his head started to diminish, and the nausea had passed. When he dared get to his feet, he half-walked, half-crawled up to the next landing to an open window. Fresh air helped a little. He looked down at the street. The black Firebird was gone.

When Tozzi returned to his aunt's apartment that evening, he found Gibbons sitting on the couch, watching Dan Rather on TV. His shirt was off, and there was a nasty red mark on his neck. He gave Tozzi the eyeball before he said anything. "Where the hell have you been?" he finally said.

Tozzi stared at the welt. He was more than a little surprised to see Gibbons sitting there in his torn T-shirt, an open can of beer on the coffee table. He'd never seen him so casual, so off-guard. The sight reminded him of some of the old retirees in this building, and that made Tozzi uneasy. "What happened? What're you doing here?"

"Some gorilla grabbed me from behind down on the second floor." Gibbons didn't have to explain any more than that. The welt and the fact that he was still alive told the rest of the story.

Tozzi looked stunned. "Who? How?"

"Varga's people, most likely," Gibbons said matter-of-factly. "They could've followed me here the day I found this place. Or maybe they found you on their own. Who knows? Why they decided to attack today is very interesting, though. I didn't think he could put the pieces together so fast. He must somehow have access to that computer monitoring system."

"You're talking to yourself, Gib. Who's got access to the monitoring system?"

"I found out who Pagano really is. Bill Kinney, the guy who's supposed to be helping me find you."

Tozzi sat down on the other end of the couch, his face frozen as he digested all this. "Kinney. That's the guy from Philly, right?"

Gibbons sipped his beer and nodded.

"What do you think we should do?" Tozzi asked.

"I think we should let Kinney lead us to Varga," Gibbons replied, expecting Tozzi to object and argue for immediate execution. For a moment he wondered whether Tozzi was nuts enough to be considering an eye-for-an-eye thing, planning to do up Kinney the way he did Lando, Blaney, and Novick. He dismissed the thought immediately. Tozzi wasn't that bad.

Tozzi leaned forward with his elbows on his knees. "What are the chances of Kinney leading us to Varga? These guys aren't stupid, you know. And Varga's the world champ in keeping his ass covered."

"What if you turned him in?" Tozzi asked. "Go over Ivers's head. Go straight to the federal prosecutor's office."

"With what? Hearsay evidence?"

Tozzi nodded thoughtfully. "Yeah, right . . . So what do you suggest?"

Gibbons picked up his shirt from the back of the couch and put it on. "Well, I found you and I uncovered Kinney. Maybe I can find Varga too."

"Yeah, sure."

"Wanna put money on it?" Gibbons flashed the crocodile smile.

"The man's a ghost. He's everywhere and he's nowhere."

"No, Tozzi, that's God you're talking about. Varga will be a little easier to find."

"Good luck." Tozzi was still doubtful.

"Listen, do you have any other hideouts?"

Tozzi shrugged. "No place clean enough to stay overnight. I'll have to rent a room somewhere."

"Okay, when you find a place, call me at this number and let me know where I can get in touch with you." He jotted down a phone number on the back of an old copy of *Reader's Digest.*

Tozzi saw the 609 area code. "Lorraine?"

Gibbons nodded as he shrugged into his jacket and stuffed his tie into the side pocket.

"What're you gonna do down there?" Tozzi asked.

Gibbons grinned slyly. "I'm going down to Princeton to play a long shot."

"What?"

"Just collect what you'll need and get out of here fast," he said, going to the door. "And don't come back."

"Hey, hold up," Tozzi said. "Do you really think you can find Varga?" There were traces of skepticism, hope, and despair in his voice.

"Won't know till I get started," Gibbons said. He slipped out the door, but that menacing grin lingered in the air like the Cheshire Cat's.

TWENTY

The afternoon sunlight filtered through the tall trees and splattered light on the old bluestone walks of the campus. It was warm but not too humid, and students from the summer session sprawled on the grass, reading, studying, kissing. Princeton really was a pretty place. It always made Gibbons wary. Things that seemed too perfect naturally made him suspicious.

Lorraine was wearing jeans and a blue work shirt with red and black burros embroidered on the front. Her hair was tied back with a leather-and-wood device that Gibbons couldn't quite figure out. She looked like a protester with the United Farm Workers, one of César Chavez's people, a throwback to the old hippie days. Walking along with him, she must've looked like she was being taken in for questioning, he thought. She looked beautiful.

They walked in silence, which wasn't unusual for them, but Gibbons felt he should say something. Too much had been left unsaid with Lorraine. He felt guilty about that. He wanted some changes made, but he wasn't exactly sure what changes. Things had to be put right between them, but it seemed inappropriate to bring it up now. She was too worried about Tozzi. So was he.

They emerged from a courtyard, and the looming Gothic chapel suddenly appeared before them. Gibbons slowed his pace to take it in. "Do you really think this kid can do it?" he asked.

Lorraine looked at him as if she just noticed he was there. "Well, he didn't think it was an impossibility. At least that's the impression

I got from him. He was one of those four high-school kids from Scarsdale who broke into the Bank of Boston computers a few years ago."

"What's this kid's name again?"

"Douglas Untermann."

"So how did you get him to agree to help me with this?"

Lorraine looked at him and grinned. "He owes me."

A flash of jealousy singed Gibbons's cheeks as he imagined some Ivy League Lothario, some Bill Kinney–type, making a play for his history professor. "What do you mean he owes you?"

"He took my Early Medieval European History course last fall and he got so far behind in the reading, he had to take an incomplete. He was supposed to take the exam in March, but he still hadn't done the reading, so he begged for more time. He put it off twice more, pleading for mercy each time. Doug needs social-science credits to graduate, you see. That's why he needs me."

"So what's his problem?"

Lorraine shrugged. "He's a nerd." She laughed when she said the word. "Did you know these computer whiz kids actually call themselves nerds? What self-images these people must have!"

"What kind of deal did you cut with him?"

"Get this. All last spring as he was putting me off, postponing his exam, he kept begging me to let him do a paper instead. When I asked him what he wanted to write on, he said he wanted to compare Henry II's reign with some character he'd invented playing that game Dungeons & Dragons."

"I don't believe it." Gibbons was beaming in disbelief.

"Absolutely true. I told him to take a hike. But when you called me the other night and asked if I knew any discreet computer geniuses, I called Doug and told him I'd reconsider letting him write his paper if he did me a little favor."

"Very nice, Professor Bernstein," Gibbons said, taking her hand. "I owe you one."

They walked down a stone path that suddenly opened up on a magnificently tended flower garden in full bloom. Standing against a background of red and white impatiens, pink gladiolas, and deep orange marigolds was a wedding party posing for photographs. The bride's white gown in the sunlight was actually radiant against all that color. The groom looked very pleased with himself.

Gibbons was suddenly very conscious of Lorraine's hand in his.

No one said anything until they'd passed through the garden. "Do you really think he can get into the Justice Department's computers?" he asked.

Lorraine shrugged. "He's been working on it all night," she said hopefully. She was trying hard to be cheery, but that desperate look of fear and distress was in her eyes.

He wished he could tell her not to worry, that it would be okay, but he couldn't lie to her.

Douglas Untermann was an eighteen-year-old sophomore. Apparently he'd skipped a grade somewhere along the line. He was extremely antisocial but not in a particularly unfriendly way. Human communication just didn't interest him as much as computers. For him computers presented infinite possibilities and yet were always predictable. People, on the other hand, were all pretty much the same but consistently unpredictable. Doug preferred predictability. Which was all for the best, Gibbons figured, particularly for a guy with the looks of a fetal pig and the personality of a five-speed power drill.

Gibbons sat at a spare desk at the computer center staring out the window as Doug hunched over his keyboard, ceaselessly punching in different combinations of whatever he was doing to get into the Justice Department in Washington. They hadn't said a word to each other since Lorraine left them over two hours ago. She had to go do something or other at her office. In that time, Gibbons had had two cups of burnt coffee, shredded both Styrofoam cups into small bits, and counted the little holes on the toes of his wingtips. He'd refrained from speaking to the kid for fear that he'd bolt like a scared rabbit. But this was getting ridiculous. If Doug was telling the truth, he'd started working on this last night at ten and he was still at it now, seventeen hours later. This was supposed to be the computer age, for chrissake.

Gibbons finally slapped his hand on the metal desktop to get the nerd's attention. "So, Doug, what's the story?"

Doug shot his palm up into the air like a traffic cop, his eyes glued to the monitor. "Wait," he blurted.

The monitor suddenly filled with numbers, scrolling down at a demon pace. When it had gone through what must have been a thousand sets of numbers, it stopped and the monitor was empty. Doug slumped in his chair like a deflated balloon. "Shit," he mumbled.

"What happened?"

"I tried everything, but I can't get around it." Doug looked like he was going to cry.

"You can't get around what?"

"Their security system! There're no back doors. I tried to find one, but the system is airtight."

Gibbons was amazed to hear that the government could actually do something right for a change. "You can't get into the Justice Department files. Is that what you're telling me?"

Doug just pouted. They'd beaten him, and he wasn't taking it well. The distant ripping sound of a dot-matrix printer in another room filled the void.

Suddenly Doug came back to life. "Goddamn them! It isn't fair."

"What isn't fair?"

"These new systems. Operators, *human* operators. It's not fair. And everybody's using them now. You've got to call an operator first and give your password. If you've got the right password, they call you back and give you access. The sneaky part is that they call you back at a predetermined phone number, so even if you figure out some authorized user's password, you've got to be at his phone to get in. It's un-fucking-fair!"

Gibbons got the feeling Doug was explaining all this to his hardware, not to him. "So they've turned it into a user's-only club, huh?" He still didn't believe that the government could be so competent. These computer kids were supposed to be able to do anything.

"Yeah, and it really sucks."

They fell silent for a while, then all of a sudden Doug started up again, like a teletype machine in an empty office.

"This used to be a lot of fun, breaking into their systems. I mean, they really did make it hard, but it could be done."

"Yeah? What was the best one you ever did?" Gibbons knew this kid didn't have a good bartender he could cry to, and anyway he was curious to hear how these guys operated.

A dreamy look of nostalgia came over Doug's pasty face. "My best one? My best one was when I found my father's girlfriend. That was the best, hands down."

"How'd you do that?"

Doug slumped down in his chair, stared into space, and gestured with his pudgy hands. "Well, my mother suspected that my father was cheating on her, but she couldn't prove it. I had a feeling he was too. My father travels a lot in his job, so he certainly had the opportunity to have an affair. He also makes a lot of money, so he could easily afford to keep a wench if he wanted to.''

''Where's he work?''

''IBM.''

It figures.

''So what I did first,'' Doug went on, ''was get his American Express account number—the business card, not the personal one—and check out where he'd been spending his time—''

Gibbons interrupted. ''How'd you get the number?''

''Out of his wallet while he was taking a shower. Anyway, when I accessed his account records, I figured out where he'd been in the past year, and one place stood out like a sore thumb: Great Barrington, Massachusetts. It stood out because it was the only place on his records where IBM doesn't have an office. After that, getting into the Great Barrington town computer was a piece of cake. See, I had a hunch and it turned out to be right. The tax records showed that my father owned a little house up there. His little hideaway.''

Doug cracked his knuckles before he continued. ''Now I knew the address of the house and I already had his Social Security number, so I patched into a few of the big DP companies and I looked around for his homeowner's insurance policy. That took some time because there's a lot of data to get through with insurance files. Anyway I finally found it after about a week. He'd insured the house through State Farm and the policy was taken out jointly with his girlfriend. That gave me her name, Social Security number, age, all that stuff. Dad was stupid. He should have put everything in her name. Guess he didn't trust her that much.''

Gibbons couldn't believe this. ''So then what did you do?''

''I made a deal with my mother. I told her that if she bought me this autodial twenty-four-hundred-baud modem I wanted, I'd give her Dad's girlfriend's name and the address of their love nest.''

''Did she go for it?'' Gibbons already knew the answer to that.

''Of course. Her lawyer sent a private detective up there to follow them around and take the incriminating pictures and all that. Their divorce finally went through at the beginning of the summer.''

Gibbons shook his head. He had to laugh. ''Nice kid. Turning on your old man like that.''

''What do you mean? I could've told Mom about all the money he had socked away in Grandma's name. I found out he was worth at least twice what he reported to the court. I saved him a bundle on alimony."

"Great. So you screwed your old lady too."

Doug winced. "She's a real pain. Anyway, my father gave me a forty-meg hard-disk AT with a color monitor for keeping my mouth shut about the money. It all worked out for the best. Dad says he's a lot happier with Emma now."

Gibbons stood up and stretched his back. "Thanks for the effort, Doug. I'll tell Lorraine you did your best."

Doug nodded and went right back to the computer.

Another good reason for not getting married again, Gibbons thought.

TWENTY-ONE

When Tozzi walked into her office, Joanne leaned back in her high-back chair and looked at him through half-closed eyes. "Is it Halloween?" she asked. She was referring to Tozzi's suit, his "Mr. Thompson" outfit.

Her unexpected sarcasm stung him. He wasn't feeling very secure, having just moved into the EZ Rest Motel right on the highway in Secaucus, taking only what belongings he could stuff into a small suitcase and a plastic Macy's bag. The room had one small window that looked out on a twenty-four-hour Exxon station. The highway traffic was loud but it was constant, like white noise, though every time a car pulled into the gas station and rolled over the pressure wires, the bells rang inside the garage, and that had kept him up most of the night.

Tozzi was wearing his suit because he figured it was only right that he dress appropriately for an office visit. It was bad enough that he was dropping in unannounced again; he couldn't embarrass her by coming in looking like—what?—an undercover cop, a wiseguy, her gigolo? Besides, he had to look decent because he'd come with the vague hope that she might invite him to stay at her place, just for a little while, at least.

She reached for a cigarette from the pack of Newports on her desk and held one between her fingers, the butane lighter poised in her other hand. "Well?" she said.

Tozzi smiled lamely. "Trick or treat." He sat down on the gray-oatmeal sofa and sank down into the cushions. He could've fallen asleep right there.

She lit her cigarette and squinted behind the rising smoke. "You look like shit. What's wrong?"

Tozzi rubbed his eye sockets with the heels of his hands and exhaled a short bitter laugh. He hesitated before he told her anything, but then went ahead and told her anyway. "That ex-, former, whatever-the-hell-he-is husband of yours—the guy I'm not supposed to mention in front of you—is out to get me. I had to leave my apartment because he knew where I was."

"You sound paranoid." She sounded unconvinced. Or unconcerned.

"You ought to see the piano-wire burns on my friend's neck, courtesy of one of Richie's gorillas. You'd be paranoid too."

"Is he dead?" Finally she looked alarmed.

Tozzi shook his head.

"How do you know Richie's responsible for this?"

Tozzi hesitated again.

"Fuck you," she suddenly snapped. "You come waltzing in here looking for sympathy, but you still don't trust me enough to tell me the whole story. Well then, just get the hell out of here."

Tozzi looked at her and sighed. He wished he could just go to sleep. "Richie's after me because I'm after Richie."

She pursed her lips and tapped her polished nails on the leather edge of her blotter. A thin wavy line of smoke rose from her cigarette. "I figured that out a long time ago," she said impatiently.

"So what else do you want to know?" This wasn't the way he'd hoped this would go.

"Who do you work for?"

"No one. I work alone."

"Really. You're a lone wolf? An avenging angel? How goddamn stupid do you think I am?"

He looked her in the eye. "I never thought you were stupid. Just the opposite."

She turned the page on her calendar with a sharp snap and shuffled papers angrily. "Then what are you doing here? What do you want from me?"

"I don't know," he said. "I just wanted to see you."

"Is that a line left over from your disco days?"

He ignored the insult. "The first time I met you, you said that any enemy of Richie Varga's was a friend of yours."

"So?"

"So help me."

She looked away, looked at anything else in the room but him. He had a feeling she was deliberately trying to maintain her fury. "Why don't you leave me alone? I don't care about him anymore. He's out of my life. I don't want him back in. Can't you understand that?"

Tozzi noticed that her hand was shaking. "I do understand. But you've got to realize that—"

"I don't have to realize anything. I don't care what Richie's doing."

Tozzi stared at her hand and wondered if he should play the card he had in mind. At this point, there was nothing to lose. "Do you care what he wants to do to me? Do you care that he wants to kill me?"

She swiveled her chair sideways and took a slow drag off her cigarette. Her face was set off by the high-back wings of the leather chair. For some reason, Tozzi thought of the profile of Alfred Hitchcock at the beginning of the old TV show.

Her phone rang then—a twittering flutter, not an actual ring. She let it go for five rings before she decided to pick up.

"Yes?" she said, sounding weary. She was still in profile as she listened to whoever was on the other end. "All right. I'll take it.

"Hi, Dale. How are you?" Suddenly she was someone else, Ms. Varga, vp. Her tone wasn't friendly, it wasn't unfriendly. It was business cordial. Formal concern, interest, but no warmth.

"Yes, that's right. We can channel your data any way you choose, and of course, as we discussed, it can be tailored to fit your needs."

Tozzi lay down on the sofa and put his heels up on the arm. It was very comfortable except that there were no pillows for his head. He crooked his forearm behind his head and watched Joanne work through heavy lids.

"We offer a basic hospital package that we've found works very well. Medical records can be kept separate from billing so that people in different departments can access only what data is pertinent to their positions. Executives are provided with pass codes that will open up the entire data source if needed. Payroll and personnel records can either be included in the package, or you can continue with your present service and leave that data separate. I believe I told you, though, that the cost of issuing biweekly paychecks goes down significantly if you shift personnel and payroll onto the total package service."

Tozzi figured she was pitching additional data-processing services to some hospital who already used DataReach for their payroll. He was impressed with her rap. She wasn't hard-sell, just hard facts. He knew the technique. She'd lay it out so logically and so matter-of-factly that the guy on the other end would feel stupid if he didn't buy her package. It was the way smart cops got perps who were caught red-handed to turn on their buddies. Spell it all out for them nice and calm. Tell them what they can expect if they cooperate and what they can expect if they don't. Tell them exactly what information you want. Work it nice and easy like an optometrist testing for the right lenses. Work it down to two choices: Is this better? Or is this? If you can do it in the wee hours of the morning before a public defender can drag his ass down to the station, nine times out of ten the felon will opt for the logical choice and spill his guts all over the floor.

"Now you do know that as part of the package," she continued, "we send out our auditors every six months to review your system. They check for inaccuracies, poor performance, overlapping services, and security leaks. If they discover any problems, we will either rectify the situation or recommend changes in your basic service that will accommodate your needs better."

Tozzi shut his eyes. Just ten minutes. That would be so nice.

"Excellent," she said into the phone. "I know you'll be glad you decided to go with the total package. Alan Lurie is the systems analyst here who handles our medical accounts. I'll have him call you today to set up an appointment so that you can review your needs with him, determine if any custom software will have to be written, and assess your existing hardware. Okay? . . . Fine. If you have any questions, give me a call. I'll be talking to you, Dale. Bye."

Joanne swung around to face the telephone console. She pressed for a dial tone, then punched in four digits.

"Alan? Joanne. Queen of Peace Medical Center finally made up their minds. They're going with the whole package."

There was a hint of triumph in her voice. About as much as a good businesswoman allowed herself, Tozzi guessed.

"The vp in charge of operations over there is Dale McIntee. I told him you'd give him a call today to make an appointment to get things rolling. Hold his hand and make him feel secure. I think he's still a little uncomfortable with the price. You know what to do."

She listened for a minute, then suddenly she tilted her head back and laughed. She looked like one of those people on the TV ads for Bell Telephone, getting a real kick out of calling some dear relative in the old country. Her office laugh was about as sincere as a commercial.

"You're right about that," she said, abruptly curtailing her mirth. "Get back to me after you've talked to him."

She hung up the phone and leaned back in her chair, smiling with satisfaction. It didn't seem to matter that Tozzi was sprawled out on her sofa, half-asleep.

"Big deal?" he asked.

"A very big deal," she answered.

She didn't seem so pissed-off now. There must have been a lot of money riding on this hospital deal. Probably a sweet bonus for her, too.

"I guess I better get going," he said, but he didn't make a move to get up. He was too comfortable.

She stood up and walked around her desk. When she sat down on the edge of the sofa where his legs were stretched out, the 9mm Beretta in his ankle holster dug into her back. She pulled away and glanced disparagingly at his leg.

"Are you really in trouble with Richie?" she asked.

"Not just Richie," he said.

"If you level with me, I'll help you any way I can."

Her tone seemed sincere now. Nothing like the woman he'd just listened to on the phone. "I'm an FBI special agent," he said. "Used to be, actually. The Bureau doesn't sanction independent contractors."

Joanne nodded. "I had a feeling," she murmured. "But why? Why are you chasing Richie? Why are you working alone like this?"

"It's a very long story. Basically, Richie's a bad guy. The Bureau doesn't always see the bad guys right away. And sometimes they don't want to see them. My problem is that I see everything. I can't help it."

"What can I do to help?"

He shook his head. "Nothing really. I just need to know you're going to be there for me, like a safety net if you know what I mean. I'm hanging out over the edge. I need to know I have someplace to fall if I slip up."

She was rubbing his chest gently with the flat of her hand. She seemed to be unaware that she was doing it. "Do you need a place to stay? You can come to my place."

He thought about it for a second and changed his mind. ''No. It would be too risky for both of us. I'm sure Richie knows where you live.''

''Do you think he knows about us?''

''Anything's possible.''

She smiled sympathetically. ''He isn't God, you know. He can't know everything.''

Tozzi stared into her eyes. He slipped his arm out from behind his head and pulled her down to him, kissing her tenderly. Her hair fell around his face, covering him like a tent. His tongue coaxed hers, and she forgot where she was, letting herself go. He didn't want to let her go. He felt warm and protected and satisfyingly horny under all that lush dark hair. He felt that maybe he and Gibbons could pull this off after all. He felt good about what he was doing, and he had a good feeling about Joanne. He felt a hell of a lot better than he did last night when he shut the door on the apartment that smelled of his aunt's gravy and anisette cookies, the apartment that was full of pictures of people he used to know a lot better. He felt rotten last night. But now he thought maybe it could be okay.

She rubbed the muscles inside his thighs and wondered how long it would be before Richie's men finally killed him. She gripped his balls and stabbed at his tongue with hers, secretly hoping it would be a little while longer.

TWENTY-TWO

The firing range was empty except for the two of them, all the lanes dark except for theirs. Kinney adjusted the headphone ear protectors, then clipped a fresh paper target to the run and sent it halfway down the length of the range on its motorized track. He picked up the 12-gauge Remington 870 Police shotgun and held it in his left hand as he fed rounds into the magazine. FBI special agents are required to have above-average proficiency with three types of weapon: the .357 Magnum handgun, the automatic assault rifle, and the pump-action shotgun. They also have to be able to shoot ambidextrously. But Kinney wasn't here at the range to work on his left-handed shotgun technique.

He glanced over at Gibbons, who was in the next stall, taking target practice with that ancient Colt of his. He squeezed off shots evenly, emptying his weapon at the standard paper target—a drawing of a grizzly thug squinting down the barrel of a revolver. Gibbons started with his target at long range.

He's a cunning old bastard, Kinney thought. I underestimated him.

He raised the shotgun, peered down the barrel, and pulled the trigger all in one motion. The recoil jolted his shoulder. A ragged hole the size of a dinner plate separated the target's head from his body.

Gibbons was really something. He may look like a straight arrow, but there was more there than met the eye. Kinney could almost admire him. After all, most people wouldn't behave as coolly as he was, knowing what he knew. How many other agents would've invited him to come along to the NYPD's Pelham Bay firing range under the pretext of being able to discuss the ''case'' in the car on the way up, knowing all along that he'd be riding with the Hun? If nothing else, Gibbons had balls.

He watched Gibbons reloading his gun, then looked at his own target. Abruptly he aimed, fired, and blew the paper thug's hands and handgun away.

All the way up here, Gibbons kept going on and on about Tozzi, his habits, his downfalls, how he hoped that Tozzi would get careless soon and leave them with a solid lead as to his whereabouts. Incredible. Gibbons knew that he was Steve Pagano. But that was about all he knew. Gibbons had no way of knowing about his connection to Lando, Blaney, and Novick. That wasn't in any file. He couldn't have found out that he was the killer, because he would've acted on it by now. No, he didn't know, and he wouldn't find out.

Kinney took aim with the shotgun and fired again. One of the paper thug's shoulders disappeared.

Being in cahoots with Tozzi makes him vulnerable, Kinney thought. I could turn him in right now. He could make counteraccusations, of course, but that's all they'd be. Empty accusations. He's got no evidence.

Gibbons had pulled his target in to close range and now he was practicing rapid discharge, emptying his load in less than three seconds. When he was through, there were five neat holes clustered around the target's heart.

Kinney glanced back at Barney, the range supervisor, who was leaving his booth again. Barney had prostate trouble—he told anyone who'd listen to him about it—and he was constantly running out to go to the john. It would be easy to get rid of Gibbons right here and now. He could say Gibbons went berserk, started threatening him with his gun. He could say he had no other choice but to use deadly force to save his own life.

But just then Barney came back in and returned to his booth. No, on second thought he couldn't kill Gibbons here. He'd need time to arrange it, make it look right. It was too risky here.

Gibbons was sending his target back again. It sailed down like a ghost and stopped between mid and long range. He took position, steadying the gun in both hands, and commenced firing, aiming each shot carefully. The paper thug took two shots in the torso. The third grazed his neck. The fourth got a shoulder. The fifth sank into the upper thigh. The sixth pierced the stomach. Gibbons wasn't a bad shot. Not great, but not bad.

Kinney raised the shotgun again and quickly pulled the trigger. This time he hit paper but missed the thug. He pumped the gun and raised to firing position again, taking his time now. He aimed carefully, fired, and got the thug in the nuts.

Varga said he'd take care of the two of them, but he fucked up. Well, what the hell do you expect when you send a jerk like Feeney in to do the job? Now Gibbons is more cautious than ever, and Tozzi has disappeared completely. "You take care of Gibbons. We'll find Tozzi," Varga said the other night. Fat bastard. He fucks things up and I'm supposed to clean up the mess all the time. The big cheese, he thinks he knows everything. Giving orders makes him feel powerful. Well, fuck him. I'll take care of Gibbons, and I'll do it right. Take my time so there won't be any loose ends they can hang me with later. Never leave any loose ends.

Gibbons was waving to him now, trying to get his attention. He pulled the ear protector off one ear. "Are you all through, Bert?"

"Yeah, I'm finished," Gibbons said. "Take your time. I'll meet you downstairs."

He watched Gibbons wave to Barney as he walked to the door. The heavy steel-reinforced door slammed shut behind him, and Barney went back to his newspaper.

Kinney exhaled deeply as he replaced the ear protectors. He reached for the toggle switch and brought his target in to close range. As he pressed the shotgun to his shoulder, he pictured the yellow school bus pulling up in front of his house that morning, and Greg and Bill Junior running across the sunny lawn to meet it. He squeezed the trigger then and blew the paper thug's head off.

TWENTY-THREE

There was a short rap on the door, and the black kid with the Frankenstein haircut and the two earrings in one ear came in. He was carrying a stack of videotapes.

"I found some more tapes for you, Mr. Gibbons."

"Thanks, James."

Gibbons took the tapes and put them with the ones he hadn't looked through yet. James was a good kid, despite the earrings. He had a very pleasant, easygoing way about him, which Gibbons thought was phony when he first met him. Now he just thought James was a homo.

On the TV monitor, a crowd of men were walking down the steps of a courthouse. They were all clustered around one man, Richie Varga. Reporters shoved microphones at him and yelled out questions, but Varga just looked at them with lazy contempt. The reporters were kept just out of reach by the circle of prosecutors and federal marshals who'd escorted Varga in and out of court every day. Gibbons had watched several weeks' worth of the television reports on the Varga trials, and each report featured this same crew.

James and Gibbons watched in silence as the cameras followed Varga getting into the back of a big green sedan and driving off with his cadre of marshals. In the next shot, a small dark man with hair too black for his age and dark bags under his eyes stood in front of the crowded courthouse and spoke into a hand mike. James turned up the sound. ". . . tomorrow when Richie Varga is scheduled to take the stand again, this time against reputed crime boss Sabatini Mistretta. This is

Mort Newman reporting from Brooklyn.'' An attractive blonde sitting at the anchor desk appeared next. Gibbons reached for the VCR and fast-forwarded the tape.

''You and Mr. Newman are old friends, aren't you?'' James said.

''How do you think I got in here?'' Gibbons turned the sound back down. He was starting and stopping the tape, searching for the next day's report on the Varga trials.

''Is it true that you're an FBI agent?''

Gibbons glanced up at James, who was leaning against the wall with his arms crossed over his chest. ''Is that what Morty told you?''

James nodded.

''Then it must be true.''

''He said he owed you a favor. Are you one of his sources?''

Gibbons's eyes were on the screen. ''No. He's one of *my* sources.''

''Come on. Morty's been a reporter for thirty years. He's got more integrity than to . . .''

''Than to what? Be a tipster for a fed?''

''Well . . . yeah.''

''Morty and I have known each other for a long time. It's more a case of 'you scratch my back and I'll scratch yours.' ''

''Did you help him with the Bernie Horowitz story?''

Gibbons turned around and looked at James. Bernie Horowitz was a serial killer who murdered fourteen young women in the New York area over an eleven-month period in 1974–75. He was a nut who claimed that the Virgin Mary told him to do it and that she spoke to him through his cat. Morty Newman was the first reporter to break the story of Horowitz's capture and arrest at his apartment in Queens. He was the only reporter to get a film crew into the apartment. Actually it was only into the doorway of the apartment, but the cameraman was able to zoom in and get a shot of the cat. Morty got a lot of mileage out of that cat. A cute little tabby, as Gibbons remembered.

''No,'' Gibbons said. ''Morty didn't get that one from me.'' Gibbons studied James's face. He didn't look old enough to remember the Horowitz murders. Blacks are funny, though. They don't age like white people. They tend to look pretty much the same age their entire lives, then age all of a sudden once they hit seventy. He'd noticed that over the years from studying mug shots on wanted posters. He was always surprised when he saw a black guy's face then read a date of birth that seemed ten, fifteen years off. Maybe James wasn't a kid. Maybe he wasn't queer either.

"Say, James, can I make a call?" Gibbons nodded toward the beige phone on the desk.

"Sure." James pressed an unlit extension button, picked up the receiver, and dialed nine to get an outside line. He handed the phone to Gibbons. "There you go."

Gibbons changed his mind. James was definitely a homo.

He took the phone and called directory assistance for the number for Amtrak at Penn Station, then he called Amtrak. "What time is the next train for Washington?" Gibbons looked at the monitor as he waited for the information. Varga was coming out of the courthouse again, dressed in a shiny steel-blue suit this time. Gibbons glanced at his watch. The clerk on the other end of the line said the next train to Washington left Penn Station at ten after noon. Gibbons looked at his wristwatch, then thanked her for the information.

"Going to see the brass in Washington?" James asked after Gibbons hung up.

Gibbons was smiling the crocodile smile. "Nope. I'm going to see this guy." He put his finger to the glass of the monitor and indicated one of the men surrounding Varga. Only the man's head was visible in the shot. He looked like a fat Popeye.

James scowled. "Brutal-looking motherfucker."

Gibbons laughed.

Gibbons poured two more fingers of whiskey into each of their glasses. George Lambert hoisted his, sneered and squinted at Gibbons, then downed half of what he had in his glass. He smacked his lips and wiped his mouth with the back of his hand. Gibbons half-expected him to grunt out, "Well, blow me down," each time he knocked back another slug. He was glad he hadn't spent money on anything better than Four Roses. Lambert wasn't a very discerning drunk.

"So what the hell *really* brings you here to my humble abode, Gib?" Lambert rolled his glass between his meaty hands and squinted at Gibbons.

Gibbons flashed his crocodile smile. "The FBI is looking for a few good men, George. They sent me down here to recruit you."

Lambert frowned. "Go fuck yourself."

Gibbons knew he'd hit a nerve with that one. Lambert was a frustrated G-man with a very large image of himself. He'd tried several times in his career as a federal marshal to transfer over to the Bureau, but they didn't want him. He was about Gibbons's age, and now he was just putting in his time, waiting for retirement. But the man still dreamed about living the dangerous, action-packed life of a special agent. Being a federal marshal must've been very frustrating for him. He only got to see the aftermath of what other federal agents did because most marshals are basically just caretakers. They baby-sit witnesses, play social worker for people under witness protection, and maintain real property seized from criminals as IGG, ill-gotten gain. One of George's recent responsibilities was a family-style restaurant in Suitland, Maryland. It would be his headache until the owner, who had been selling cocaine out of the kitchen, exhausted his appeals, which could take George right up to his retirement.

Gibbons freshened up Lambert's drink. Cosigning meat orders and talking to pushy restaurant suppliers was a hell of a way for a tough guy to finish up his career. Gibbons genuinely felt for him.

Lambert suddenly stood up. "I'll be right back," he grumbled as he headed for the bathroom. Gibbons had already seen the can. It was a great place to get sick in if that was what he was going to do. Lambert's wife, Dora, had left him years ago, but her mark was still on the house. Frilly curtains in the living room. Cream-white Chippendale-style dining-room furniture with gold curlicue trim. And lilac fixtures in the bathroom. Lambert hadn't bothered to change anything in the house, and now everything looked generally shabby and frayed. Maybe letting the place go to seed was his way of getting back at Dora. Still, Gibbons couldn't image getting up every morning and pissing in a lilac toilet.

When Lambert returned, Gibbons could see he was a little unsteady on his feet. He was a big guy, and that made his balance look that much more precarious. He made it to the table and sat down hard. The chair groaned.

"You remember Pete Ianelli?" Gibbons asked. He knew Lambert would. Ianelli was one of the first people to enter the Witness Security Program, a Las Vegas hood who decided to testify against the mob to get out from under an unbelievable gambling debt. The Justice Department decided to send him east, thinking it was easier to hide someone in a densely populated area. Lambert had been assigned as his babysitter, and because the program was new, Gibbons had been assigned to assist in securing Ianelli's new location in Bethpage, out on Long Island.

Lambert chuckled. "What a goddamn pain in the ass he was. Did you know we had to move him out of New York after all that?"

"No," Gibbons said. In fact he did know. To Kentucky.

"The jerk couldn't keep his big yap shut. The son-of-a-bitch loved to blow his own horn, tell people what a big deal he had been in Vegas. He claimed he only told the old lady at the Italian deli where he bought his cold cuts. He said he thought she was just a nice old lady. Next thing you know I'm getting urgent calls from the FBI in Vegas. One of your undercover guys reported that the mob out there knew where Ianelli was holed up and they had a contract out on him. I had to go up to Bethpage and get him out of there on the double. Who knows how close they got to him? I saved the little jerk's life."

Leave it to George to make a car trip from DC to Long Island sound like the Entebbe rescue.

"Is Ianelli still around?"

"Oh, yeah." Lambert sighed, shaking his head like the wise old patriarch of a large extended family. "Still part of my caseload." He drained his glass and poured himself a little more.

Gibbons assumed that Varga was also part of his caseload. If that was true, Varga was probably his star client, the biggest fish he'd ever handled. That would make watching over Richie Varga Lambert's claim to fame. It was what entitled him to drink with the big boys.

Gibbons watched Lambert raise the whiskey to his lips, watched how he squeezed his tiny eyes shut when he swallowed as if the booze caused him pain. The bottle only had about four fingers left in it. The bastard could really drink. Gibbons felt a little light-headed himself. Of course he had to drink his share to keep Lambert going. He just wished to hell the bastard would keel over before they'd have to go to a second bottle, which would have to be from Lambert's stash. Lambert liked cheap gin, straight, and to Gibbons, drinking straight gin was like swilling witch hazel.

He reconsidered asking Lambert outright, but he knew what the answer would be. Lambert would put on this smarmy high-and-mighty look as he quoted chapter and verse on Justice Department policy for making formal inquiries about people under the protection of the Witness Security Program. Besides, Lambert would want to know why Gibbons was asking about Richie Varga, and if Gibbons knew Lambert, he'd blab it to more than just the old lady he bought cold cuts from. Gibbons just wished the hell he'd hurry up and pass out.

"Hey, George," Gibbons said.

Lambert fixed a glassy-eyed stare on Gibbons. "What?"

"You ever hear from Dora?"

Lambert grunted and snuffled. "Who gives a shit about her?" he slurred. All of a sudden he seemed very drunk.

What a dunce Lambert was. He should've tried patching things up with her. Dora wasn't so bad. Except for her taste in decorating, she always seemed all right.

"Beautiful woman," Gibbons said with a note of regret. "Last time I saw her you were still married. Most women let themselves go to hell after they've been married for a while, but not Dora. She had some figure. You have to admit she was a fine-looking woman, George."

"You didn't have to live with her."

"True." Gibbons didn't live with anybody, but he didn't want to talk about that. He thought about Lorraine. She sure as hell would never put in a lilac toilet. "True," he repeated sadly.

"I don't want to talk about Dora," Lambert ordered gruffly. He hauled himself out of his seat, turned the rest of the bottle into his glass, then wandered into the living room. He dropped into a brown vinyl recliner with a noticeable tear on one of the arms. Gibbons suspected that the chair came after Dora had left, his first attempt at decorating revenge. "You want more?" he called to Gibbons. "It's in the kitchen, in the cupboard. I got gin. Maybe something else, I dunno, look in the back."

"Sure." Gibbons went into the kitchen, which Dora had apparently remodeled when avocado and burnt orange were the "in" colors, and opened cupboards until he found the booze. There was a half-gallon of Gilbey's, a fifth of Gordon's, and an unopened fifth of Boodles. He must've been saving the Boodles for a special occasion. Behind the gin, there were a few dusty bottles. Gibbons pulled down a very old bottle of Lemon Hart rum with the Gilbey's. If they had to keep this up, he'd be damned if he was going to drink straight gin.

He opened the refrigerator and looked for something to eat. He figured he better eat something to soak up the alcohol or else he'd be passing out too, which would make this another goddamn wasted trip. Gibbons's plan was to search the place for an address book, a ledger, something that might give him a clue as to where the government was hiding Varga. If only goddamn Lambert would just give his liver a break and fall asleep.

He found the end of a loaf of white bread in a plastic bag and some liverwurst so he made a sandwich with a lot of meat on one slice of bread. The bread was very dry. After the first bite, he opened a jar of mayonnaise and dipped the sandwich in.

Just as he was about to go back out to Lambert, it occurred to Gibbons that he could use a little ice to go with the rum. He opened the freezer and reached into a plastic bin full of loose cubes. He grabbed a handful, but his finger snagged on something. When he pulled his hand out, there was a small plastic bag dangling from his ring finger. Inside the bag there was a small black book.

''Well, fuck me.'' Gibbons grinned.

Untying the tight knot in the bag was a challenge in Gibbons's condition, but he eventually got it undone. As he suspected, the little black book was an address book. Gibbons flipped through it. There were just names and phone numbers, no addresses. He noticed right away that the names weren't written under the right letters in the book. Mr. Thorval was on the F page, and Mrs. Myers was on the G page. The first entry on the D page was Dora. That was the only name with an address.

Gibbons shook his head. He couldn't believe Lambert could be so obvious as to put his address book in the freezer. What a dunce. Gibbons guessed that the names in the book were the new identities of the protected witnesses in his charge. They were probably entered under the last initial of their real names, which Lambert figured he wouldn't forget.

On the V page, there were only two entries: one for a Jim Hennessey, the other for a Mark Davis. Gibbons took out his notebook and scribbled down the names and phone numbers. If he was right about Lambert's system, one of these guys was Richie Varga.

When Gibbons finished copying, he put the bag with the book in it back into the freezer and covered it with ice cubes. He then put the ice cubes in his empty glass back into the bin so Lambert wouldn't think he'd been in the freezer.

''Hey, what the hell're you doing in there?'' Lambert yelled from the living room.

''Making a sandwich. You want one?''

''No.''

Lambert was sitting perfectly still in the recliner when Gibbons returned. He looked like the statue of Lincoln at the Lincoln Memorial, Abe Lincoln with an empty glass in his hand.

''If I ask you something, Gib, will you tell me the truth?''

''Sure, why not?''

''You ever sleep with Dora?''

''Not on a bet, George.''

Lambert sighed and looked into his empty glass. Gibbons went to pour him some gin, but he pushed it away. The man was a picture of troubles.

Gibbons screwed the cap back on the gin. He suddenly felt pretty low himself. ''You're a good man, George.''

TWENTY-FOUR

His suit hung in the closet all by itself. The suitcase was open on the turquoise vinyl chair, a blue dress shirt draped over the back. The clean clothes were in the suitcase; the dirty stuff was in a pile on the floor. Under the clean underwear there were three boxes of bullets: .38 hollow points, .44 soft points, and 9mm jacketed hollow points. On the bed, his arsenal was laid out on pieces of yesterday's *Daily News*. The Beretta 9mm automatic and the Charter Arms .44 Bulldog were off to one side. The Ruger .38 Special was broken down for cleaning. Gun solvent stained the newspaper. It highlighted the little picture of Jimmy Breslin next to his column.

It was hot as a bastard outside and the goddamn air conditioner was all but useless. Even on high, it barely threw a breeze. It did cut the humidity in the room some, but it wasn't loud enough to block out the ringing of the gas-station bell next door. It was evening rush-hour now, and the damn bell was ringing constantly.

Tozzi was going nuts. He was cleaning his guns because he had nothing better to do. Subconsciously he figured that if he got ready for something to happen, something would happen. He was like a writer with writer's block sharpening a whole pack of pencils, subconsciously hoping that an idea would come to him by the time he got to the last pencil. It was Boy Scout logic: Be prepared. But the problem with this kind of thinking was that eventually the preparations can become the goal, and nothing ever gets accomplished. Tozzi realized that as he worked the small wire brush around the chambers of the revolver's cylinder, and it only made him more impatient.

He'd been at this crummy motel a week and a half now and he hated the place, but he didn't want to move until he spoke to Gibbons and goddamn Gibbons hadn't answered his phone in days. Tozzi had been cursing him all day for not having an answering machine, even though he'd probably be very wary of putting his voice on tape and thus creating physical evidence that could be used against both him and Gibbons.

Tozzi was no good with time on his hands, he never had been. He started thinking about things, analyzing his life, and that always got him depressed. The fact that everything he owned in the world was in this seedy motel room depressed him. The fact that he had more guns than pairs of shoes depressed him. The fact that he was beyond the point of no return really depressed him.

Tozzi had checked in on Thursday after he found Gibbons watching TV at his aunt's place. On Friday he called Gibbons at Lorraine's to let him know where he was, then took a ride over to Bobo's video rental shop. Bobo nearly shit his pants when he saw Tozzi walk in, but when Tozzi took him to the back room, Bobo had nothing new to tell him, except that he'd heard that Paulie Tortorella had been picked up for torching that store in Woodbridge and that now he was out on bail.

On Saturday morning he got in the car and just drove, heading for Joanne's place in a roundabout way because he didn't want to admit to himself that he really wanted to see her. When he saw a Dunkin' Donuts on the road, he stopped and bought a half-dozen croissants. He figured she'd prefer croissants to doughnuts; she was that type. The croissants were his excuse for dropping in for brunch.

When he got there, she looked in the bag and asked him why he hadn't bought doughnuts. She said for future reference, she really liked cinammon crullers. After coffee and croissants, he went out grocery shopping with her. She offered to make beef Stroganoff. He watched the Mets game while she cooked. He stayed for dinner, and somewhere in the middle of the second bottle of Beaujolais, they snuggled up on the couch with the TV on. When he put on MTV, she ridiculed him for wanting to watch the all-rock video channel, but he said he'd never seen it before and he was curious. Videos are an insult to your intelligence, she said, but he still wouldn't change the channel, so she started rubbing his crotch and wouldn't stop. Tina Turner's "What's Love Got to Do With It" video came on then, and Joanne jumped him, pouting and mugging in his face, lip-synching to the music. They wrestled on the couch, laughing and groping, tearing each other's clothes off. When they finally managed to stop laughing, they did it on the floor. He needed a good laugh. He ended up staying the night.

Spending time with Joanne had always been nice, but this time it depressed him afterward, and now he was still depressed. He kept thinking about the possibility of making some kind of life with her. He tried to figure out step by step how he could bring his life back to a state of normality. He was wanted for murder. He'd gone AWOL from the Bureau. Even if he could beat the murder raps, how could he ever get a job? Who'd hire him? What did he know how to do except catch bad guys? Maybe he could join the union and work construction. But somehow he didn't see himself coming home to Joanne's place in dusty work boots and a hard hat. That wasn't her idea of a husband. He thought about having kids with her, but that seemed too remote to even consider.

Everything in his life seemed disorganized, half-finished, impossible. That morning he cruised around his old neighborhood in Newark, trying to remember when things were okay. He had a pretty good pepper-and-egg sandwich at a little sub shop that used to be Lee's Chinese Laundry. His mother and his aunts never took anything to old Mr. Lee except bed sheets that had gotten gray. They claimed those Chinese worked wonders with linens, but the rest of the laundry they could do better themselves. Mr. Lee had to be dead by now. Tozzi drove back to the motel after lunch and decided to clean his guns. He had to put something in order.

He inserted the cylinder back into the frame of the .38 with a sharp snap. The bell at the Exxon station started to ring again, and this time it didn't stop. "Goddamn," Tozzi muttered. When the bell still didn't stop, he bounced off the bed, wielding the revolver like a gunslinger. He went to the grimy window and saw a woman in a white Volkswagen Rabbit stopped with her front tires right on the black hose. She had no idea she was the one making all the noise. "Get off the bell," he screamed through the closed window. "Stupid bitch, pull up!"

His hands were trembling, and in his fury he pointed the gun at her windshield and squinted down the barrel.

"Pull up!" he yelled.

Suddenly he pulled the trigger and flinched, expecting glass to shatter. But the gun wasn't loaded. The click of the hammer nearly made his heart stop. He stepped back from the window and sat down on the bed, his heart pounding as he pictured that stupid woman slumped over the wheel, blood staining her dress. He wondered what the hell was wrong with him.

The next thing he knew the phone was ringing. He stood up to get it and quickly glanced out the window. The white Volkswagen was gone.

"Hello?"

"I didn't think I'd find you in." It was Gibbons.

"Where the hell do you think I'd be?" Tozzi snapped. "I've been waiting to hear from you all week. Where the fuck've you been, man?"

Gibbons didn't respond right away. "You going for an Academy Award or what?"

Tozzi sighed and rubbed the tight muscles at the base of his neck. "What's going on?"

"I think I found him."

"What?"

"Get ready. We're going for a ride."

"What do you mean you found him?" Tozzi got up and started to pace.

"I paid a visit on a federal marshal I know. I made a good guess that he was our friend's liaison with the Witness Security Program."

"And this guy just told you where to find him?"

"No, stupid, listen. I found the guy's address book in the freezer. There were two names entered under V—a Mr. Hennessey and a Mr. Davis. Both had telephone numbers, but no addresses—"

"Call Bell Security. They'll give you the addresses for those numbers. Don't worry. They melt when they hear 'FBI.' "

"I know the drill. Just shut up and let me talk," Gibbons said. "I already got the addresses. One is in Pennsylvania, East Stroudsburg, the other in St. Paul, Minnesota—"

"Okay, which one do you want?"

"Stay put, will ya? I saved us some legwork."

"What did you do?"

"I called credit rating companies in both areas. I said I was selling my house by myself without a broker and I wanted to run a credit check to make sure my prospective buyer was on the up-and-up. I gave them a song and dance about how I was retired and I was anxious to sell my place so I could get down to Florida. For an extra fee they said they could put a rush on it. I wired them the money, and the printouts came in the mail today.''

''Weren't they a little suspicious that your address is an apartment building, not a private house?''

''I used Lorraine's address.''

''So what did you find out?''

''Mr. Hennessey owes about ten grand on a whole slew of credit cards,'' Gibbons said. ''Mr. Davis's sheet was blank.''

''Davis has no credit history?'' Tozzi asked skeptically. ''I thought Justice had gotten hip to that. Supposedly they were giving witnesses made-up credit histories with their new identities so they could get loans and stuff like that.''

''That's only in the last year or so that they've been doctoring the credit histories. My guess is that Hennessey is a recent member of the club. Davis must be a veteran with the program, and Justice hasn't gotten around to fixing up credit records for the people who've been in place for a while.''

''So you think Davis is our man.''

''It just might be—'' Gibbons was cut off by a recorded announcement telling him that his three minutes were up and to signal when through for additional charges.

''Hello? You still there?'' Tozzi asked.

''Yeah, I'm here. Listen, I'll pick you up around seven.''

''Where're we going?''

''East Stroudsburg. To Mr. Mark Davis's house.''

Tozzi nodded. ''Okay. I'll see you at seven.''

''Right.''

Tozzi hung up the phone. The bell at the Exxon station started ringing again, but he didn't hear it now. The .38 was still clutched tight in his hand. Unconsciously he cocked the hammer and pulled the trigger, listening to the click of metal on metal. He did it again and again. He was thinking about Varga. He was getting ready.

TWENTY-FIVE

"So what are we waiting for?" Tozzi said. He was sitting in the passenger seat of Gibbons's car, fingering the grain of the vinyl dashboard, staring at the house, getting itchy.

In the driver's seat Gibbons stared at the small Cape Cod situated on a small lot between two bigger houses. It had white aluminum siding and dark green shutters. Even in the dark he could see that the grass needed cutting. There were no lights on in the house except for a dim one upstairs. Gibbons figured it was probably a night-light in the hallway. He ignored Tozzi's impatience.

Crickets chirped in the bushes beside the car. The night was humid, and every house on the street hummed with air conditioners. The back of Tozzi's shirt was wet with perspiration. The .44 in the belt clip was chafing his side. There were no other cars parked on the street, and that was making him nervous. It was quarter after twelve, and this was the kind of neighborhood where nervous ladies call the cops when they see unfamiliar cars parked on the street. They didn't need cops now. Cops get very indignant when they find FBI people in their jurisdiction, and they don't like being bullshitted, which is what they'd have to do if a cruiser came along and asked them what they were doing there. The patrolmen wouldn't simply check their IDs and go away. They'd want to go down to the station, probably call the field office for verification. No, Tozzi didn't need cops now.

"We've been staring at this damn house since eight o'clock, Gib. There's nobody else in there but him. The lights went out an hour ago. He must be asleep by now. Let's go get him."

Gibbons nodded, his eyes stayed on the house. ''Yeah, I think he's in there alone.'' He said it to himself, as if he were finally convinced. This was Gibbons's legendary caution, the caution that had often driven Tozzi up a wall when they had worked together. Look before you leap, watch your step, don't be hasty. As Tozzi thought about it, it occurred to him that his partner's infuriating degree of caution might have been one of the contributing factors to his going renegade. A minor factor but still a factor.

''How do we know it's really him?'' Gibbons asked.

Tozzi pounded a steady nervous rhythm on the dashboard. ''What can I say, Gib? You traced him to this address.''

''Hmmm.'' Gibbons was wearing his hat. The half-light of the street lamp illuminated his profile. His eyes were pinpoints focused on that house. His profile reminded Tozzi of Dick Tracy.

''Suppose it is Varga,'' Gibbons suddenly said. ''What do we do then? He's not going to just break down and confess to killing Lando, Blaney, and Novick simply because we found him.''

Tozzi sighed in annoyance. ''I'll stick my gun in his eye and tell him point-blank that we know he killed three FBI agents. Then if he doesn't start blubbering the way he should, we tell him we have Bill Kinney and that Kinney fingered him for the murders. He'll deny it and blame it all on Kinney. Then I stay here with him and you go back to New York to do the same with Kinney. Kinney will deny it and pin it all on Varga. What do I have to do? Paint a picture for you, Gib?''

''What if it doesn't go that way?''

''Then you'll step out of the room and I'll take care of Varga my way.''

''No.'' Gibbons said it evenly but with absolute authority. Tozzi decided not to debate the point now.

''Gib, we'll never find out anything if we just sit here.''

Gibbons pulled on his nose, then looked at his watch. ''Fifteen more minutes,'' he said. ''Let him get into a deep sleep.''

Tozzi rolled his eyes and rubbed the flesh on his hip where the gun clip was irritating him.

The little Cape Cod didn't have central air-conditioning, just individual units in most of the rooms. People always want to save electricity, though, so they open windows to get whatever breeze they can, and a lot of times they forget to lock their windows before they go to bed.

That's why the dog days of summer were burglar harvest time. Varga had been under witness protection long enough to be careless, Tozzi figured, but he figured wrong. The only window he could find not secured by a vent lock was the small, high window in the downstairs bathroom. He had to stand on a wire-mesh patio chair so he could poke two holes in the bottom corners of the screen and get his fingers in to release the spring latches and lift the screen. The spindly legs of the chair kept sinking into the soft soil of the flower bed, which made hauling himself up and in quietly more of a challenge.

Once he was inside, he leaned out and whispered to Gibbons. "Come around the side. I'll let you in through the kitchen."

"No. Just give me a hand."

Tozzi wanted to object, but anything he'd say at this point would be taken as an insult. The guy wasn't that old, after all. He should still be able to climb a window. But how quietly was another question.

Gibbons had powerful arms and once he had all his weight on his hands on the sill, he was able to maneuver himself in without a sound. Quieter than Tozzi had been, they both noted to themselves.

Tozzi had his gun drawn, ready to proceed, when Gibbons put a hand on his arm. "Wait up a minute," he whispered.

The next sound Tozzi heard was a stream of piss hitting the water of the toilet.

"Don't forget to flush," Tozzi said sarcastically.

"Fuck you. I had to go."

Tozzi briefly wondered if Gibbons's bladder was the real reason he finally agreed to break in.

"Okay," Gibbons said as he zipped up. "In a house like this there are probably only two bedrooms on the second floor. When we get upstairs, you check the one on the near end. I'll take the other."

Tozzi nodded and watched Gibbons pull out Excalibur. The gun's familiar blue finish in the dim light reminded him of the good old days before he went renegade. No time for regrets now, he thought.

Together they stepped out of the bathroom and rounded the corner into the living room. The walls were covered with pictures of horses, most of them framed prints of line drawings with soft pastel colorings. They were fox-and-hound–type pictures. It was the kind of decor a purchasing agent for the Justice Department might pick for a man living alone, Tozzi thought.

As he walked into the room, Tozzi's eye went directly to the lighted numbers beaming from the wall unit opposite the couch. He froze, thinking this might be some kind of electronic alarm system, but then he realized that the blue numbers were on the face of the VCR, and the red "27" was the channel selector on the cable box.

On the shelf above the television there was a collection of toys, small plastic windup toys. A robot dinosaur, a dachshund, a bear on roller skates, a matching King Kong and Godzilla, a clown, a penguin wearing a top hat, and a crawling eye. Tozzi examined the metal glint behind the creatures and discovered a Slinky. It was hard to imagine Joanne married to a guy who played with a Slinky.

He took a second look at the crawling eye and gritted his teeth. Lando, Blaney, and Novick.

Tozzi also noticed a Willy Nelson album on top of the turntable, and a copy of *Forum* on the coffee table. Country music and dirty books. It certainly did seem like a lonesome buckaroo's bunkhouse.

He felt Gibbons's hand on his shoulder. Gibbons signaled with his head toward the stairs, which fortunately were carpeted. Gibbons started to climb and Tozzi followed, pointing the .44 up the stairwell to cover his partner.

The stairs squeaked under their weight, but the carpeting muffled the sound. As Gibbons reached the top, Tozzi suddenly wondered whether Varga had any pets. A dog sleeping by his side could be trouble. Also, with friends like his, Varga would certainly be armed.

As Tozzi rounded the stairs, he saw Gibbons pointing with Excalibur at the room that he was supposed to cover. The door was open. By the light of the night-light in the hall, he could see a single bed littered with disheveled clothing. The room was cluttered with cardboard boxes, and there was a tabletop hockey game on the floor.

Across the hall, the bathroom door was open. There was a cat's scratching post between the sink and the toilet. Tozzi checked the floor. He didn't want to step on a goddamn cat.

As they approached the second bedroom, Tozzi could hear the air conditioner buzzing in a loose window frame. It made enough noise to cover any sounds they might have made, but Tozzi was still suspicious. Varga could be waiting in there for them. Tozzi thought maybe he should be leading the way instead of Gibbons.

They took their positions on either side of the door. Tozzi was glad to see that the doorknob was on Gibbons's side, which meant he'd have to reach across and open the door himself. He opened it a crack.

A weird light glowed from the side of the room behind the door. All he could see was this watery light on the noisy air conditioner.

He opened it a little more and saw a sleeping figure under a sheet. The entire bed was cast in this wavery light.

Gibbons touched his arm and gestured with a jerk of his thumb. Tozzi nodded. He took a breath, felt to make sure the safety on his gun was off, then threw the door open so hard it smashed against the wall behind and wobbled on its hinges.

The sheets flew up and the startled sleeper sat up, ready to bolt.

"Freeze," Tozzi shouted, holding the .44 in both hands, which were leveled right in front of the man's face so he could see it.

The man was speechless, his mouth hanging open. He put his hands up, dropped them, then put them up again. He didn't know what to do. Then he suddenly noticed Gibbons and Excalibur at the side of the bed, and instinctively he backed toward the headboard in fear.

Tozzi glanced quickly at the source of the weird light. It was coming from a fish tank on the bureau.

"Get up," Gibbons said. "And keep your hands where I can see them."

"Hey, guys, what do you want? Just tell me, okay?"

Tozzi looked him over closely. Big hairy belly, double chin, heavy blunt-end mustache, dark wavy hair. "We want to know a few things, Richie."

"Who?" He smiled nervously. "Hey, you got the wrong guy. My name is Davis."

"Yeah, Mark Davis," Gibbons said. "Also known as Richie Varga."

"No, you must have the wrong guy. Really. I don't know who you're talking about."

Tozzi thrust the muzzle of his gun in the man's cheek. "You want to see how fast I can undo your plastic surgery, Richie? Let's play it straight, okay?"

"Jesus fucking Christ," he cried, gasping for breath. "Jesus, Jesus." He kept repeating "Jesus" as if it was the only word he could remember.

Tozzi shoved him back onto the bed. He fell on his back like a board, and Tozzi jammed the .44 into his neck. "I'm gonna ask you this once, Richie. That's all." Tozzi could feel the pulse of his jugular through his gun. "We want to hear the story you didn't tell in court. Are you with me? We want to hear the one about the three guys who—"

"Wait a minute," Gibbons interrupted. "This isn't Varga."

Tozzi glared at his partner. "What do you mean this isn't Varga?"

"I've seen a lot of pictures of Varga. I don't think this is him. Not even with plastic surgery."

Gibbons was stalling, being goddamn cautious again. Damn it all. But then Tozzi thought of something. "Get up, fatso," he ordered the man on the bed.

The man didn't move. He was too scared.

"I said get up!" Tozzi shouted.

When he still didn't move, Tozzi grabbed the waistband of his boxer shorts and pulled. He yanked and cursed until they started to rip. He tore the fabric off him and exposed the man's genitals.

Tozzi stared at him in the watery light, then turned on the bedside lamp to get a better look. "Fuck! Varga only has one ball. This bastard is hung like a goddamn horse."

Gibbons looked at Tozzi with surprise and indignation. "How'd you know about that?"

"Somebody told me."

"Yeah, and I bet I know who."

"Fuck," Tozzi repeated. "This guy's a fucking ringer. Varga hired a fucking ringer to take his place in the Witness Security Program. Unbelievable!"

Tozzi suddenly smelled piss. He looked down and saw that "Mr. Davis" had peed all over himself.

"Did Richie Varga hire you to be his fucking ringer?" he shouted at the man.

"Mr. Davis" couldn't form the words, but he nodded wildly in a nervous stutter motion.

"Goddamn him!" Tozzi's body was shaking with rage. He wanted to shoot, but instead he picked up the phone on the night table, ripped it out of the wall, and threw it at the fish tank. It hit the wall just above the tank, knocked the lid off, and splashed down into the water. It sank to the bottom as small iridescent-blue fish darted frantically around the turbulent water.

"Don't you dare move out of that bed until the sun comes up," Tozzi yelled at the prone man. "You understand me?"

The man kept nodding and mouthing unformed words. Tozzi was pretty sure the scared little shit would stay put for a while. But just in case, he was going to yank the cord on the downstairs phone on his way out. "Come on, let's go," he said to Gibbons, backing toward the door.

"Somebody told you, huh?" Gibbons muttered to Tozzi on the stairs. "That's some pillow talk you have."

Tozzi ignored the crack and rushed down the stairs with Gibbons snickering right behind him.

TWENTY-SIX

The Kinney dining room sounded like a mess hall and looked like a scene from a sitcom. The kids—the oldest a fourteen-year-old girl, the youngest a two-and-a-half-year-old boy—sat along the flanks of a long oak table, three on one side, three on the other.

Mrs. Kinney, a small woman with melancholy eyes and tipped blond hair, sat at one end, telling the two older boys that she wasn't even going to discuss the issue of getting another television for their room. Four televisions in one house is enough, she said.

The teenager was sulking about something, waiting for someone to ask her what was wrong so she could refuse to answer.

The younger girls, ages seven and almost nine, were trading slaps under the table and giggling with malicious glee.

At the other end of the table, Bill Kinney was cutting up a slice of roast beef into small pieces for the little one. His sleeves were rolled back and his tie was loosened. The commotion around the table pleased him, soothed him almost. It made him feel like the benevolent despot of a busy realm. Fatherhood made him glow.

"There you go, Sean," he said, setting the plate under the little boy's chin. "Eat it all up."

The heavy silver fork swayed in Sean's little fist for a moment, then he put it down and picked up a square of meat with his fingers.

Kinney smiled.

"Father?" Mrs. Kinney called across the table with exasperated irony. "Will you please tell these two why we cannot have another TV in this house?"

Kinney raised his eyebrows and tugged on his earlobe. He looked at the boys. "Another television, huh?" He nodded solemnly. "We'll take it under consideration," he said, smiling.

The boys grinned in triumph.

Mrs. Kinney shot her husband a withering look and sighed. He always let the kids win.

He gave her a reassuring look as he reached for the string beans. Just then the phone rang.

The sullen teenager promptly stood up and went into the kitchen to answer it. She walked with her eyes downcast and her back straight, like a nun. Kinney knew this was her way of punishing someone, most likely her mother.

A moment later she reentered the dining room and went back to her seat. "It's for you, Dad," she said after she sat down.

"Who is it, honey?"

"Mrs. Davis," she mumbled.

"Did you say Mrs. Davis or Mr. Davis?"

"*Mrs.*"

Kinney looked at his wife with an annoyed expression. "Now what?" he grumbled.

Mrs. Kinney watched him walk around the table. The Davises called every now and then, and she knew they had something to do with Bill's work. She'd taught herself long ago not to ask for details about his work. After sixteen years of marriage, she wasn't even curious anymore.

In the kitchen, the receiver of the red wall phone was resting on the counter. Kinney picked it up and stretched the cord all the way to the breakfast nook. He looked out the window at the backyard, which was littered with balls, bikes, and toys. The grass needed cutting again.

"Hello?" he said.

"Hi. How are you?" It was Joanne Varga.

"Okay. What's up?"

"Your friend Gibbons and his pal Tozzi paid a visit on a friend of ours in Pennsylvania. East Stroudsburg."

Kinney felt a tightening in his chest. "When?"

"Very late last night."

"What happened?"

"They didn't find who they were looking for, that's what happened. Looks did not deceive in this case. We're not happy about this."

Kinney started to pace. "How the hell did they find their way to East Stroudsburg?"

"I don't know and I don't care. What I do care about is that they blew Richie's cover. You were supposed to take care of Gibbons. What happened?"

"I'm putting together a plan right now, but I had no idea he'd figured out that much. Jesus, this is bad."

"Not as bad as it could get. I assume these two are playing for bigger stakes than catching a federal witness who plays hooky. They must have something else in mind. After all, Tozzi needs a very good deed to his credit if he's ever going to come in out of the cold."

"Tozzi's facing time for murder. Good deeds won't help his case."

"Still, the two of them seem very anxious to find Richie." Joanne had a way of speaking with a certain kind of double-edged irony that made everything sound like a vague threat.

Kinney fingered his pocketwatch in his pants pocket, nervously opening the lid and clicking it shut over and over again. "Well," he said, "what do you think?"

There was a slight pause. Kinney could hear faint ghost voices filtering through the line.

"What do *you* think I think?"

Kinney knew. Gibbons and Tozzi had to die. As soon as possible.

"Feeney's crew will help you on this," Joanne said.

Kinney pictured that wiseass Feeney and his two punk sidekicks. "Listen, why don't you let me see what I can do—"

"Just get in touch with Feeney. He'll know how Richie wants this handled."

"You sure you don't want me to try to handle this alone first?"

"Things have gotten out of hand. Richie wants this done his way," she stated flatly. "I don't think I have to remind you. If they get close enough to start putting real pressure on Richie, *you'll* be our first bargaining chip."

Kinney stared out at the kids' swing set. He saw the three eyeless heads on the empty swings. His heart was pounding.

"Okay. I'll get in touch with Feeney."

"Good. The sooner these two are out of the picture the better."

"You're right."

A sudden uproar sounded from the dining room, and Kinney's heart leapt. Then he heard the boys laughing.

"We really have no other option now," she said.

"You're absolutely right. I'll take care of it."

"I know you will," she said. "Also, don't forget about Atlantic City. We want that rolling soon."

"Right. I'm on top of it. Don't worry."

"Just make sure we don't have to."

Kinney blew air out of his cheeks as he hung up the phone. "Bitch," he whispered.

Before he went back to the table, he took a deep breath and put on a stern fatherly grin. "What's all the noise about?" he said as he entered the room.

"The boys are being mean to Chrissie," his wife reported.

"About what?"

The sullen teenager suddenly burst into plaintive anguish. "They always get away with murder, but I can never do anything."

"Specifically what are you referring to, Chrissie?" he asked.

Mrs. Kinney answered. "She wants her curfew extended to midnight. She says all her friends stay out that late." The disapproval was evident in her voice.

The two boys puckered their lips and made soft kissing sounds. Chrissie shot up from her chair and stood over the table with her fists clenched at her side. "See what I mean?" she screamed. "You let them get away with murder." She ran out of the room and up the stairs in tears.

Kinney glowered at the two boys. "After dinner I want to talk to you two in your room."

"Does this mean we don't get the TV?" the younger one whined.

"We'll discuss that later," he said.

A door slammed on the second floor and shook the house. The dining room was suddenly quiet.

"Finish your dinners," Kinney pronounced. It was so unusually quiet he could actually hear his knife scraping the plate as he cut through the thin slices of rare roast beef.

TWENTY-SEVEN

Foley Square was hazy blue with all the rush-hour exhaust fumes held at ground level by the merciless humidity. Gibbons walked out of the parking garage scowling at the day. He'd heard on the radio while driving in that morning that the overnight low temperature hadn't gotten below eighty and that at seven-thirty it was already eighty-seven degrees. He'd spotted a digital time/temperature sign in the window of a Chase Manhattan branch as he turned off Broadway. It said ninety, and it was only twenty after nine. Now as he crossed Centre Street, he could taste the pollution.

He was in a shitty mood. It seemed like he'd been having a continuous headache for the past two days. It started on the drive back from Pennsylvania with Tozzi after they rousted Varga's ringer. Even though he kept asking Tozzi to shut up, Tozzi kept yammering on about Varga and Kinney and Lando, Blaney, and Novick, harping on what they had to do now, how they had to find Varga, how they would have to use Kinney as bait, how he *had* to nail Kinney and Varga, how he *had* to do it for Lando. It was almost four in the morning when he got back to his apartment, and although he did get some sleep that night, it was more like passing out than sleeping. When he got to the office the next morning, Kinney was there, but if he was wise to anything, he didn't let on. And seeing Kinney in all his golden-boy glory just made the headache worse.

He felt like he'd slammed up against a brick wall because he didn't have a clue as to what he was going to do next. If he went to Ivers with what he knew, it might compromise Tozzi. He considered tailing

Kinney after work but vetoed that immediately. An experienced agent can pick up on a tail in no time. He thought about confronting Kinney directly, but that was too risky. They had no real proof that Kinney was Varga's hangman, so Kinney could deny everything, and then if he brought the matter to Ivers, Gibbons would have to face a lot of questions he didn't want to answer. It was frustrating knowing as much as he did about Varga and Kinney. He felt like he was sitting at a poker game with a pair of aces in his hand but he just didn't know how to play them. He was up most of the night, trying to come up with a solution.

Right now Gibbons needed coffee badly. He went into the Chock Full O' Nuts coffee shop where he always had breakfast, and shuffled through the crush of people lined up for take-out orders. Everybody was complaining about the heat. The air-conditioning inside was minimal, but at least it was a relief from the humidity outside. Office workers sat shoulder-to-shoulder at the winding counter, lingering over their coffees, no doubt trying to forestall going outside for a few more minutes. Gibbons was scanning the place for an empty stool when he spotted someone in back waving to him. It was Kinney, and he just happened to have an empty seat next to him. What a coincidence.

"Morning, Bert," he said brightly as Gibbons came over.

"Morning." Gibbons sat down and saw that Kinney was eating one of those all-in-one breakfast sandwiches—a slice of ham, a fried egg, and a slice of cheese on a toasted English muffin. He wondered if Kinney knew that he knew.

"Those any good?" he asked, indicating Kinney's sandwich.

"They're okay."

The waitress came over, her pencil already poised over her order pad. She was about eighty years old with a face like Whistler's mother, but she was built like a bowling ball and she knew how to hustle. Gibbons noticed her every morning, swerving around the young girls who took their time about everything. "Can I help you?" she asked. There was the bare hint of a Slavic accent in her voice.

Gibbons glanced at Kinney's sandwich again. "Coffee and a sweet roll," he said.

"Heat the sweet roll?" she asked.

"No thanks."

She reached under the counter and came up with a sweet roll in a wax-paper bag. She set it down in front of Gibbons with an empty mug which she filled quickly and accurately. The other waitresses always spilled a little. Sometimes they spilled a lot, but the old lady never missed.

After she left, Kinney said, "So . . . I hear you were in Pennsylvania recently."

Gibbons stirred his coffee with a wooden stick, looking down at his breakfast. Kinney was an aggressive player. Gibbons considered playing dumb, but Kinney had no time for his deliberations.

"Our friend Mr. Davis in East Stroudsburg," he said. "I heard all about your little visit the other night."

Gibbons unwrapped his sweet roll. "News travels fast."

Kinney didn't respond.

Gibbons blew on his coffee and took a sip. "I suppose now there's a contract out on Tozzi and me."

Kinney shrugged and bit into his sandwich. "I wouldn't know anything about that."

"No? You're the butcher of Buchenwald, aren't you? I thought slicing up agents was your specialty."

Kinney took a long sip of his coffee. Gibbons caught the gleam of the garnet stone in his big college ring. "You're treading on thin ice, Bert."

"Am I?"

"Think about it. If you go telling tales about me, I'll tell some tales of my own about you and Tozzi. Aiding and abetting a renegade agent suspected of murder is a very nasty charge."

"You're blowing smoke, Kinney."

"I have pictures."

"I'm sure you do."

"You want to see?"

"I believe you."

The old waitress scooted back with a fresh pot of coffee. "More?" she asked.

"Please," Kinney said, pushing his mug toward her. The bastard had the manners of a prince.

"I'm okay," Gibbons said to her and she passed on to the next customer. "Suppose I went ahead and told Ivers about your moonlight job. You could make all kinds of charges against me in retaliation. But what about Tozzi? He's crazy, and he's got nothing to lose. He'd come gunning for you sure as shit."

Kinney smiled. ''Tozzi's no problem. We'll find him.'' He was getting cocky now.

''I'm a pretty old guy,'' Gibbons said. ''With a good lawyer, I could do like the mob bosses do, play sick, stretch out my appeals, use all those tactics. What if I decide it's worth facing prosecution just to nail your ass to the wall?''

Kinney picked up his check. ''Who knows?'' He dug into his pocket and counted out the exact amount.

The old waitress whizzed by and scooped up his money and the check as soon as he put it down. Kinney swiveled on his stool to get up.

''Tell me something,'' Gibbons said. Kinney stopped to face him. ''Is it hard to cut a guy's head off?''

The corners of Kinney's lips turned up as he shook his head. ''Not at all. I recommend a heavy machete with a sharp edge. Start from the throat, not the back of the neck. It's easier that way.'' He stood up and reached into his pocket. ''It's the eyes that are tricky.'' He put a quarter down on the counter. ''See you around, Bert,'' he said.

Gibbons watched him walk out the door, as straight and confident and unwrinkled as a senior-class president.

He finished the last piece of his sweet roll and drained his cup. The waitress appeared instantly for a refill, but Gibbons declined. She immediately moved on to offer refills to her other customers, a model of early-morning service and efficiency. As he stood up to go, he stared at the miserly tip Kinney had left. Gibbons picked up the quarter, put it in his pocket, and replaced it with a dollar bill.

Walking toward the door, he was conscious of Kinney's quarter in his pocket the same way you're conscious of the bottom of your shoe even after you've scraped off the dogshit. He pushed through the glass doors and went outside. It was like moving through warm Jell-O out there. For a moment he wondered whether Kinney was really human.

TWENTY-EIGHT

Tozzi wandered through the big old house and picked up information all around him like a video camera. The teenage girl's name was Chrissie. It was engraved on a locket Tozzi found on her bureau: *"To Chrissie with all our love—Mom and Dad."* Two of the boys shared a very cluttered room with bunk beds. There was a handmade sign on their door: "DO NOT TRESPASS—ALL TRESPASSERS WILL BE SHOT ON SIGHT—GREGORY KINNEY AND BILL KINNEY, JR., PROPRIETORS." The two younger girls shared another room, a very pink room. One was named Virginia; Tozzi saw it written on the page edges of a geography textbook. The other girl's name remained a mystery. In a small room no bigger than a good-sized closet, Tozzi found the little boy's room. It was the room on the second floor directly over the foyer. Tozzi leaned over the crib and parted the curtains with the barrel of the .38. He was a little nervous about the Buick. It had been in this neighborhood since nine o'clock this morning, and now it was just after two. His wasn't the only car parked on the street, though, so there was no reason for the cops to get suspicious. And actually the big old sedan looked like the kind of car someone's maid might drive.

Sitting in the Buick that morning, he'd watched the house, watched a school bus come for the two boys and the two younger girls, probably taking them to day camp. He watched the mailman making his rounds, watched gardeners and plumbers come and go, watched housewives leave then return with bags of groceries. Surveillance was always boring, and it made him edgy. Tozzi started worrying that he'd never get a look at Kinney's wife. But just as he was about to chuck it all and get some lunch, a small blonde finally came out the front door. She had the little boy with her, holding his hand as they walked down the front path. Tozzi could see that she was talking to him. When they got to the driveway, she scooped the kid up, kissed him, and put him in the car seat in the back of a metallic-blue Dodge Caravan. She got behind the wheel, turned the engine over, and backed out of the drive.

Women never let their cars warm up, Tozzi noticed. If you don't let the oil circulate for a minute or so, it can be murder on the valves down the line. Tozzi imagined Kinney lecturing his wife about the expense of a valve job. He'd never met Kinney, but he imagined him as being pompous and critical. Gibbons described him as an Ivy League type. Observing his home, Tozzi pictured him as a Yuppie. But Kinney was also a trained professional with strong psychopathic tendencies, capable of committing murder to accomplish his dubious goals. It was a description that could also fit himself, Tozzi realized. He was sure that was how Ivers viewed his little runaway.

Gibbons had called late last night at the motel and told him about his breakfast meeting with Kinney. He gave Tozzi an address in Montclair, New Jersey, told him it was Kinney's home address.

''Check out the place in daylight,'' Gibbons had suggested. ''Watch his wife, get a description for me, the kids too and where they go to school. Find out what kind of cars they drive. I need to know intimate things about his home life so I can make him think twice before he does anything. We mean business too, I want him to understand that. Right now he thinks we're sitting ducks. We've got to make him realize that retaliation is part of the game.''

''You sound like me,'' Tozzi said.

Gibbons didn't respond.

''How'd you manage to get his address?'' All agents had to have unlisted home phone numbers, and only SACs, their assistants, and the brass in Washington had access to personnel files.

''I followed him when he went out for lunch. He went to a discount sporting-goods store over by City Hall and bought himself a pair of sneakers. I saw that he paid with a credit card. Later that afternoon, I waited till he went to the File Room, then I went to his cubicle. The sneakers were in a plastic bag behind his desk. He left his MasterCard receipt in the bag. As I suspected, he had to write his address and home phone on the slip.''

"You'd think he'd be more careful."

"Well, he wasn't."

Walking through the silent house now, Tozzi wondered if he could be so careless. A simple oversight like that could cost him his life. He thought back over his actions of the past couple of days, looking for the fatal mistake. He couldn't think of any. But of course, Kinney's carelessness probably wouldn't occur to him right away either. Not until it was too late.

Tozzi left the toddler's room and went into the master bedroom, which was dominated by a large four-poster bed. The oak posts were thick and imposing; the tops were carved pineapples. It crossed his mind that the Kinneys might be kinky.

On the dresser there were some family pictures. Tozzi studied the group shot of the kids sitting in a line back to front. It must have been taken a few years ago because Chrissie still looked like a kid. Tozzi had seen a more recent photo in her room. She was cute.

There was a picture of Mrs. Kinney sitting on a donkey with a big sombrero on her head. She looked happier in this picture than she did in person. The Kinneys' wedding picture was also there, a studio portrait, him in a tux sidled up behind his beaming bride. Tozzi studied Kinney's face. He had the sharp features of a go-getter and a Kennedy haircut. In fact, he looked like he could be some distant cousin of the Kennedys. He had that look of aggressive privilege. What he didn't already have he'd go out and get for himself.

Tozzi glanced back at the picture of mousy Mrs. Kinney sitting on the donkey and he thought about Joanne. Why was it that guys like Kinney always have everything? Wife, family, nice house in an upscale neighborhood. Even if he hadn't chosen to go renegade, Tozzi doubted that he could ever have all this. Certainly not with Joanne. Maybe the Irish just assimilated better than the Italians. Italians are born suspicious, and their suspicion makes them suspicious to others, automatic outsiders. Who knows? Maybe he'd just made the wrong choices. He'd become the wrong kind of criminal. A vigilante just isn't bad enough to get the kind of rewards Kinney got. What was that phrase he saw on a hooker's T-shirt once?—"Good girls go to heaven, but bad girls go everywhere."

In the bathroom off the master bedroom, Tozzi found a pair of beat-up New Balance running shoes, size ten. On a hook behind the door hung a pair of blue nylon running shorts and a heavyweight gray T-shirt. There was an L.L. Bean label in the neck of the shirt. On the sink there was a tube of Aim toothpaste. Opening the medicine cabinet, Tozzi saw that they had both Anacin and Tylenol. Mrs. Kinney also had a prescription for Placidyl, a mild tranquilizer. He saw from the prescription that her first name was Elaine. Tozzi poked around some more and discovered Mrs. Kinney's diaphragm next to a crushed tube of spermicidal jelly. A woman with six kids wasn't much of a recommendation for the diaphragm, he thought.

Suddenly he heard something. He stopped breathing, the gun clutched in his hand, pointed up. It came from downstairs, sounded like a door closing.

"Anybody home?" It was a girl's voice, most likely Chrissie the teenager, though it could've been Elaine Kinney.

Tozzi went back into the bedroom and stood by the open doorway, listening.

"Any of you assholes home?" she repeated bitterly. It had to be the teenager.

Tozzi heard some banging, and he imagined her just getting home from a summer job or maybe summer school, dropping her bag on the wood floor, and moodily skulking around the house. He wondered what he'd do if she found him there. She was just a kid, no threat, and so what if she saw his face? Still, it would be better if Chrissie didn't see an intruder in the house. Kinney should remain confident of his family's security. It would shake him up all the more when Gibbons let him know that his home had been violated.

Tozzi peered out the doorway and waited for Chrissie to give him an indication of where she was so he could decide how he'd get out of the house. Then in the small antique mirror hanging at the top of the stairs, he saw her. She was coming upstairs. She had a can of soda in one hand, a cigarette in the other.

He stepped away from the doorway and got behind the door. He could hear her going into the bathroom off the hallway. It was on the other side of the wall right behind him. He could feel her presence in there.

"Shit." She said it in a prolonged whine.

He felt her footsteps leaving the bathroom. He moved closer to the doorway. He waited. When he dared to peer out into the hall again, he saw that the phone that had been on a table at the top of the stairway was gone and the cord extended into Chrissie's room.

Good, he thought as he rolled up his pant leg and put the .38 in his ankle holster. Once she started yakking, he could slip downstairs and out the side door through the kitchen, the same way he came in.

Treading carefully, he went out into the hallway, concentrating on getting past Chrissie's door. He was relieved when he saw that she'd closed her door and he hurried to get to the stairs, but as he stepped over the telephone wire he could hear that she was sobbing. He gently pressed his back against the wall and listened for a moment.

"No," she whined. "Nothing. I just checked . . . They've been sore all week . . . No, not in the morning. It's always just before dinner. I don't think any of them know I've been throwing up every day, but they're gonna find out sooner or later, I know it. What am I gonna do?"

Her sobs were heartbreaking. Tozzi stayed and listened.

"No, that's no good . . . How can you say that, Jenny? He didn't do it on purpose . . . I can't tell him, are you crazy? I don't want anyone to know. Come on, Jenny, think of something. Do you think your sister might let me use her driver's license? . . . So I can get an abortion without my parents knowing about it, that's why. Sometimes you're so stupid . . ."

Tozzi started down the stairs. He'd heard enough to know the story. He just wasn't sure whether he'd tell Gibbons. Hearing the news about his daughter's pregnancy from Gibbons's mouth would certainly rattle Kinney, but it made Tozzi uncomfortable. It didn't seem right to take advantage of the kid's situation. She had enough problems. He'd have to think about this.

He got to the bottom of the stairs and headed for the kitchen. It was the kind of kitchen you see in commercials for floor wax, everything clean and shining. The appliances seemed relatively new, and though the counters were cluttered and the refrigerator door was a display space for crayon drawings held up by magnets shaped like barnyard animals, this kitchen just didn't have the appropriate amount of wear and tear that a family of eight should give it. Tozzi hated it for its pristine condition. It was so perfect, such a deception. Lando's wife kept their kitchen spotless, but he deserved perfection. Any man who could kill the way Kinney killed Lando, Blaney, and Novick deserved to eat in a slaughterhouse.

Suddenly he heard the front door opening. Loud voices, the boys. Tozzi looked around the room frantically for something he could steal, something he could take away from Kinney. He wanted to hurt this monster, get back at him any way he could.

The morning's mail lay on the counter: a few bills, a letter, the latest *Redbook,* a flier from ShopRite. Quickly Tozzi snatched the envelopes and slipped out the side door. His head was throbbing as he hid in the shrubs and waited for Kinney's kids to get inside and shut the door. The school bus was pulling away from the curb. They must've just gotten back from day camp. When the kids were inside and the bus was gone, Tozzi walked briskly across the lawn and headed for the Buick. The envelopes were crumpled in his hand. He was furious. Kinney didn't deserve all this, the bastard. It wasn't fair.

TWENTY-NINE

Gibbons had a lot on his mind. He looked at his watch again as he walked down Centre Street. It was just after ten A.M. Kinney would be late for his meeting at the U.S. Attorney's office. Good.

The heat had let up some, but Gibbons really hadn't noticed. He did notice that the traffic in the city was somewhat lighter than usual, the pace of the pedestrians a little more relaxed. Late August in Manhattan was always like this, slow and lazy.

But Gibbons couldn't relax. He had too much on his mind. The names of Kinney's children rolled around in his head like glass marbles, colliding with all the other miscellaneous information Tozzi had picked up about the Kinney family. He imagined the eight Kinneys and how they lived their lives, and his head became their big Victorian house. He wondered about them. He wondered whether Elaine Kinney had any inkling that she was married to a killer. He wondered how screwed up the kids would become after they found out the truth about their father. He wondered which ones would become bitter and resentful of their father and which ones would defend him with blind loyalty. He wondered if it would be better for them if New York had the death penalty so that at least Kinney's physical presence could be obliterated. He wondered about Chrissie and whether he should use what he knew about her being pregnant. He wondered about Tozzi, whether he found the key or not. He wondered whether Tozzi remembered to get everything. He wondered about a lot of unimportant things so that he didn't have to wonder about himself. Because if he started worrying about himself, he'd smell like bait for sure.

He kept walking until Centre Street widened at Foley Square. The courthouse with its imposing row of Greek columns loomed over the square, and Gibbons suddenly remembered something a female defense attorney had once told him. Walking up those courthouse steps scares the shit out of everyone who goes on trial here, she'd said. The sight of those columns just kills any hope you might have had left because they tell the future. Defendants see prison bars in those columns. They see cops standing at attention, they see gun barrels. Defendants who'd already served some time see rock-hard dicks, and they cringe at the thought of going back to jail. Gibbons always remembered these images when he came down this way. He also remembered that it was the first time he'd ever heard a woman use the word "dick." She was a judge now.

He headed for the small park across the street from the courthouse. Kinney was standing with his foot up on a bench right where Gibbons told him to be. As usual Kinney looked poised, relaxed, and confident. Kinney looked like an ad for the black pinstripe suit he was wearing. He hardly looked like someone who was already fifteen minutes late for an important meeting.

"What's so urgent, Bert?" Kinney's tone had the kind of smugness rich people use with workmen, a false friendliness meant to underline his perceived position of control. Gibbons wondered whether Varga used that tone with him, and now Kinney finally had the opportunity to use it on someone else.

Gibbons stared at the courthouse. "Eighty-five Dodge Caravan, metallic blue, Jersey plates ATJ–79H."

The smirk disappeared from Kinney's face.

"68 Mount Holly Avenue. A yellow Victorian with blue trim."

"It's buff, not yellow," Kinney said.

Gibbons focused on the column just to the right of the front doors and continued. "The master bedroom is dark blue and light brown. You sleep in a four-poster bed with pineapples on the heads. The master bathroom has speckled tan tiles. You like New Balance jogging shoes. There's a dirty gray T-shirt and blue nylon shorts hanging up behind the door. You use Aim toothpaste and Mitchum deodorant. Your wife rode a burro once and wore a sombrero."

"If this is your best shot at blackmail, my friend—"

Gibbons cut him off. "Gregory and Bill Junior share a room. They both go to the Frelingheysen Middle School. Chrissie goes to Montclair

High. The younger girls go to Grover Cleveland Elementary. Your little boy's name is Sean, and there are clowns on the wallpaper in his room."

"Very stupid, Bert. Why tell me that Tozzi broke into my house? Now that I know, do you think I'll let it happen again? You wasted your best shot."

Gibbons could hear the tension in his voice. Kinney was trying very hard to maintain his air of smug superiority.

"Your wife is a dyed blonde, about five-one or -two. She smokes Trues and takes Placidyl for her nerves. She uses a diaphragm and jelly."

"I'm singularly unimpressed, Bert. This is the senseless, useless, and desperate act of a doomed man. No, two doomed men."

Gibbons clenched his fist. He had no choice. Kinney had to be pushed as far as possible. "Your daughter Chrissie doesn't use anything," Gibbons said flatly. "She just found out she's pregnant."

He could hear Kinney's erratic breathing. When he glanced at his face, Gibbons finally caught a glimpse of Steve "the Hun" Pagano. Kinney's face contained all the pure, mindless hate of an attack Doberman baring its teeth at a stranger. *This* was the monster who slaughtered Lando, Blaney, and Novick.

The revelation was brief, and it chilled Gibbons to the bone, but he was satisfied that he'd accomplished his goal. He looked Kinney in the eye to seal the dare, then turned his back on the courthouse and walked away. It was then that one of the rare moments in the city happened to occur. By some fluke of traffic control, there were no cars, buses, or trucks within earshot, and Gibbons could hear his own footsteps on the pavement as he headed back to the field office.

There was a man on first and a man on third, and Gary Carter was up at bat. The count was two and one. Tozzi strained to see the TV in the living room as he unpacked the groceries in Gibbons's closet of a kitchen. Goddamn cheap son-of-a-bitch. A thirteen-inch black and white. Nobody's got black and white anymore.

Tozzi wasn't much of a baseball fan, but he turned on the Mets game as soon as he got into the apartment. He was nervous and he needed some noise. He wished the hell Carter would blast the next one. He was itchy for some action.

He left the jar of instant coffee out on the counter and put the big plastic bottles of Coke in the refrigerator. Get a lot of stuff with caffeine, Gibbons had told him.

The cans of Spam, beans, and vegetables went into the cupboard with the big can of Crisco. Tozzi was still skeptical about Gibbons's greasy-food theory. He claimed that back in the bad old days when the Bureau looked the other way on marathon interrogation sessions, one of the tricks was to feed the suspect the greasiest shit you could make. Once the sludge started to build up in the suspect's stomach, his resistance started to melt. A few days' worth of Crisco-fried everything served with a bottomless cup of muddy coffee often lubricated the lips. It sounded a little too *Dragnet* for Tozzi, but Gibbons swore that it had broken some pretty hard-ass punks in his day, and Gibbons seemed pretty eager to take care of Kinney the old-fashioned way. Tozzi was prepared to eat a lot of take-out for the next few days.

From what he knew about Kinney, though, Tozzi doubted that this guy would admit to anything. Which was fine with Tozzi. If Kinney didn't want to confess, he was prepared to take care of him the way he took care of Vinnie Clams and the faggot congressman and the lawyer Lefkowitz. He didn't believe that Kinney was the only way to get to Varga. He could see Kinney clamming up and just sitting tight through all this because Kinney probably knew there was no hard evidence that could be used against him in court. But that was okay because there was no way that Tozzi was going to let Kinney fly, no matter what Gibbons said. Right now all Tozzi was worried about was Kinney taking the bait and following Gibbons back here. As Tozzi saw it, it all depended on how pissed off Kinney would get about having his privacy violated and how reckless it would make him. But unfortunately Kinney didn't get ruffled easily. He was *very* cool. Tozzi hoped Gibbons decided to tell him about his daughter.

Tozzi grabbed a beer from the refrigerator and sat down on the couch. The pitcher threw the ball and Carter just watched it sail by. It looked like a strike to Tozzi, but the umpire called it a ball. Carter walked and now the bases were loaded.

"Fuck you, Carter," he said as he popped the top on the beer can.

Tozzi wanted to see a homer.

From the entrance of the underground parking garage on Centre Street, Gibbons could see Kinney's silver Volvo double-parked up the block. He was being too obvious, and that made Gibbons suspicious. Gibbons hoped that this carelessness was due to his rage. Otherwise what Kinney was doing was playing decoy, which meant he had called Varga for support troops. Even on short notice, Varga could probably provide shooters.

Gibbons scanned the area around him. It was about five-thirty. There was a pack of executives waiting for their cars to be brought up. There was the crew of attendants. There were plenty of pedestrians passing by. Any one of them could be a shooter, and every one of them could end up an innocent victim. He kept his right hand free just in case he needed Excalibur in a hurry.

Cars kept coming up the ramp, and Gibbons wondered whether one of them would have a shooter slumped down in the backseat. Kinney probably regretted that this wasn't one of those garages where you went to get your own car. That would've been perfect for a hit. Kinney probably could've handled that alone.

When his green Ford LTD arrived, Gibbons tensed. He walked around the back of the car and checked the backseat. Empty. The Puerto Rican attendant must've thought Gibbons was checking to see if he stole anything. He got out of his car and shoved the ticket at Gibbons. "Thirteen-seventy-five," he said belligerently. "Pay the cashier."

Gibbons already had a twenty ready. "Here, you pay the cashier," he said. "I'm in a hurry. Keep the change."

The Puerto Rican didn't object. Gibbons didn't want to get tied up with change.

He glanced into the backseat once more before he got into the car. He put it in gear with his right hand, then steered with his left, replacing his right on the butt of his gun under his jacket.

He drove past the silver Volvo and caught the light at the corner. In the rearview mirror he saw the Volvo pull into traffic and get in line behind him. There was a cab between them. He waited, watching the mirrors. When the light turned green, Gibbons turned left onto a side street, heading for Church Street. At Church Street he turned right and proceeded north. As he crossed Canal Street, traffic started to flow a little better and he took the wheel with his other hand.

Tozzi tuned the radio back to Gibbons's all-news station, then shut it off. He went to the window in the living room and looked down at the back alley and the line of garage stalls where Gibbons parked his car. Gibbons had told him that he wouldn't be able to see his space from the apartment because it was down near the end of the alley, but Tozzi looked anyway. He knew Gibbons should be on his way home now. He'd be coming through the Lincoln Tunnel, taking the first exit, then following Boulevard East into Weehawken to his apartment just one block off the palisades that overlooked the river. Tozzi could see the tallest buildings on the Manhattan skyline over the top of the apartment on the other side of the alley. His eye went right to the twin towers of the World Trade Center. It was about a ten-minute walk from the field office.

He'd watched the Mets lose it in the tenth inning, then switched to the Yankees-Tigers game, which was just starting up in Detroit. Smokey Robinson sang the "Star-Spangled Banner" and did an amazingly catchy rendition. After two dull, scoreless innings, Tozzi turned off the TV, tuned in a classic-rock'n'roll station on the radio, and read the newspaper. He'd listened until they played "Suite: Judy Blue Eyes," then he shut it off. He'd hated Crosby, Stills, and Nash in the sixties, and he still hated them.

The plan was pretty straightforward. He was supposed to wait in the apartment, out of sight, while Gibbons lured Kinney up to his place. They figured it was likely that Kinney would pull a gun on Gibbons and order him upstairs. When they got inside, Tozzi would ambush him and disarm him. Simple.

Right. Unless, of course, Kinney didn't take the bait. Or he called for support troops. Or he ambushed Gibbons before they got to the apartment. Or, or, or . . .

There was too much room for a screwup. Maybe their plan was simpleminded, not simple. The FBI operates on three basic principles: overwhelming manpower, overwhelming firepower, and the element of surprise. That's the way Tozzi learned it at Quantico. But as he thought about what Kinney did to Lando, Blaney, and Novick, he wasn't so sure two against one was overwhelming enough. Tozzi realized that there were too many variables they'd overlooked. They were counting on Kinney becoming irrational, but so far he'd shown no signs of ever losing his cool. And what about Gibbons? Was he really up to this? Were his age and the time he'd spent in retirement factors to consider? Tozzi worried that they were.

He shut off the air conditioner and opened a window. If it was too cool when they walked in, Kinney would be suspicious. Tozzi looked down at the alley again, then picked up the paper from the coffee table. He returned to the couch and started reading the personals to take his mind off his concerns for his old partner.

Gibbons turned into the cobblestone alley, and all he could hear over the whoosh of the air conditioner were the thumps and squeaks of his tires going over the uneven stones. Rush-hour traffic was as bad as usual, and this short trip down the alley always came as a welcome relief. But not today.

He'd lost the silver Volvo somewhere on the approach to the Lincoln Tunnel, but that didn't matter. Kinney was a clever guy and an experienced agent. If Gibbons could find out where he lived, he could find out where Gibbons lived.

Pulling up to his stall, Gibbons wondered if Kinney could've possibly beaten him through the tunnel. He put the car into reverse and started to back into his space. A blazing orange sun reflected off the windows of the building across the alley. He wondered if Tozzi was ready. In the rearview mirror he could see the cool shadows under the stall, then the glint of his approaching back-up lights on the fenders of the cars on either side. When he cut the engine and put it in park, he just sat there for a moment. It was quiet and dark and insulated under there. For a moment, Gibbons almost felt safe.

Tozzi was going nuts. It was twenty of seven and no one had showed. Something had gone wrong. He was worried about Gibbons.

Suddenly there was an insistent knock on the door, four quick raps.

Tozzi drew his weapon and got behind the door. Why was he knocking? Why *would* he be knocking?

The knocking turned into pounding. "Hey, anybody home?" an annoyed voice called through the door.

Tozzi pictured the door flying open, followed by a hail of gunfire. "Who is it?" he answered, his heart pounding.

"Pizza."

"What?"

"Pizza, pizza. I got a pizza for 6D. Gibbons, right?"

Tozzi paused. It was a trap, he knew it. He crossed the doorway quickly and put on the chain lock. Standing away from the door, gun ready, he opened it a crack. There was a woolly-headed black kid in bright yellow high-top sneakers holding a pizza box. The name "Gibbons" was scrawled on the box in black crayon.

"Take it, man. It's already paid for," the kid said.

"What do you mean it's already paid for?"

"Look, man, I just deliver them."

Tozzi didn't move.

"Hey, look, Jack, I got no time for this. I'll just leave it right here, okay?" The kid put the box down on the floor and left.

Tozzi stared at it. His throat was so constricted it ached. Lando, Blaney, and Novick. Oh, God.

He stared at it for a few minutes, afraid to open the door because he was afraid to open the box. But he had to know. Sliding the chain from the plate, he opened the door and peered out, right and left, the .38 clutched in his hand. The hall was empty.

He slid the pizza box in with his foot, then shut the door and locked it. He stared down at it for a moment before he picked it up and laid it on the table. He broke the tape on the sides and front, then slowly opened the lid.

Sitting in the middle of the pizza was a gun, a .38 Colt revolver, Gibbons's gun, Excalibur. It lay there on its side in a puddle of tomato-tainted oil like a dead fish.

Strings of mozzarella cheese clung to Excalibur as he lifted it from the pizza. His hand was trembling as he stared at it. "Oh, shit," he murmured.

THIRTY

Gibbons was on his hands and knees, his head tucked into his chest, taking slow shallow breaths to minimize the pain that racked his body. It was all he could do, handcuffed to the steampipe the way he was. Conserve your strength, he kept telling himself. But what for? Another whack with the rubber hose? He looked at his watch. This had been going on for fifty minutes now, and he had a feeling Kinney was just beginning.

Just then another punishing blow landed on that same shoulder. He kept thinking it must be separated by now, though he had no idea what a seperated shoulder should feel like.

Kinney performed with that damn length of black hose, like a ballet dancer, slowly getting up on his toes for every stroke, whipping it down backhand across Gibbons's back and shoulders, always careful with his follow-through. Kinney took his time and placed the blows precisely, pausing now and then to explain his method.

"Never go fast with a beating, Bert," he said, pausing to take aim again, this time making Gibbons's tailbone throb. "Speed anesthetizes the experience. You fall into a rhythm and mentally the victim prepares for the blows. The hose does the damage, yes, but it's pain without fear, and that defeats the purpose. Your man has to wonder when it's coming next. He's got to taste that terror of anticipation, Bert." Suddenly the hose ripped into the back of Gibbons's head. "Give him time to think that maybe it's finally over. Present him with hope . . . then take it away."

Gibbons waited, watching his own blood drip from his brows to the dusty wooden floor. He waited and told himself it wasn't over yet, refusing to hold out any kind of hope. But then, without warning, the black hose dropped right in front of him, the hose but without the hand. It was well within reach.

He could hear Kinney's soft laugh. He looked at the hose and he was tempted. Just one good smack at the bastard, that's all. Just one good one right in the face. Maybe put his eye out, the bastard.

"Go ahead, Bert. Take it," Kinney whispered, mocking him. "You're not that old. You can still take care of yourself, can't you? Go for it."

And without thinking, Gibbons grabbed for the hose with burning hate in his heart, but before his fingers could grasp it, Kinney's foot slammed into his windpipe, the toe of the heavy black wingtip he'd been looking at for nearly an hour finding the delicate cavity just above the sternum. Gibbons arched back and clutched his chest with his free hand, thinking Heart attack, when Kinney delivered a hard uppercut into his face, drawing blood over the cheekbone. Gibbons fell back. The handcuff on his right wrist rattled down the steampipe as he landed flat on his back.

Through the haze of numbing pain, Gibbons could see Kinney's face clearly now. The bastard kicked him in the ribs, and instinctively he tried to grab Kinney's ankle and trip him, but he was too weak to react fast enough. Kinney kept kicking, his gleeful glinting eyes set in an otherwise placid face that smiled in winces whenever he delivered a new blow. A mindless frozen Doberman smile that Gibbons saw in strobe flashes between kicks, again and again and again, never changing, a mask carved in ice . . .

When Gibbons woke up again, it was dark out. He went to look at his watch, but the face was smashed. His head throbbed, he was sore all over, and the flesh around his eye felt stiff and lifeless. So this is what it feels like to be knocked out twice in one day, he thought.

He was slumped on the floor, his back against the radiator. As soon as he tried to stand up, his head started to spin. He went to clutch his temples, but the handcuffs stopped him. He stared at the cuffs in confusion for a moment. He'd forgotten about them.

Sitting up slowly, he was able to peer over the sill of the dirty casement windows and see a panoramic view of the Statue of Liberty's backside with the World Trade Center in the background. He knew he was still in Jersey from the proximity of Lady Liberty, in an abandoned warehouse somewhere on the waterfront in Jersey City or Bayonne. He didn't like the fact that they weren't trying to keep their location a secret from him. It didn't bode well, as Lorraine might say.

His face was crusty with blood, particularly the area around his left eye. That goddamn college ring, the garnet stone.

He couldn't remember passing out, but from the way he felt and the way Kinney had behaved, he just assumed that the bastard continued to beat him while he was unconscious. It was easy to understand why they called him "the Hun." Gibbons wondered if Lando, Blaney, and Novick were treated to this kind of torture before Kinney cut them up. A sickening hollowness opened up in the pit of his stomach as he remembered the coroner's report on those three. He was lucky he still had his eyes.

"Hey, you 'wake, ole man?"

Gibbons looked up. Someone was standing over him. He had a metal folding chair in his hand. Instinctively Gibbons grabbed his head.

"Take it easy, man, take it easy. I'm not gonna hit you with it." He unfolded the chair and set it down next to Gibbons. "I already hit you once today. That's enough."

Gibbons leaned on the chair and painfully hauled himself up and into the seat. In the dim light he focused on the face that went with the heavily accented voice. He was short, dark, and wiry with a razor-trimmed mustache and glittering eyes. A tight muscle T-shirt showed off well-developed arms, and there was an automatic in the waistband of his pants, right above the fly. The pants were shiny and green, and he wore them with pale yellow suspenders. Spic chic.

"E-man! What the fuck're you doin' over there?"

Gibbons followed the new voice to the other side of the long room where two figures sat hunched over a table. There was a stand-up lamp with a battered shade next to the table. Gibbons felt like he was in a dark cave looking out.

"He's up, man," E-man called back. "What're we supposed to do with him?"

"Nothin'."

E-man crossed his arms over his chest and nodded. "You don't remember me, do you, man?"

"Should I?" He had an overwhelming urge to kick this little asshole's teeth in.

"So you didn't see me at all? Not even in your side mirror when you got out of the car?"

"What're you talking about?"

"I was in your trunk, man. After you parked in that alley I got out nice and quiet, came up behind you, and *wham!* took you down with my sap. Pretty slick, huh?"

"You want a merit badge?"

"A what?" E-man's smile faded. "What's that you said?"

Gibbons didn't answer. He knew it drove Latins wild when they thought they were being made fun of but didn't know enough English to be sure.

"Hey, what're you two yakking about over here?" The other two sauntered up and stood over Gibbons. One was tall, lean, and full of nervous energy; he bounced on the balls of his feet like Jimmy Cagney. The other was broader and slower. They both had the same shanty-Irish face, though. Long bony head, beady eyes, and pig nostrils. Gibbons assumed they were brothers.

"He thinks he's real bad for an old dude." The little muscle man sneered. "How 'bout it, Feeney? Can I show him how bad I am?"

The lean one smiled with a mouthful of horse teeth and kept bouncing. "Not yet. Mr. K said to chill out until he gets back."

The little man shrugged his shoulders and shuffled his feet in place. "Yeah? When's that gonna be?"

Feeney shrugged. "He said he'd be back before morning. Louis, what time is it?"

Gibbons noticed that the broad-shouldered mick had one of those tiny three-inch televisions in the palm of his hand. "Must be five o'clock. *Here's Lucy* just went on." Light from the little screen flashed eerily across his face and lit up the inside of Louis's nose.

"He should be here soon," Feeney said. "Come on." He headed back to the table, and the other two followed loyally.

Assholes, Gibbons thought angrily, but his anger only made his headache worse. He tried to sit quietly, hoping to make the pain subside. Whatever they were doing over there, the three punks were quiet, and the quiet helped his head. After a while he realized that the night had turned to gray dawn, and he stared out at a black-and-white world, enveloped in his thoughts. He wondered if they'd gotten Tozzi too.

Sometime later Gibbons was pulled out of his trance by the sound of a bell ringing. He immediately pictured those cheap electric bells kids hook up to twelve-volt batteries for school science projects. Across the room, E-man and Louis jumped up and rushed to the freight elevator. Feeney, the leader, strolled over. When the slow elevator finally arrived, E-man lifted the gate and out walked the bastard himself.

Kinney was carrying Dunkin' Donuts bags, which Louis immediately took from him. E-man and Louis clustered around Kinney like kids around their dad just home from work. Feeney kept a respectable distance. He was the head of this crew after all.

Gibbons overheard Kinney telling them to take their breakfasts and go downstairs for some air. Feeney huddled with his boss for a second before he joined Louis and E-man in the elevator.

When they were gone, Kinney turned toward Gibbons. The morning light from the windows above Gibbons's head highlighted the golden boy, who was wearing a crisp tan suit today. "Morning, Bert," he called affably as he picked up a folding chair and walked toward the sunlight. He was carrying a Dunkin' Donuts cup in his other hand.

If Kinney got close enough, Gibbons swore he'd stick his fingers in the bastard's eyes and rip his fucking face off.

"I brought you a coffee," Kinney said as he set down the chair.

"You know what you can do with it, don't you?"

Kinney shrugged and sat down backward on the chair. As he carefully pried the lid off the cup, Gibbons considered the distances and decided that he was too far away to get a decent shot at him.

"Where's Tozzi?"

Kinney ignored the question and sipped gingerly. The garnet in his college ring sparkled brilliantly in the sunlight.

"You planning on cutting my head off too?"

Kinney frowned. "We haven't decided yet, Bert." This was the public Kinney talking, the future Special Agent in Charge. The Hun had gone back into his coffin for the night. Gibbons had to marvel at how different this Kinney was from the animal who'd savaged him last night.

"Tell me why," Gibbons said, squinting at him.

"Why what? Why I went over to the mob? Or why I killed Lando, Blaney, and Novick?" Kinney smiled brightly.

Gibbons's stomach was burning with pure hate. "Both."

Kinney closed his eyes and laughed. "What do you want me to tell you? How about 'love'? That's always a good one. I did it for love."

"I think you did it because you're a fucking wack. You get off on killing. You're sick."

"Much too simple, Bert. The insanity defense is overused. It's what they say when they've got nothing else to blame. You know that."

"Then why?"

"Why do people do anything these days, Bert? For money. Pure and simple."

"Is that how Varga converted you? Just with money?"

Kinney stared at Gibbons for a long moment before he answered. "When I was undercover in the Philly mob, Richie Varga and I sort of naturally gravitated toward each other. He wanted to be made in the worse way, but he knew it would never happen in the Philadelphia family because they thought he was a little jerk who just happened to be Jules Collesano's son-in-law. Richie had a lot of good ideas, though, and I was impressed with him. He asked me if I'd support him. I said yes, but I didn't tell him I was a fed until after he'd screwed his father-in-law. I wanted to be sure he really was a rising star before I committed myself."

"Why the hell would he trust you after you told him you were a fed?"

"As I said, we're kindred spirits. As a matter of fact, I gave him the original idea for turning on the New York bosses. The heads were my idea too. But you have to understand something, Bert. Richie and I fit each other's needs. He wanted power, and I wanted money. Together, we got what we wanted."

Gibbons scowled. "You're full of shit. It wasn't just the money."

Kinney sipped his coffee. "You wouldn't understand, Bert. You live like a monk, you clearly don't like material things, and most importantly, you don't have kids. Money doesn't mean the same thing to you that it means to me."

"Yeah, right. And your mother needs an operation."

"College costs are soaring, Bert. Right now it costs about sixty thousand dollars for a decent college education, and that's just for a bachelor's degree. Given inflation and the ages of my children, I figure I'll need at least six hundred and fifty thousand to send them all to school. You know what a special agent makes, Bert. Even if they made me director tomorrow, I'd never be able to afford it."

"Send 'em to tech school. The girls can be hairdressers." He just said that to get back at Kinney.

Kinney grinned. "Not my kids, Bert. No, I want my kids to have at the very least what I had. Because, face it, the world just gets harder all the time, and the competition they'll have to face will be enormous."

Gibbons just shook his head. He refused to credit this shit with a response. It was unbelievable how guys like this could rationalize anything, even murder, for their own benefit. Not only rationalize it, but make it seem as natural and logical as getting in out of the rain. Damn him.

"Believe me," Kinney said, "I tried to figure out another way, but Varga presented me with a once-in-a-lifetime opportunity, as they say. I saw it as a workable solution to my financial dilemma. I had no other choice, really. You sure you don't want a coffee? There's an extra one."

Gibbons looked at his feet. Kinney was making him sick.

Kinney exhaled loudly and stood up. "Well, if it's any consolation to you, I've instructed the boys to leave you alone for the time being. We won't do anything until we have your friend Tozzi. Then I'll just have to figure out who gets to watch the other one die. Of course, maybe by then I'll have thought of something simultaneous so you can both watch." He took another sip. "Later, Bert."

Gibbons listened to his footsteps as he walked the length of the big room, hating that bastard more than he'd ever hated anyone in his entire life.

THIRTY-ONE

Tozzi peered through a row of hemlock bushes, his feet sinking in the soft soil, his back up against the stockade fence. He could see the whole house from here. Chrissie was downstairs watching TV. The other kids were probably in bed; it was almost eleven. Mrs. Kinney was upstairs doing something in the bedroom, walking around the room in her bathrobe. Kinney was in his study, sitting at his desk. He'd been on the phone for the past half hour.

Tozzi felt the scratch on his cheek where the low branch of a short-needled spruce tree had caught him as he was hopping a fence a few doors down. He'd been thinking about dogs at the time and he wasn't paying attention. The lawn in that yard was bare and there was a dog run attached to the back of the house. He was afraid some goddamn dog would come charging out and wake up the whole neighborhood. The dog must've been inside, though, because he crossed that yard with no trouble. Sneaking through the backyards was the only way he could get to Kinney's house unnoticed, he'd decided. In fact, he hadn't even bothered to check out Kinney's street. He was certain there'd be a couple of Varga's men sitting in a car out front waiting for him. He'd counted on there not being anyone covering the backyard or stationed inside the house. If Kinney invited the heavies inside, he'd have a lot of explaining to do to his wife. Conducting business at home was strongly discouraged by the Bureau—Mrs. Kinney probably knew that—and if Varga's muscle all looked like the pair of greaseballs Tozzi spotted that morning, Kinney would have a hard time convincing his wife that these guys were FBI colleagues.

Watching Kinney through the window, Tozzi assumed that some of these phone calls he'd been making had to do with him. Probably ordering up more torpedoes to go out looking for "the other one."

Tozzi was weary and worried about Gibbons. He wanted to put a bullet between Kinney's eyes so bad. He'd spent the whole night and day plotting and planning, trying to outpsych this son-of-a-bitch, and now he was just sick and tired of thinking about him.

It had been a frantic twenty-four hours. After the pizza had arrived at Gibbons's apartment, Tozzi had wasted no time getting out of there. He figured he was being watched, but he had a gut feeling that they wouldn't try to take him. Not yet. The situation was too perfect for Kinney to pass up. Tozzi was a wanted man and Gibbons was supposed to be hunting him down. If Kinney's thugs could corner Tozzi somewhere where there wouldn't be any witnesses, they could take Tozzi down, then bring Gibbons along later and shoot him with one of Tozzi's guns to make it all look like a shoot-out, the good agent taking a fatal bullet while trying to apprehend the renegade. Kinney, of course, would claim to be the only witness, which would make him the hero who finally succeeded in neutralizing the maniac renegade. It was perfect. Not only would Kinney eliminate the threat of exposure, he'd pick up a gold star in the process and go to the head of the class, the son-of-a-bitch.

After Tozzi had left Gibbons's place, he'd stashed Excalibur in the trunk of the Buick with his other guns and took off, heading north along the river, taking local roads so he could spot a tail. By the time he'd reached the George Washington Bridge in Fort Lee, he was pretty certain no one was following him, but that's when he panicked. He suddenly realized he had nothing that could lead him to Gibbons, and he couldn't stop thinking about what Kinney might be doing to him. Kinney was insane, he was a butcher. That's when Tozzi started to doubt his theory about Kinney's plan for staging a shoot-out. Maybe Kinney had already sliced up Gibbons, pulled another Lando, Blaney, and Novick. Maybe he didn't care how much Tozzi knew about him because he figured no one who mattered would listen to a renegade agent. Maybe Kinney figured it was better to get rid of Gibbons right away and worry about Tozzi later.

Gunning the Buick south down the Turnpike Extension, Tozzi had broken out into a cold sweat thinking about all this. He had to find Gibbons, fast. It occurred to him that maybe Kinney had someone staked out at the motel in Secaucus where he'd been staying. He hoped to God Kinney did have someone there. Even if it was all part of Kinney's plan to use Gibbons as bait to nail him, Tozzi didn't care. He had to risk it to get a lead on Gibbons's location before Kinney went blade-crazy again.

When he'd gotten to Secaucus, he pulled into the Exxon station next to the EZ Rest Motel and told the attendant to fill it. That's when he spotted them. He was looking right at them, not thirty yards away. Two slimy-looking disco retreads sitting in a navy-blue T-bird with an orangy-tan vinyl roof parked on the side of the motel, waiting. He had no way of knowing for sure who they were, but instinctively he knew. He could read their stories in their weaselly faces—two young torpedoes eager to make an impression with the big boss and increase their chances of getting made in Varga's family. They were yakking away at each other like two old ladies at the old-age home. The sight of them made him crazy. He wondered if these two assholes would really know where Gibbons was. Doubtful, he decided. Shaking them down probably wouldn't be worth the risk. Tozzi pounded the steering wheel with his fist in frustration. He had to do something, though.

The attendant reappeared at his window and he paid for the gas with a twenty. As the man counted out his change, it suddenly came to Tozzi. Not a plan or a strategy, just something he could do right now that would send Kinney a message. He wanted Kinney to know that he may be running, but he wasn't hiding.

It had appeared in his mind full-blown, as if he were seeing it in a movie; then he just followed through and repeated what he saw, not really thinking about it. He guided the Buick around the back of the gas station, crossed over a mound of burnt-out grass into the motel's back lot, pulled up behind the building, put it in reverse, and backed into the narrow drive nice and easy until he was about twenty-five feet from the two gabbing torpedoes. Then he floored it and rammed the T-bird. He kept his foot on the gas, pushing their car out into highway traffic. He heard the torpedoes yelling, the bumpers crunching, their tires screeching, then felt the tremendous crash vibrate his wheel as a U-Haul van plowed into the T-bird and dragged it all the way to the motel sign at the other end of the lot. Tozzi spun the steering wheel, turned around, and tore out into the highway, veering around the wreckage of the demolished T-bird pinned between the van and the steel uprights of the neon EZ Rest sign.

Driving away, Tozzi couldn't believe he did that. It was crazy. Innocent people could've been hurt in that crash. It was a stupid thing to do. He'd heard on the radio later that no one had been seriously hurt. The radio announcer made a joke of the torpedoes' claim that they were deliberately pushed out into the middle of Route 3. The police reported that a quantity of an unidentified white powder was found in their car. Tozzi hoped the radio announcer's skepticism reflected the police's feelings about their story and that no one was looking for a 1977 copper-brown Buick LeSabre with a mangled rear bumper.

After the motel incident, Tozzi just drove. He drove so he could think, sort things out, put together some kind of plan. First thing, he knew he needed a place to stay, at least for the night, and Joanne seemed to be the logical solution, but as he drove out to her place, he began to have doubts about her. It was possible that she wasn't entirely on the up-and-up, he'd thought. She'd been married to Varga, and despite all that she'd said about him, they were never formally divorced. Maybe she was cooperating with Varga, maybe she was just keeping him busy that first night they spent together so that Varga's people could put the bomb in his cousin's car. It was possible. He changed his mind and decided not to go to Joanne's. He ended up spending the night in the Buick parked at the Vince Lombardi Service Exit off the Turnpike. But before he dozed off in the front seat, he changed his mind about her again. He was just being paranoid again, he'd decided. He'd seen her plenty of times in the past few weeks. There were more than enough opportunities for Varga to take him out when he was with her. She was really all right after all. He was just being paranoid about her, that's all. And as it was, he was paranoid enough about everything else.

He stood there in the shadows behind the hemlocks now, watching Kinney with the phone to his face. Kinney was burning the midnight oil, and Tozzi knew it wasn't for the FBI. If only he had a tap on that phone, he thought. If only. Tozzi moved quietly behind the hemlocks, walking along the perimeter of the yard through the neglected vegetable garden. So who needs a tap? he thought.

He got to the edge of the driveway and slipped between the Volvo sedan and the family van, mounting the three steps that led to the side door. The kitchen was dark inside. He remembered that there was a wall phone next to the refrigerator, a red wall phone. Tozzi carefully opened the screen door and tried the inside door. It was unlocked. Locking up was probably Kinney's duty. Last one to bed locks up, and Dad usually worked late in his study.

Light from the den shone into the otherwise dark kitchen and reflected off the sparkling appliances. He could hear the television, some shitty rock song he'd heard before but couldn't identify. Chrissie was probably watching MTV. He went to the doorway and peered into the den. He could see the image on the screen of a long-haired blond guy in tights and a raggy top leaping all over the stage, mugging into the camera, and generally making an ass out of himself. He could see Chrissie's knees behind the arm of the couch. He hoped she wouldn't decide to get up and fix herself a midnight snack.

The phone was just to the right of the doorway. Hanging on the wall next to it was a plastic organizer with compartments for coupons, memos, and bills and a shopping-list pad on the bottom. The top sheet of the pad had a few items scribbled down, not nearly enough for a full shopping. Tozzi pulled out the pack of envelopes from the bill compartment and flipped through it. There was nothing unusual: gas and electric, Visa, the local pharmacy, and the phone bill. He thought about taking the phone bill, but then rejected the idea. Tracing the long-distance calls could be useful, but he didn't have the time and he didn't have the resources to have that done anymore. Real agents can do that, not him. Real agents like Kinney. He put the bills back in their slot.

He reached for the phone then, carefully lifting the receiver, covering the mouthpiece with his hand, and putting it to his ear. Kinney was still on the phone.

". . . goes into your account when the job's completed. That's the way we've done it all along," Kinney was saying.

"Yeah, yeah, direct deposit, I know, man. But I got a little problem with a shylock, you know? All I need is two grand to get him off my back for a while. That's all I need, two grand in advance. Is that a big thing I'm asking for?"

The whiny voice on the other end sounded a lot like Paulie Tortorella.

"That's not the way we set it up," Kinney said coldly.

"Fuck the way we set it up! Have I ever let you down? No. Now I'm asking for one favor and you're giving me fucking grief. How the hell am I supposed to operate for you when I got this shylock's legbreaker following me around? You tell me that?"

There was a pause. Kinney was considering it. "All right," he finally said. "I've got to get the keys for the place in the Bronx to you anyway. You know where Kill Van Kull Park is in Bayonne?"

"Where?"

"The park under the Bayonne Bridge."

"You mean where all the tugboats go by?"

"That's it. Meet me there tomorrow at noon, by the basketball courts. I'll have the money for you."

"Great. Thanks, man."

"And let's not make a habit out of this, Paulie. Okay?"

"Yeah, sure. Never again. See you tomorrow."

"Right."

They hung up and Tozzi quickly remembered to press the hook so Kinney would get a dial tone. He waited for Kinney to make his next call. After a minute he released the hook, but all he heard was Kinney's breathing. Kinney was probably looking up a number, he assumed.

"Chrissie?" Kinney's voice simultaneously came through the receiver and echoed down the hallway.

"What?"

"I'm trying to work, Chrissie. I thought we had an understanding about the phone when I'm working."

"I'm watching TV, Dad. I didn't touch the stupid phone."

Oh, shit. Kinney must've heard a difference in the dial tone or something. He must have good ears. Tozzi quickly hung up the phone and moved toward the door.

But just as he reached for the knob, the overhead lights flickered on. He turned and saw Kinney in the doorway with a claw hammer in his hand.

"Tozzi," he said in a hiss. There was evil in his eyes. His face was at war with itself, twitching, battling between sadistic glee and mad fury.

Tozzi dropped to one knee, went for the .38 in his ankle holster, but Kinney leapt across the kitchen, wielding the hammer like a savage with a tomahawk. Tozzi moved to get out of the way, but the hammer blow intended for his head smashed down on the top of his shoulder and sent a shooting pain down his arm and up the back of his neck. He bolted up in reaction to the pain and in the process flipped Kinney on his back. Seeing the opportunity for retaliation, Tozzi delivered a sharp knuckle punch under Kinney's armpit, knocking the wind out of him. Kinney tried to swing the hammer, but Tozzi was kneeling on his chest, twisting his wrist until he released the hammer. Tozzi felt the heft of the hammer in his hand, another opportunity. He lifted it over his head, intent on beating Kinney's brains out. He wanted to see that deceitful Ivy League face smashed to bloody pulp. He wanted fucking revenge for everything.

"Daddy!" Chrissie screamed from the doorway. Her hand was poised over her mouth in horror.

Tozzi froze. The son-of-a-bitch. He was making him play his game. Tozzi's grip went slack. He'd be goddamned if he was going to stoop to Kinney's level and play the psychopath. No, he was better than Kinney, goddamn it. No matter what they said, he was better than that. Gibbons knew. Gibbons. It didn't make sense right now, but he kept telling himself that Kinney had to live so that Gibbons wouldn't die.

Tozzi's hand was shaking. His brain couldn't analyze everything his gut was throwing at him. He wanted to hurt this bastard, but his brain kept saying no, spitting out reasons he couldn't deal with right now.

The girl screamed again. He could hear people scrambling out of bed upstairs. Kinney was struggling. Finally his gut took over and he pinned Kinney's hand against the floor and hammered it—once, twice—into the shining linoleum.

Kinney grunted and rolled over on his wound. Tozzi ran for the door as the two boys rushed into the kitchen.

He sprinted across the back lawn and hopped the fence. If Kinney did have torpedoes watching out front, he hoped they were slow and stupid.

THIRTY-TWO

Slumped down behind the wheel of the Buick, Tozzi could see the street, the park, the basketball court, and the shimmering water of Kill Van Kull, the narrow straits that separate Staten Island from New Jersey. He could see Paulie Tortorella in a black and pink Hawaiian shirt sitting up high on the back of a bench, drinking a can of soda, watching the tugs go by. He'd been there about twenty minutes. Tozzi had spent the night there.

At noon on the dot, the silver Volvo arrived. A gold Chevy Caprice that had been hogging two spaces at the curb moved back to make room for the Volvo. Tozzi had noticed the three guys sitting in the Chevy a long time ago. They'd been there since eleven.

When Kinney got out of his car, Tozzi saw that his hand was bandaged, the pinky and ring finger set with curved metal splints that made his hand look like a claw. Tozzi thought back to last night in Kinney's kitchen. He'd swung the hammer with his right hand and smashed Kinney's left hand. He regretted that he hadn't thought about that at the time and ruined Kinney's right.

Kinney had come alone in the Volvo. The three guys from the Caprice fanned out around him as he walked toward the basketball court. He spoke briefly to only one of the torpedoes, who immediately fell back behind Kinney after they'd finished. They seemed to know better than to get too close to the Hun. Surprisingly these guys weren't the usual Nicky Newark types. These three wore dark suits and shades, top buttons buttoned, ties up. They looked like pallbearers—or FBI agents.

Kinney was wearing a light blue seersucker suit, and he seemed unaffected by the blistering noonday sun. The merciless rays beamed off every piece of chrome and glass in Tozzi's line of vision, and he had to keep moving his head to get a clear view of Kinney and his entourage. The park was packed with kids running around like nuts. A bunch of them had set up a plywood ramp on the basketball court and they were playing Evel Knievel on their skateboards. It would be a hell of a place for a gun battle. But Tozzi had a feeling Kinney didn't give a shit about that.

Last night Tozzi had expected Kinney to change the location of his meet with Tortorella, figuring that Kinney would assume that he'd overheard the details of his telephone conversation. Then he thought about it. Kinney wants him dead because he knows too much about Kinney's relationship with Varga. Obviously the three torpedoes weren't there to protect Kinney from Tortorella. Kinney was hoping this meet would lure Tozzi out again.

Tozzi was beginning to think like Kinney. That's how they told you how to do it at Quantico. But was Kinney beginning to think like Tozzi? Tozzi frowned at the thought.

Kinney strolled over to Tortorella's bench. He put his foot up on the bench, leaned on his knee, and gazed out at the water. Another tug sailed by, a red one with a big white M painted on the stack.

Tozzi saw Tortorella shaking his head no. Kinney must've asked him if he'd been followed. A stupid question. If someone had followed Paulie, obviously he wouldn't have stuck around. On the other hand, maybe he would've. He needed that money.

Kinney went into his breast pocket and pulled out an envelope. He tapped the seatback with it as he explained something to Tortorella, who kept his eye on the envelope. Tozzi imagined Kinney lecturing the little man, making sure he understood that this was a big favor and a one-time deal and that he shouldn't ask for anything like this ever again. Kinney had to put Paulie in his place before he let him have the cash. Kinney was really into power, that was clear.

When Kinney finally deigned to give Tortorella the envelope, the little man hopped down off the bench, said thanks a lot, and made an abrupt exit. Tortorella wasn't into groveling, that was clear too. Kinney stayed and watched another tug pass by, then went back to his car, escorted by the three pallbearers. They got into the Caprice and waited for the Volvo to pull out. When the Volvo was almost out of sight, they pulled out of their space and followed.

Tozzi held the key in the ignition, forcing himself to wait. When the Caprice was nearly out of sight, he started his engine and drove after them, hoping Kinney hadn't thought of doubling back to see who was following the pallbearers. That's the way he would do it.

Fortunately, that wasn't the way Kinney did it. Tozzi followed the gold Caprice north to the causeway that led to Liberty State Park, just a stone's throw from the statue. Tozzi always thought it was significant that even though Lady Liberty was just off shore, the bitch kept her back to Jersey. When they first put her up, they could've turned her a little bit so it wouldn't have been such a blatant snub.

This causeway also led to an entrance to the Turnpike, so luckily there was enough traffic here to keep the Buick from looking suspicious. But when the Caprice turned left instead of going straight into the park, Tozzi had to slow down. There wasn't much traffic down that road. He slowed down and waited for a sixteen-wheeler to turn left, then tailgated the truck for cover until it turned off at a paper factory. Tozzi kept driving, hoping the pallbearers didn't realize that the brown Buick was following them. He couldn't slow down; it would look too suspicious on this road. There was nothing out here, just an empty field on the river side, and a junkyard where hopeless wrecks were stacked six high on the other. Tozzi glanced at the sprung trunks on some of those ruined cars and thought about compactors and Gibbons. He was relieved when the Caprice didn't turn into the junkyard.

The road curved around the waterfront. The Caprice was out of sight now, hidden behind tall grass and high ragweed on the bend. Tozzi stayed on the main road when he came out of the bend instead of taking the one that forked to the right. He knew the area. That road ended at the old railway station where the immigrants from Ellis Island were dumped. He remembered his grandpa telling him that once they got past the physical exam at Ellis Island, the new arrivals were asked if they wanted to go to the city or the country. If you said the city, they shipped you to the Lower East Side. If you said the country, they sent you to Jersey City. Grandpa opted for the country, but he only had enough money to get him as far as Newark. In two generations, the Tozzis hadn't made it any farther west.

Suddenly the main road went from blacktop to cobblestones, rattling the old Buick. Tozzi saw the trestle bridge up ahead and a few abandoned factories and warehouses tucked under the gloom of the black steel structure. The gold Caprice and the silver Volvo caught his eye right away. They were parked next to a line of abandoned trailers in the rutted dirt lot of an old two-story brick warehouse. Tozzi drove on in case someone was watching. There were more factories and warehouses on the other side of the bridge, a few of these still in operation. Tozzi parked on the first side street he came to, then got out and doubled back on foot.

Tozzi circled around the warehouse, crouching through the tall grass. He could see the loading dock and the fronts of the two cars. There was a third car, a black Firebird Trans Am, tucked away in the tall grass behind the trailers. Two of the pallbearers were leaning on the hood of the Caprice. Three scruffy-looking punks sat on the edge of the loading dock, pawing through two white take-out bags, stuffing their faces with whatever they found. The big Irish kid looked like he was going to eat the bags. The short Latino punk was trying to make conversation with the two pallbearers, but they were ignoring him. The pallbearers apparently considered themselves a higher order of torpedo and didn't want to associate with the punks. Tozzi watched this scene until the punks finished eating and went back inside. Tozzi could hear the warning bell of the freight elevator coming down to get them. He saw the Latino give the pallbearers the finger as he backstepped into the elevator.

When the elevator came down again a few minutes later, Kinney and the third pallbearer stepped out. They joined the other two pallbearers, got into their respective cars, and left, bouncing over the deep ruts in the dirt lot. Tozzi grinned. If Gibbons was up there, he was still alive. Corpses don't need guards.

Tozzi went directly to the loading dock and looked into the empty elevator. He was going to have to improvise. He had to get their attention first. He stuck the .38 in his waistband, cupped his hands around his mouth, and started to sing the first thing that came into his head. "O-o say can you see . . ." He was thinking of Smokey Robinson's version. ". . . by the dawn's early light . . ." He started singing louder just in case they couldn't hear him.

A moment later he heard the elevator starting its slow ascent. Tozzi grinned. He leapt off the loading dock and rushed over to the row of rusty trailers with their doors hanging open like old whores, still singing.

When the elevator reappeared on the loading dock, the big Irish kid and the little Latino stepped out slowly, leading with their guns. The little guy looked mean; the big mick looked spooked. Tozzi kept singing. ". . . Gave proof thro' the night that our flag was still there . . ."

E-man pointed to the trailers with his gun. They hopped off the loading dock and stalked the trailers. "Hey, tweety bird!" E-man yelled. "Come on out. We want your fuckin' autograph."

The strained singing didn't stop. They walked up slowly to the open trailers, ready to plug the first thing that moved. Suddenly the singing stopped.

"Come on out, asshole," Louis shouted. He tried to sound tough.

"Shut up," E-man sneered. Feeney was upstairs with the old guy so it was his turn to be Wyatt Earp.

Suddenly Louis jumped. He heard something in the trailer on the far end. E-man heard it too. He pointed his gun into that black hole and stared at it hard.

"Come on," he whispered to Louis. "In this one."

When Tozzi saw their legs leave the ground and disappear into the middle trailer, he couldn't believe it. He was on his back under the end trailer. He'd kicked the underside of it to get them to come closer so he could grab their ankles from below and pull them down. But this was ridiculous. They were making it too fucking easy. Now he could hear them whispering inside the belly of the middle trailer. "Okay, now!" one of them said, and immediately close-range gunfire ripped into the side of their trailer. Apparently they figured they were drilling the song bird inside the next trailer. Spent bullets hit the ground next to Tozzi's leg. These two evidently knew shit about ballistics. You'd have to be packing elephant cartridges to penetrate two insulated steel walls and stay on course. Assholes.

As the two punks made themselves deaf inside the trailer, Tozzi scrambled under their trailer, crouched to his feet under the tailgate, reached up, and shut the doors on them. He felt the sting of their redirected bullets hitting the doors and he yanked down on the rusty latch with all his weight to close it. He found a discarded u-bolt in the dirt, which he dropped into the hasp for insurance.

What assholes, he thought as he went back to the loading dock.

There was a padlocked steel door on the loading dock. Tozzi shot the lock and forced the door open. The stink made his eyes water. Dirty light beamed into the stairwell from a window on the landing above. The stairs were littered with debris, and the landing and hallway were crowded with steel drums. The smell was overpowering. Illegally dumped toxic waste, no doubt. The brew that made New Jersey famous.

Tozzi climbed the steps, worrying about rat teeth and high-stepping the whole way up. He shoved heavy sloshing barrels aside when he got to the top, making his way to the door. His throat was burning. He kicked the fire door and kept kicking until it opened enough to let him in.

Inside he was greeted by a slug zinging off the corner of the metal door just a few inches from his fingers. Tozzi hit the floor rolling.

"Throw the piece to me, jerkoff, or your friend here is a memory," Feeney yelled. He was standing over Gibbons, who was slumped down on the floor, handcuffed to the steampipe. There was an automatic in Feeney's hand leveled at Gibbons's head.

Tozzi froze, lying on his belly, his heart pumping hard. He stared at the pig-faced boy and thought of that famous picture of a Viet Cong blowing the top of some South Vietnamese guy's head off. Or was it the other way around?

"Say goodbye, FBI. Both of yous." The pig-faced boy was a cocky son-of-a-bitch. "Now toss the gun, I said, or else I waste him."

"Who's he?" Tozzi yelled back. "I don't know him."

"Hey, fuck you, you—"

Gibbons suddenly woke up and grabbed Feeney's wrist. The automatic discharged into the brick wall. Gibbons held on. Tozzi got up and charged, slamming his hip into Feeney's chest, both hands clasped around his gun hand. Together they smashed into the window, breaking glass. Tozzi snatched the gun away from him and threw it down.

"You fucking little shit—" Tozzi grabbed him by the flesh under his chin and shoved his head through a cracked windowpane and pulled it out again. He started throwing punches to Feeney's gut and face, but they weren't landing hard enough to satisfy Tozzi. He wanted to hurt this little bastard. He wanted the little fuck to suffer. Then he remembered Kinney's face coming at him with the hammer and he stopped.

Feeney slumped to the floor. He was like a crab that had been left in the refrigerator overnight, no sign of life other than a little movement in the legs. Blood flowed out of his piggy nostrils.

"You finished?" Gibbons asked. He looked like hell, but he sounded fine.

"I think so," Tozzi said.

"Watch your face," Gibbons said. He held Feeney's gun to the chain on the handcuffs, turned away, and fired. He pulled on the hot mangled links until he was free, then hauled himself up and went over to Feeney. He found the handcuff key in Feeney's pants pocket and unlocked the cuff.

"I would've gotten the key for you," Tozzi said. "Why didn't you just ask?"

Gibbons ignored the question. "I was just about to throw him out the window when you barged in," he said, sounding pissed off. "You fucked up my whole plan."

"Sorry," Tozzi said. It was good to see the old son-of-a-bitch alive.

"Come on." Gibbons started for the stairwell.

"Wait up," Tozzi said, then got down on one knee and lifted his pant leg. He pulled Excalibur out of his ankle holster and handed it to Gibbons. "Here, take this. I'm tired of carrying it."

Gibbons took his gun and examined it. Then he looked Tozzi in the eye. "Thanks."

Tozzi thought he detected an aborted attempt at a smile of gratitude. Maybe not, though.

Gibbons stuck Excalibur in the pocket of his jacket. He weighed Feeney's automatic in his hand before he reared back and flung it through the window and into the tall grass outside. Shards of tinkling glass rained down on Feeney's chest and stuck to his bloody face.

"You want to take these guys in?" Tozzi asked.

Gibbons looked at Feeney for a moment and thought about it. "They're dumb enough to be stand-up guys and protect Kinney. Fuck 'em."

Tozzi shrugged. The stink from the stairwell was beginning to fill the room.

"Come on, let's go," Gibbons said.

THIRTY-THREE

"What do you think?" Gibbons said, holding a Styrofoam cup of lukewarm coffee to his lips.

"I want to take a look," Tozzi said, curling his fingers around the steering wheel of the LeSabre.

They sat in the car watching the fire inspectors pack up their gear. They'd been there all afternoon, sifting through the rubble. There were two of them—the senior guy wore a suit and high rubber boots; the other one, who actually did the dirty work, was in khakis. The guy in khakis was loading up the sample cases he'd been filling all afternoon, picking through the smoldering remains of the brick buildings that used to be Kantor's Army and Navy Store and Brothers Audio-Video Discount Center on Jerome Avenue in the Bronx. The Thom McAn Shoe Store next door to the Brothers site had sustained quite a bit of damage. A city building inspector had come by earlier, stared at the shoe store for a while, and concluded that this building should come down too. The fire inspectors were more thorough and methodical. They were investigating a possible crime scene, so they took their time. The guy in the suit supervised, conferring with his man, making suggestions from the safe side of the police barricades, occasionally calling in on the radio in the red NYFD station wagon, but mostly schmoozing with the cops securing the scene. Gibbons had noticed that whenever the workhorse wanted to get away from his boss, he went into the charred remains of the building and disappeared for a while. The suit didn't go in that far.

Gibbons looked at his watch. ''They'll be gone soon.''

''Says who?'' Tozzi asked.

''It's almost five. The suit's management, and management doesn't get paid overtime.''

Tozzi shook his head. ''Another dedicated civil servant,'' he said. ''You think they found anything?''

''Doubtful. They know it was set, but it's a hard thing to prove. Unless the torch was a real dummy and left gas cans behind.''

''Tortorella knows what he's doing. I've seen him work.''

Gibbons sipped his coffee. ''You seem pretty sure this was Tortorella's work.''

''I'm not sure about anything.'' Tozzi rubbed the back of his neck. ''All I know is that I saw Tortorella torch a store like this in Edison, and then I heard him and Kinney talking about a job in the Bronx.'' Tozzi looked beat.

''Didn't you sleep last night?'' Gibbons asked. They'd spent the night at Lorraine's house. Gibbons had suggested that they go there, saying that it would be safer out in the country. In fact, it wasn't any safer there than anywhere else, except that Lorraine was there, and after sleeping on a splintered floor handcuffed to a steampipe for the past two nights, he had an urgent need to be with her. He also wanted her to see that her cousin was all right.

''I slept okay,'' Tozzi said. ''I'm glad we went down there. I wanted to see her once more before— It was good seeing her.''

Gibbons nodded pensively. ''Yes. It was.''

The inspector in khakis packed up his cases and got into the red station wagon. The suit was already behind the wheel. The station wagon pulled away from the curb and made a right at the first corner. As soon as it was out of sight, one of the two police officers got into their patrol car and took off down Jerome Avenue in the same direction, leaving his partner behind to watch the scene. Getting out of the Buick and crossing the street, Gibbons noticed for the first time that the cop who was left on guard was a woman. She was tall but slight, and the uniform made her look like a kid playing dress-up. Why the hell didn't the department get these broads uniforms that fit right? Gibbons thought. No wonder punks give them shit, looking like that.

Gibbons cut in front of Tozzi and walked right up to the cop. ''FBI,'' he said, showing her his ID. Tozzi stood back, poker-faced. ''We want to take a look at the scene,'' Gibbons said.

She touched the edge of the ID in his hand as she examined it. "Sure, go ahead," she finally said.

"You here alone?" he asked. He could hardly see her eyes under the visor of her hat.

"My partner went for dinner," she said.

The sun was going down over the ghetto. It was Miller time. You mean your partner went for a few beers, Gibbons wanted to say. This was a borderline neighborhood, borderline between bad and worse. He bet she was glad to have them there.

Gibbons squeezed through the police sawhorses. Tozzi followed without a word to the cop. They split up and started poking around.

Gibbons stepped over charred bricks, wet carpeting, melted plastic, soaked cardboard boxes, the blackened electronic insides of one thing or another. As far as fires go, it looked kosher to him, but FBI agents don't know a whole lot about arson. Unless it's a federal facility that's burned, arson is always handled by the local police. He kept looking, though. He might get lucky. You never can tell with these things.

"There ain't shit here, man. Just like the other place."

Gibbons peered over a pile of bricks, plaster, and lathing. A gang of black kids was looking through the rubble, searching for salvageable goods, no doubt. They angrily shoved beams and hunks of plaster out of their way. "Shit . . . shit . . . shit . . ." The one wearing a black nylon do-rag around his head cursed every time he tossed a brick and came up empty.

"Not even a fucking Walkman," a kid with no front teeth said. "This is jive."

It was then that Gibbons realized these weren't kids. These were what the papers called "youths" and politicians not up for reelection called the "hardcore unemployed." Cops usually called them "fucking dangerous."

"Maceo," the one in the purple muscle T-shirt called, "you say that other store was like this?"

"Shit, yeah," the guy with no front teeth said. "Sound King, on a Hundred Sixty-ninth, you know? Burned down just like this place, but there was nothing to take there neither. And that time I know I was the first dude to get down there. Damn."

"I need me a box, man," the do-rag declared. "Yo, white man! What you doing there?"

They spotted Tozzi coming around back from the alley side, and they all raised their backs like cats at the sight of him. Tozzi was dressed in jeans, a black T-shirt, and a bush jacket. He didn't look like a cop to them.

Gibbons then saw the flash of blades and narrow-eyed faces. These guys felt cheated, and they were ready to take it out on someone.

Tozzi squared off. He had that look on his face that Gibbons didn't like. Gibbons looked back toward the cop on the sidewalk, but she made like she didn't hear and kept her back to the whole affair, the bitch. The feds can take care of themselves, she must've figured. Let the feds hang themselves, who cares? Feds are the PD's natural enemy. Damn cops watch too much TV.

Gibbons pulled his gun and cocked the trigger so everyone could hear it, just like they do in the movies. "Okay, boys, time to go home."

Mean faces snapped around in his direction. "Eat it, old man," one of them said. Two of them turned to take him on. Blades against bullets—hardcore wasn't the word for this bunch.

Tozzi reached into his jacket, and the purple muscle shirt made a move toward him. Gibbons winced, waiting for the muzzle flash, but just the sight of Tozzi's 9mm was enough. The gang left in a cloud of mumbles and curses.

Gibbons put away Excalibur and took out his notepad. He scribbled down *"Sound King—169th."*

Tozzi climbed over a charred beam. "Taking notes for your memoirs," he asked.

"The brothers said something about another fire just like this one. No salvageable merchandise there either."

"You think it's a bust-out scam?"

"Could be. Empty out the merchandise before the blaze, collect on the insurance, then sell the merchandise or move it to another store and have it 'burn' again. They can keep moving the stuff and collecting on it until it's outdated."

Tozzi folded his arms and looked at the ground. "It's not hard to find surplus hardware to burn. Melted plastic, pressboard cabinets, fried circuit boards—it all looks pretty authentic."

"So Varga's running a bust-out scam with Kinney as his foreman," Gibbons said.

Tozzi shook his head. "Doesn't really make sense. You can burn down two, maybe three stores, but that's it. The insurance companies must get hip to what's going on. Varga's financing a whole new family, for chrissake. Can't buy that much dope with the profits of an operation like this. How many men could he afford to keep on the payroll? I mean, how much do you think it's costing him to keep Kinney alone in his pocket?''

Gibbons looked at their long, jagged shadows on the rubble. ''Varga's pretty inventive. He may have put a new wrinkle on this scam.''

''You have any ideas?''

He did, but he didn't want to tell Tozzi yet. He knew Tozzi was touchy about certain things, and there was no sense getting him all riled up if his hunch turned out to be wrong. ''Nothing definite,'' he said. ''Tomorrow I'll see what I can dig up at the office.''

''What about Ivers? Isn't he going to want to know where you've been all week?''

''Probably.''

''What will you tell him?''

Gibbons shrugged. ''If I'm lucky, he won't be in and I won't have to lie to him. I'll make sure I show up late. He's usually tied up in meetings after ten. Come on, my throat's dry. I need something to drink.''

They headed back toward the police barricades.

''Find what you were looking for?'' the lady cop asked. She didn't even try to hide the sarcasm in her voice. Gibbons remembered a time when uniform cops bit their tongues in the presence of special agents, a time when the only women in uniform were crossing guards.

''Sorry, I can't talk about ongoing investigations,'' he said politely. ''By the way, what happened to your partner, officer?''

''He's on dinner break, I told you.''

''Oh, that's right.'' Gibbons nodded and tapped his forehead. ''You did say that. Well, would you like us to stay until he returns?''

''Fuck off,'' she growled.

Tozzi squeezed his nose and snorted a laugh.

''Suit yourself,'' Gibbons said, turning away and crossing the street.

As they drove away in the Buick, he could see her long shadow on the pavement as she stood alone guarding nothing. The sky was hot orange behind the grim tenements. He could hear congas beating on the rooftops, rap blaring from ghetto blasters in the street. Her partner had some sense of humor. For her sake, Gibbons hoped he had a little mercy too.

THIRTY-FOUR

She wore a black leotard and black spiked heels, that's all, and she kept running her pointy red fingernails through the mounds of white blond hair that piled on her shoulders and spilled down her back as she dug her feet in and ground her ass into the front plate-glass window of Spyro's on Eighth Avenue. Tozzi took another bite of his souvlaki and marveled at the hooker's ingenuity. She was working the street outside while coming on to him inside at the same time. And the way she was goosing that window, there'd be big kiss marks on the glass pretty soon. He had to admit it was advertising that worked. He was hard as a rock.

Tozzi sat at the window table, watching the hooker's ass, occasionally glancing around her to see the afternoon rush-hour crush, people marching down Eighth Avenue toward the Port Authority to catch a bus home, cars backed up on Forty-seventh Street inching toward the entrance to the Lincoln Tunnel at Fortieth and Ninth Avenue. The Times Square vicinity was a funny place at this time of day, like two simultaneous spirit worlds occupying the same space. The hookers and hustlers went about their business while the secretaries and businessmen floated around them, the straight people all moving in the same basic direction, eyes ahead, undistracted, like an army of zombies.

Back at the counter, Spyro was ladling fat drippings over the huge hunk of lamb turning on a towering vertical spit. The fat sizzled, caught fire, and flared dramatically as it dripped off the meat, but Tozzi had gotten used to the sound by now and didn't even pay attention. Spyro did this every five minutes or so.

Tozzi wanted to know where the hell Gibbons was. He said he'd be here between five and six, and though it was only twenty to six, Tozzi was concerned. Gibbons was always early. He wondered if Gibbons met Kinney at the office today. Maybe Kinney had followed Gibbons from the office and now Gibbons was trying to lose him. Tozzi remembered a few years back when there was a mob hit on a big-wheel real-estate developer right in front of a fancy steak house on East Forty-fourth at rush hour. The hit man pumped three bullets into the back of the guy's head, then calmly walked around the corner and disappeared into the crowd. Rush hour was the perfect time for a hit. Where the hell was he?

He looked at the hooker again. She'd stopped rubbing her ass on the glass. She was negotiating with a beefy-looking guy in a Brooks Brothers suit whose glasses were too small for his head. Tozzi examined the line of her legs and the curve of her ass. It was a very tight little bod. When she walked off with the john in tow, Tozzi felt slightly rejected. He thought he'd at least get a friendly goodbye wink or something. Tozzi picked up his sandwich and took another bite.

A few minutes later the door opened, setting off the electric buzzer that alerted Spyro that someone was there in case he was in the back or stuck on the can. Tozzi had noticed that Spyro greeted his customers as if they were invading Turks, glaring at them with his flashing black olive eyes, his grim mouth covered by a thick handlebar mustache. When Tozzi realized that the latest arrival was Gibbons, he figured for once Spyro's suspicions were justified. Gibbons looked meaner than usual, and today that pissed-off Indian-chief face even made him uneasy.

"What happened?" Tozzi asked as Gibbons sat down at his table. "Was he there?"

"No. He—"

"Can I help you?" Spyro demanded belligerently.

"Yeah. Just bring me a coffee."

"One-dollar-fifty-cent minimum."

Gibbons glared at the Greek.

"And a baklava," Tozzi intervened. He turned back to Gibbons, and Spyro went away. "Kinney wasn't at the office?"

"He was there this morning. He asked around if anybody had seen me lately. One of the guys told me he left the office around eleven."

"So what did you find out?"

Spyro returned with Gibbons's order. There was as much coffee in the saucer as there was in the cup, and the small brown honey-glazed lump looked exactly like what Gibbons thought of it. Gibbons pushed the plate to Tozzi as soon as Spyro set it down.

Gibbons lifted the lid of the stainless-steel pitcher and sniffed the milk before he poured it into his coffee. "I got some interesting information," he said. "I was on the phone most of the afternoon. I got hold of an Inspector Langer at the fire department who was unusually cooperative. He heard FBI and I guess he was impressed. Anyway, I asked him about the fires in the Bronx, Brothers Discount Center and Sound King. He told me about another similar fire in Forest Hills. In all three cases, the fires seemed suspicious, but they couldn't prove arson. Langer was also kind enough to give me the names of the insurance companies who covered those stores."

Tozzi grinned as he chewed another bite of his sandwich. "You love it when they spread their legs for you. Did you threaten him with prosecution for obstruction of justice? That used to be your favorite."

Gibbons ignored the remark and continued. "I called the insurance companies and talked to people in the security and fraud departments. One guy at Praesidio Mutual had a lot to say. He was a former cop named Ramirez who was fed up with his job and needed to let off some steam. According to Mr. Ramirez, all insurance companies expect to pay out on a certain number of total- or partial-disaster fires every year. It's only after they reach their quota that they start getting sticky about paying out on fire claims. But the interesting thing is the more fires a company pays out on, the more they can up their premiums the next year. Ramirez told me the companies actually want to meet their fire quotas and even surpass them a little because what they pay out in claims is nothing compared to the higher rates they can justifiably charge. And according to Ramirez, that's standard for the industry."

Tozzi speared a corner off the pastry and ate it. "Yeah, so what's this got to do with anything?"

Gibbons winced at the turd on the plate. "Ramirez also told me that before a company reaches its quota, whatever investigations they conduct are just for show. That's why he's so fed up with his job, he said."

Tozzi took another piece of the turd. "So what's the point?"

"Suppose Varga knew which companies hadn't met their yearly fire quotas. He could target those companies specifically and keep the bust-out scam going, increasing his yield considerably. Before the quota is reached, payoffs are made faster and the investigations are worthless."

Tozzi set down his fork. He could see what was coming. "And how would Varga know which companies to hit on?"

Gibbons pressed his lips together and sighed. "Aside from paying out on recent total-disaster fire claims on audio-video stores, the three insurance companies I called today had something else in common. They all have their computerized files handled by the same data-processing firm—a company in Jersey called DataReach. That's where what's-her-name is a vp, isn't it?"

Tozzi nodded. Gibbons knew what Joanne's goddamn name was and he knew she worked for DataReach. Playing dumb was his asinine way of softening the blow, making her seem less important than she actually was.

Gibbons leaned over the table and tasted his coffee. "So what do you think?"

"I think we ought to take a trip out to see what's-her-name."

"You call the play on this one, Toz. We handle it any way you want."

This was Gibbons's way of saying he didn't know how strong Tozzi really felt about Joanne Varga. It was his way of offering consolation for being stupid and trusting her in the first place. Tozzi appreciated Gibbons's concern for his feelings, but he was angry with himself and he felt like a fool. He didn't want anyone's understanding. He wanted to nail Kinney and Varga and bring down Joanne with them. He didn't want to dwell on his feelings. He wanted to feel smart. He wanted to win.

Tozzi stood up abruptly, took out his wallet, and left a ten on the check. "Come on," he said to his partner. "Let's get going."

Tozzi felt funny being in Joanne's apartment alone with Gibbons. No one had answered the doorbell so they let themselves in. Tozzi used the keys Joanne had given him, and he felt culpable for having them. The keys were just another facet of her deception, something else to win his trust. Gibbons walked in behind him, giving him a wide berth, and his solicitude was aggravating Tozzi.

Tozzi stood in the living room and looked around. The scene of the crime, he kept thinking. He'd spent a fair amount of time here, and he knew where everything was. He'd used her toilet, washed up in her shower, watched TV on her couch, cooked with her pots, slept in her bed. He knew more about this place than he should've. He kept thinking about that old saying about how a criminal always returns to the scene of the crime.

Gibbons walked around with his hands in his pockets like a browser in an antique shop. He found his way to the kitchen, and from the living room Tozzi heard him opening the refrigerator. Tozzi wandered in and saw his partner sniffing a quart of milk to see if it had gone sour. He was looking for signs of recent occupancy. Gibbons hunkered down and pulled out the produce drawer.

"The lettuce looks pretty fresh," he said. "No yellow spots on the broccoli."

He stood up and opened the freezer compartment. He pulled out a package of chicken breasts and held it at arm's length so he could read the label. " 'Sell by September 6.' That's . . . Saturday, right? She probably went shopping yesterday, maybe even this morning."

She went shopping last night, Tozzi knew. She always shopped at night.

They moved back into the living room. Gibbons checked the date on the *TV Guide* on the black-lacquered coffee table. It was next week's. Tozzi wondered what he'd say to her when he saw her again. This wasn't a simple betrayal. Under different circumstances, he'd prefer to settle things with her by himself, confront her directly, do what he should've done with Roberta way back when. If there weren't major felonies involved, if this were just a matter between the two of them, he wondered how he'd handle it. Screaming accusations? Mournful disappointment? Righteous indignation? Anguish and pain? Violence? He tried each one on like a hat. There was no perfect fit.

He saw Gibbons standing over the tub in the bathroom. It was a modern cream-colored tub with handles built into the sides. He didn't have to see it; he remembered it.

"There's a little water around the drain," Gibbons reported matter-of-factly. "The bar of soap's still wet. Somebody took a shower not too long ago."

Tozzi went to the medicine cabinet, avoiding his own reflection in the mirror, and examined the contents of the second shelf from the top. It wasn't there, the blue plastic clam, her diaphragm case. Wherever she went, she took it with her. Wherever she was, she was going to be staying overnight. Tozzi looked over the other shelves just to make sure the diaphragm wasn't there, but it was gone. He shut the cabinet and squinted at himself in the mirror.

Gibbons had already moved on to the bedroom. He was looking in the closet, probably looking for the absence of a suitcase. Tozzi could've told him not to bother. Joanne had an array of luggage and overnight bags, too many to use all at one time. But he didn't say anything.

He looked at the quilt hanging on the wall. It was a real Amish quilt, she'd told him. The design was called the log-cabin design. It consisted of varying lengths of black, red, and blue strips set at right angles, but to him it still looked too modern to be called a log-cabin design. He'd said that to her when she first told him about it, but she insisted that it was really a very old design. She said one of the reasons she bought it was because it looked modern yet it was really old. He'd spent a lot of time lying in bed staring at that quilt. By the morning light, it dominated the room. Tozzi looked at the left side of the queen-size bed, the side he slept on, the side with the empty night table.

"Does she always make her bed like this?" Gibbons asked.

Tozzi shook his head. "Only on weekends."

Gibbons went to her night table. He pressed a button on the clock-radio and the red digital numbers switched from the present time to the time the alarm was set for, 6:55. Gibbons switched on the radio. An alto sax played bebop at low volume.

Gibbons listened for a moment. "Charlie Parker," he said, then he shut it off and left the radio the way he'd found it.

Next to the clock-radio was a white Trimline phone on top of a Panasonic answering machine. The lights on the answering machine weren't blinking, which meant there hadn't been any calls since she'd last monitored it. Gibbons turned the playback switch to listen to her old messages. The first thing they heard was a hang-up followed by a few seconds of dial tone. Then a man's voice came through the machine.

"This is your father," the voice said with a self-conscious chuckle. "I guess you've already left, right? Okay, so we'll see you later tonight then. In case you haven't left yet, we may all go down to the casino for a while, but I'll make sure I'm back early. Okay? Drive carefully, baby. There're a lot of nuts on the road. See you later."

Jules Collesano sounded a lot more coherent than he did the day Tozzi met him. Tozzi stood over the bed, staring at the pastel plaid bedspread. He had a feeling he'd been seeing some terrific acting jobs lately. Unfortunately even the bedroom scenes. The tape kept running, but there were only more hangups.

THIRTY-FIVE

The Imperial Casino where Tozzi said he had met Jules Collesano was packed. It was almost eleven, and from the looks of things there were a lot of paychecks being blown tonight. Whirring slot machines, clicking big-six wheels, spinning roulette wheels, rolling dice, the soft but steady snap of cards on felt, the nervous silence of winners, the hubbub of losers. Gibbons took in the Imperial's Roman Empire decor, the plaster columns, the statues of the emperors gazing at each other across a battlefield of greed and false hope. Driving in on the Atlantic City Expressway and seeing the huge, brightly lit casinos standing tall over the landscape, Gibbons thought of false idols, of Sodom and Gomorrah. But here in the casino, he could only shake his head and think of the legendary decadence that preceded the fall of the Roman Empire.

Gibbons stood with Tozzi on the carpeted landing that led down to the casino, looking out at the madness. "What does Collesano like to play?" he asked Tozzi.

"He was playing blackjack the day I met him."

Gibbons grunted. There were about eighty blackjack tables here, and they weren't all in the same place. "What are you going to do if we find him?"

"Ask him where his daughter is."

"Then what?"

Tozzi sighed and pulled on his nose. "I don't know."

That was the part Gibbons was worried about. Tozzi was in an evil mood, and caution had never been his strong suit. "Come on, let's look around," he said, wishing he knew a good way to keep his partner on a short leash.

Walking through the casino, Gibbons got a sense of the class system of gambling. Poor blacks and retirees played the slots; these were the plebeians. Citizens played the bigger-money games, particularly blackjack. Craps was a man's game; women favored roulette and big six. At the blackjack tables, men preferred to play with men, women with women. The patrician class played baccarat in an exclusive alcove set apart from the hoi polloi.

"Hey," Tozzi said, indicating one of the roulette tables, "check that out."

A dumpy housewife type with a terrible dye job was standing over a mountain of chips, betting heavily and winning heavily. No one at the table reacted one way or another, although a small crowd of onlookers had gathered around the table. Gibbons noticed a second croupier at the table, an Oriental guy, arranging stacks of chips with the meticulous care of a sushi chef.

Another small crowd had gathered around an old black man in a crushed ten-gallon hat working two colossal slot machines simultaneously. These machines stood seven feet tall and had computerized screens that simulated the spinning face of a conventional slot machine. He pulled down on the huge arms with cakewalk grace, feeding coins into the giants, then pulling down, moving back and forth in an uninterrupted rhythm. Gibbons noticed that the man didn't even bother to look at the results. Even when he won, he just kept on going. It was only the loud clanking of those heavy casino slugs hitting the stainless-steel trays under the machines that told him he'd won. If gambling was a sickness, this was the delirium.

Tozzi touched his arm and gestured impatiently with his head. He wanted to move on, keep looking. In a way, Gibbons hoped they didn't find Collesano or his daughter tonight. He was afraid Tozzi would get carried away in this bacchanalian atmosphere.

They turned down an aisle of blackjack tables and Gibbons's eye combed the faces. The gamblers weren't all lowlifes, not by a long shot. He was surprised at the number of middle-aged, middle-management types, somber-faced white guys steadily tapping the felt for yet another card, praying for twenty-one, staring at the vicissitudes of the cards and keeping a lid on their emotions, winning some hands, losing most. They reminded Gibbons of Bill Kinney, and he thought about what it must have been like when he was undercover in the Philly mob, playing Steve Pagano. It must have been hard for him to reconcile the hard realities of a special agent's life with the opulent lifestyles of Richie Varga and his pals. With all those kids of his, he must've been terrified by the looming financial responsibilities he knew he had to face. It must've been very easy for him to be seduced by the luxury, the power, and the comfort that he saw money could buy. Slipping from Bill Kinney to Steve "the Hun" Pagano probably became pretty effortless for him. That's what can happen when guys go undercover. They forget who they really are. Changing personalities probably became so easy for him, eventually he figured he could make it work for him so he could take the best of both worlds and leave the rest. The successful Ivy Leaguer, rising star in the FBI, benevolent patriarch, provider and protector could be bankrolled by the Hun. In his mind it was probably the perfect balancing act. Gibbons could almost understand the guy's motivations.

But then he saw three eyeless heads, and that could never be forgiven.

He sighed and scanned as many faces as he could see, knowing that this was a useless exercise. He only knew Collesano from pictures. If he saw him here in the flesh, most likely he wouldn't recognize the man. This was all for Tozzi's benefit. His smoldering guinea temper was having a field day with being the betrayed lover. Well, this was as good a place as any to get it out of his system, Gibbons supposed.

But then a face caught his eye. Not Collesano, but a younger man. A huge fat face and a strange body, heavier in the chest and shoulders than in the gut. Then he remembered where he had seen that face. The guy in that black Trans Am parked outside Tozzi's aunt's apartment in Bloomfield, the dogs in the backseat. He'd been eating an ice-cream cone. Gibbons distinctly remembered that he'd thought this guy looked like an oversized baby.

Gibbons stared at the man's impassive face as he threw down chips on a craps table, betting heavily. The dark wavy hair. The cold eyes. It could be him, he thought. It definitely could be Richie Varga.

Standing next to the heavy man, throwing the dice, was a stocky older man. "Tozzi," Gibbons said. "See the fat guy at that craps table over there? The guy next to him. Is that Collesano?"

Tozzi looked. "Yeah, that's him."

"The fat guy's Varga," Gibbons said. "I'll put money on it."

Tozzi looked at Gibbons, then looked back at the fat man. He was about to say something when he noticed another face in his line of vision. Feeney, the punk from the abandoned warehouse, was standing in the next aisle, and he was staring right at them. There was a white bandage plastered across his hairline. His hand was inside his jacket, and he was wearing a sneer that broadcast sweet revenge. Instinctively Tozzi glanced right and left. Kinney's pallbearers were blocking the aisle.

Tozzi looked back at the pig-faced boy who was chuckling confidently now. He had them hemmed in. They were outnumbered. There was nothing they could do.

Gibbons spotted the pallbearers closing in on them. He looked at Tozzi and didn't like the look in his eye. "There are innocent people here," he warned.

"I don't give a fuck," Tozzi said.

"Not here!"

But out of the corner of his eye, Tozzi could see two of the pallbearers coming up fast behind Gibbons. One had his gun drawn, and he was trying to hide it behind his buddy, but Tozzi had already spotted the extended barrel of a silencer.

"Get down," Tozzi yelled and went for his gun. "Everybody, get down," he yelled. Then he saw the muzzle flash. A woman sitting at a blackjack table next to him screamed and fell off her stool. Tozzi saw a clear shot and fired at the pallbearers.

"Get 'em," Feeney screamed as he leapt up on the nearest craps table, drew his gun, and pointed down at Tozzi.

Tozzi wheeled around and dropped to one knee. He saw Feeney's gun and he fired twice. A chunk of Feeney's head flew across the aisle. Blood splattered across a croupier's white blouse. Feeney's knees buckled and he collapsed on the felt, faceup.

Tozzi stood up, gripping the automatic in both hands, ready to take on the pallbearers from the other side, but the sight of Excalibur in Gibbons's hand had apparently dissuaded them. They were nowhere to be seen now.

Gibbons was gritting his teeth. "You're one fucking asshole, Tozzi!"

Tozzi didn't answer. He looked back across the aisle. Varga and Collesano were gone. "Come on. Let's get out of here."

"Yeah? How?" Gibbons shot back.

Armed security guards were running toward them, guns held high, pushing their way through the crush of hysterical people fleeing for their lives.

Tozzi spotted a tray full of chips, thousands of dollars' worth of casino chips. He grabbed it and heaved it in the direction of the security guards. The chips flew out over the tables and rained down on the crowd. Gamblers shouted, shoved, and dove for the freebies. More chips fell, pelting their backs as they scrambled on their hands and knees.

By the time the guards reached the source of the shooting, they found a dead man in a black suit sprawled in the aisle with a silenced automatic in his crumpled hand. A second corpse was laid out faceup on a craps table, sprinkled with chips. There was a hundred-dollar chip on the spot where Feeney's other eye should have been. The other two guys were gone.

THIRTY-SIX

They were sitting at the dining-room table having cake and coffee. Jules was at one end, Varga at the other, Joanne in the middle facing the windows. There was a big bowl of fruit on the table between the coffee cake and the pot of coffee. Two big ugly dogs were asleep under the table. The men's appetites apparently hadn't been affected by the carnage at the casino. They all looked pretty content. It was a real homey scene.

Tozzi stood at the sliding glass patio door, looking in. He wondered why those dogs didn't sense his presence. Useless mutts. He glanced along the length of the house. Gibbons was just turning the corner, heading for the side door at the kitchen. He looked back in and focused on Varga stirring sugar into his coffee. From where Tozzi stood he had a clear shot at the fat son-of-a-bitch.

He switched the Beretta to his left hand, wiped his palm on his pants, then took the gun back in his right.

He wished to hell Gibbons would hurry up. But of course that wasn't his way of doing things. They even had to have a debate in the car as to whether this was really the house or not. Gibbons had never trusted his partner's hunches, but Tozzi had more than just a gut feeling about this one. This was the house he caught Joanne staring at when he came down here with her, the one she said her friend lived in, the politician's daughter. Thinking back, Tozzi figured she must have told him to drive by here on purpose that time so that she could check the house, see what cars were in the driveway. There were three cars in the drive right now. Her maroon Saab, a black Fleetwood Brougham, and a smoke-gray Mercedes. He guessed that the Caddy was her father's, the Mercedes Varga's. He looked at her through the glass. Jules was telling a story, gesturing with his hand as if it were a gun, and she was laughing. Tozzi wondered if that whole story about the Barbie doll was a crock too.

Suddenly Tozzi heard the crash of glass breaking and immediately saw their alarmed faces as they all turned toward the clamor of Gibbons breaking the corner pane of the kitchen door. Tozzi banged hard on the glass patio doors to get their attention before anyone made a move. They saw him right away and he made sure they saw the gun. Even the dogs looked stunned. Tozzi tried the door, expecting it to be locked. Surprisingly the heavy glass slid open easily.

One of the dogs finally started to growl. It was about time.

Jules jumped when the swinging door behind him flew open and Gibbons came in from the kitchen leading with Excalibur. "Hey, what the hell is this?" Jules sputtered.

"Watch out for the dogs," Tozzi said to Gibbons. Both Blitz and Krieg were growling low, but neither one moved from under the table. Still, they were mean-looking mothers and Tozzi didn't trust them.

"Rottweilers," Gibbons said as if making a note for himself.

"You fucking stupids," Jules shouted. "Get the hell out of my house."

"You're under arrest," Gibbons shouted over him. "All of you."

"For what?" Joanne asked coolly. She laced her fingers and stared imperiously at Tozzi. The Ice Queen.

"Computer fraud in your case," Gibbons said. "And conspiracy, complicity in arson, and insurance fraud."

The dogs growled a little louder now.

"Really?" Joanne said, arching her brows. "And how does that stack up against helping a renegade FBI agent? Isn't that conspiracy too? And how about complicity in the murders he committed?"

Gibbons didn't answer her. He was looking at Varga. "Same charges for you, Varga. Plus murder for the deaths of FBI special agents Joel Lando, Alex Blaney, and James Novick."

Varga seemed to wake up then. His eyes brightened and a rubbery grin stretched across his hanging jaw. "Who's Varga?" he said in a soft, high voice. "You've got the wrong guy." The grin stretched wider.

Tozzi couldn't hold it in any longer. "You said you hated him," he shouted at Joanne. "You said he fucked your father over. But all along you were really in cahoots with him. I don't get you."

Joanne threw her head back and laughed softly. "Well, maybe you're just not as smart as you think you are, Tozzi."

Jules snickered into his hand.

"Oh, no? Well, just how dumb do you think I am?" The woman was evil. He could feel the muscles in his jaw twitching. "You said he used to beat you. What happened? Did you miss it?" He wanted to hurt her the way she'd hurt him.

"Business is business, Tozzi. What can I tell you?"

"What's that supposed to mean?"

She just shrugged and smiled.

"What is it about this guy?" Tozzi said, pointing at Varga with his gun. "Somehow he gets people to do whatever he wants, doesn't he? Maybe that business about him not being able to get it up was just a story. I mean, he must be some kind of stud for you to still be rolling over and spreading your legs for him every time he snaps his fingers."

She glared at him. "You know, people like you refuse to understand anything because you don't want to live in the present. Don't tell me about the past, that's history."

"Well, then tell me about the present. I'm listening."

She shook her head, exasperated with him.

"Come on, tell me a good story."

"You want a good story? I'll tell you one—"

"Joanne," her father warned sternly, "don't say a thing."

"No," she protested vehemently, "he wants a story. I'll give him a good one." She looked Tozzi in the eye and shifted to her business manner. "About two years ago, Richie came back to me with an opportunity, and I took it. Simple as that. He had a sound plan, and the risk factor was very low since he'd already eliminated all the competition with his grand jury testimony. With the information I had access to at DataReach, I knew that bilking insurance companies would be incredibly easy. The profit potential was phenomenal. As part of our deal he promised to give my father his old job back, *capo* of Atlantic City. And as for me, I wanted a title as well as a share in the profits. In time Joanne Varga will be known as the first woman underboss in the history of La Cosa Nostra and, I might add, underboss of the single most powerful crime family this country has ever seen.'' She laughed scornfully and looked at Gibbons. ''Now go try to sell that fairy tale back at the field office.''

Her explanation had the same arrogant ring as Kinney's reasoning for killing Lando, Blaney, and Novick. It wasn't their fault. Nothing was anybody's fault. It was just the fortuitous meeting of opportunity with circumstance. That's all. Blame it on the moon.

Jules slapped the table and made the silverware jump, laughing like a jackass.

Varga sipped his coffee and tittered smugly behind his cup. The bastard didn't seem very upset that his cover had been blown.

''More coffee?'' Joanne asked him, reaching for the pot.

''Sure, why not,'' he said.

She reached for the pot and refilled his cup, glancing up at Tozzi from under her dark lashes. ''Business is business,'' she repeated with a mocking laugh. After she filled Varga's cup, she leaned across the table and kissed her husband on the lips. They lingered over that kiss, playing it for the balcony. The fat under Varga's chin bobbled and shook. It reminded Tozzi of a giant slug devouring its prey.

He just couldn't take any more of this shit. His hands were steady as he leveled his gun at Varga's fat head and cocked the hammer. Then unexpectedly he heard the click of another hammer. Very close to his ear. Out of the corner of his eye he saw the blue metal barrel about two feet from his head. Excalibur.

''Forget it, Tozzi,'' Gibbons said.

The dogs growled.

THIRTY-SEVEN

"Don't do it," Gibbons said, holding his gun on Tozzi. "You do it and I'll have to take you in. You're not the law. Let a jury decide what he deserves. Let me take Varga in, the right way."

"But what about Lando, Blaney—?"

Without warning gunshots exploded. Gibbons felt the impact of the bullet and automatically recoiled before he actually felt the pain. "Shit," he grunted, clutching his elbow with his gun hand.

Tozzi discharged his weapon at the source of the gunfire without hesitation. Joanne screamed and fell forward onto the table. The gun she'd fired bounced off the tabletop and hit the carpet. She was on the edge of the table, struggling with her head to get her balance as she clutched her bloody hip with both hands. "Help me," she demanded, but neither her husband nor her father moved. Her struggling only made her slide on the polished table, and she toppled over on her back. She cursed and whimpered at the pain. Her ivory-colored blouse was stained with coffee, and sticky flecks of coffee cake clung to her hair and face. Her hands were covered with her own blood.

"Goddamn you!" she said. "Goddamn you!" she kept repeating, but Gibbons wasn't sure if it was meant for Tozzi or Varga. He got the feeling the indignity of being helpless on the floor upset her more than the slug in her hip.

The dogs were quiet now. One sniffed tentatively at her hip.

"Oh, my God," Jules whispered in shock. "Oh, baby . . ." He slid to his knees to go to his daughter, but Tozzi chased him back into his seat with the muzzle of his gun.

"Hands on the table where I can see them. Fingers spread, both of you." Tozzi backed up a step and trained the gun from one to the other. "You okay?" he asked Gibbons.

"My elbow," he said tersely, shaking out a handkerchief to make a tourniquet. "I'll live."

"Don't count on it, Bert."

Gibbons turned toward the new voice. Blitz and Krieg started growling again. Bill Kinney was standing in the doorway to the kitchen, the swinging door against his back. His tan suit was wrinkled and he needed a shave. There was a machine pistol in his right hand. The left was still bandaged around the curved metal splints. Gibbons noticed that his watch fob was wrapped around his bandaged hand, the antique gold watch dangling between his two good fingers. "No, I wouldn't count on it at all, Bert." He had that Mr. Hyde look again.

Gibbons exhaled slowly and swallowed hard.

"As they say in the movies, drop your guns, boys."

In the face of an Uzi at close range, Gibbons and Tozzi knew better than to argue. They let their weapons fall. Tozzi's gun clacked against the small .22 automatic Joanne had used. Varga must've slipped it to her under the table when they kissed. Gibbons raked the two guns far out of Joanne's reach with his foot.

"I heard about the shootout at the Imperial," Kinney said. He shook his head and smirked. "I came right over. Figured you'd need someone competent to clean up the mess, Richie."

No one said a word. Gibbons's eye fell on the serrated bread knife Joanne had used to cut the coffeecake. It was at the edge of the table just above Joanne. He looked at Kinney, who was also looking at the knife.

"Say, Richie. If you'd like I could take care of Mr. Gibbons and Mr. Tozzi for you. The same way I took care of Lando, Blaney, and Novick, I mean."

Varga said nothing, but that smug grin had disappeared.

"You don't have any of those Japanese knives, do you, Jules?" Kinney asked. "You know the ones they advertise on TV? The ones you can cut through a beer can with? They'd be good."

Jules forced a laugh. "Hey, Kinney, watch where you point that goddamn thing, will ya?"

Kinney swung the gun around and pressed the short barrel into Jules's cheek. "I'll point it wherever I goddamn want," he said through clenched teeth.

Jules looked imploringly to Varga, whose dead stare never left Kinney.

When he removed the gun from Collesano's face, he tracked the room slowly with it, pointing from Jules to Gibbons to Tozzi to Joanne to Varga and back. He did this as he talked. "Remember what a hell of a time I had with the eyes, Richie? Very hard to get them out without making a mess. What you need is something like a grapefruit spoon, something curved with a long handle and a sharp serrated edge. That would be perfect. Yeah, the eyes are tricky." Kinney nodded to himself. "Taking the heads off is no problem. All you really need is strong blade. The strength of the metal is really just as important as the sharpness of the edge, I think, because you've got to get through that neck bone."

Joanne was looking very pale. "Make him stop, Richie," she hissed, gulping for air.

"Yeah, what you need is good tempered steel," Kinney said. "You know what I'm talking about, Richie. I mean, *I* could probably do it with a good pizza cutter if I had to. You must have a good pizza cutter here, Jules. I mean, you're Italian, after all."

Christ, Gibbons thought.

"What're you looking at me like that for, Tozzi? You think you're better than me? I'm Jack the Ripper, but you're Robin Hood, right? No, no, no, no. That's not the way it is." He gestured vehemently with his claw hand. "Sure, we're both killers, but I'm smart and you're not. I was looking out for my future; you were just out for vengeance. I had a plan; you just had a mission, some stupid cause."

"I've got a clear conscience," Tozzi said.

"That and a dollar will get you on the subway." He weighed the Uzi nervously in his hand. "You know, the two of you really are something. So high and mighty, so righteous. Is that what they taught you when you went through training, Bert? I know when Tozzi and I went through Quantico it was the *law* that was important. The laws were written to be enforced. Agents don't write the laws and it's not up to them to interpret those laws. They just enforce them. That's how they told it to us. Maybe in Hoover's day they taught it differently. Things were looser then, from what I understand."

"No. It was just easier to tell the good guys from the bad guys back then," Gibbons said.

Kinney laughed. "I doubt it. Everybody's a bad guy unless he's paid not to be. Except you two aberrations."

"But you had it both ways, right?" Gibbons wanted to keep him talking. "A good guy and a bad guy at the same time."

"You could say that. But I prefer to think of myself as a *smart* guy. I'm one of the very few people in this world who knows how to use the intelligence I was born with. Just give me a year, and I'll be running this whole operation." His eyes widened as he looked at Varga. He was clutching the watch tightly. "Do I scare you, Richie?" His derisive laugh degenerated into a wet cough.

"So what do you say, Richie?" Kinney raised his voice, waving the Uzi. "You're still the boss. I haven't taken over yet. Tell me what you want me to do? Come on. Show some initiative. You want me to make cold cuts out of them, I'll do it. Just say the word."

Gibbons looked at Varga looking at Kinney. His stare was cold and unwavering, a weird combination of intense hate and disdain. Under the table he tapped one of the dogs on the flank with the side of his shoe. Then he said one word in a flat monotone: *"Blitzkrieg."*

Instantly the two dogs sprang up and attacked, faster than Gibbons thought those fat, lazy animals could ever move. One latched onto Kinney's knee; the other took a flying leap at his chest and knocked him back through the swinging door. From the kitchen a short burst of automatic fire briefly drowned out the hellish sounds of the Rottweilers doing their work.

Tozzi quickly stooped down, retrieved his gun, and covered Varga and Jules. Gibbons wound the handkerchief around his arm, then picked up his gun and pocketed the .22.

They heard a wet gurgling scream and more intense growling. Tozzi made a move toward the door, but Jules stopped him. "Don't go in there," he said earnestly.

When the door opened again, Blitz and Krieg came trotting into the dining room, the door swinging gently behind them. The second dog had a severed hand in her maw, the index finger still crooked around the trigger guard of the dangling Uzi. The dog dripped blood on the carpet from the doorway all the way to Varga, then dropped Kinney's hand at her master's feet. Both animals dropped to their haunches in front of Varga and panted through jowly dog smiles, waiting for praise.

THIRTY-EIGHT

Special Agent in Charge Brant Ivers sat behind his big mahogany desk, flipping through Gibbons's report on the arrests of Richie Varga, Joanne Collesano Varga, and Jules Collesano, a report that included an account of the death of Special Agent William Kinney and all the evidence connecting him with the murders of Special Agents Joel Lando, Alex Blaney, and James Novick.

Gibbons sat back in the leather chair across from the SAC and watched him read. Ivers was wearing a navy three-piece suit and a two-tone blue rep tie, a rather conservative outfit for him. Ivers had just gotten the report that morning and now he looked a little pale. Undoubtedly he was thinking about the detour his career was going to take once Washington got ahold of that report. Gibbons smiled like a crocodile.

Ivers nodded mechanically, his lips pressed together tightly. "Congratulations, Bert. This is top-notch work." He spoke quietly. Today he looked his age.

Ivers closed the report and stared at it on his desk. He wrinkled his brow and shook his head. "Those pictures of Kinney's body, what those dogs did to his neck—" He winced. "How in God's name can people train dogs to do something so monstrous?"

It was a rhetorical question from a man who didn't know what else to say, but Gibbons figured he'd answer it anyway. "There's a long precedent for this kind of thing with Rottweilers. The Romans originally used them to herd cattle. The legions found them useful in driving off an enemy's herds during a campaign in order to limit their food supply.

They'd just let a pack of these dogs go and they'd chase the cows off. If a bull tried to make a stand against them, they were trained to attack the bull and kill it. I can imagine one of these brutes going up against a bull. It must've been quite a sight."

Ivers shook his head. "Monstrous and inhumane," he murmured.

"The dogs or Kinney?" Gibbons asked.

"Kinney was a very sick man," Ivers pronounced somberly. "I only wish we had gotten some indication of his problem earlier. I think he could've been helped."

Gibbons wasn't used to this kind of reverence from the SAC. He liked him better as a pompous ass, and this humble routine was boring. "I'm not so sure anything could've changed Kinney," he said. "The real Kinney was a killer. He was like a guy with a secret fetish. If Varga hadn't given him the opportunity to come out of the closet, though, he might've kept the lid on, the way most of us do."

Ivers raised his eyebrows. "Not unlike Tozzi."

Gibbons shrugged. "Maybe."

"It's regrettable that Tozzi was able to escape in the fray that night," Ivers said gravely.

Gibbons puckered his lips and stroked the lines around his mouth with his thumb and index finger. You asshole, he thought. We solved Lando, Blaney, and Novick, broke up the biggest bust-out scam anyone's ever seen, apprehended the mob boss no one even knew existed, and caught a bad agent. What the hell else do you want?

"That pocket watch Kinney was holding when he died," Ivers said. "Very interesting. We did some checking and found that it was a family heirloom, belonged to his great-grandfather. According to his wife, it meant quite a lot to him. The inscription on the lid reads, 'To my son and all my son's sons—May excellence abound in us all.' His great-grandfather was a security guard at Harvard. Apparently he won the watch from a professor in a poker game."

"Interesting." It figures.

Ivers leaned forward over his desk as if he were about to tell Gibbons a secret. "You know, Bert," he confided mournfully, "the Bureau had no idea Varga had formed a new family. The Director won't be pleased when he reads this. It's going to be quite an embarrassment for us."

"Well, you can thank Tozzi for flushing him out."

Ivers ignored the mention of Tozzi's name. "One thing I don't understand is why Varga sicced the dogs on Kinney after Kinney had already implicated him in the murders. You'd already heard it all, so there was nothing to be gained by silencing him.''

''It might've been a heat-of-the-moment reaction,'' Gibbons speculated. ''Kinney was being pretty abusive. He was also talking crazy. I suspect that when I testify as to what Kinney said about killing Lando, Blaney, and Novick on Varga's orders, Varga's lawyers will try to discredit my testimony by proving that Kinney was nuts. Kinney had definitely snapped, but I don't think they'll have much of a case. It won't stop them from giving it a shot, though. By the way, I heard the U.S. Attorney's office is talking about making a deal with Phillip Giovinazzo. They'll reduce some of the pending charges against him if he'll testify to being at Gilberto's in Brooklyn when Varga and Kinney brought out the heads.''

''But even if Giovinazzo doesn't cooperate,'' Ivers said, ''Varga will be convicted for Kinney's murder. Kinney was armed and technically he was trespassing when he entered Collesano's house. Nevertheless, the use of trained attack dogs constitutes first-degree murder. The grizzly nature of the killing should override any extenuating circumstances in the minds of a jury.''

Gibbons nodded to make Ivers feel good. He was trying to sound impressive with his knowledge of the law to bolster his own spirits. Ivers was full of shit, but there was no sense in busting his balls now. They were going to be black and blue soon enough.

''How about Joanne? What's she looking at?''

''Besides the criminal charges she's facing, DataReach will sue her. The insurance companies that were burned in the bust-out scam will all sue DataReach. DataReach will have no choice but to sue her in turn and hope that they can recover enough in damages to pay back the insurance companies and stay in business. Though I can't imagine who would trust their files with them when this gets out.''

''Who knows? They may land on their feet. Business is a funny world,'' Gibbons said, recalling Joanne's reasoning for her return to Richie Varga. ''Business is business, as they say.''

''Jules Collesano's participation in all this seems to have been comparatively minor, but he'll be hit with the usual racketeering charges. Under the circumstances, he'll surely serve some time.''

''I'd say it was a pretty good haul,'' Gibbons said.

''Yes, it was.'' Ivers sucked in his breath and held it for a moment. He looked constipated.

''And what do we do about Tozzi?'' Gibbons asked.

"Well . . . we'll continue to handle his case in-house . . . until headquarters decides otherwise." Ivers looked *really* constipated.

The crocodile grin returned to Gibbons's lips as he stood up and went over to the windows behind Ivers's desk. He lifted one of the slats of the stained-wood venetian blinds and looked down at the street.

Ivers looked puzzled as he swiveled around in his chair to see what Gibbons was doing.

Gibbons reached for the cord and pulled up the blinds. "See that ice-cream vendor in front of the courthouse?"

Ivers screwed up his face and squinted out the window.

"See the bench just to the left? Take a look at the guy sitting on the bench, the one wearing jeans."

Ivers strained to locate the person Gibbons was pointing out. Then he spotted him. It was Tozzi, sitting there with his legs crossed, eating an ice-cream sandwich. He was looking right up at them.

"Holy shit!" Ivers cursed under his breath as he swiveled around and reached for the phone.

Gibbons slapped his hand on the receiver and kept Ivers from picking it up. "Hold on, hold on."

"Goddamn it, he's right there! He'll get away!"

"No, he won't. Not if you play ball."

Ivers's face rapidly turned an angry shade of red. "I knew it. I knew this could happen, but I kept telling myself that it wouldn't. How stupid! Goddamn it all! You've been protecting him, haven't you?"

Gibbons nodded.

"Why?"

Gibbons stared at him. "I always side with the good guys."

"What the hell's that supposed to mean?"

"It means Tozzi was right. He's the one who deserves the congratulations for this entire bust. I think you should take him back."

Ivers reacted as if Gibbons had thrown boiling water in his face. "Are you serious? Tozzi's a killer, he's—"

"He's one hell of an agent."

"I'm—I'm shocked. You're as much as confessing your collusion with that madman." Ivers pointed out the window as if Godzilla were out there.

"I'm not confessing to anything, Ivers. I'm here to make a deal with you." Gibbons reached into his inside pocket and pulled out a sheaf of papers folded in half vertically. "It's very simple. You forget about Tozzi's little freelance escapade and let him back into the Bureau, and I'll give you this." He held up the papers.

"What's that?"

"Another report. This version leaves out the business about Kinney working for Varga and plays down the extent of Varga's family. This one makes it sound like we nipped Varga's operation in the bud. And in this version, Kinney's killed in the line of duty, an unfortunate casualty in the attempt to apprehend Varga." Gibbons held the new report over Ivers's head, waiting for him to jump like a dog for a bone.

"It won't work," Ivers mumbled angrily.

"Sure it will. Only you and I know the extent of Tozzi's renegade activities, and Washington still doesn't know he was ever gone. We'll make up a good story for the boys here at the office, say it was all a mistake. You can make it wash."

"It won't work," Ivers repeated. "Varga knows all about Kinney. It'll eventually come out in court."

"Wake up, will ya? Varga's lawyers won't bring up Kinney. If they claim that Kinney was bad and that he was secretly working for Varga, it will only strengthen the prosecution's case against Varga for the murders of Lando, Blaney, and Novick. They won't do that."

"You're in big trouble, Gibbons," Ivers threatened, furious that Gibbons was bullying him with a bargain he really wanted to accept. His brow was beaded with sweat.

"Cut the shit, Ivers. The bottom line here is that this report will make you look like an able administrator. The one you've got will put your career in the toilet."

Ivers just glared at him.

"Assistant In-House Coordinator of Public Relations. The job is vacant again, Ivers. In case you don't know, that's the guy who's in charge of running the free tours down at headquarters in Washington. Talking to civic groups is also part of the job description. And answering letters from high-school kids who want to know more about the Bureau for their term papers. The guy who's retiring from the job used to be the SAC in Sacramento. McManus is his name. I'm sure you heard the story. He got the job after it was discovered that one of his special agents was running interference for a couple of Russian spies. The poor guy didn't know a thing about it until he heard about it from the Director."

Ivers's jaw was clenched. He was sweating like a pig. "No . . . I can't . . ."

"Last chance, Ivers. Take the deal or I take my story to the press."

The SAC's eyes popped out of his head. "You wouldn't dare."

"Why wouldn't I? My career isn't at stake. I'm retired. I've got nothing to lose."

"You'll go to jail. The government doesn't look kindly on ex-employees talking out of school."

"When was the last time you can think of that a reporter gave up his source? Those guys feel very strongly about the First Amendment."

"You've got all the answers, don't you, Gibbons?"

Gibbons put the report back in his pocket. "All right, have it your way, Ivers. I don't give a shit." He started for the door.

Ivers suddenly pictured himself on the dais at a Daughters of the Revolution tea. "Goddamn you, Gibbons. Give me that report."

Gibbons stopped and turned back to see Ivers holding out the old report in his fist. After they traded reports, Gibbons went back to the window, lowered the blinds, and pulled the cord up and down, flashing the blinds. When he looked out again, Tozzi was standing at the curb in front of the bench, nodding and grinning.

Ivers stood up slowly, glanced at Gibbons, then raised the blinds all the way. Out the window, he could see Tozzi waving to him. The SAC sighed deeply and nodded his assent so Tozzi could see. Tozzi nodded back and smiled like a crocodile.